VOICES OF THE DEAD

'Astonishing'
MARK BILLINGHAM

'Compelling'
FINANCIAL TIMES

'Atmospheric, enthralling . . . Victorian Edinburgh comes
thrillingly to life'
JENNY COLGAN

'Full of twists and turns – a great read'
EVENING TIMES

'Dark and visceral, gritty and charming, with a twisting plot
and compelling characters'
JESS KIDD

'The historical setting is fascinating, and all of Brookmyre's
wit and storytelling verve are evident'
THE TIMES

VOICES OF THE DEAD

AMBROSE PARRY

CANONGATE

This paperback edition published in Great Britain, the USA
and Canada in 2024 by Canongate Books

First published in Great Britain, the USA and Canada in 2023
by Canongate Books Ltd, 14 High Street, Edinburgh EH1 1TE

Distributed in the USA by Publishers Group West and
in Canada by Publishers Group Canada

canongate.co.uk

1

British Library Cataloguing-in-Publication Data
A catalogue record for this book is available on
request from the British Library

ISBN 978 1 83885 551 2

Typeset in Van Dijck by Palimpsest Book Production Ltd,
Falkirk, Stirlingshire

Printed and bound by CPI Group (UK) Ltd, Croydon CR0 4YY

In memory of Thalia Proctor

PROLOGUE

he smell of oil was all around him, sharp and yet cloying. He had splashed it about the stage until the can was empty, taking care to make sure its grim centrepiece in particular was thoroughly doused.

Sometimes you do not choose the part. Sometimes it is the part that chooses you. A life in thrall to the theatre ought to have prepared him for that. The course of his future had changed in a matter of moments. Though he could not have conceived of it mere hours ago, the new path before him was clear: what he had to do, who he had to become. The role he had to play.

He was grateful that the body had stopped twitching. It seemed strange to say, but he bore the dead man no ill-will. He wished it could have gone differently, wished their fates had not become entangled. However, he had been given no choice. The man had come here and confronted him with a direct accusation. More than an accusation: they both knew the truth of what he had done. It was pointless to pretend otherwise.

What followed had felt repulsive and yet inevitable, an action he was compelled to pursue. But once that compulsion was spent and the act was done, he understood that in carrying out this fatal deed, he had killed himself also. He was undone by his own hand, everything he had worked towards and striven for destroyed. It appeared his whole world was at an end, his situation hopeless. Then he had looked again and remembered where he was.

The theatre was where he had spent so many of his happiest times, and it had given him one more gift. He loved it because it was a place of infinite escape and of boundless possibility, thus reminding him that he was the kind of man who could always clothe himself anew.

He stepped away from the stage before striking the match, flicking it onto the boards.

He was not ready for the ferocity with which it caught. With precipitate terror he realised that his sleeve was alight, the heat immediate and relentless. He threw himself to the floor, quickly shedding the jacket and tossing it away. Some of the oil must have splashed back onto it as he shook the can. Fortunately, he had not got any on the hat.

The rising flames held his gaze longer than was prudent. He watched the scenery transformed in tongues of orange and red, Elsinore engulfed, until one of the flats collapsed onto the already burning body. He needed to satisfy himself that it would be truly consumed, but having seen that, it was time to leave.

He exited through a side door into the darkness of an alley, aware he could not afford to be seen upon the street. Not yet.

He knew he needed to make haste, for he now had a journey ahead of him, one from which he could never return. Despite that, he tarried just a moment at the corner, unable to look away quite yet as the smoke billowed beneath the theatre's colonnade and the flames lit up the night.

EDINBURGH

APRIL 1853

ONE

aven's heartbeat surged as he woke to the sound of screaming and a presence at the end of his bed. Not screaming, wailing. He recognised his mother's cries, mournful and distraught, while the cause of them loomed in the half light. His father was not dead. He was standing mere feet away, returned to avenge himself upon the son who had stood up to him.

Then both sound and image shifted, resolving themselves into more rational truths. What he could hear was the crying not of his mother, but of a child, the familiar discordant symphony that for almost two years had punctuated his days and his nights. The menacing shape was simply the coat he had hung over the edge of the wardrobe door. There was no ghost, no phantom, yet only moments ago it had appeared so vividly real. How much the mind extemporised from the merest glimmer of suggestion.

As he came to, he found himself wishing it truly had been his father. The man had been a drunken brute but at least he would relent once his rage was spent. Raven was now in thrall to a worse tyrant.

Crying was good, he had been told. A silent child was far more troubling.

Raven had foresworn all quietening syrups; Godfrey's Cordial in particular was not permitted in the house, particularly given its association with the shocking events of summer 1850, but the perpetual noise was wearing away at his resolve. He now understood the pervasiveness and popularity of such soporific draughts.

Raven sighed, resigning himself to yet another early start. He counselled himself that Dr Simpson would probably be up already, writing letters to the *Lancet* and preparing papers for presentation at the Edinburgh Medico-Chirurgical Society. Raven envied his energy: he seemed to have an endless supply. Raven also envied Simpson's ease with his children, the way he could play with them as though he was a care-free child too.

Little James seemed eternally displeased, erupting in outrage at the slightest frustration, as though permanently resentful at having been brought into existence. Raven had been assured that it would get better when the child could crawl, and then when he could walk, but in each case, James's greater mobility merely expanded the ambit of things he could be tearful about.

Simpson's children all seemed to be of milder natures than Raven's. He wondered, was this because Simpson's attentions served to imbue them with his own infectious calm? By contrast, the more time Raven spent around James, the more agitated the boy became. Or was it that Simpson's children had inherited the professor's gentle nature, while Raven's son inherited his rage?

When he had suggested this to Sarah, she was scornful. 'No one is born angry, Will,' she told him.

His wife was with the little one now, already awake for who knew how long, toiling to keep the child amused in their less than expansive home. He knew she was tired and strained but she remained indefatigably more patient than him despite being heavily pregnant with their second. Which was not to say her patience was limitless; just that these days she had far more of it for James than for Raven.

She had been particularly angry with him last night. It had been her stated intention that the three of them spend the day together as a family, but Raven had found a reason to be somewhere else. It was true that he had been asked to attend a birth, but he had been disingenuous regarding just how urgent it had been. And more disingenuous still regarding how long the delivery had taken. Raven felt a hollowing shame about this now, but there was a limit to how much tearful disgruntlement he could subject himself to, and that was just from the bairn.

Yesterday had been a Sunday. That used to be his day of rest. These days when Monday came around, he was grateful to be going to work. Number 52 Queen Street used to feel like chaos: a menagerie of children and animals roaming unfettered as the day washed an unpredictable tide of souls through the front door for Raven to deal with. Now it felt like an oasis, a sanctuary.

As though to emphasise the point, his bedroom door swung open, crashing noisily against the wall as James burst into the room. His mother was upon him like a falcon, scooping him up and quietly urging 'We must let Daddy sleep' as she spun the boy's grasping arms away from where Raven lay.

She had spoken as though she was protecting Raven from interruption, mindful of his rest as the household provider, but he couldn't help thinking that in truth she was acting to protect the child from him.

He began pulling on his clothes, stubbing his toe on the wooden chest at the end of the bed, which did nothing to improve his mood. He briefly distracted himself with the thought of the breakfast that would be served at Queen Street, then calculated that this would not be for almost three more hours. Time enough for a dozen further tempestuous tantrums.

He was wondering how long he could stretch out his ablutions when he heard the jingle of the doorbell.

Raven stuck his head into the hall as a man was shown inside, clutching a note. He looked rather old to be a messenger boy. Then Raven took in the whip clutched in his other hand. A driver.

'It's from Dr Littlejohn,' the man said, handing him the note.

I require your urgent assistance at Surgeons' Hall on a matter that requires the utmost discretion. My apologies for the early intrusion. I will be greatly in your debt.

No, Raven thought, as James began howling once again: it will be I who is in yours.

There was a bitter wind whipping in off the Forth as the carriage climbed North Frederick Street, but the sky was clear and the morning's colours vivid. Raven instinctively welcomed the spring and its lengthening days, but as James was adapting to the changing season by waking with the first beam of sunshine, he thought that the winter had had its consolations.

Edinburgh was a city beginning its day. He was seldom on the street at this time, and it offered different sights to later hours. From the coach he watched bakers' boys carrying their trays of fresh loaves and warm rolls to hotels along Princes Street. Raven had known a time when he was not above lightening their loads undetected, and counselled himself that perhaps he didn't have so much to complain about these days. There had been a time when he dreamed of having what he had now. It wasn't that he lacked gratitude for his lot; but despite how much had changed, he still worried whether it would be enough, particularly now it wasn't just himself he had to provide for.

The driver took him over the North Bridge and along to Nicolson Street, where the Roman columns of Surgeons' Hall loomed before them. Raven was a licentiate of the College of Surgeons, but he could not displace the sense that he was approaching enemy territory. The surgeons were increasingly inclined to see obstetricians as an upstart breed, an attitude typified by Professor Syme recently suggesting they be categorised alongside veterinarians, and the appointment of Dr Archibald Christie as the College's new head was unlikely to pour oil on troubled waters. He was new both to his position and to the city, but his reputation had preceded him. He was renowned for being as combative as he was ambitious, a man restlessly in search of new enemies to conquer. Consequently, he had been nicknamed 'Corpus' behind his back, less for the bodies he had dissected than for those he had climbed over to get where he was.

'I dinnae envy you venturing inside,' said the driver, bringing his horses to a halt.

Raven was briefly unsettled by this statement, thinking the man was referring to Dr Christie before realising he must mean something else.

'Why would that be?' he asked, curious as to what superstition or misapprehension the man might be about to share.

'Heard they found a hacked-up corpse in there.'

'I don't doubt it,' Raven replied. 'And quite necessary for the subject of anatomy to be adequately taught.'

'Porter told me he saw guts and livers and all sorts, a severed leg still dripping blood.'

It must have been the porter's first day, Raven thought. Wandered into the dissecting room without warning.

'It's common enough to have specimens on display,' Raven reassured him.

'On display, aye,' the coachman said. 'Not in somebody's desk drawer.'

As Raven stepped down from the carriage, he saw his friend Henry striding to greet him, and a second man hurrying from the building at his back. Henry was recently returned from Selkirk, where the country diet had evidently been to his liking. He looked relieved to see Raven, his impatience and anxiety evidently deriving from the presence of the stern figure behind him. Corpus Christie was marching grim-faced across the flagstones, his brow knitted together in a mixture of consternation and disapproval, a man with questions to which he already knew he would not like the answers.

'You've called for someone else?' Christie asked, taking in Raven's arrival much as he might the delivery of a wheelbarrow full of cow dung. 'I asked for discretion.'

Henry sent Raven a look conveying both gratitude and apology for what he was being dragged into.

'I appreciate that, sir,' Henry replied, 'but I explained that I would need some assistance in conducting my enquiries. That

meant engaging either Dr Raven or Mr McLevy. Which would you
have preferred?'

This spiked Dr Christie's ire. Nobody wanted the belligerent
Irish detective at their door, even someone as preeminent as the
head of the College of Surgeons. This also made Raven reassess
why he had been summoned, having initially assumed his role
would involve administering chloroform. Henry was assistant
pathologist at the Infirmary, but he was also assistant to the
police surgeon, Dr Struthers, which lent weight to his remarks
regarding McLevy.

Dr Christie seemed to remember himself and belatedly
offered a greeting. This was in keeping with what Raven had
heard about the man. It was said he was garrulous around men
of status but had little time for anyone who could not directly
further his goals.

'Dr Archibald Christie,' he said gruffly, like he grudged the
breath.

Christie was a tall and ascetically slender man with a dark mane
of flowing hair, about which he was reputedly vain.

'Dr Will Raven.'

'Ah, yes. Assistant to Simpson.'

The great man's coat-tails had been of substantial benefit to
Raven, but on this occasion he quickly ascertained the association
would serve him ill. Christie had not referred to his mentor as
Professor or even Doctor; merely 'Simpson'.

'Where is the patient?' Raven asked.

'I think it's a little late for that,' said Henry.

Christie tutted at this, visibly agitated.

Raven gave them both a quizzical look.

'Best that we simply show you,' said Henry.

Raven glanced up as they led him beneath the columns of the
building's imposing facade. He wondered why such monuments
always strove to evoke the Romans or the Greeks. Raven's schooling
had served to instruct him that they were brutal and bloodthirsty
times. He suspected the wealthy men who had commissioned them

did so in tribute to epochs when slavery had been altogether less controversial.

Raven's mother had given him the name Wilberforce, after the man who led the campaign to abolish slavery towards the end of the last century. He consequently saw it as his duty to be a driver of progress, and to look to the future rather than the past. Simpson had been an inspiration in that regard. Not only had the professor changed the course of medicine with his discovery of the effects of chloroform, but he was a strident sceptic of humbug and quackery. A duty to progress was a duty to scientific enquiry.

'It's Professor Cooper,' said Henry, leading Raven along a corridor.

'We don't know if it's Professor Cooper,' insisted Christie.

'I meant to say it's Professor Cooper we're concerned with.'

'What about him?' Raven asked, the words of the coach driver coming back to him and taking on a new and sinister resonance.

Christie opened a door on the left and led Raven into a well-appointed suite of offices. The room was warm, despite the fact that the furnace in the corner appeared to be unlit. The walls were wood-lined, three of them covered floor to ceiling with shelves of books and of preserved specimens. The sight of these alone might have been sufficient to startle whoever the driver had spoken to, but even allowing for exaggeration, they were hardly the stuff of nightmares.

Something was wrong here, something both Christie and Henry were reluctant to describe. Instead they wished Raven to see for himself, and the closer he got to doing so, the less Raven relished the prospect.

Remembering the driver's words, he glanced at the desk, a sturdy and expansive bureau covered in volumes and papers. Its drawers were closed. Henry and Christie had already walked past it anyway. They made for a wall press, a shallow cupboard adjacent to the windows, its door conspicuously open.

As he approached it, he could see more shelves, bearing vials, boxes and yet more books. Raven remained unable to discern what had occasioned either urgency or concern. Then he saw that on the floor of the cupboard was a dark grey blanket, its contours vaguely describing a shape underneath.

Henry delicately tugged it away to reveal a human foot. A left foot. It wasn't still dripping blood and it could not be described as a leg, but the carriage driver was right about one thing. It did look freshly severed.

Raven felt a hollowing inside himself. Mere yards away, human specimens were dissected every day: sights, smells and sensations with which he had developed a quotidian familiarity. But something hidden in a cupboard and covered beneath a blanket spoke not of scientific exploration but of darker deeds.

Raven took it in for a moment then turned to Henry and Christie, the latter looking simultaneously agitated and affronted; whether by the presence of the foot or of Raven he was not sure.

'I'm a little confused as to my role here,' Raven confessed.

'As am I,' said Christie, addressing Henry. 'Other than his not being James McLevy, what do we gain from Dr Raven being here?'

'He has a proven record of making discreet enquiries. The matter of the French midwife a few years ago, and of the notorious Mrs King.'

'I would hardly call the latter discreet,' Christie observed distastefully. 'It was the talk of the city.'

'The city knew only a fraction of the truth,' Raven said, for there were aspects of that affair that would shake the town to its volcanic core were he ever to reveal them.

'We don't know where Professor Cooper is,' Christie volunteered. 'He was last seen on Friday.'

'And was he walking with a bit of a limp?'

'This is no matter for levity, Dr Raven,' Christie grumbled.

'I merely mean to ask whether you believe this to be part of Dr Cooper.'

'This was discovered by one of our porters late last night,' Christie said. 'He informed me, and I sought Dr Cooper at his house. He was not at home. I returned here a few hours ago and summoned Dr Littlejohn.'

'Is Dr Cooper a tall man?'

'Of average height.'

'It's just that this looks a small foot to me. I assume this is not a specimen from the dissecting room?'

'There is only one cadaver being anatomised at the moment, and it has the full complement of feet,' Christie replied. 'We do not know who this belongs to or where it came from. There might be a perfectly mundane explanation for it, which is what I am hoping Dr Littlejohn might be able to arrive at.'

Raven looked again at the foot, which struck him as having been concealed hurriedly rather than carefully hidden. He noted too the lack of evidence suggesting violence had happened here, far less the messy business of hacking through a limb.

'I can think of an explanation that excludes Dr Cooper having murdered anyone or having been murdered himself,' Raven said. 'Unfortunately, it is not one that would continue to exclude Mr McLevy.'

Christie looked at him with an uncomfortable combination of expectation and apprehension.

'Perhaps someone has been acquiring dissection specimens, shall we say, independently,' Raven suggested.

Since the Anatomy Act of twenty years before, any unclaimed bodies could be used for dissection, so there was usually a sufficient supply. Nonetheless, some doctors were still not above procuring specimens by underhand means, particularly if they were unusual in some way.

Christie's expression indicated that an explanation involving murder might now seem preferable. The man had only recently taken up his post and anything suggestive of body-snatching would provide a calamitous start to his tenure.

'Is it possible to make some discreet enquiries at the Infirmary?' Raven suggested.

'I will certainly ask,' Henry replied. 'But if a body had turned up anywhere in this town missing a foot, it would already have attracted the attention of Struthers, and therefore McLevy. We should be grateful that does not appear to be the case.'

Christie did not look grateful. 'Until such time as we are able to account for this, it is imperative that the matter remains confidential. I do not wish to invite speculation or public alarm.'

He then turned so that his simmering glare took in Raven too.

'I realise that I am new to this city, so let me state very plainly that I am not a man who deals well with disappointment. I expect this matter to be resolved without the unnecessary involvement of anyone who is not already present in this room. Is that understood?'

'Yes, of course, Dr Christie,' Henry replied.

Raven remained silent. His thoughts turned to the driver who had brought him here. It might have been a porter he had spoken to, but his would not be the only wagging tongue. The fishwives of Newhaven were as nothing compared to the doctors of this city when it came to trading gossip and rumour.

Little in Edinburgh stayed secret for long. Apart from those things that stayed secret for ever.

TWO

arah added a handful of oats to the basin and gave it
a stir, watching as the warm water turned a milky
white. She lifted the baby from his cradle and placed
him in the bath. He loved this morning ritual and
thrashed about, sending a shower of droplets in her direction,
pebbling the front of her dress. She let him splash for a while but,
ever aware of the temperature in the room, she had to draw the
proceedings to a close before he became chilled. She lifted him out
and towelled him down, examining his skin for signs of inflammation, but there were none. He was pristine, unlike Dr Simpson's
third son Jamie, who had been afflicted by a disfiguring eczema
from a young age.

Sarah let herself cuddle her small charge for a while, breathing
in his baby scent. A feeling of serenity enveloped her, a blissful
moment of calm before the rigours of the day. As she pressed her
cheek against the fuzz of his head, she heard her name being called.
Reluctantly, she stepped out of the room and peered over the
banister to see Jarvis hovering at the bottom of the stairs. He
looked flustered. Given the rarity of such a sight, it was not a
good sign.

'Sarah, we need you,' he said somewhat tersely, before disappearing from view.

Sarah returned to the nursery and handed the baby, Alexander, over to Ruth, the nursery nurse, who was marshalling the rest of her troops: Jessie, William and Jamie. Auburn-haired Jessie was her father's favourite. He called her 'Sunbeam' and was particularly attentive towards her because she was fragile like Jamie. As usual Jessie was feeding her porridge to Nelson, the nursery dog, a Newfoundland whose great size belied his gentle nature. William was hauling on the poor beast's ears while the dog waited patiently for the crusts from William's toast.

Sarah gave a brief apology to Ruth and then headed for the stairs. She found Jarvis standing outside the downstairs waiting room.

'It's a young woman,' he said. 'Complaining of back pain.'

Jarvis looked worried. Given that the butler had been with the Simpson family for many years and was generally inured to the sights, sounds and smells of the various diseases to be found within the confines of the doctor's waiting room, Sarah began to feel apprehensive. As he reached for the door handle, Jarvis added: 'I realise that this is not my area of expertise, but I don't believe her back is the problem.'

Sarah entered the room to find the woman in question bent over a chair. She was quiet but her breathing was laboured, as if she had been running hard. At the other end of the room the rest of the early arrivals had gathered at the opposite doorway, watching from a safe distance.

Jarvis shooed them out just as the woman reared up and began to moan. Sarah approached her and swiftly ascertained that the butler had been correct in his assessment. The problem was not her back.

Sarah looked at Jarvis. 'Dr Simpson?'

'Not here,' he replied. 'Called out in the night and yet to return.'

'Dr Raven?'

Jarvis shook his head.

The woman's moan had now become a roar, followed by the unmistakable sound of second-stage bearing down. Sarah suggested that they get her onto the floor, but the woman was not for moving. Having no alternative, Sarah hoisted the woman's skirts as Jarvis turned to face the wall.

'She's crowning.'

'Is that bad?' Jarvis asked.

'No, but you'd better get me some towels before this baby drops onto the floor.'

Half an hour later the child was delivered, followed mercifully by the placenta. The woman was now on her back, propped up by pillows and nursing her daughter, while Sarah kept a hand on the abdomen ensuring that the uterus was firm. She allowed herself a smile. She had delivered a few infants in her time, but on all previous occasions she had been supervised by someone qualified to take over should any complications arise.

Sarah had guided the baby's head out, protecting the perineum with one hand as she had been taught. There had been no rents or tears and only minimal bleeding. Even so, and despite Sarah's best efforts, the carpet was a sodden mess of blood and fluid. She didn't relish the thought of telling Lizzie the housemaid about it.

Sarah stood and stretched her own aching back. As she looked down at the new mother and child she felt a familiar pang, a sensation that she always struggled to name. Was it regret? Or envy? She could never be sure. Sarah had been pregnant once too but had lost the baby and almost died herself. She now swithered between wanting what other people had and being grateful for finding herself entirely unencumbered by such responsibilities.

She had been married too — well, of course she had. Finding herself unmarried and pregnant would have made for a very different story. Her husband had been a young doctor whom she met at Queen Street when he had been undergoing treatment for what turned out to be a terminal illness. It had been a brief window of happiness tainted by the knowledge that it was to be short-lived. Sarah was now a widow and had been for several years. She felt a little young to bear such a soubriquet but had to admit that it conferred certain advantages. A widow was entitled to a degree of freedom that an unmarried woman did not enjoy, and while she missed the companionship of married life, she also was keenly aware of the expectations that being a wife came with. Sarah had other plans.

Satisfied that the risk of haemorrhage had passed, Sarah helped the woman to her feet, aware that the waiting room was needed for its intended purpose. She was leading mother and baby through to one of the consulting rooms to recover from the ordeal when Lizzie entered from the opposite end with her bucket and brush, scowling as she took in the multiple stains on the carpet. She set her pail down roughly, soapy water sloshing over the side, and stared venomously at Sarah as though all of this was somehow her fault.

Through the door that Lizzie had left open, Sarah glimpsed the throng of patients that now filled the hallway. Although Dr Simpson was an obstetrician, deliveries in the waiting room were a rare event. Tongues would be wagging.

Sarah settled the new mother onto the upholstered examination couch in Raven's consulting room. She fetched some blankets and a bassinet for the baby. The mother was soon asleep and her daughter, now fed, followed suit. Sarah watched them for a while, feeling a small glow of satisfaction at a job well done. But that little spark of self-congratulation was soon extinguished as she realised that this was entirely the sort of thing that gave her ideas above her station and not infrequently led her into trouble. Her frustration sometimes made her angry and she frequently tested the boundaries of what other people considered acceptable for a woman in her position. Her years of working with Dr Simpson had furnished her with a set of skills and knowledge that she was ever keen to apply, and yet being a woman meant that she was always limited in what she was permitted to do. She was a nurse, an assistant, and that did not seem enough for her.

Sarah harboured dangerous desires. She wanted to be a doctor. She had followed the career of Dr Elizabeth Blackwell with interest and had even travelled to Europe to meet with her, but it had been made clear that obtaining a medical degree and then attempting to practice medicine as a woman was close to impossible. There was no university in the Empire that would admit a woman, and even the American institution that had accepted Dr Blackwell had declined to repeat the experiment.

Sarah looked down at her dress and noticed that, like the waiting-room carpet, it was heavily stained. She would have to change it.

She had been leaning on Raven's desk, and when she stood up to leave, she knocked a few loose papers to the floor. She picked them up and returned them to the desk, noticing a theatre bill amongst the mess.

'The Great Kimble: Do the Spirits Return?' it read.

She wondered what Raven was doing with that. It was not his kind of thing at all.

Back in her own room, Sarah sat on her bed and allowed herself a moment to rest. The day had barely begun and already she was fatigued. She looked over at her desk. Her notebook sat where she had left it, her lecture notes still waiting to be completed. She had been up late the night before trying to catch up on her reading.

She was attending lectures three times per week at the Scottish Institution for the Education of Young Ladies at Moray Place, trying to bolster her knowledge of botany, physiology, natural history and chemistry. The institution was substantially funded by Amelia Bettencourt, partly at Sarah's suggestion, the education of women being an area in which she and the spiky aristocrat had found common ground. Sarah had been doing well but lately was struggling to keep up with her studies. Her other work, assisting Dr Simpson here at Queen Street, was equally important, but seemed to take up an increasing amount of her time. She also found herself helping out in the nursery when Ruth became overwhelmed, which was frequently. There didn't seem to be enough hours in the day to accomplish all that she wanted to do. She sometimes wished she could pull a lever to stop the world and give herself time to complete all of her tasks.

And yet she persisted. Why did she push herself so hard when there was little prospect of ever achieving what she desired?

She stood up and removed her soiled dress, struggling with some of the buttons at the back, thinking about the time when there had been someone to help her with such things; someone to care for her. She examined the dress by the light of the window, scratching with her fingernail at some of the larger stains on the floral cotton fabric. It had been one of her favourites and would need a thorough soaking in salt water if the blood stains were to come out of it.

She threw the dress onto the floor and stood at the washstand in her chemise, wishing she had warmer water to wash with, but reluctant to descend the stairs again for fear of encountering Lizzie. Lizzie in a foul temper was generally best avoided.

She heard footsteps on the stairs, and she tensed as her door opened, but it was not Lizzie coming to remonstrate with her. It was Will Raven.

Sarah grabbed a towel from the rail and held it up, shielding herself.

'You didn't knock.'

Raven smiled at her. 'Whatever you've got, I've seen it before.'

Sarah had said the same words to him the first time they met. She had been a housemaid then and had helped him bathe and tend the wounds he had sustained in a brawl. His manners had improved little since then.

They had also lain together once, before Raven was married. It had left a bittersweet mixture of conflicting emotions she had never quite been able to reconcile. Consequently, it was a memory she fought to suppress whenever it arose, though some days she fought harder than others. She wouldn't countenance such a thing now, of course. Although she sometimes wondered if he would. She often caught him looking at her but was unsure what that meant, or if it meant anything at all.

'I heard that there was some excitement this morning,' Raven said. 'Seems to be a day for it.'

He seemed to be amused, which irked her.

'Just a normal delivery,' she said, though it did not feel ordinary to her.

'Jarvis was impressed.'

This was a surprise as Jarvis rarely expressed approval of anything.

'He actually said that?'

'Indeed. And he sent me to tell you that Dr Simpson has returned and a late breakfast is now being served in the dining room. Largely in your honour.'

He looked her up and down, still smiling.

'Although it might be best if you got dressed first.'

THREE

aven entered the dining room and was greeted by the unmistakable smell of kippers. He sat himself down and reached for some toast. He was halfway through his first slice when Dr Simpson entered, looking a little the worse for wear. Usually a meticulous dresser, and ever fond of a brightly coloured waistcoat, his dark suit was distinctly crumpled, and his necktie askew.

'Bad night?' Raven asked.

'Is there ever any other kind?' the doctor said as he sat down heavily at the table. 'I'm in desperate need of a little respite from the night bell.'

'I thought that was what Viewbank was for.'

Viewbank was a recent purchase, a small house in Trinity, a village a few miles from the town. Dr Simpson had bought it as a rural retreat, escaping in the evenings at the end of a busy day to tend the garden there. Tea and egg and a sunset were all that he needed to replenish himself, he said. Although looking at him now Raven felt it might take considerably more than that.

'They still find me,' he said, shaking his head sadly. 'I've taken to hiding my hat so that no one can tell that I'm there.'

Raven poured the professor some tea and offered him a slice of toast. They munched in silence for a while until Sarah joined them. She was wearing her red woollen dress with the lace collar, a colour that suited her. She looked flushed, perhaps in her hurry to get dressed or perhaps because he had interrupted her ablutions. He was aware that he was being too familiar with her, but he enjoyed the friendly intimacy they shared and would not wish it otherwise. He did not desire to see any stuffy formality corroding their friendship and the closeness that they had long enjoyed.

It was also, he had to admit, a relief to be on friendly terms with a woman when his wife seemed intent on rendering their every conversation hostile, an excuse to recite a litany of his deficiencies as husband and father. He was either too busy, or not busy enough. He did not spend enough time at home but was also not making enough money to support them in an appropriate fashion. Too attached to Queen Street. Too attached to Dr Simpson to make his way on his own. He was weary of Eugenie's perpetual complaints and wondered if he would ever be able to meet her exacting standards; if he would ever be able to make her happy.

Sarah sat down and reached for the teapot. Her hand shook a little as she poured.

'I hear congratulations are in order,' Dr Simpson said. 'A difficult situation handled with great aplomb.'

'It was nothing,' Sarah said, sipping her tea.

'I disagree. The ability to remain calm in such a situation is extremely valuable. You should not discount it.' He smiled at her. 'I don't know what we would do without you, Sarah.'

The professor turned to Raven. 'I gather you were detained elsewhere, hence Sarah having to step into the breach. What was so urgent?'

'Henry Littlejohn requested my assistance, at Surgeons' Hall.'

'A medical case, or . . . ? Surely not a police matter?' Simpson asked.

'That is what Henry means to ascertain, and Dr Christie hopes fervently to avoid. It is a matter of some delicacy.'

Raven glanced towards Sarah. She responded with a withering look.

'You are *not* going to tell me it's too grim for my female sensibilities.'

'No. I mean to stress that it is strictly confidential. We promised Dr Christie the utmost discretion.'

As soon as the words were out, Raven realised his mistake. The professor looked thoroughly intrigued now.

Raven thought of Christie's veiled threats and explicit entreaty. He did say *unnecessary* involvement, though.

'A dismembered foot was discovered in a wall press in Dr Cooper's office.'

'A specimen?'

'We don't know. Dr Cooper himself is as yet unaccounted for.'

'And how does Henry imagine you might assist?' asked Sarah.

'Just as I am doing here: asking around and making discreet enquiries. I think Henry assumes I can still do so in less salubrious circles than this. He doesn't realise that I have become altogether more respectable during his time in Selkirk.'

'Quite,' agreed Sarah. 'It must be almost three years since I last had to treat you for a knife wound.'

Raven's hand went automatically to the site on his arm, but as always, the touch of the scar made him think not of the attack, but what happened in the hours after Sarah stitched it. He suspected her thoughts had gone there too, for she coloured a little and changed the subject.

'I see you're planning a trip to the theatre,' she said.

'How did you know that?'

'I saw the handbill on your desk.'

'It isn't my idea,' Raven said, looking to the professor for the explanation.

Simpson brightened, sitting straighter in his chair.

'My esteemed friend, the eminent theologian Reverend Guthrie, has become disturbed by talk of spiritualists and their claims to summon the dead. It's all nonsense of course, but he wishes to see for himself what this Kimble fellow is up to, and he thought that being accompanied by a couple of medical gentlemen might prove advantageous.'

'In what way?' Sarah asked. It seemed a genuine enquiry rather than an expression of doubt about their abilities.

'That being men of science we may be able to see through his subterfuge,' the professor replied.

'Is that a good idea? I mean, aren't you worried? After the *Lancet* business?'

Raven was surprised that she knew about this, although he shouldn't have been. She was a more conscientious reader of the medical literature than he was. There had been a recent letter in the *Lancet* denouncing Simpson as a purveyor of quackery, a scurrilous piece of nonsense that had caused a considerable degree of upset. The correspondent had used a pseudonym, but was strongly rumoured to be Dr Christie, an early shot across the bows following his arrival in Edinburgh.

'I like to keep an open mind about most things,' Simpson replied. 'Give everything a fair trial. And that letter was incorrect in just about every particular, as I pointed out in my reply. I will not curtail my activities because I have been falsely accused. I find that I am becoming inured to the criticisms thrown at me by fellow members of the profession.'

'I am more than happy to accompany you, Dr Simpson,' Raven said, keen to show his support. 'Genuine quackery ought to be exposed. The only problem is that my intended attendance has disappointed my wife.'

'How so? Eugenie doesn't believe in this sort of nonsense, does she?'

'No, of course not. But she had wanted me to accompany her to a salon where there is to be a scientific demonstration of mesmerism. I have had to let her down. Again. Not that I consider there to be much that is scientific about it.'

'What do you mean?' Sarah asked.

'Well, mesmerism has been entirely discredited, hasn't it? But alas, much like homeopathy it seems intent on being resurrected.'

'In what way discredited? I was under the impression many doctors believe there might be something in it,' Sarah said, looking to the professor for confirmation.

'It's true that I have dabbled with it,' Simpson said. 'Sleeplessness, toothache, that kind of thing. I had a lengthy correspondence with a surgeon named Esdaile in Calcutta. He claimed to have considerable success using it for operations on the natives there.' He rubbed his chin, a prelude to his summing up of the subject. 'While it is quite evident that some patients are exquisitely susceptible to suggestion, I think in general it is very limited in application and subject to great abuse at the hands of unscrupulous practitioners.'

'That is what's so galling about this,' Raven said. 'It's a medical man promoting it. A Dr H.P. Malham.'

'Never heard of him.'

'American, apparently. He recently gave a demonstration in some New Town drawing room and now people are talking about mesmerism with renewed credence. Hence Eugenie's enthusiasm to attend this salon.'

'I'll go with her,' said Sarah.

'Really?'

'Yes. I'd like to.'

Raven wasn't sure what he was most surprised about. That Sarah wanted to go to a demonstration of mesmerism or that she wanted to go with Eugenie.

Further discussion was interrupted by Jarvis, who entered the room bearing a letter for the professor. Dr Simpson slipped a nail under the wax seal and opened it, a smile brightening his tired face almost as soon as he started to read.

'This is from Sir James Clark, the Queen's physician.'

'If it's about the birth of Prince Leopold, we know about that already,' said Raven. 'I don't believe there is a person in the realm who remains in ignorance of the news.'

Dr Simpson looked at them both, a twinkle in his eye.

'The Queen had chloroform.'

Raven put his cup down. This *was* news.

'But I thought they were all against it. No place for it in normal labour and all that.'

Dr Simpson read from the letter:

'You will be pleased to hear the Queen had chloroform administered to her during her late confinement. It acted admirably. It was not given at any time so strongly as to render the Queen insensible, and an ounce of chloroform was scarcely consumed during the whole time. Her Majesty was greatly pleased and has never had a better recovery. I know this information will please you, and I have no doubt that it will lead to a more general use of chloroform in midwifery practice in this quarter than has hitherto prevailed.'

He put the letter down and looked at Sarah.

'This is why there is no longer any place for mesmerism.'

FOUR

triding along Queen Street at Dr Simpson's side, Raven took in his familiar sealskin coat and the hat which would drown a lesser head. The professor was an unmistakable sight, not merely to Raven but to half of the city, and as they proceeded east towards Leith Walk, it struck Raven that the man's attendance at tonight's spectacle would not go unnoticed.

They were on their way to the Adelphi Theatre at the top of Broughton Street. Raven's mind went to the performances he had seen there, the wondrous sense of escape it had offered when he was a child. His mother had taken him on occasion, and for a few hours he had been transported to realms where danger was only imaginary and evil men were vanquished.

'Perhaps you'll be taking the wee fellow to the theatre one day soon,' Simpson suggested, as though able to see into Raven's mind.

Only if I wished to ruin it for everyone else, Raven thought. He kept the sentiment to himself, but his expression betrayed him.

'Is young James not filling your heart with joy these days?'

Raven sighed. 'He exists in a state of permanent discontent and highly vocal frustration. Apart from when he is asleep, the only time he does not appear to be on the verge of tears is when he is already crying.'

'That's a noted sign of great intelligence. An enquiring mind is never at rest, and at that age, unable to satisfy itself, it gives vent by the only means available.'

'Really?' Raven asked, buoyed by the consolation this offered.

'I've no idea,' Simpson replied. 'But when you're dealing with tears, tantrums and flailing limbs, it's easier if you tell yourself it's an overture to greatness.'

Raven felt the consolation quickly wane.

'I am uneasy with the boy, and I fear he senses that. I think it best if I simply stay out of the way. I thought it would get better over time, but two years on and with another on the way, I fear I am not made to be a father.'

Simpson put a hand on his back. 'Everyone feels like they don't know what they're doing at first.'

'When does that change?'

He smiled. 'If it ever does, I'll let you know.'

Simpson's arm rose in animated greeting as they neared their destination, hailing the Reverend Guthrie as the minister crossed at the top of Leith Walk.

Guthrie was a tall, austere-looking man, and although a popular preacher he had an air of scrutinising disapproval about him that made Raven instinctively wary. To his mind, the world was replete enough with joyless folk without seeking out more of them, though Raven was aware that he wasn't the soul of good humour himself these days.

Raven never knew what to expect when meeting one of Simpson's acquaintances. They certainly did not conform to any type, disposition or outlook. Simpson was a tolerant man, curious about what he might learn from people, though not averse to provoking them and quietly gauging their reaction to his mischief. Raven, by contrast, was always in a hurry to reach the people from whom he imagined he could learn the most, while being quick to dismiss those he instinctively found objectionable.

Again, he wondered: Had Simpson always been this way, or was such patience something Raven could learn in time?

Simpson introduced them, the churchman's features transformed by a smile as soon as he encountered company. Guthrie's
hand was cold as Raven shook it, but there was warmth in his
greeting. The professor had told Raven of Guthrie's charitable
endeavours, funding the Ragged Schools which aimed to feed, clothe
and educate the poor children of the city. There was little arguing
with that.

'I hope you are not already trembling at the prospect of what
supernatural wonders we might witness,' Simpson said.

'More at what damage a charlatan might wreak,' said Guthrie.
'I know better than most what a powerful draught faith can be.
And like your chloroform, it should not be entrusted to the hands
of the untrained.'

They joined the short queue beneath the Adelphi's colonnade,
which was when Raven saw something that he had not anticipated.

'I didn't realise they would be charging a fee for admission,'
Raven said with some dismay.

'Dr Raven is always concerned for his pocket,' Simpson said to
Guthrie. 'It's his way of implying I do not pay him enough.'

'No, it's just that . . .' He glanced at Guthrie. 'I suppose
with the religious connotations, I assumed . . .' Raven did not
complete the sentence, embarrassed to make his misapprehension
so explicit.

'That can be your first lesson in detecting charlatanry, Dr
Raven,' Simpson said. 'No matter how it is dressed up, as soon as
someone puts his hand out for money, you know that is the purpose
of the exercise and the sum of his intentions.'

Raven reached reluctantly into his pocket, glancing at a poster
advertising the evening, a larger version of the handbill he had
been given. He did not expect to see proof that the spirits returned,
but in the presence of the professor, he suspected he might get his
money's worth nonetheless.

As they took their seats, Raven had the impression that a
religious service might have been better attended. The stalls were
barely half full, and the circle had not been opened. The Adelphi

had clearly seen better days, and it did not appear that Kimble's contribution was likely to alter its fortunes. However, from what he could overhear, it appeared those in attendance were making up in anticipation and enthusiasm what they lacked in number.

'I felt such a sense of my Alfred's presence the last time,' said a woman in the next row to her companion. 'When Kimble spoke to him, he told me things only Alfred could have known. I could feel him in the room, like he was sitting close by.'

'I would give anything to feel my Sadie was close again. It's been three years.'

'I would warn you it is overwhelming. I cried when I got home. I was moved to feel Alfred near me after all this time, but I also revisited the pain of losing him.'

'I would take that pain,' the other lady affirmed.

Raven watched a gentleman take the stage, recognising him from the front of house as the theatre manager. Evidently this was not an elaborate production, nor an expensive one. The backdrop was a simple curtain, before which sat a wooden cabinet, like a wardrobe with a fitted bench inside where otherwise there might be shelves or a clothes rack. In front of the cabinet was a low table upon which sat a tambourine and a violin.

'Ladies and gentlemen, thank you for coming to the Adelphi this evening,' the man announced. His demeanour was solemn, not the barker these surroundings might indicate. 'I will now leave you in the presence of Mr Richard Kimble.'

The man who took the stage was short and thin. At a distance and in the poor light, Raven could not accurately estimate his age but guessed him to be in his late forties or early fifties. His suit was presentable, though showing signs of wear. It was not the attire of a showman, but perhaps that was the first act of deception. There was something delicate about his gait, as though suffering from yesterday's excess. Raven was not the only one to notice.

'I suspect he has been communing with the spirits quite recently,' Simpson muttered under his breath.

Kimble held up both his hands, arms spread wide.

'Death is not the end,' he announced. His voice sounded soft and yet it carried clearly. A man used to the stage. 'You are all here because you know this. It is why those of us who are bereaved find it so difficult to understand how the person we knew yesterday can be gone today, never to return. But the reason their absence feels so impossible is because we look at it wrongly. That person has not truly gone. They are somewhere else, true, but the barrier between us is thinner than we imagine.

'I learned long ago that I was one of those blessed to be able to penetrate it. I resisted this at first, but in time I came to accept it as a responsibility. The spirits can reach into our world, and they do so because the loss feels as painful to them as it does to us. If I can alleviate that pain, then it is my duty to do so.'

Kimble made a subtle gesture and another member of staff, the young woman who had sold Raven his ticket, began moving down the centre aisle, passing envelopes to the audience on either side.

'In order to penetrate the barrier, it helps to focus on what connects you to those you have lost, so please write down their name and their relationship to you. But the spirits are only summoned if the message is meant expressly for them. If I cast my eyes upon it, the thought is dispelled, so put your card inside the envelope. Fold it closed, then write your name on the outside.'

Raven watched Simpson scribble something hurriedly and slip the card into the envelope. He wrote his name on the front but also marked a large X on the back.

The young woman gathered the envelopes into a basket and handed it to Kimble before retreating up the aisle. Kimble placed it to one side and turned his attention to the cabinet.

'The spirits wish to make themselves known, and to that end I must be their vessel. But first, I wish to let them make themselves *heard* in the only way available to them.'

Kimble indicated the musical instruments before him on the table.

'I do not wish what you experience tonight to be clouded by

doubt and suspicion, and so I must ensure that I cannot influence events. To that end, I require some assistance in restraining me within this cabinet.'

Raven felt a sharp elbow to the ribs.

'Make yourself useful,' said Simpson.

Raven got to his feet, as did a handful of other gentlemen, though he expected that one of them must be Kimble's confederate, the one who would be chosen.

'You, sir,' Kimble said. To Raven's surprise, Kimble was pointing at him.

Raven mounted the stage via a short staircase at the side, the steps audibly creaking under his weight.

Kimble handed him one of several lengths of rope from inside the cabinet, then sat down upon the bench. There was an unmistakable whiff of alcohol about him: not merely that of one who had recently imbibed, but one who seldom went more than a few hours without.

'Tie my hands here and bind my ankles to the bench,' Kimble instructed, placing his hands together behind his back. Raven looped the rope twice around both wrists and pulled it taut, then tied it in a strong knot. He bound Kimble's ankles to the legs of the bench, then Kimble instructed him to close the cabinet door and secure it with the heavy padlock that hung from a hasp.

It clunked into place and Raven gave it a firm tug, suspecting the hasp itself might be rigged to come loose from the board. To his disappointment, it did not.

'And now place the key on the table,' Kimble ordered, his voice now muffled, 'far from reach.'

Raven briefly considered pocketing the key and replying that it would be well out of reach that way, but opted to comply rather than start an altercation.

He had no sooner made his way back to his seat than the gaslights went down and plunged the house into darkness. The theatre was silent for a few moments, not so much as a cough to be heard as the place collectively paused in expectation.

Then there were gasps as the tambourine sounded, jingling gently at first, then louder. Moments later, the violin's strings were plucked. Again, it was faint but in the darkness it seemed all the more vivid.

Then the gasps became shrieks as a faintly glowing entity briefly appeared, that of a disembodied hand. It was there for just a moment, long enough to be seen, brief enough to wonder if it had been imagined.

The tambourine sounded again, continuing to shake, then stopped, and barely a second later the lights came back up, revealing the instruments to be where they were on the table and the cabinet still locked. The key remained where Raven had put it, though he wished he had taken note of which way round it had been.

'If someone would be so good,' Kimble said from inside the cabinet, and a man seated nearer the front climbed the creaking staircase to undo the padlock and reveal Kimble still tied within.

There was a smattering of applause as Kimble was released from his bonds. He then strode forward and lifted the basket of envelopes, placing it down on the table. He addressed the audience in controlled tones, though Raven thought he detected a slight tremor in his voice.

'Now, as you will remember, I asked you to write your initials on the outside of your envelope. I will choose one now and see if the spirit named within can be called forth.'

Raven thought he must have misheard or misunderstood when Kimble gave out his instructions before. He was sure the man had said to write your name, not your initials, but following the distraction of the cabinet spectacle he could not remember for sure.

Kimble picked an envelope from the basket and held it at arm's length, its blank back to the audience.

'The initials are CM,' he said. 'And there is a spirit seeking someone. Seeking Catherine.'

A woman in one of the rows behind Raven squealed. He turned around and she was mouthing the next word even as Kimble spoke.

'Massey.'

'That's my name,' she announced, excited. 'I am Catherine Massey.'

'The spirit says her name is Ivy.'

At this, the woman's voice choked. 'My daughter. My wee girl.'

'Yes,' said Kimble. 'She seeks her mother. Stand up, madam, come forward that I can see you.'

Mrs Massey stepped into the aisle, using seat-backs for support as she appeared so tremulous as to be in fear of collapse. She looked to be no more than Raven's age.

'You were parted from each other too early,' Kimble said. 'Oh, she was so young. Only three years.'

Mrs Massey gently shook her head. 'No, she was two.'

Kimble paused for a moment. 'Yes, but to Ivy you were together for three years, for you carried her nine months. She is clutching a toy, a doll.'

Mrs Massey nodded. 'Not a doll, but she used to clutch a blanket.'

'Yes, I thought a doll as I can see her holding something close. She held it for comfort in the dark then, and it comforts her in the dark still.'

Mrs Massey was sobbing now, tears running down her cheeks. At Kimble's summoning, her friend stepped forward and helped her back to her seat. As she did so, Kimble opened the card and briefly examined it, as though confirming what had been established.

Kimble repeated the routine, this time naming a woman close to the front and then calling upon her late son.

'He is in fine clothes,' he said.

'His uniform,' the woman told him.

'Yes. A soldier.'

She nodded, eyes filling.

'He died far away.'

'Burma,' she said.

'He talks of the heat. But also of blades and cannons. He wants you to know he did not suffer at the end.'

She shook her head in pained confusion. 'The letter said he was run through. He died . . . after two days.'

'Yes, but at the *end* he went peacefully because his thoughts were of you.'

Simpson barely suppressed a tut.

After another couple of such encounters, Raven observed that Kimble was now holding out an envelope with an X on the reverse. Simpson sat up straighter, an eagerness to his expression.

'The next spirit seeks a . . . Thomas . . . Langton.'

A gentleman across the aisle stood up excitedly. 'That's me.'

Simpson gave Raven a knowing look.

'Mr Langton, I am in contact with a spirit who says you are his father. The name I am hearing is— '

'Humbug!' shouted Simpson. 'That is the only name worthy of this nonsense, for the back of the envelope you are holding bears my mark, a cross.'

Kimble turned the envelope around. His eyes widened briefly as he realised he was undone, but he recovered his calm expression, perhaps hoping to brazen it out.

'The contents of the cards are not for my eyes,' Kimble insisted. 'They call to the spirits named therein. I often pull a card and find that the spirit summoned is not the one named in that message, but somewhere else in the basket. They do not always form an orderly queue,' he added with a forced chuckle.

'I wish to hear from my boy,' said Mr Langton, sounding at once impatient and worried his chance was lost.

'And this man here is toying with your grief,' said Simpson. 'Had I not exposed him, he would claim the next card he drew to bear *my* name, just as he holds my card and calls out yours, Mr Langton. This is no more than a parlour trick.'

There was murmuring around the room, a sense of growing anger, though initially it was not clear whether the bulk of it was directed at Kimble for being a cheat, or at Simpson for interrupting him.

The professor turned to take in the whole theatre.

'Did anyone write merely their initials on the card? Or their full name?'

More murmuring. Everybody had assumed they were the only one who had misheard or made a mistake.

Kimble's face was grim. He looked much as Raven imagined he must have when he woke up that morning, sweat laced with alcohol seeping through his pores.

An object hit Kimble in the chest, thrown from the stalls. It was a half-eaten apple.

'Please, ladies and gentlemen,' he appealed. 'The spirits respond to our emotions. It only serves to dispel them when there are those present who do not believe.'

At this, the Reverend Guthrie stood up and made himself known. The place was instantly silenced as people recognised his minister's collar.

'I believe,' he stated loudly, 'that you are a charlatan.'

And with that, a dam broke. People began shouting angrily at Kimble, forcing him to retreat from the stage, while others hurried towards the foyer, stating their intention to demand their money back.

Raven was of the opinion that his had been well spent.

Not everybody was pleased with Simpson, however. Mr Langton challenged him, aggrieved at what he felt had been taken away.

'What does it matter whether he asked for a name or for initials?' he demanded. 'He got all the other things right. Things he could not have known.'

'We only remember the names of the horses that won, don't we,' Simpson replied calmly. 'Kimble got many things wrong, and all that he got right was told to him.'

Mr Langton shook his head in disgust, unmoved by Simpson's arguments. Nor was he the only one struggling to accept what had unfolded. As they stepped back out into the night, Raven saw Mrs Massey standing against one of the columns of the portico. Her face was a tearful mixture of longing, pain and confusion.

'It is cruel to dabble in such things,' Simpson murmured, looking at Mrs Massey. 'The need to believe is the most powerful part of the deception.'

FIVE

I can assure you that what Eugenie and I witnessed at the salon last night was no vulgar spectacle,' Sarah said, having listened to Raven recount the farcical events he had seen at the Adelphi. 'We watched a young woman taken from the audience and mesmerised,' she continued. 'She fell into a trance, and it was as though she had breathed ether or chloroform. She was completely oblivious to painful stimuli. I saw members of the audience pull her hair, tug at her earlobes and shout into her face. None of it roused her.'

They had repaired to the kitchen after the morning clinic, drawn there by hunger and the smell of freshly baked bread. Sarah fetched two plates and a bread knife, while Raven acted more directly, gouging a piece from beneath the crust with his fingers. Sarah slapped his hand away. There was a comfortable familiarity about it, though she wondered if he showed better table manners before his wife.

'Not quite the equivalent of having a leg off though, is it?' Raven said.

'Agreed. But what Dr Malham demonstrated last night still demands serious investigation.'

'Which university did this Malham attend?' he asked.

'Harvard, I think.'

'What is he doing in Edinburgh?'

'He regards it as the medical centre of the world, and therefore more open to new ideas than London or Boston.'

Raven rolled his eyes. 'People were impressed by Mesmer at first too. What you ought to investigate is the debacle involving John Elliotson at University College Hospital in London. It begins with simple enough demonstrations of young women in trances, but before you know it, people are claiming powers of clairvoyance and all sorts of other nonsense.'

Sarah began cutting the bread into slices.

'Then let us talk about what I did actually see, not what anyone claimed. I saw this young woman withstand considerable pain without the slightest flinch. I was distressed enough just watching. You could not have tolerated it, believe me. If mesmerism can produce this degree of analgesia, shouldn't we explore it and perhaps put it to use?'

'I don't know how she tolerated being poked and prodded, but just because I cannot say how something was done does not mean it constitutes proof of animal magnetism or some other magical force.'

Raven reached for a slice of bread, but Sarah batted his hand away, less playfully this time.

'I didn't say it was magical. And Dr Malham said specifically that he does not believe in animal magnetism. Just because we don't know how something works does not mean we can deny its effects. You can't tell me *how* chloroform works, but you would never suggest we stop using it.'

'I notice it only works if you inhale the vapour,' Raven countered. 'And I know where the vapour comes from.'

'You cannot see it though, and you don't know why it has the effect that it does. We cannot see electricity or gravity, or indeed magnetism, but these forces are undeniably present.'

'Yes, but the effects of all of those, like the effects of chloroform, are measurable, predictable and repeatable.'

Sarah suppressed a sigh, denying him the satisfaction of her frustration.

'But that is precisely my point. How can it be subject to rational scientific study if we simply dismiss it out of hand?' she asked.

With her attention on him and not the loaf, Raven snatched a slice of bread and bit into it, speaking as he chewed. 'Elliotson and Mesmer's misconduct have clearly demonstrated that there *is* no field to study,' he said with a self-satisfied smile.

She should have known he would be this way. Raven sat there secure in his position as a doctor, assistant to Professor Simpson no less, with a fine education behind him and excellent prospects before him. He could afford to dismiss the possibilities of mesmerism. Sarah, who could not attend university, could not study medicine, could not pursue the career of her choosing, had to exploit whatever opportunities presented themselves.

Sarah was not some wide-eyed dupe, intoxicated by wonder. She knew all about Elliotson and Mesmer's unscientific excesses, but she also knew about James Braid in Manchester and the process he was calling 'hypnosis'. She knew about the likes of Kimble and the Fox sisters, turning a profit from parlour tricks dressed up as supernatural phenomena. But she also knew that was not what she had seen last night. People might pay to hear messages from the dead and invisible spirits play musical instruments, but it would make for poor entertainment merely to watch someone have their hair pulled or their earlobe tweaked without flinching. And crucially, the salon was by invitation only and payment was not sought for admission.

There was more to be known about mesmerism. It *was* a field of study. But most importantly it was a field that men such as Raven had not already claimed. That it was not accepted as an established discipline of medicine was also the reason it offered Sarah an opportunity. Unlike Raven, she had to sift through the chaff discarded by others in the hope of finding something they had overlooked. Sarah could not afford to dismiss the potential of any new field in case it was the avenue by which she might establish herself as some form of practitioner.

She was reaching for the cheese when she recognised the sound of Jarvis's footsteps coming down the stairs.

'Dr Littlejohn is here to see you,' the butler announced.

Raven stood up, eyeing the loaf.

'Please ensure there's some of that left when I return,' he said.

'Actually,' said Jarvis, 'I was speaking to Miss Fisher.'

It would be difficult to say whether she or Raven was the more curious as they hurried up the stairs.

Henry was standing in the entrance hall, a wooden box next to him on the floor.

'Is this regarding the foot?' Sarah asked.

'Indeed. I was hoping you might be able to shed some light on something.'

Raven looked askance at the wooden box. 'You surely haven't brought it with you?'

'As you are aware, it is imperative that I keep the matter quiet for now. Can you imagine the attention that would be generated by my bringing Miss Fisher inside Surgeons' Hall?'

'Understood.'

Henry lifted the box and they followed Raven towards his consulting room.

'You didn't hear of any mutilated patients presenting themselves at the Infirmary?' Raven asked.

'None missing a foot, anyway,' Henry replied. 'And nor have any bodies shown up minus the requisite appendage. I don't suppose you've happened upon any information since yesterday?'

'No, but I've been keeping my eyes open for signs of suspicious hopping. What of Dr Cooper?'

Raven held the door open and Henry placed the box on his desk.

'I am pleased to say he has returned, all in one piece, irritated by the fuss and adamant that he has no knowledge of why there should be a foot at the bottom of his press.'

'He would say that though, wouldn't he,' Raven observed. 'Did you ascertain whether he was in dispute with anyone?'

'It's Surgeons' Hall,' replied Henry drily. 'Everyone is always in a dispute with everyone else. But I did hear that Dr Cooper has had cross words with a few colleagues regarding his growing interest in mesmerism. He is of the opinion that it is not to be lightly dismissed.'

Sarah failed to resist sending Raven a look of vindication.

'This is not a popular position among his peers,' Henry added, which Sarah knew to be quite the understatement. No less a figure than the late Robert Liston had declared himself an enemy of mesmerism and rallied fellow surgeons to his banner. Indeed, his famous words upon the first successful use of ether in one of his operations had been: 'This Yankee dodge beats mesmerism hollow.'

Henry opened the box and removed the foot, still wrapped in the same cloth. He placed it on Raven's desk, in a spot where the morning sunlight struck it.

'Is there any way of telling if it's male or female?' asked Sarah.

'No. I would say it's small enough to be a woman's but not so dainty as to preclude being a man's.'

Henry began to delicately pull back the cloth, revealing the grisly item beneath. Sarah's eyes fixed upon it, cool and unruffled.

'And what do you hope I can do for you, Henry?'

'Having had the opportunity to properly examine the foot in better light, I observed damage to it other than that inflicted in its removal. I came to speak to you, Sarah, because in accordance with the forcefully expressed wishes of Dr Christie, I am hoping to delay the moment at which I am obliged to inform Mr McLevy. I am of the opinion that the damage indicates an application of some kind of corrosive. Of the three of us, you seem to be the most up to date on matters of chemistry.'

Sarah was pleased to observe that Raven did not attempt to dispute this.

'You see this discolouration here?' Henry pointed at the medial aspect of the foot. 'And the flesh here is soft and easily broken.'

'It does look as though some caustic substance has been applied,' Sarah agreed.

'Was someone attempting to dissolve it, do you think? And if so, what would they use?'

'Potash would do it. But it would take a while. Or nitric acid. Potash would be best, though, as it can be used in any receptacle. Nitric acid would require porcelain or glass.'

Raven arched an eyebrow at her.

'What?' Sarah said.

'How do you know this stuff? Have you been making experiments?'

Sarah tutted. 'I read. Widely.'

'Could someone at Surgeons' Hall have been investigating the effect of corrosives?' Henry suggested.

'In Cooper's rooms without his knowledge?' Raven countered. 'Doesn't seem likely, does it?'

'So, we're back to dissolution,' Sarah said. 'As a means of disposal, presumably.'

'Though I am curious,' Raven added, 'as to what manner of man would first try to dispose of such an appendage by dissolving it, and upon failing, resort to merely hiding it in a cupboard.'

'There are many aspects I find curious about this,' said Henry. 'But there are two questions we must answer before we are likely to learn more about any of them: who does this foot belong to, and where is the rest of them?'

SIX

ee James was running in increasingly erratic patterns on the grass of Queen Street Gardens, chasing pigeons with apparently murderous intent. As he bore down on one of them, Raven was suddenly moved to scoop him up. The child squealed with delight as he was unexpectedly lofted from the ground. Raven tossed him fully into the air, then caught him under the arms and held him to his chest.

There was a feeling of warmth that went far beyond the mere physical heat of it. For all the boy could drive him to distraction, the love Raven felt for him was sometimes uncontainable.

When Raven heard James laugh and saw his smile, he saw everything he wanted in this world, but equally when he saw James's look of rage and heard his cries of anger and frustration, he saw everything he feared that he might instil in the boy, or that the boy might have inherited already.

He often wondered whether the best way to do right by the child was simply to provide for him and to offer him an example whilst keeping a distance. It was not uncommon. So many of the fathers he knew enjoyed privacy from their families, the children only permitted to approach their father at his bidding; never allowed to interrupt his important work or his quiet times. But then there were moments like this, which made him think of the joy he had witnessed in Simpson's children and in Simpson himself through being fully involved with them, the great professor acting like a child when he was with them.

Raven could also starkly remember the feeling of his own father's indifference, and that had been on the good days.

A moment later James decided he had had enough of this restraint. He began struggling, his feet kicking at Raven, and soon he was voicing his familiarly vociferous displeasure.

'Down! Down, Daddy, down.'

Eugenie smiled at him from her place on a nearby bench. Raven took in the bulge of her stomach and felt something uncontainable towards her too.

'My father visited while you were at the Maternity Hospital this afternoon,' she said.

Raven tried to maintain a neutral expression, concealing how he truly felt as he anticipated where this was going. He so much wanted to do right by both of them – all three of them soon enough – but felt such worry, such fear of failing them. He could not afford a misstep.

'With our second child due soon, he is concerned that our place in Castle Street is too small. We need more space, Will, and that means more money. Certainly more money than Dr Simpson is paying you.'

One of the things Raven had come to learn about marriage was how often you could have the same conversations while both pretending you hadn't each said your side of it a dozen times before. Eugenie was impatient for Raven to set up his own practice. She had been brought up in the household of one of the most successful doctors in Edinburgh, Cameron Todd having a vast roster of wealthy patients, and she seemed to be under the impression that the same would be true for Raven as soon as he opened his doors. Unfortunately, it did not work like that.

'If I wish to build up a practice, I will need to offer something that patients cannot find elsewhere,' he argued. 'As I intend to specialise in gynaecology, it would be unwise to leave Queen Street when there is still so much to learn.'

'But when will it be enough, Will? I know how fond you are of Dr Simpson and I know how valuable his instruction has been, but there will always be more to learn. You have to step out on your own some time. Or is he not the only thing keeping you there?'

Raven knew what she was alluding to and understood that her emotions were running high if she was doing so directly. His wife had always been sensitive about his relationship with Sarah, not least because it predated their own, but she rarely raised it explicitly.

'If I struck out on my own right now, it would be a great risk. At least at Queen Street I have a steady income. Setting up a new practice will be an expensive business, and it could be a long time before it generated a decent return.'

'Yes, which is why my father has offered to lend you the money until your practice is established. I don't understand why you remain so reluctant to accept.'

'I wish to stand on my own two feet, not be beholden to anyone else.'

'It's my father, Raven, not some Old Town cut-throat.'

Eugenie knew a little of Raven's past dealings with such people, and how it had occasioned the scar on his cheek. She knew less of what it had taught him regarding the nature of all such relationships, no matter who held the note. Raven had been in the debt of a ruthless and extremely dangerous money-lender by the name of Flint: a combustible individual with whom Raven had not so much a relationship as a fragile truce. Flint was confoundingly resourceful, with an unfailing eye for human weakness, a man who knew more about what went on in the darker parts of this city than James McLevy could ever pretend to.

Sarah's father meant well, but Raven's experience with Flint had taught him that the power exerted by those one owes becomes something they are reluctant to relinquish. Such men found ways to ensure that the ledger was never clear. Even when Raven's debts were paid, Flint had found new ways to keep his hooks in him, and similarly he suspected Cameron Todd would not easily give up any leverage he had over his son-in-law.

'I know your father wants only the best for you, as do I,' Raven told her. 'But we both know that he likes things his own way. He would be always at my shoulder, demanding a say in how the practice was run.'

Eugenie placed a hand on her belly. 'Time is marching on, Will. And I do not think our modest place in Castle Street is big enough to accommodate two children and your pride.'

She was right, he knew. Eugenie had grown up in a large town-house on St Andrew Square and was feeling the strain of her reduced circumstances. Raven wanted to give her more, but feared that if he moved on too soon, he might only be half the doctor he would otherwise become.

The spectre of Flint had not troubled him in years, nor had he seen or heard from the man. The last time they exchanged words, Flint had held a Forsyth pistol to Raven's head, Raven a Liston knife to Flint's throat. The only reason he would ever wish to encounter him again would be so that Flint could witness how much better Raven's life had become, and thus know which of them was ultimately the victor.

Raven watched his son race across the grass in the evening sunshine, his place of employment visible just along the street. He worried constantly about the future, but this was already a better future than he might once have imagined.

Then he saw Eugenie rise from the bench and, despite the encumbrance of her belly, move to sweep up James with a haste Raven recognised. It was an instinctive precaution whenever she saw her son get close to anyone she did not like the look of, and she would be forgiven for not liking the look of this.

There was a huge figure lumbering towards them, awkward of gait, uncommon of stature and misshapen of visage. He was seven feet tall, but awkwardly proportioned, like a version of Mary Shelley's creature put together from oversize parts of other men. His head alone was the size of a barrel, his features oddly stretched apart by his affliction. He was a frightening sight to those who did not recognise him, more frightening still to many who did.

But not to all.

'Don't worry,' Raven told his wife. 'He is known to me. He means you no harm.'

Raven doubted the giant meant him any harm either, but in his experience his presence was seldom a harbinger of anything good.

'How are you, Gregor?'

'I've been better, Dr Raven, but as I only see worse days ahead, I am grateful for how I feel right now.'

'It has been a long time,' Raven acknowledged. He had once taken an interest in Gregor's welfare, but family life had given him more immediate responsibilities.

'I did not mean to alarm you, madam,' Gregor told Eugenie, offering a smile. His teeth were like a derelict graveyard, gaps between them not merely from rot but as a result of how certain parts of him seemed to grow at a different pace to others.

Eugenie looked further disturbed by the smile, but James responded in kind, letting out a chuckle. Raven hoped this did not mean the child had inherited an instinct for trouble and was happily welcoming when he recognised it.

'I need your help,' said Gregor.

'Is it a medical matter?'

'Yes and no,' he replied.

'Is it urgent?'

'Again, yes and no. Urgent for me, at least, but . . .' His huge face creased with strained apology. 'It is not something I wish to discuss in public. You will need to come with me.'

Raven glanced at Eugenie, keeping her distance a few feet away. From her impatient expression he could tell that she believed their discussions regarding his prospects and her father's offer were not concluded. Raven walked closer to her, mussing James's hair where he hung in her arms.

'I am urgently required elsewhere,' he told her. 'A medical matter.'

Eugenie frowned, but she was unable to dispute this, for Gregor did not look well. He was pallid and gaunt, as though he had not been eating.

Gregor led Raven out of the gardens onto Queen Street, where he hailed a carriage and told the driver an address in the Old Town, near Nicolson Square. They climbed aboard, the big man having to contort himself to fit through the covered carriage's small door. Raven took it as a sign of being accorded greater respect that this was the manner of conveyance. In the past, Gregor had on occasion bundled him into the back of an open cart.

'Who lives at that address?' Raven asked as the carriage picked up speed. 'Have you gone up in the world? And please do not answer yes and no.'

'It concerns one Laurence Butters,' Gregor said. 'Do you know the name?'

Raven did not. 'Why would I?'

'Perhaps from a playbill. He is an actor.'

'And how does he concern you?'

Gregor paused, fixing Raven with a weary expression, part apology, part acknowledgement of the inevitable.

'He owes money.'

Raven confined his response to one word, though it contained multitudes.

'Flint.'

Among those multitudes was the troubling implication that if Gregor knew where to find Raven, then Flint knew where he lived. Where his family lived.

Raven felt strangely annoyed with himself. It was as though thinking about Flint had conjured him up again, brought him back into existence.

Gregor had been – and evidently still was – Flint's enforcer and collector, and Raven's introduction to him was something of which his face bore a permanent reminder. Equally, Raven's profession had not endeared him to Gregor, but in time they had each redeemed themselves in the other's eyes, to the extent that they had an unspoken understanding. Nonetheless, Flint engendered a surprising amount of loyalty in Gregor, and not merely because he was the man who put money in his pocket. Raven suspected that Flint and his crew were the closest thing to family that Gregor knew.

'Does this Mr Butters require medical attention?' he asked.

'That remains to be seen. Primarily it's my own welfare I'm concerned with right now.'

Raven's face conveyed his exasperation at Gregor talking in riddles. The big man gestured towards the driver.

'As I said, it's best if you see for yourself.'

The carriage sped along South Bridge and past Surgeons' Hall. It turned onto Nicolson Square, where it stopped and they disembarked. Raven noted the proximity of the address to where the foot had been found.

Gregor led him into Nicolson Square Court, through a back entrance and up some stairs. He had to stop for breath at the first landing. He really did not look well.

Before learning his true name, Raven had nicknamed him Gargantua, but he looked back on this with a degree of shame, for he had failed to see the human being within the hulking form. And that hulking form was the result of the man's illness. Gregor was painfully familiar with the story of Charles Byrne, the so-called Irish Giant, enough to know that Byrne died aged only twenty-two. It was a matter of pride to Gregor that he had lasted longer than that, but his health was in visibly rapid decline.

'I was sent to collect,' he explained. 'Though I'm not sure how capable I am of pressing the matter these days.'

Raven thought of last night's performance. Many things, even in the everyday, were a matter of illusion. If Gregor turned up at your door demanding money, you would be terrified at the mere sight of him, but in truth it was taking all his strength just to keep himself upright. The greatest damage he could inflict would be if he were to collapse on top of you.

'Butters owes Flint a sizable sum,' Gregor said, resuming his climb. 'Been rising with interest for some time, but the rumour was he had come into some money, hence me being dispatched to collect. He's a hard man to track down, though: a real bag of tricks. Flint warned me that nothing about him is what you would assume. His days on the stage have apparently made him very adept at pretending to be other people. That's why I was sent here to break in and take whatever I could find.'

As they reached the next landing, Raven saw that a door had been forced.

Gregor led him inside, where Raven was immediately struck by a familiar smell, not overpowering but still unmistakable. Blood. Days stale yet still hanging in the air. Otherwise it was a modest but well-maintained dwelling, neatly decorated in bright colours, the walls adorned with playbills featuring Butters' name. There was undeniably a woman's touch about the place.

'Is he married?'

'Yes. But there's been no sign of her either. There's nothing fresh in the larder and the stove has not been lit in a while.'

'Do you think they've absconded?'

'Well, one of them has. The other can't have got very far.'

'How do you know that?'

Gregor led Raven into the kitchen, where the smell was stronger. There was dark staining on the floorboards – a lot of it – and burgundy speckles on the walls.

Gregor crouched down with laborious effort.

'I was looking for hidey holes where he might have stashed some money. Under the floorboards is a common choice, and they all reckon they're the only one to think of it. Usually under a heavy bit of furniture. Anyway, I found this.'

Gregor indicated a trunk on the floor. It was padlocked but the hasp had been broken off, gouged clear of the wood.

'Was this you or was someone here before you?' Raven asked.

'Looks that way,' said Gregor. 'But if there was any money in it, it couldn't have been much. It's full to the brim with this old rubbish.'

Gregor reached in and lifted out a sheaf of old playbills and pages from newspapers and magazines. There were dozens of them: mementoes of Butters' performances down the years. A life in yellowing print.

'That's not what I want to show you.'

Gregor hauled the trunk aside and wedged up a floorboard beneath it, revealing a narrow channel between the joists. There, squeezed in between the boards, was a human foot, the flesh ragged and rotten where it had been hacked off.

'A medical matter, but not urgent,' Raven acknowledged.

'That's not all.' Gregor pulled up the next floorboard. The light through the kitchen's small window was not strong, but it was enough for Raven to recognise a section of femur with a piece of muscle still attached.

'This Laurence Butters, was he a tall man?'

'Short.'

Raven thought of the foot at Surgeons' Hall. It had been a left; this was a right.

'So this could be his.'

'Yes,' agreed Gregor. 'Which would be very bad news for Mr Flint.'

'What do you want me to do about it?'

'I don't want the blame for this,' the big man replied. 'People don't forget the sight of me coming and going. I don't want McLevy fixing me for murder. Once he happens upon a satisfactory conclusion, he doesn't worry much if there's some steps missing from how he gets there. You know how he works.'

'Only too well,' Raven said.

'I reckoned it would be better if this came to his attention through the right channels. It's known you're friends with Dr Littlejohn who assists the police surgeon. I'm presenting it to you so you can present it to him.'

'You could have contacted Dr Littlejohn yourself.'

'I don't know him. I know you. But it's not just that.'

Gregor's face took on that weary look again, knowing Raven wouldn't like what he was about to say next.

'Mr Flint wants to be kept informed. If this turns out to be Butters, he doesn't want McLevy thinking he was behind it. And if it's not Butters, he wants to know where the bugger is, quick smart.'

'I can't see what use I would be in that matter. Finding people is not my forte. When you're a doctor they tend to come and find you.'

'He remembers you as a resourceful man.'

'Does he also remember how well-disposed I am towards him?'

'Mr Flint is a good man to have owing you a favour,' Gregor said.

'There is no favour I would wish from him.'

'And a bad man to have bearing you a grudge,' he added.

Raven sighed. 'Understood,' he said. 'If I learn anything, I will pass it on. I was rather hoping Flint had forgotten about me, just as I had largely forgotten about him. I note he has not changed. Still lending money and sending you to collect.'

'I don't actually see so much of him any more,' Gregor replied. 'He is the one going up in the world. Fancies himself the businessman these days.'

'What kind of business?'

'Nothing that he would confide in the likes of me. But I know he is directing his funds into legitimate enterprises. I think he has something big in the offing, which is why he's calling in debts.'

Gregor carefully replaced the floorboards over the foot and thigh.

'You will make sure Dr Littlejohn knows I only found this and reported it, won't you?'

'For sure, Gregor. But once Henry knows, there will be no keeping McLevy out of this.'

This didn't seem to trouble Gregor, and nor should it particularly. Raven thought of the foot at Surgeons' Hall. He didn't imagine Dr Christie would have quite as sanguine a reaction when he learned the same news. Nor did he relish the fact that Henry would be obliged to tell McLevy how he came by the discovery.

Gregor climbed to his feet, his head almost brushing the kitchen's ceiling. He clutched his hands together.

'Thank you. I am much obliged towards you, Dr Raven. But you are still obliged to me, if you understand my meaning.'

Raven did, unmistakably.

Gregor had initially borne great enmity and suspicion towards Raven because of how his profession had mistreated Charles Byrne. The anatomist John Hunter had been determined to procure the Irish Giant's body, asking to purchase it even before the man had died. Byrne, a religious man, was horrified at the prospect, and had sworn his friends to protect his remains. Unfortunately, Hunter's coin proved too tempting, and the giant was betrayed before he could be laid to rest. Most disgracefully, Hunter did not even dissect his prize. The scandal attending his acquisition caused him to boil the man down to his bones and hide them away, only assembling Byrne's skeleton years later, by which time it was merely a trophy. Gregor had been vocal in his condemnation: *Five hundred pounds, Hunter paid. Do you think Charles Byrne earned a fraction of that his whole life? Men like you see men like me as worth more dead than alive.*

It had been a long road, but in time Gregor had come to understand that Raven should not be judged by the worst deeds of his profession. They had come to an agreement whereby Raven would ensure Gregor's remains met a more dignified fate.

'I may need that favour soon. I am not long for this world,' he said.

Raven wished he could argue the point, but it would be to insult the man's intelligence and make light of his suffering.

'I want to be buried somewhere the anatomists can never get at me. You'll do that for me, won't you, Dr Raven? You remember what I did for you, and for Miss Fisher.'

'I do indeed, Gregor. I have not forgotten. You have my word.'

eppermint?'

Catherine Crowe held out a crumpled paper bag.

Sarah popped one into her mouth and began crunching it immediately. The rustling and the crunching seemed to annoy their immediate neighbours, who turned in their seats and gave them a sour look. Mrs Crowe blithely ignored them.

They were seated towards the back of a small meeting room on the first floor of a building in Potter Row. Sarah had noticed that there was a larger space downstairs, but evidently not the numbers to fill it.

There had been a notice in the *Scotsman* the day before about the recent establishment of an Edinburgh Mesmeric Association, which would be holding regular meetings 'to share knowledge and encourage the promulgation of the science of mesmerism'. Sarah had been keen to attend but reluctant to go on her own, and with Eugenie's curiosity proving sated by the salon, had sought out Mrs Crowe instead.

Mrs Crowe was an author who attended dinners at Queen Street on occasion, often surprising the other guests with her enthusiasm for the intoxicating effects of inhaling chloroform and ether, and indulging in the most salacious gossip (which was probably the reason Dr Simpson invited her). Sarah had come to know her independently through her involvement in progressive causes. If there was a meeting to advocate the rights of women or to highlight the plight of the poor, Mrs Crowe would be there. However, she also had a boundless enthusiasm for fringe interests such as spiritualism, homeopathy and phrenology. Sarah did not know on which side of the debate Mrs Crowe's interest in mesmerism might fall, but she could be confident that it would be pursued with gusto.

She had briefly considered asking Raven but decided against it. She wanted to hear what the members of this nascent association had to say without having to endure his disparaging remarks. He had made up his mind and there seemed to be no changing it. She would have to present him with incontrovertible evidence, and even then she was not sure he would budge. He often accused her of being stubborn, perhaps because it was a trait he was well-equipped to recognise.

Sarah had entered the room and been unsurprised to find that she and Mrs Crowe were the only women there. Perhaps more surprising was the presence of so many medical men, a sight that would have dismayed Raven. The pair of them had drawn quite a few curious looks, but Sarah could not rightly say whether this was down to their gender or that her companion was sporting a voluminous purple cape and matching hat, finished with a towering ostrich feather that would have obscured the view of anyone sitting behind her. No one was.

Sarah was of the opinion that when intruding into male-dominated territory it was best to do so in a stealthy manner, without attracting too much attention. As Eugenie liked to say, if a woman sits quietly in a corner, the men around her will frequently behave as though she is not there. Mrs Crowe evidently did not share this approach and unapologetically took up space wherever she went. Sarah was beginning to think that this tactic was worthy of emulation, though perhaps minus the exuberant millinery.

Mrs Crowe knew everyone and everyone's business and so pointed out the most notable attendees as they took their seats – generally at a distance from Mrs Crowe herself.

'There's Dr Davey, Association Secretary and keen acolyte of Mesmer. He's done me, you know.'

'You've been mesmerised?'

'Of course. You know me. Keen to try everything.'

'What was it like?'

'I'm quite susceptible to the old mesmeric forces apparently. Dropped off to sleep in a jiffy. Quite relaxing. Felt a sense of calm for a while afterwards, though it didn't do much for the pain in my back. But then it often takes more than one treatment. Sometimes weeks of therapy are necessary, hence the keen interest of this lot. Multiple treatments, multiple fees.'

Mrs Crowe popped another peppermint into her mouth.

'And here comes Dr Johnstone. Rumour has it that he has been taking part in spiritualist séances at his home, trying to contact his dead wife.'

'Why would he do that?' Sarah asked.

'Grief is a curious thing. Makes you vulnerable to the shady promises of charlatans. The only reason I would have to contact my husband after his death would be to make sure he was getting his just deserts, in the bad place, being tormented by demons.'

Sarah had heard this sentiment expressed before, but still felt a little shocked by the older woman's candour. Mrs Crowe had famously left her violent husband and had turned to writing as a means of supporting herself.

'And here is our Dr Malham. Quite splendid, isn't he.'

Dr Harland Malham walked in wearing a green brocade jacket, which seemed rather ostentatious for a medical man; those of Sarah's acquaintance were almost universally clad in a sombre black. Sarah wondered if Mrs Crowe was referring to the man himself or merely his sartorial choices.

'Do you know much about him?' Sarah asked.

'Worked in Boston before coming here,' Mrs Crowe replied. 'He was an associate of the man Morton, who discovered ether. I'm told he helped with the experiments but then Morton refused to share the credit. Malham became disillusioned and decided to try his luck here.'

Malham was in the company of two men Sarah did not recognise, one of them almost as flamboyantly attired as he, the other slightly more soberly dressed, but his suit of fine quality nonetheless. Mrs Crowe of course knew who they were.

'That's Mr Somerville,' she said, indicating the more formally attired and business-like of the two. There was an energy about him, Sarah thought, someone else not so much unapologetic for his presence as making a subtle statement of intent.

'He's buying up property all over the city,' Mrs Crowe went on. 'He has plans to purchase this building and offer preferential rates if the association expands to take over the whole place. Naturally, he is demanding a share of the profits, should any accrue.'

'And who is the third?' Sarah asked.

'That's Mr Gethyn, the tailor. A Welshman. Not long arrived in Edinburgh but already very much in demand.'

The low murmur of muted conversation in the room was terminated when Professor Gregory stood to open the meeting. Gregory was Professor of Chemistry at the university and author of Sarah's well-thumbed textbook on the subject. He was an unusual case – a university academic who seemed able to pursue his more controversial interests, such as phrenology and mesmerism, without attracting the opprobrium of his fellow professors. This was down to his being a mild-mannered man who avoided direct confrontation with his peers – easier said than done in this city – and to the fact that he rigidly stuck to chemistry when teaching students.

The professor stood at the front of the room and cleared his throat. 'Mesmerism,' he said, 'is capable of treating disease that ordinary medical therapies cannot reach. This is quite evident by the multiple experiments made by learned colleagues. Unfortunately, the medical profession in general has shown an injudicious disregard and even a needless hostility towards it. We must take some comfort from the fact that some of the ablest writers on the subject and some of the most influential leaders of the movement are physicians of eminence in various countries. Further proof of this is here before us tonight in the form of Dr Malham, all the way from America.'

Dr Malham got to his feet. He was of average size but had a commanding presence. He gestured with his hands as he spoke, communicating to the audience the great passion he felt for his subject.

'I do not believe in animal magnetism,' he said. 'I do not believe in an invisible magnetised fluid that courses through all living things. What I *do* believe in is the power of the mind, a power that with the correct knowledge and skill, can be tapped into. Its remarkable effects are of scientific interest, but what of the applications of these phenomena? There is an ever-growing list of afflictions, some of them of long standing and resistant to the efforts of modern medicine, which can be relieved by recourse to mesmerism. Tic douloureux, rheumatism, megrims and seizures, to name but a few. The establishment of this association is an important first step in promoting this remarkable method of treatment and of cure.'

Following a smattering of polite applause, there followed a vigorous discussion about various aspects of the mesmeric cure: whether it was always necessary to induce mesmeric sleep, whether cures could be achieved by local mesmerism with passes made over the affected part.

One man stood up on unsteady feet.

'Ah, poor old Dr Baird,' Mrs Crowe said. 'He has a case of the shaking palsy.'

Sarah looked over at the man in question. His left arm was making rhythmic movements that seemed to be outwith his control. 'What are we to do about the lack of suitable operators?' he said, his voice a little tremulous. 'Everyone I know has more cases than they can possibly attend to. Many applications for treatment have to be delayed as a result.'

'You make an excellent point, sir,' said Dr Malham. 'Now that funds have been raised for an institute, even though it is for the moment only a few rooms, we should consider classes for those who wish to learn the technique.'

Dr Baird was quick to dismiss this suggestion.

'I do not believe that there is much appetite within the profession for such instruction.'

'Then I suggest we cast our net a little wider,' Malham replied.

'This is far better kept within the medical community, I should think,' said Professor Gregory, rising to his feet. 'I would be wary of placing such a potent instrument into the hands of the ignorant.'

There was a low susurrus of agreement.

'But think of the benefits that could be accrued by sharing this knowledge,' Malham countered.

'You risk further alienation of the profession if you commence instructing all and sundry to do this work,' Professor Gregory cautioned as he took his seat again, the discussion effectively terminated.

The meeting drew to a close soon after, the contentious issue of teaching the great unwashed shelved for the time being. The ladies kept their seats, watching as the men gradually filed out.

The discussion – and its truncation – kindled something in Sarah, as she recognised the process taking place before her: of men fortifying their positions and cutting off access to the levers of power. They had already done this with every established medical discipline, but there was still a chance to act before they had entirely staked their claim on this emerging one.

'I think I should like to learn this technique,' Sarah said in a low voice to her companion. 'If it is as effective as they say, it would be very valuable at Queen Street. I could contribute more. Be of greater use.'

'From what I hear, you are indispensable as it is,' Mrs Crowe said.

'Given their attitude to instructing the general public, sadly I think it unlikely they would consider women as suitable candidates. It is said that we lack the magnetic power necessary for successful treatment.'

'How convenient,' Mrs Crowe muttered, putting on her coat. 'You are really keen to learn?' she asked.

Sarah nodded.

'Then you must approach the person you believe to be most sympathetic. The gentleman who begins every meeting by expressing his scepticism about magnetism and magnetic power. Dr Malham is your man.'

'How do I convince him to take me on as a pupil?'

'When it comes to men there are three ways to get what you want.'

'And what would they be?'

'Number one – flirtation. Fluttering of the eyelashes can be very effective.'

Grateful as she was for the advice, Sarah's face made it clear what she thought of that option.

Undeterred, Mrs Crowe continued. 'Number two – flattery. A fanning of the male vanity. Very potent. Almost irresistible.'

'And number three?' Sarah asked, hoping for something a bit more palatable.

'Money,' said Mrs Crowe. 'Offer him a fat fee.'

EIGHT

aven and Henry stood either side of the table that dominated the police surgeon's room, a makeshift facility down the hall from the front desk and McLevy's office. Over the years that Raven had been coming here, very little had changed. It was a ramshackle place with an air of the temporary about it, but that had doubtless been the case for two decades. Nothing about it felt clinical, fitted as it was with furniture that looked like it had been scavenged, and a table that, while sturdy, looked better suited to butchery than dissection.

McLevy was not there, but his presence clung to the place like a stink; one Raven was all the more conscious of due to having been summoned here not at Henry's request but that of the detective himself. Raven had brought Henry to Nicolson Square and Henry in turn had summoned the detective, Raven having made himself scarce. He had, like Gregor, naively hoped his role in the chain of discovery could be kept anonymous.

The body parts that Gregor had discovered were lying on the table now, the femur and the foot looking smaller in these circumstances, but no less perplexing.

'What does the Ulsterman make of it?' Raven asked.

'Too early to say,' Henry replied. 'He's not happy, but that's a given. McLevy prefers property cases. He likes catching thieves and reuniting rich people with *almost* all of what was taken. Dead people offer less scope for gratitude or personal enrichment.'

'And what's his view on the Surgeons' Hall connection?'

Henry looked sheepish. 'I haven't told him.'

'You haven't? They were found barely a quarter mile apart.'

'You heard Christie. He's head of the College, and he doesn't make empty threats. I wanted to make sure that there *is* a connection before drawing McLevy into Surgeons' Hall. This is my first chance to compare the specimens. If it turns out they're not a match, then there's no need for him to know about it quite yet.'

Henry went to a cupboard and produced the wooden box he had brought to Queen Street, placing it on the table next to the foot and the femur.

Before he could open it, McLevy burst through the door.

'So, when were yous going to tell me about this?' he boomed, slapping a sheet of paper down on the table with a report that echoed around the room's stark walls.

It was a scandal sheet, a cheap folded pamphlet penned by someone calling themselves 'the Hoolet'. 'Gruesome Remains Found at Surgeons' Hall', it gleefully announced. 'Murder Among the Sawbones – Or a Return of the Resurrectionists?'

The Ulsterman had thumped it down next to the dismembered body parts, but it was the pamphlet that Raven now found the more troubling sight.

McLevy in the flesh was shorter than Raven remembered, but no less intimidating for it. He realised that the image of him that he kept in his head was larger because McLevy's stature was not about his mere physical size. He was the kind of man you remembered as towering over you when in fact he may have remained seated throughout the conversation. He gave off an air of restless menace, a malevolent energy permanently in search of its next target. As he was fond of putting it himself, he believed 'a bold front is the best baton', though he engaged the latter with some alacrity when the former proved insufficient.

As Gregor had alluded, McLevy loved to boast about getting

his man for every crime, when it would be more accurate to say he was proficient in getting *a* man for every crime. The detective's laissez-faire relationship with reason and evidence had once caused Raven to come terrifyingly close to taking the blame for murder. Not only had Raven been innocent, but in that instance it transpired there had not even been a murder.

Raven turned over the pamphlet's front page, rotating it slightly so that Henry could read it from his side of the table. Inside was a highly exaggerated account, expanding upon the nonsense Raven had heard from the coachman. Now as well as guts, livers and a severed leg, as the driver had wrongly stated, there were lungs, arms and a torso, all discovered in an office awash with blood.

Raven and Henry looked at each other helplessly for a moment.

'What?' said McLevy. 'Are you going to tell me that neither of you two *doctors* had heard anything about this?'

'I had heard something,' Henry faltered, 'but had not ascertained its significance.'

'Body parts found in two different locations a stone's throw apart and you didn't think it was significant?'

'Body part, singular, in the case of Surgeons' Hall,' said Raven, holding up the pamphlet. 'This is ninety per cent nonsense.'

Raven had decided he would take the brunt of the detective's ire, on the grounds that McLevy hated him already, whereas Henry, having ambitions to succeed Struthers as police surgeon, needed to stay in his good graces. Raven didn't quite understand why Henry was so keen on this notion when he surely had other options available to him, but he was firm in his resolve and Raven wished to assist.

The detective rounded on him.

'It must be years since I've seen you, Dr Raven, but little has changed. Your presence still augurs mischief.'

He turned back to Henry. 'Tell me more about the ten per cent.'

Henry flipped open the wooden box.

'This is all that was found,' he said. 'The rest is sensationalism made up to sell scandal sheets. It was found in a cupboard in the office of one of the surgeons. As you know, body parts are hardly a rarity at that locus, and we were endeavouring to find out more. We hoped to conclude the matter without troubling you with it.'

'Never mind your cringing excuses. What can you tell me about the meat? Are these feet both from the same body?'

Seeing the two close together on the table, although one was a left and the other a right, Raven could not say for sure that they were a match.

'As you can see, they are each of a different hue,' said Henry, 'and the one found at Surgeons' Hall is slightly larger. However, neither of these observations preclude the feet being from the same body. The difference in size is not pronounced and is quite common. On most human beings, one foot or hand is slightly larger than the other.'

'They do tend to be the same colour, though,' grumbled McLevy.

'The discoloration of the Surgeons' Hall foot is likely because it has been subject to corrosives in an unsuccessful attempt to dissolve it.'

McLevy put a hand to his chin and fell silent as he considered what was before him, the energies that fuelled his anger channelled into cognition instead. While he was occasionally given to starting with his desired conclusion and assembling the evidence to fit, McLevy did have a keen mind and a talent for understanding the thoughts of a criminal.

His voice was quieter when he spoke again.

'It is my contention that whoever did this was attempting to dispose of the body in instalments,' McLevy said. 'It is less conspicuous to dispose of a corpse in small pieces. There were bloodstains on the floor at Nicolson Square; splashes on the walls too, indicative not merely of a murder having happened there, but the dismemberment too.'

'Posing the question of what has happened to the rest of the victim,' said Henry. He turned to Raven. 'We took up all the floorboards,' he said. 'This was all we found.'

McLevy winced.

'Did I misspeak?' Henry asked.

McLevy's expression remained a grimace. 'No, it's my lumbago. A lingering complaint. The potion-pushers have been useless to me about it, but seeing as you're here, Dr Raven, you might be able to assist.'

'Would you like me to examine you?' Raven replied, taken aback by the notion.

'No, it's that I've been hearing great things about this Dr Malham, the American mesmerist. I'm told he can get results where others have failed, and I would appreciate your perspective as to whether it's an avenue worth exploring.'

Raven took a moment, pretending he needed to martial his thoughts, then said, 'Mesmerism is the province of mountebanks. It makes great claims but is of no medical value.'

McLevy nodded. 'Thank you. If you say it has nothing to commend it, then that is precisely the endorsement I needed to hear. I will be seeking Dr Malham out forthwith. I suspected you pill-mongers might regard mesmerism as a threat, so I wanted to get that from the horse's mouth.'

'Was this why you summoned me here?' Raven asked, surprised but not entirely incredulous. McLevy had a reputation for tenacity, but Raven knew that this also extended to his capacity and endurance for holding a grudge.

'Of course not. I summoned you because you were the one who brought the Nicolson Square discovery to Dr Littlejohn's attention. What do you know about this Laurence Butters? His name is familiar but I can't think why.'

'Perhaps it is because he is an actor.'

McLevy frowned. 'No, it's not that. When I recall a name, they're either a thief or some other manner of miscreant.'

'All I know of him is that he owes money to a certain Mr Flint. This discovery was reported to me by one of Flint's men, who had been sent to collect on this debt.'

'Interesting,' said McLevy. 'But despite the low regard in which

I hold Mr Flint it makes little sense that he should be responsible for Mr Butters' death, if Mr Butters this is.'

'It is my understanding that Flint is eager to establish that, as he still hopes to collect. I am told Butters had come into some money, hence Flint deciding to call in the debt.'

'It troubles me that we haven't been able to locate Mrs Butters either,' said Henry. 'These could as easily be a woman's feet.'

'Perhaps one of them decided they'd rather not share the windfall,' Raven suggested.

'We need to find out more about Mr Butters,' said the detective. 'Who he knows, who he crossed, what enemies he might have had.'

'Enemies?' Raven said, failing to keep the scorn from his voice. 'A critic, perhaps, offended by his Falstaff? He's an actor.'

'And the world of theatre has more grudges, jealousies and back-stabbing enmity than you would believe, Dr Raven. Actors, playwrights, theatre-owners: in my experience, they are fiercely jealous of one another, and quite ruthless in pursuit of money and fame.'

Raven thought of Kimble and realised the extent of his misapprehension. He was a man with no compunction about tormenting the bereaved, milking their suffering for profit and adulation. Flint's practices were honest and compassionate by comparison.

Raven became aware of hurried footsteps coming down the corridor. Moments later, a ruddy-faced, red-haired constable came through the door, the urgency of his mission evident in the expression on his face.

'Mr McLevy, sir.'

'What is it, Skinner?'

'More remains, sir. Human remains, I mean.'

'Where were they found?'

'Buried in a grave.'

McLevy looked at Raven as though beseeching him to understand what he had to deal with.

'Lord help us, Skinner. Next thing you'll be telling us there's a thief in the Calton Jail.'

The young policeman realised how he had misspoken.

'Sorry, sir, I mean remains that were not supposed to be there. All chopped up into bits.'

'What bits?'

'Not sure, sir. It looked like a butcher's midden.'

They all looked at the items on the table. Two feet and a thigh.

'Lead on,' ordered the detective, heading for the door.

Raven trailed along at Henry's back, deciding that he would indulge his curiosity while McLevy was not forbidding it. For the moment, he seemed too intent upon his purpose to care.

Then the detective stopped on his way to the exit, stepping briefly into his office. Through the open door, Raven watched him retrieve a dog-eared, yellowed document from a drawer, peruse it briefly then give a nod of satisfaction.

'I remembered where I knew the name Butters,' McLevy explained. 'Skinner here shunted my memory. I never encountered him myself, but my predecessor left a file for me when I took over here in 1832. It was a list of suspects for unproven activities, people to keep an eye on. There he is: Larry Butters, as he was then.'

'Why is he on the list?' asked Henry.

'He was a body-snatcher.'

NINE

aven had seen many a grave, many a corpse, and yet there was something disturbingly incongruous about what he witnessed at Greyfriars Kirkyard. Perhaps it was the connotations of love, loss and grief, the inherent value of human life and dignity to which those feelings testified, which made it seem not merely a crime, but an affront, an atrocity. Human remains were supposed to be laid to rest respectfully. Even those undergoing dissection had to be accorded appropriate consideration towards the human being they once were, although that was not always the case. There were constant rumours circulating about what medical students got up to with the bodies when no one was looking, and he knew from his own university days that some of those rumours were true.

Raven saw a human head still partly submerged in the earth, its face staring up in hollow-eyed shock, a permanent expression of hopelessness and fear. It sat next to the upper parts of two arms and a single severed hand, the cut ends of the radius and ulna clearly visible.

Skinner was right: it had all been dumped like so much rubbish, thrown away rather than laid to rest.

Raven had walked with Henry to the churchyard, the distance from the police office being insufficient to merit a cab. McLevy raced ahead with Skinner and another of his men. Raven was still wondering why the detective had not dismissed him and fired off a warning about meddling in police business. Raven being the one who brought the matter to the police's attention had perhaps given McLevy reason to keep him close, which was not a comforting thought.

There were two gravediggers waiting for them when they arrived, an older man and a lad of no more than fifteen. The boy's eyes were bloodshot, testament to recent tears.

Another of McLevy's men had remained while Skinner fetched their boss, standing sentry to ward off anyone who happened by. A sheet of sackcloth had been laid down over the scene, pulled back briefly for McLevy and Henry to inspect it.

'What's the story?' McLevy asked the gravediggers.

'We were preparing the plot for Peggy Morrison,' said the older man. 'She's due to be buried tomorrow. Six days a widow.'

'Six days?' asked McLevy.

'Aye. Her husband died not a full week past. They were married forty year. Inseparable. According to the family, no sooner had she put the last of her affairs in order than she followed him.'

'So the grave was fresh,' said McLevy, deriving the significance. 'Soft, like.'

'I had been telling the boy here we'd be getting our money easy today. Just shows how wrong you can be.'

He put a hand on the back of the lad's head, ruffling his hair. Father and son, Raven deduced, recognising the subtle affection, a sign he'd have missed two years ago.

'Somebody's noticed the grave was recent and has seen the chance to dispose of this lot,' said McLevy. 'When did you bury Mr Morrison?'

'Would be five days back.'

'You didn't notice anything in between?'

The gravedigger looked uneasy. Clearly he knew who McLevy was, and didn't want to be on the wrong side of anything he said.

'There's little that meets the eye to distinguish a grave that's been covered over one day or one week.'

'So we've only providence to thank for the plot needing to be dug again so soon.'

If the grim spectacle of the remains themselves was disturbing, there was a more distressing sight to come. Raven saw a woman being escorted by one of the constables and anticipated the reason for her being brought here.

'A Mrs Annabel Bryant,' the constable announced. 'She lives on the floor below Mr and Mrs Butters.'

Mrs Bryant was an older lady, bird-like in build, picking her footsteps carefully on the rutted path. She had a knitted shawl wrapped around her, which she was clutching to herself. She already looked tremulous.

'It's not a pleasant sight, but we need you to take a wee look,' said McLevy.

He gestured to one of his men, who pulled the sheet back with an enthusiastic motion that was a little too close to a flourish.

She must only have caught a mere glimpse, but it was enough to cause her legs to buckle. Raven, having anticipated this, moved in to catch her before she fully collapsed, taking her weight and helping her gently to the ground.

McLevy tutted, annoyed at his men. 'Did you not prepare her for what she was about to see?' he asked.

'I told her we feared we had found her neighbour,' said the constable who had fetched her.

'At least we can take that as a positive identification,' suggested another.

'Why, do you reckon she'd have barely blinked had she seen a severed head she *didn't* recognise?'

Henry reached into his bag and produced a vial of sal volatile. He unstoppered it and let it waft gently beneath the woman's nostrils while Raven cradled her head. Mrs Bryant roused, twitching her nose and blinking. Henry had positioned himself so that he was screening her from the grave.

'Are you alright?' McLevy asked, before she even had time to remember where she was.

'I just . . .' She closed her eyes for a moment, then let out a sigh before opening them again. She was deathly pale, and Raven feared she might vomit, but she was able to raise her head without support.

'Can you tell us if you recognise this person?' McLevy asked.

She shook her head. 'I got such a shock. I barely saw. I'll look again, though.'

She gestured to Henry, who stepped aside.

Raven felt her tense at the sight, but this time she remained steady.

'Oh, dear God,' she said.

'Do you know who this is?' asked McLevy.

She nodded, tears forming.

'That's Lydia Butters.'

Raven helped Mrs Bryant to a bench out of sight of the grave, assisted by Henry and accompanied by McLevy. She was unable to say much for a while, being too gripped by shock.

'The pity of it,' she kept repeating. 'That poor woman. The pity of it.'

'You were close, then?' McLevy asked, his voice softer than Raven would have imagined. Raven had only ever seen him solicit co-operation through threats and intimidation, but he should have anticipated that the man could draw upon other means. He didn't only speak to thieves and claimants, after all.

Mrs Bryant clutched the shawl to herself.

'Not especially, but I saw her in the street and on the stairs.'

'Was she always at home, or did she work?'

'Oh, she worked. She was in the theatre too, like Mr Butters. She was a seamstress. Worked on the costumes. I know she was handy with a needle because she repaired a coat for me once, and you'd never have known it had torn.'

'How were relations with her husband?' McLevy asked. 'Did you hear raised voices?'

Mrs Bryant took a moment to consider this, and it seemed telling that there was something to consider.

'They were an odd couple, in a way. Maybe this is just me, and I don't want to be disrespectful under the circumstances, but if you knew them separately, you wouldn't imagine them together, you know? You seldom *saw* them together, in fact. They came and went at different times. I know they had friends, though; or rather, he did, for it was always men that I saw visiting. Some strange types, but that's theatre folk.'

'Again, did you hear discord? Arguments?'

'I would often hear Mr Butters' voice raised, and sometimes he sounded furious, but then I would hear him say the same thing a moment later and realise he was rehearsing. I do recall hearing some shouting a few nights ago, though. Sounded like someone had their dander up, but it stopped just as suddenly.'

'Did you hear anything about Mr Butters coming into a windfall?' asked Raven, drawing a look from McLevy. He instantly regretted the intervention. Raven was worried McLevy had forgotten this detail, but now feared the detective might think he was acting as a proxy for Flint's interests, or even worse, that he had an interest of his own.

'No,' Mrs Bryant replied. 'I wouldn't know anything about that, but I do know he isn't good with money. The kind of man who has it spent as soon as it's in his hand, Lydia said. Safe to say his talents lie elsewhere.'

'So have you seen him perform?' McLevy asked.

'Oh, yes. Several times. He was good. I saw him most recently at the Adelphi, in *The Bride of Lammermoor*. I also saw him in *Rob Roy* and as Tam o' Shanter. Each time, I had to remind myself that he was my neighbour. Face, clothes, hair, voice. He was utterly transformed.'

TEN

arah once again found herself outside the building on Potter Row, this time feeling conspicuously unaccompanied and altogether less certain about the purpose of her visit. It was not the most salubrious address, but far from the least, being a few streets back from Nicolson Street where the College of Surgeons was situated.

She climbed the front steps and tried the door, which was open. She wandered into the dingy vestibule, where she could hear music and footsteps from the large meeting room off the lobby. It had been empty before, but today she saw a group of young women being instructed in formal dancing, chairs lining the walls. Clearly the building's rooms were rented out for various purposes.

Sarah ascended the stairs, and as she approached the room where the association meeting had taken place, she became aware of raised voices coming from another room across the hall. The door was slightly ajar and she stood outside, listening. One sounded very much like Malham: he had an American accent, though he sounded altogether less sanguine than the previous times she had heard him.

'We can't build our institute if we are confined to this tiny place,' he was saying. 'Surely there are other banks you have yet to try.'

'Where the answer is likely to be the same,' his companion

complained. 'No bank is going to touch a man like me without a cautioner. Isn't there some way you can demonstrate the value of your holdings back home?'

'Of course, but by that time, someone is bound to have beaten us to the purchase.'

'I don't suppose you could mesmerise some wealthy client, convince them to advance some credit or guarantee a loan.'

Malham gave a bitter laugh. 'What's all the more galling is that my property in New York is worth far more than what we are trying to borrow, but until the sale is concluded, it is of no use to me.'

There was a scrape of a chair and the sound of footsteps, enough warning to allow Sarah to back away from the door before it opened further to reveal Malham and Mr Somerville, the gentleman she had seen with Malham at the meeting.

Somerville acknowledged her with a polite nod before descending the stairs, a leather document folder under his arm. There was the sound of a door closing elsewhere in the building.

'Can I help you, madam?' Malham asked. 'Do you have an appointment?'

'No. Sorry. Presumptuous of me to just turn up, I suppose.'

She realised her error was due to the working practices at Queen Street, where patients who wished to be seen simply presented themselves and waited their turn.

Malham smiled at her. 'I have some time now. Would you care to come in?'

The office was in better condition than the other parts of the building she had seen. Light was streaming in through two large windows, the room warm despite the April chill outside. There was a large mahogany desk to one side, a good Turkey rug on the floor, and a chaise-longue, presumably for patients to recline upon. Sarah wondered if she would be asked to lie down and was relieved when offered a chair. Malham sat behind his desk.

'What can I do for you, Miss . . . ?'

'Fisher,' Sarah stated. She wondered how best to proceed, briefly considering Mrs Crowe's suggestion of flattery, but opted for a more direct approach. 'I attended the association meeting last night. I wish to study mesmerism and would like you to teach me.'

Malham's eyes widened in surprise. He steepled his fingers in front of pursed lips for a moment, composing his response.

'If you were at the meeting, you would know that the association is unwilling to open up instruction to persons not belonging to the medical profession.'

'Yes. But I was under the impression you were not in agreement with that.'

Malham sighed. 'Changing opinions takes time, Miss Fisher. It would be unwise to disregard my colleagues' concerns at this time. Especially as I am a newcomer, and a foreigner to boot.'

'But what if you were to prove that mesmerism can be taught not just to someone outwith the profession, but to a woman? Would that not convince them?'

Malham glanced heavenwards. Sarah could not tell whether he was weighing a response or seeking strength. Either way, she could tell that he had nothing useful to offer her.

'Miss Fisher, much as I admire your forthright manner and the sincerity of your intentions, I have just explained to you why it is incumbent upon me to step lightly in dealing with my new peers. What you are proposing would be interpreted as a blatant act of provocation, and while part of me would like to see the resultant expressions on certain faces, I hope you will understand why I must take the cautious path for now.'

Sarah stepped back out onto the street. She felt sunshine on her face and breathed in the spring air, but neither was much consolation against what in retrospect seemed an inevitable disappointment.

A cloud covered the sun, and the street became instantly much darker. She stood for a moment, trying to decide on the best route home. The street seemed empty, eerily quiet.

She started walking. Suddenly there were footsteps behind

her, a gust of air and then someone was trying to wrench the bag she was carrying from her hand. She turned to see a face uncomfortably close, masked with a scarf, bloodshot eyes staring wildly into her own. For some reason she held on to the bag, refusing to relinquish it. That proved to be a mistake. Her attacker was stronger than she and simply pushed her to the ground, the shock of the fall causing her to let go of the bag. Her assailant took off at speed while behind her she heard more footsteps approach. Someone raced past her, shouting at the man who had attacked her. Both men rounded a corner and disappeared from sight.

Sarah sat for a moment, reeling from what had happened. She had just managed to get to her feet when her assailant's pursuer returned. She wobbled a bit and he put out a hand to steady her. It was only now that Sarah recognised him as Mr Somerville.

'Are you hurt?' he asked.

Sarah took a moment to answer.

'I don't think so.'

Her voice sounded as though it was coming from a distance.

'You're bleeding.'

Sarah looked down and noticed an abrasion on the heel of her left hand, a livid red studded with bits of gravel from the road. Her hand was shaking, as was the rest of her.

Mr Somerville took a handkerchief from his pocket and wrapped it gently around her injured hand.

'Brandy, I think,' he said. 'I know a place.'

Mr Somerville took her arm and led her round a corner and down some steps into a basement whisky shop, the kind of place where working men could buy a dram for a penny. Mr Somerville seemed to know the proprietor, and with a nod of acknowledgement he led Sarah straight through the small shop and through a door at the back. He sat her down in the small windowless room, disappeared briefly and then returned with two glasses containing what Sarah assumed to be brandy.

She realised that she had just entered the back room of a whisky shop with a complete stranger. It was as though she had temporarily taken leave of her senses. She hoped that her rescuer was just that and not some opportunist about to cash in on her transitory vulnerability. She remembered the raised voices coming from Malham's office, the anger and frustration that was so audibly expressed by this man.

Sarah took a sip, trying not to look at the glass too closely; she had grave doubts as to its cleanliness. She felt a comforting warmth spread across her chest and the shaking of her hands started to subside. She put her glass down and took a good look at the man opposite. He was well dressed, clean-shaven. He smelled of tobacco and shaving soap. He was maybe ten years older than her, his features sharply defined, a ruggedness to him that belied the fine clothes. He smiled at her, a smile that seemed warm and unthreatening. Nonetheless she wondered how soon she could leave, wondered if her legs would carry her.

'Feeling better?'

Sarah nodded.

'I suppose I should introduce myself. Name's Somerville.'

'Sarah Fisher.' She managed a small smile. She didn't want to seem ungrateful. 'Thank you for your assistance, Mr Somerville.'

'If only I had been that wee bit faster, I might have been able to return your property to you. Was there anything valuable in your bag?'

'Not really. My notebook. A library book. It is the bag itself that is of value to me.'

'Describe it to me. I might be able to get it back.'

'How?'

'Let's just say I know people hereabouts. I grew up round here.'

This explained much. He expressed himself articulately, but his accent spoke more of Old Town than New.

'Well, it's black leather. Like a doctor's bag. And it has the initials JYS in gold lettering.'

'JYS?'

'James Young Simpson.'

'The chloroform man? How did such a thing come to be in your possession?'

'He gave it to me.'

Mr Somerville looked at her quizzically.

'I work for him.'

'So, what were you doing wandering the streets round here? Not a part of the town a young woman should be venturing into on her own.'

'It's where the offices of the Mesmeric Association are located.'

'You were after some therapy?'

'No. I simply wished to learn more about the practice. But it is yet another door closed to women. By virtue of my sex, I cannot be taught.'

She surprised herself with her candour. It was mostly driven by anger, and the need to express her frustration.

'You want to learn how to perform mesmerism yourself?'

'If you don't mind, Mr Somerville, I would rather not talk about it,' Sarah said.

A moment of awkward silence passed between them.

Mr Somerville looked down at her hand, still wrapped in his handkerchief. Sarah unwound the temporary bandage and held it out to him but stopped when she noticed the blood on it.

'Perhaps I should wash it first,' she said.

Somerville took it from her. 'No need. It's seen far worse.'

As he shoved the handkerchief into his pocket, he nodded at the wedding ring now visible on her left hand.

'What does your husband think of all this? If you were my wife, I wouldn't be letting you wander about on your own. It's not safe.'

'I don't have a husband. I'm a widow.'

'Then we have that much in common. I lost my wife too. Did he die recently?'

Sarah had no wish to discuss this either, no matter how kind and attentive the man seemed to be.

'What is *your* interest in the association?' she asked him.

Mr Somerville frowned a little at the abrupt change of subject, the brusqueness of her question. He took a sip of brandy and paused before answering.

'My interest is two-fold, I suppose. I reckon mesmerism has the potential to be a boon for the afflicted, particularly those who haven't been helped by other means. So, from that point of view, obviously it ought to be encouraged and supported. But frankly, if mesmerism is as effective as they say, then there's money to be made from those who can afford to pay. I am a businessman after all.'

'But one who is struggling to secure a loan.'

Mr Somerville's expression was suddenly wary.

'I overheard your conversation with Dr Malham.'

His frown deepened and Sarah worried that she had taken things too far.

'I apologise. I know it is not my concern,' she added hurriedly. With some relief, she saw his face relax.

'It's difficult to make your way in this town without the proper connections,' he said. 'We are trying to establish an institute, and I have identified the perfect property, but without a guarantor, it's likely to slip through my fingers. And without a place in Edinburgh big enough for his ambitions, Malham will move on and try again elsewhere.'

Somerville was concerned about an opportunity slipping away but Sarah suddenly saw one present itself. She realised she had a solution that might please all parties. She was not without some proper connections herself.

'Perhaps I can help,' she told him.

'You? Is your Dr Simpson an enthusiast for mesmerism then?'

'No, unfortunately not. But if it is a guarantor for your loan that you require, I know of someone who might be willing to do that for you.'

'Someone of sufficient rank and station?' He sounded sceptical and Sarah couldn't blame him for that. 'Who did you have in mind?'

'Amelia Bettencourt.'

Somerville let out a low whistle. 'Cannae get much higher in rank and station than that, short of royalty. How do you know her?'

'It's a long story but I'm sure she would be interested. Although I suspect that she would stipulate a condition.'

'And what might that be?'

'That the association would have to open up tuition to everyone. Including women.'

Mr Somerville's eyes widened in surprise. It might even have been relief. He raised his glass.

'That is a condition I could heartily agree to.'

ELEVEN

here was a mildness to the breeze as Raven walked along Heriot Row, the early morning wind lacking its usual bite. Raven was taking a circuitous route to work, having strode east along George Street and then north on St Andrew Square towards Queen Street Gardens before looping back. His home on Castle Street was just around the corner from Simpson's house, barely two hundred paces, but he needed time to clear his head, a buffer between the noise and tension of home and the challenges that would greet him at the morning clinic.

He had woken early and gone to James's room while Eugenie was still sleeping, hoping to let her get some more rest. The boy was, unusually, not already crying, as he seemed to do most days immediately upon waking. Instead he was rapping on the wooden side of his bed, entertained by the noise he was making. Raven had joined in for a while, but James had evidently decided he was doing it wrong, or perhaps that he shouldn't be doing it at all, and began bawling for his mother.

When James's features were twisted into an angry howl like that, Raven sometimes caught a glimpse of his own father in his son's face. Sarah had insisted such things were not passed on in the blood, but if it was nurture rather than nature that shaped a child's disposition, did James instinctively sense the disquiet in

Raven and respond to it? When Eugenie appeared at the nursery door, her first words had been to ask Raven what he had done to upset the child, and it had all deteriorated from there into another argument about the usual subject.

As he contemplated the waiting chaos of another Queen Street clinic, he acknowledged that Eugenie was not the only one impatient for him to be running his own practice. It was something he had always intended when the time was right. But how would he decide that to be so? Was it cowardice holding him back? The other issue, of course, was the money, and the obligation that came with it. The longer he worked with Simpson, the greater his reputation would be, and this would be all the more important if he was to feel that he was not merely running an extension of Cameron Todd's practice.

Raven heard hurried footsteps at his back and instinctively turned, bunching his fists as he did so, an ingrained response from his years in the Old Town. There was no threat bearing down upon him though, only Henry, brandishing another pamphlet.

'Have you seen this?' he asked.

'Fiend on the Loose', it declared, above a line drawing of a cloaked figure clutching a blood-dripping blade.

Raven flipped it open. There were illustrations of severed body parts, though clearly not done by anyone who had studied anatomy. '"The madman has been chopping up his victims and depositing the gory results across the city,"' he read aloud. '"The first body parts were found at Surgeons' Hall, the next at Greyfriars Kirkyard – recently buried and only discovered by chance. We must ask ourselves: How long has this fiend been abroad? How many graves conceal the remains of unfortunates other than those named on the headstone above? And is anyone in Edinburgh safe while this menace stalks the street unseen?"'

'McLevy is going to be furious,' said Henry as they continued to walk towards Queen Street.

'Who is publishing this drivel?'

'I know no more than you.'

'He signs himself "The Hoolet". An owl.'

'Watchful and wise,' Henry replied.

'Not that watchful. He doesn't know about the discovery at Nicolson Square.'

'Yes, but I fear it's only a matter of time before he finds out and prints the name of the victim.'

'Christie can't be happy about Surgeons' Hall being associated with this,' Raven said. 'Or having McLevy knocking on his door.'

'I have managed to postpone the latter, for now. I persuaded McLevy to let me investigate the Surgeons' Hall end of things, but unless I come up with sufficient information to satisfy him, he'll be going there himself. The story is spreading across the city and the taint of scandal grows ever larger, especially with rubbish like this selling on street corners. I need all the help I can get, Will.'

'Don't you think I have enough to occupy myself? I have clinics every morning, Minto House in the afternoons, not to mention another baby on the way.'

Henry took on a plaintive look. 'I'm sorry to put it this way, Will, but Dr Christie already regards you as part of this. You'll be getting a share of the blame if he doesn't like the outcome, so you have reason to ensure otherwise. Also, it's worth bearing in mind that having such a man's approval would surely be valuable to someone looking to set up their own practice.'

This somewhat quenched Raven's annoyance. What Henry had said certainly sugared the pill. But Christie's approval was not the only consideration.

'Does McLevy know you intend to bring me further into this?'

'McLevy lacks manpower, and that which he does have is not well suited to the task. Loath as he would be to admit it, I suspect he would be grateful to have your eyes upon the matter. He hasn't forgotten your part in finding the infamous Mrs King, or in the matter of our mutual friend now resident in the Caribbean.'

Raven thought of McLevy's ambivalence towards him at Greyfriars, in contrast to the outright hostility he normally exhibited. If finding favour with Dr Christie did not come at the price of antagonising the detective, then there was little reason not to assist his friend.

'Have you concluded anything from examining what was found at the cemetery?' he asked. 'Cause of death, for instance?'

'Not yet, but I don't have a full body to examine. The corpses I usually deal with tend to come fully assembled. Though I think it safe to conclude that what we have found so far belongs to the same person, despite the hysterical nonsense in that pamphlet.'

A coal cart had stopped in front of one of the townhouses. They gave it a wide berth, mindful of the coal dust that billowed about it.

'Let me ask you, Will. If you had murdered someone and you wished to dispose of the body without being seen, how would you go about it?'

Raven glanced at the coalmen. This was not the kind of conversation he wanted anyone eavesdropping on out of context, particularly as he barely needed to think about his answer.

'Much the same as our suspect here. I would cut it down into smaller pieces so that I could transport it inconspicuously. That would require several trips, and therefore increase the risk, but not as much as trying to move a body intact.'

'Yes,' Henry said, 'but how would you go about the cutting?'

Raven wasn't sure what he was getting at but gave the logical answer.

'Disarticulation, I should think. Go through the joints. Bit easier than sawing through bone.'

'These were my thoughts too. But our suspect *has* gone through bone. The limbs seem to have been removed from the thorax in a very irregular and unscientific manner. Also, the neck was a ragged mess, indicative I think of cutting through from the back.'

'Entirely the wrong way to approach it,' observed Raven. 'That would suggest Butters killed his wife in anger, but when the rage was spent and he had to act to conceal the deed, he found he could not look at her face.'

'I agree. And I am certain it must have been Butters rather

than someone from Surgeons' Hall, because this butchery was not the work of a doctor.'

'I think you overestimate the competence of some of our colleagues,' said Raven, 'but I concur. Nonetheless, something must connect Butters to Surgeons' Hall. According to McLevy, he was once a suspected body-snatcher, which might make him familiar with the notion of dismemberment but not the surgical practice. This was more than twenty years ago, though.'

'Presumably he knew enough of Surgeons' Hall to think he might find a means of dissolving the body there,' Henry suggested. 'Perhaps he took one small piece to Dr Cooper's office to test it with whatever he could find. I assume he was interrupted, or feared he might be, which was why he hid the foot in the cupboard.'

'What's his connection to Dr Cooper? And why would he go to that bother with one foot, then bury the rest of her at Greyfriars?'

'It wasn't quite the rest of her,' Henry reminded him. 'We are still missing some parts. But I suspect that idea came to him later, perhaps seeing a funeral or noticing the fresh grave as he passed. Though it leaves the question of why there would still be pieces under his own floorboards.'

'I assume he would only have risked moving a limited quantity at a time. Perhaps he meant to come back for the rest, but before he could do so, Gregor broke in and pulled up the floorboards looking for money.'

Henry nodded, but there was little satisfaction in his agreement.

'That being so, I suspect Butters returned to the house while Gregor went to fetch you. When the place was searched more thoroughly, only women's garments were found. None belonging to him. It very much appears he murdered his wife, buried her – or most of her – and then absconded when he realised he was discovered.'

Raven saw the problem.

'Meaning he's been gone for two days,' he said.

'He could be in London by now,' Henry mourned. 'Or on a ship to God knows where.'

TWELVE

Raven was greeted by the usual cacophony of coughing from the waiting room as he entered 52 Queen Street, a sound that often left him wondering how many patients left with more diseases than they came in with. He made his way briskly to his consulting room, not wishing to be waylaid by anybody en route. He observed Dr Simpson's old leather bag on the hall table, a note to Sarah sitting beside it. He wondered what that was about.

Sarah was in the consulting room when he entered, getting things prepared for the morning clinic. She looked pale, distracted. Not her usual self. He noticed a bandage tied loosely around her left hand.

'What have you done to yourself?'

Sarah looked up from what she was doing. It seemed to take her a moment to realise what he was talking about.

'Oh, this. I fell over in the street.'

'Let me see.'

She hesitated for a moment and then held out her arm. He took her hand in his and carefully unwrapped it. There was a large abrasion on the hypothenar eminence which still had bits of dirt ingrained in it.

'I couldn't seem to get it all out,' she said by way of explanation. 'Difficult to do it one-handed. I'll need to scrub it.'

Sarah grimaced at the prospect but did not disagree.

He fetched some warm water from the kitchen, keen to see to her injury before dealing with anything else, then sat her down and slowly, gently, began scrubbing at the abrasion with a bristled brush.

'How did you fall?' he asked.

'Tripped over a loose cobblestone,' she said, wincing a little as he removed a particularly adherent piece of grit.

'Makes a change,' he said.

'What does?'

'Me tending to your injuries rather than the other way round.'

Satisfied that the wound was as clean as he could make it, he reapplied the bandage. He felt a sudden urge to kiss the injured hand but managed to stop himself just in time. That would not do at all.

Raven's first patient of the day was Miss Poole, a frequent attender and not one of his favourites. Even Dr Simpson had grown tired of her recurrent complaints and now left Raven to see her whenever she turned up, which was at least once a week.

Her symptoms were always of a vague and mobile kind, sensations that travelled around her body and refused to situate themselves anywhere in particular. Raven wondered if she was merely misinterpreting the normal sensations of her body going about its business and assuming that these feelings were in fact indicators of disease. But how to convince her? She was confident that her complaints were a precursor to an imminent decline and almost certain death.

'Miss Poole,' Raven said as she entered, trying to summon up some enthusiasm for whatever she had decided was wrong with her today.

'Oh, Dr Raven. I'm in such distress. I have pain all over my body.'

'Please take a seat,' he said and watched as she hobbled across the room. She eased herself into a chair and frowned at him.

'Where is the pain most pronounced?' he asked.

'All over.'

'And what is the nature of the pain?'

'It's an ache. No, more of a tenderness. Sometimes there is a prickling sensation under my skin.'

'Are you sleeping?'

'Not at all.'

'Eating?'

'I have no appetite whatsoever.'

There was plenty of meat on her bones, thought Raven. No imminent threat of starvation.

'Bowels?'

'Costive.'

He toyed with asking about whether she had phosphorescent stools but decided against it.

He reached for some paper to write out a prescription – an aperient and a tonic which would of course 'do nothing for her', meaning she would likely be back within the week.

He thought about Sarah's enthusiasm for mesmerism. Perhaps there could in fact be some benefits if she took it up: he could divert patients such as this to Sarah for prolonged courses of treatment, leaving him free to deal with more significant pathologies. He was due to perform an amputation of the cervix for a cancroid tumour this afternoon, with every possibility of effecting a lifesaving cure. Consequently, he had little patience for this sort of stuff.

He passed the prescription over to Miss Poole with a reassuring smile.

'I have every confidence that this will sort the problem for you,' he said, feeling no confidence whatsoever.

Suddenly they both became aware of a disturbance without, the sound of raised voices coming from the waiting room. Raven was almost pleased: a good excuse for bringing this consultation to an end before Miss Poole could think of something else to complain about.

He escorted Miss Poole to the door and looked along the hallway to see the Great Kimble, standing in his rumpled suit, swaying slightly with fists raised and shouting something too garbled to make out.

Raven saw Sarah intercept the man before he could proceed any further. She was speaking to him in a low voice, trying to calm him down. Raven walked up behind her, ready to intervene should things take a more violent turn.

'What is the nature of your complaint?' Sarah was asking.

'He's ruined me!' Kimble bellowed. 'That's the nature of my complaint.'

'What are you talking about?' She was using the voice she sometimes employed to subdue rowdy children. 'Who has ruined you?'

By this point Dr Simpson had descended the stairs to investigate the commotion.

Kimble pointed at him. 'He has.'

Jarvis tried to escort Kimble into the downstairs waiting room, but he was not for moving. He stood his ground, fists still raised, although Raven was sure that in his inebriated state, the man was incapable of landing a punch.

'I demand satisfaction,' Kimble said.

Surely the man wasn't suggesting a duel, Raven thought. He could hardly stand upright.

'What do you mean by that?' Raven asked. By now, Raven, Sarah and Jarvis were standing between Kimble and the professor.

Kimble paused, as though unsure of his answer.

'I wish to have another opportunity to demonstrate my skills,' he said. 'I wish to hold a séance here at Queen Street.'

'Here?' Raven said, surprised. 'Why?'

'As I have been ejected from the Adelphi, I think it's the least you could do.'

Raven was tempted to reply that the least they could do was nothing at all but stopped himself. Kimble was angry, drunk and potentially unstable, and it was unwise to provoke him further.

'A public display at your home, Dr Simpson, has the potential to restore my reputation. If I can convince a man such as yourself, it will go some way towards persuading the general public that I am no cheap trickster.'

'Right, that's enough,' Jarvis said, clearly having come to the end of his patience. 'You've said your piece, now be off with you. You've interrupted the professor's work.'

'And he has ended mine.'

Jarvis grabbed Kimble's collar, a prelude to marching him out of the front door.

'Wait,' said Dr Simpson. 'Leave your card, Mr Kimble. Let me consider your proposal. And Jarvis?'

'Yes, sir.'

'Give the man some tea and a dish of oatmeal before he goes. He looks like he is in sore need of some nourishment.'

Raven looked at his hands.

Clean, nails scrubbed with a brush. Steady. No hint of tremor.

He felt completely calm, though it had not always been like this. When he first began performing procedures with Dr Simpson, he was always nervous. Keen to make a good impression, anxious not to be a disappointment. It was a great honour to work with the man and Raven wanted to merit his place, first as apprentice and then as assistant. Many would give an eye to be where he was now.

He remembered the first time he had attempted to aspirate an ovarian cyst through the abdominal wall. The semi-gelatinous contents had hit him full in the face, soaking his hair and his clothes, necessitating Dr Simpson's intervention. He was embarrassed about it even now.

When had he developed this degree of composure? He couldn't say for sure. It was something that had crept up on him, garnered by many long hours working alongside his mentor.

He looked up to see Sarah measuring out a few drops of chloroform onto a cone-shaped flannel. She encouraged the patient to take deep breaths and watched carefully as she subsided into sleep.

Raven waited for the signal that a sufficient depth of anaesthesia had been attained. Starting before Sarah had sanctioned it was always a mistake.

Dr Simpson stood to one side, happy to let Raven proceed. Raven inserted the speculum.

'Can you see it? Do you have a clear view?'

'Yes,' Raven replied

'There has been no extension of the tumour since last we looked?'

'No.'

'Then apply the vulsellum distinctly above the line of the diseased part.'

Although the professor was giving instructions, there was no need. Raven had performed an amputation of the cervix several times before. As though acknowledging that this was the case, the professor began discussing the procedure with Sarah.

'Sometimes in cancroid disease of the cervix, the growth is as large as a fist. This one is not so large as that and can be removed in this way because it has not extended further than the cervix itself.'

He held up the ecraseur so that Sarah could see it, a T-shaped instrument with a plunger for tightening a loop of wire on the end.

'I used to use a pair of strong scissors or a knife, but this instrument is far superior. Much less bleeding.'

Raven held out his hand for the instrument in question and proceeded to loop it around the cervix. He looked at Sarah to check that all was well at her end and then slowly tightened the instrument, severing tumour and cervix together. The bleeding was less than he had expected. He packed the vagina with lint to soak up what little blood there was and placed the specimen in a jar. Dr Simpson wished to preserve it and add it to his collection. The patient slept on, oblivious.

Raven washed his hands as Dr Simpson examined the tumour.

'Did you mean it?' Raven asked. 'What you said to Kimble? That you would consider letting him hold a séance here?'

'I think that I might.'

'Why?'

'Curiosity, I suppose. Let him perform his parlour tricks. What harm is there in that?'

'I don't think it's a good idea to encourage him,' Raven replied.

'Maybe it will be an opportunity to learn something new,' Dr Simpson suggested.

'Like how to contact the dead?'

'Of course not. But perhaps we will discover how he manages to convince other people that he can. And I do wonder whether he genuinely has faith in his own abilities or whether he is knowingly duping those with a willingness to believe.'

The patient was snoring a little so Raven helped Sarah turn the woman onto her side. Her breathing settled again, and Sarah checked the pulse.

'All is well,' she reported.

'I still don't think it's a good idea,' Raven said, unwilling to let the matter rest.

'Think of it as an experiment,' Dr Simpson replied. 'One over which we have a degree of control. He will be outside his usual theatrical environment, and we will be careful in what we divulge. Those poor creatures at the theatre were willingly offering up information and completely ignoring his errors.'

'I'm just not sure what there is to be gained.'

'Perhaps if we expose his impostures he will cease and desist. Stop taking money from the recently bereaved, which to my mind is, at the very least, morally dubious.'

Dr Simpson held up the jar containing the tumour again, his face wrinkling in a frown as he examined it.

'I fear I will have to replace you, Will Raven,' he said.

Raven felt a surge of anxiety, wondering what he had missed. 'Why?'

'Because it appears I have nothing left to teach you.'

THIRTEEN

aven was hurrying along South Bridge, trying to balance the danger of being late against the danger of being a sweat-soaked mess when he reached his destination. Dr Christie had arranged for him and Henry to meet with Dr Cooper, but Raven had been detained by a complicated delivery at the Maternity Hospital, and his primary fear was that Dr Cooper would have left for the day by the time he got there.

His head was still in a spin from what Dr Simpson had said to him earlier. He knew it was not merely a compliment on a job well done; even as he took pride in the professor's words, he had also felt sadness because this was Simpson telling Raven that his time working for him would soon be at an end. He had always known that this must happen eventually but in truth he had preferred not to think about it. Eugenie was right about that much. He was too attached to Queen Street, comfortable there despite its quirks and challenges. But with Simpson himself judging him ready to move on, any reluctance to do so now would be a matter of cowardice.

The attraction of setting up his own practice was independence, and therein lay the primary obstacle. He had an association with Dr Simpson which he could trade upon, but Cameron Todd's name also carried a great deal of weight in this city, and Raven did not wish to move out of one man's shadow merely into another. It was important that he cultivate a reputation of his own.

Eugenie assured him that her father's offer of a loan would not come with an expectation of interest, but Raven knew there would be other strings attached. And it was not merely Dr Todd's public reputation that made him wary: it was that which people *didn't* know about him. Raven sometimes thought that it was as well he had fallen for Eugenie before he learned certain truths about her father, for he would have had concerns over the nature of anyone who had grown up with him as an example. However, in practice he knew that Eugenie was not corrupted by his influence, largely because Dr Todd had kept certain aspects of his conduct secret from her.

When he reached Surgeons' Hall, he found Henry on the pavement, his attention fixed on the gutter rather than watching for Raven's arrival. Henry had a gift for seeming relaxed, which belied the strength of his ambitions. What Raven didn't quite understand was why he was so keen on the role of police surgeon. It paid poorly compared to the money a physician might make from patients in the New Town, to say nothing of the contrast in clientele.

'I'm sorry I'm late,' Raven said. 'Footling breech. Difficult delivery. I was worried we might miss him.'

'No, no. He's still teaching. Well known for over-running, as many an aspiring surgeon knows to his cost.'

'What's so interesting in the gutter?' Raven asked.

'People talk about the divides in this city,' Henry replied. 'Rich and poor, Old Town, New Town. But that only describes obvious things that we already know. I believe that a deeper understanding lies in studying its interconnectedness: the effects of apparently disparate elements.'

'Are you telling me that staring down a stank could shed light on where Laurence Butters has gone?'

'Not directly.'

'Then let us away and find Dr Cooper.'

They discovered him in the corridor outside the lecture room.

The last of his students were filing out, two having tarried to ask a question.

Dr Cooper looked at Henry and Raven with confusion as they approached.

'Dr Christie said you would speak with us,' Henry explained.

Cooper rolled his eyes, indicating he had forgotten about this and had rather hoped everyone else had too.

'Best come to my office,' he said with a sigh.

Dr Cooper's office was exactly as Raven remembered it, the only immediately observable difference being that the furnace was lit this time. There was a slight odour of brimstone in the air, causing Raven to wrinkle his nose.

'Have you been fumigating the place?'

'Yes,' Cooper replied. 'Thought that a bit of sulphur was called for.'

What was he worried about, Raven thought. Plague?

'It is an odd notion,' Cooper continued. 'One deals with cadavers and dissection all day, but there is something disconcerting about the knowledge of such things having been left mouldering in one's private space without one's knowledge.'

'We believe the foot found in your office cupboard belonged to a woman by the name of Lydia Butters,' Henry said. 'Was she known to you in any capacity?'

'Not that I am aware of. I heard about the discovery at Greyfriars. Was that where the rest of her was found?'

'Almost,' Henry replied. 'There are still pieces unaccounted for. We may have to undertake a more thorough search of this place.'

Cooper frowned. 'If there was anything further still hidden in here, we'd all be smelling it by now, believe me.'

'Does the name Laurence Butters mean anything to you?' asked Raven. 'He was her husband.'

'Is he a physician?'

'No. An actor.'

Cooper's eyes widened in surprised recognition. 'Oh. Yes, I

think I do know who you mean now. I wouldn't say I know him, but we met recently and exchanged a few words. I told him I had seen him in *Coriolanus* at the Adelphi and I complimented him on his performance.'

'You recognised him from the stage?' Raven asked.

Cooper laughed dismissively. 'No. In the flesh, he looked nothing like he had done in character. But we were introduced because he was known to an acquaintance of mine.'

'Who was that?'

'William Lewis. He is the Professor of Rhetoric at the university.'

Raven took note of this, an unworthy part of him welcoming another excuse to delay his return home on a subsequent day.

'Where did you meet Butters?' Henry asked.

'At a salon, a gathering at an acquaintance's house.'

'Who was the acquaintance?'

'Denzil Gethyn. My tailor.'

'Butters was giving a private performance?'

'No, we were both there to witness a demonstration.'

'Did you happen to discuss anything involving corrosive materials?' Raven asked.

Cooper scoffed. 'Corrosive materials? No. Unsurprisingly that did not come up during our brief interaction.'

'Dr Christie said you could not be found on Sunday,' Raven said. 'Where were you?'

'I was in Fife for a few days. Fishing. I'm sure I mentioned it to Dr Christie, but he can't have been paying attention.'

'Can you think of any reason Butters might have sought out your office?' asked Henry.

'I don't recall my place of work being discussed.'

'What *did* you talk about?'

'We were there to see an exhibition of mesmerism. We mostly talked about that.'

'You're an advocate for mesmerism, Dr Cooper?' Raven asked, trying not to make it sound like an accusation. Henry, knowing Raven's views on the subject, hastily intervened.

'And that is where you met Butters?'

'Yes. It was after the demonstration that I noticed my friend Professor Lewis in attendance. He was talking to Butters when I approached.'

'And what did he make of the demonstration?' Henry asked.

'He was decidedly underwhelmed. I suspect William was anticipating a little more spectacle or frivolous amusement.'

'I meant what did Mr Butters make of it?' Henry clarified.

Cooper rolled his eyes again, as though finding it tedious to reprise his previous answer regarding what little he and Butters had discussed. But then he bridled as though he had uncovered an unexpected memory, and not an entirely comfortable one from the look of it.

'His reaction was more pronounced, though I recall being rather struck by the incongruity of his calm manner, given the import of his words. He said that what he had witnessed there that night would change his life.'

'So, he was pleased?' Raven asked, confused by Cooper's unease.

'Undoubtedly, but . . .' Cooper's expression darkened.

'What?'

'Little as I know the man, I cannot judge his character. But I got the impression that his delight was tinged with malevolence. Whatever changes he imagined this might effect in his life, they were not benign in their nature.'

FOURTEEN

arah was shown into an ornate parlour by a diminutive young girl wearing an apron that was several sizes too big for her. Sarah wondered who she had inherited it from. Mrs Crowe rustled in behind her, having agreed to accompany Sarah to Malham's rooms on Gloucester Place.

The room seemed overcrowded. There were several sofas, armchairs, cushions, side tables, lamps, and a profusion of potted ferns. A bookcase crammed with medical texts stood in one corner alongside a display cabinet hosting several skulls and various other bits of bone.

'Malham has accumulated a fair number of accoutrements in his time in Edinburgh,' Mrs Crowe commented. 'If my skirt was any wider, I wouldn't be able to turn round.'

The door to the parlour opened and Dr Malham entered, Mr Somerville at his back. Greetings were exchanged and the ladies invited to sit.

'I am pleased to see you looking so well, Miss Fisher,' Malham said. 'I assume you have recovered from your ordeal.'

'There was no real damage done,' Sarah replied, even though that was not strictly true. She found that she was now reluctant to venture out on her own and hoped that this would be a temporary difficulty. 'I believe I have you to thank, Mr Somerville, for the return of my bag.'

The bag had been delivered to Queen Street along with a note offering Somerville's services as escort and protector, should she need it. Although touched by his solicitude, she considered this a step too far.

'Were the contents of your bag intact?' Mr Somerville asked.

'They were, thank you. Perhaps my attacker was not much of a reader.'

'Given that it was a doctor's bag perhaps he was hoping for something more medicinal.'

'Blue pills and calomel?'

'Or morphine and opium.'

Sarah thought of Dr Simpson's bag, which often contained little more than a jar of lard and some forceps. And if his medicine tin contained any morphine, it was usually in the form of suppositories. Perhaps not quite what the thief would have been looking for.

'However did you find it?' Mrs Crowe asked. 'And so soon? I don't think even James McLevy himself could have done a better job.'

'I have my sources,' Somerville said rather self-consciously, as though it were something he did not wish to dwell upon.

'And it would seem that Mr Somerville's good turn has been repaid,' Malham said, smiling.

'Yes,' Somerville agreed. 'Our prospective business venture has been resurrected thanks to your Mrs Bettencourt.'

'She agreed to stand as guarantor?'

'She did indeed,' Somerville replied. 'With, of course, her support being contingent upon tuition at the association being made available to all.'

'I must admit that I was initially concerned about that stipulation,' Malham said. 'But I'm sure the association can be persuaded if it means we can extend its meeting rooms to a whole building and establish an institute. But they will have to be persuaded, hence our little experiment.'

Sarah considered it prudent not to point out that said experiment was to be conducted discreetly at Malham's home, rather than under the public auspices of the Mesmeric Association.

He turned his attention to Mrs Crowe.

'How has your back pain been since your last treatment?'

'Can't say that I've noticed much of an improvement,' she replied.

Sarah smiled. Mrs Crowe was never one for sugar-coating unpalatable truths.

'Would you be willing to let Sarah try?' he asked.

'Of course. I have every faith in this young woman. Although you're not going to charge me, are you dear?'

Sarah laughed and shook her head but noticed that Malham looked briefly discomfited. Today's course of instruction was now denying him a fee.

'I think we ought to try to induce mesmeric sleep and then make passes over the affected area,' he said, standing up.

He guided Mrs Crowe into a straight-backed chair and fussed a bit, ensuring she was both upright and comfortable. He then placed Sarah in a similar chair facing her patient, so close together that their knees were touching. He instructed Sarah to take Mrs Crowe's hands in her own.

'Now, much as we did before, Mrs Crowe, look into Sarah's eyes. Concentrate on them. Sarah, hold your gaze steady. Do not look away. And Mrs Crowe?'

'Yes, dear.'

'No talking.'

Sarah held Mrs Crowe's hands and stared intently into her eyes. It was a remarkably intimate thing to do, and initially she felt uncomfortable. She decided to concentrate on what she knew about this woman. A successful novelist, Mrs Crowe had veered in more recent times towards the supernatural, which had in no way harmed her sales, *The Night Side of Nature* being her most popular work. She was an advocate of phrenology and spiritualism as well as mesmerism, and Sarah wondered if this overlapping of interests was entirely healthy. Was she a little too credulous? It was not ideal for the furtherance of mesmerism if some of its champions were so undiscerning in following the latest fad.

Sarah thought that perhaps she should try to control her own thoughts and wondered why Malham had given her so little instruction. Just stare. On the surface it seemed such an easy thing to do, but in practice it was so much harder than she would have assumed.

She decided to concentrate on the eyes themselves. The intense colour of the iris compared to the off-white of the sclera. Was that blue-green or hazel, and what was that small nodule on her lower eyelid?

Many long minutes passed, during which the interaction gradually progressed from feeling awkward to something altogether stranger. It was as though the rest of the room had faded and only the two of them remained, locked in an increasingly intense connection.

Eventually Mrs Crowe's eyelids began to droop, then closed completely, and her head dropped down onto her chest.

After a few minutes Malham indicated that Sarah should rise and stand behind Mrs Crowe's chair. He showed her how to pass her hands from the top of Mrs Crow's head to the bottom of her back, palms forward, close to the body and the chair, but touching neither. This went on for some time – up and down, up and down – and Sarah began to grow hot, sweat beading her hairline. Mrs Crowe continued to sleep.

'And now to demesmerise,' Malham said. 'Stand in front of her and reverse the movements of your hands. From bottom to top with palms facing you. In a few moments Mrs Crowe will awake as though from a restful slumber.'

Sarah did as she was asked. Notwithstanding the effects she was witnessing she felt a bit silly. She could see herself from the outside, waving her hands in front of a sleeping woman and could easily imagine what Raven would have to say about it.

In spite of Sarah's reservations regarding the technique, Mrs Crowe did start to rouse. She blinked a few times and looked about herself as though she had forgotten where she was.

'Well, that was marvellous,' she said. 'I feel much better already.'

'My dear Miss Fisher,' Malham said, 'that went far better than

I could have hoped. You appear to have a natural talent for it. Although it must be said that our Mrs Crowe is particularly susceptible to the mesmeric influence.'

Mrs Crowe was still in her chair, a beatific smile on her face.

Malham seemed energised by this early success. 'We must find another candidate,' he said. 'More challenging this time. Mr Somerville, would you oblige?'

Mr Somerville looked a little shocked at the suggestion and did not rush to comply with Malham's request.

'Come now, Mr Somerville. There is nothing to be afraid of.'

Somerville looked thunderous for a moment at the suggestion of cowardice on his part, but his polite smile swiftly returned, and he sat himself down on the chair that Mrs Crowe had reluctantly vacated.

'Is there any complaint that you wish to be rid of?' Malham asked, his tone smooth and buttery.

'My left shoulder gets a bit stiff in cold weather.'

'That all? Nothing else?'

Somerville shrugged. 'What can I say? Made of strong stuff.'

'Is it always necessary to touch the patient?' Sarah asked. She was reluctant to be in the same position with Somerville that she had been with Mrs Crowe, hands and knees in contact. 'You didn't during your demonstration,' she added, hoping to save herself from any unnecessary physical proximity to a man she barely knew.

Malham gave her the type of condescending look that she was well used to.

'I have spent many years mastering the technique, Miss Fisher. You cannot expect to run before you can walk. But— ' He held up an imperious hand ' —in the true spirit of scientific enquiry, let us attempt a localised version, concentrating on the affected part, without inducing sleep.'

Sarah was relieved, and she noticed that Mr Somerville seemed to be too. She detected a shyness in him that was in contrast to his confident demeanour. A man of layers, she suspected. She was well used to those too.

Malham instructed her to rub her hands together to generate a little heat, and then stand behind Somerville as she made passes close to his left shoulder, always in the same direction, close to but not touching him. She could smell the wet wool of his jacket, the distinctive scent of his shaving soap. This too felt strangely intimate and she wondered, despite her earlier success, if it could possibly have any effect.

Malham kept up a commentary as she moved her hands, using words such as flow, restoration, balance. Was this necessary for the treatment? She would have to ask.

After about ten minutes of this Sarah was all for giving up. Her armpits were damp now and she could feel the material of her cotton dress sticking to her back. Fortunately, at that point Malham held up his hand again and announced that the treatment was over. No need to demesmerise the shoulder then. She would have to ask about that as well.

Somerville stood up and moved his left arm, squeezing his left shoulder with his right hand.

'Do you know,' he said, 'that feels much better.'

Sarah didn't believe him, and she suspected he knew that. He gave Sarah an odd look, not so much as if he were being polite as that they were both complicit in humouring Dr Malham.

With the treatments concluded Malham insisted that they take tea together. A tray was brought in. There was fruit cake and Mrs Crowe began to demolish a slice with a relish that seemed distinctly unfeminine. Sarah heartily approved.

'I think that your newest pupil is rather gifted,' Mrs Crowe said as she speared a runaway sultana with her fork. 'A protégé?'

'This is certainly a promising start,' Malham conceded. 'We shall continue with your instruction, Miss Fisher, and when the time is right, we will stage a demonstration of your skills in front of the association. In the meantime, practise, practise, practise.'

Sarah sipped her tea, the warmth a balm against the knot of anxiety forming at the prospect of a public demonstration.

'And what do you make of this latest scandal?' Mrs Crowe asked, eyeing up another slice of cake.

'To what do you refer, Mrs Crowe?' Malham replied. 'What impropriety has stoked your ire today?' He smiled as he said this, part indulgent and part patronising, as gentlemen were wont to be when they thought they were being polite.

'There's a madman on the loose, or hadn't you heard? He's disposing of body parts around the city.'

Malham stopped smiling. This was not the inconsequential tittle-tattle he had been anticipating.

Somerville looked sombre. 'I had heard something about that,' he admitted. 'Terrible business.'

'Is there a suspect?' Malham asked.

'Not that I know of,' Mrs Crowe conceded. 'But it's said there was a gory scene inside Surgeons' Hall. The new head of the College is fit to be tied. Given the history in this city, any taint of scandal can besmirch the whole profession.'

Malham considered this for a moment, the thought evidently not displeasing him.

'Then perhaps it is the perfect time for the rise of a new discipline,' he said.

FIFTEEN

Raven glanced at the clock in the hall, aware that everyone was already seated. It was a quarter after three. Kimble was late, but not yet late enough.

Raven was hoping that the spiritualist would not appear at all, but short of that there was a threshold of tardiness that the professor would regard as a disqualifying level of discourtesy. Either of those scenarios would allow the foolhardy notion of this séance to be abandoned, after which they could all forget about the whole boiling.

Then Raven heard the doorbell and felt the weight of an inevitability. He recognised the mark of a showman in making his audience wait.

Jarvis opened the door and greeted the man with a degree of politeness it had taken Raven several years to earn.

'Mr Kimble. Welcome back.'

Jarvis took Kimble's coat from him and hung it on the rack. Beneath it he wore a loose-fitting suit, suggestive that he had lost some weight, or perhaps that he had bought it second hand. The smell of drink about him was less pronounced than the previous times Raven had encountered him, though not altogether absent. He suspected Kimble had shown greater discipline ahead of a demonstration where the stakes were higher than that night at the Adelphi Theatre. Less inebriated, there was a liveliness to his features, a greater alertness as he took in his surroundings.

Jarvis escorted Kimble towards the dining room, where the demonstration was to take place. Raven remained in the hall, attempting to peer into the outside pocket of Kimble's coat. He was unable to see anything and was reaching a hand towards it when Jarvis reappeared, quicker than he had anticipated.

'What are you doing, Dr Raven?'

There was no point in denying it. Not with Jarvis, who saw all.

'I do not trust this man, Jarvis, and I do not feel comfortable letting him walk in here with our guard down. I would like to know what chicanery he has planned.'

'Dr Raven, any props, devices or methods of deception would need to be about Mr Kimble's person right now, and not in the coat he has left in the hall, wouldn't you agree? Dr Simpson has invited Mr Kimble into his household. He will therefore be afforded the same dignity and courtesy as anyone else. Even you,' he added.

Raven slunk towards the dining room feeling his cheeks burn with shame, where only moments ago he had burned with moral righteousness. He regretted his actions, but his judgement had been impaired by his outrage, and he was right to be angry about this.

He had read an account of Anton Mesmer and his so-called magnetic séances. Mesmer would seat his subjects, mostly impressionable ladies with more money than sense, around an oval bath filled with bottles containing water and iron filings. The tub was then covered with an iron lid, which was supposed to conduct the magnetic force. Those gathered each grasped one of several iron rods protruding from the lid, while Mesmer's assistants, all handsome young men, sat behind the ladies, some clasping them between their knees and others gently massaging their breasts. Reportedly the subjects were induced into a state of excitement so elevated as to resemble convulsive fits. There was a powerful force at work there, for sure, but it was nothing to do with magnetism.

Nonsense like this was getting in the way of true knowledge

and progress. Genuine understanding was being held back by quacks and frauds. There was nothing to be learned from men such as Kimble, performing tricks and illusions while claiming them to be the results of greater powers.

The gathering was seated around the dining-room table. The professor sat in his usual seat at the head, while Kimble had been allocated a chair at the opposite end. Mrs Simpson was on Simpson's right, Mrs Catherine Crowe to his left. Sarah was seated halfway down the table. Raven took his place directly opposite her.

If Kimble wished to engender an atmosphere conducive to the gloomy mystery of spiritualism, then he was immediately thwarted by the sounds of dogs barking and several curious children swarming into the room. The nanny soon herded them out again with a redundant note of apology, Simpson chuckling indulgently in response. He looked reluctant to see them go, as though perhaps having second thoughts about giving up part of a Sunday afternoon that could better be spent in their company. Raven thought of how, by contrast, he was cultivating new opportunities to keep himself out of the house and away from his own son.

Choosing her moment now that there were fewer mobile hazards underfoot, Mrs Lyndsay arrived, assisted by Lizzie, between them bearing tea and a tray of cakes. Lizzie's usual scowl was temporarily absent, on pain of some threat from the cook, no doubt, though why a special courtesy should be extended for this company Raven did not know.

They drank the tea and ate the cakes while exchanging platitudes and pleasantries. They talked about the spring weather, the breezes that had kept the smog at bay of late, and how long it might last. Kimble talked about how he had come to settle in the city but was a native of Durham.

Eventually, during an awkward lull, the professor made a bid to bring the proceedings to a head.

'When do you intend to commence your demonstration, Mr Kimble?'

Kimble had been in no position to make demands, but he had

nonetheless requested the presence of external witnesses, citing the need for an objective account. To that end, Sarah had been roped in, but as Kimble seemed to know that she worked for Simpson, he had requested that there be someone present who was not part of the household. Sarah had obliged by suggesting Catherine Crowe, which proved acceptable to both parties. Simpson was familiar with Mrs Crowe, having entertained her at the house several times. Given the readiness with which he agreed, Raven suspected Kimble was familiar with her also. Raven had concerns over her tendency towards credulity, aware of her interest in fringe causes, including her participation in the mesmerism demonstration Sarah had recently attended.

Nonetheless, there would be no stage, no darkness, no unseen confederates and no willing dupes gushing forth information. Raven realised Simpson was right about bringing Kimble here. If there was an opportunity to deduce his methods and to further expose him for a knave, then it should be seized. And Raven would enjoy watching him struggle.

Kimble put down his cup, placed his hands together and issued a gentle sigh.

'From my point of view, the demonstration began some time ago, as soon as I walked through the door. I will admit that at the Adelphi, I had to embellish my impressions to an extent.'

'To an extent,' scoffed Raven, but this drew an admonishing look from the professor.

Kimble gave a shrug. 'Theatres are not, as it happens, the most conducive environments for what I can do. Thus, you believe what you witnessed there disproves my gift. But if I wish to upset the law that all crows are black, I mustn't seek to show that no crows are. It is enough if I prove one single crow to be white.'

Kimble looked about himself, all around the room, as though there was an audience other than those seated.

'I am not here today to give a performance,' he said quietly. 'Merely to observe and report. And there has been so much to take in. So many voices. This house has seen so much life. It is a house with an import that will echo down the years, perhaps the centuries, because of what happened here in this room. But it is not great events that leave indelible traces in a place such as this. It is people, for it is first and foremost a home.'

Mrs Simpson smiled warmly at this. The professor did too, though perhaps more so out of politeness. Raven had to bite his tongue lest he ask Kimble whether his special gift was for pointing out the starkly obvious. But then Kimble shifted onto his preferred terrain.

'Even in death they gather here, finding it hard to leave. Those who once lived here remain. Even those who did not live here, they know they are welcome. There is an older man, one who never came here in life. The animals gather to him. They come to him because he heals them. Just as people come here to be healed. It is a house of healing.'

Raven felt a tingle of unease. Simpson's grandfather had been a farrier and was renowned as a healer of animals. This was hardly private knowledge, however.

'The animals love this house. I mean in this world,' he added with a chuckle. 'Such a lively place. The dogs, and, my goodness, a parrot.'

Simpson's parrot was in the front room upstairs in its usual spot, and to Raven's knowledge had not made any noise. Perhaps Kimble had simply seen it from the street, or else his keen ears had heard it over the barking and the shrieking of the children, all of which Raven had trained himself to filter out.

'A parrot and yet a doctor?' Kimble asked, as though talking to someone not at the table. 'That cannot be right. How can a parrot be a doctor?'

'It is— ' began Mrs Crowe with a grin, but the professor silenced her with a cough, a reminder that she had been schooled not to volunteer anything.

'Dr John Gray,' said Kimble. 'That is the parrot's name.'

Mrs Simpson looked taken aback.

'The parrot's name is Polly,' Raven countered, but everyone in the family knew that it had taken to referring to itself as 'Dr John Gray', for reasons no one could fathom. Raven's private suspicion was that Simpson had taught the bird to do so for his own mischievous amusement. Once again, this was hardly occult information. Tales of the parrot must have spread. Mrs Crowe already knew it, and she was far from discreet.

'Animals and the sounds of children,' Kimble went on. 'So many children's voices tinkling about the place, their laughter. Tears, though, too. So much love in this house, and yet so much pain in that love. And I hear talk of another animal, one even more exotic than a parrot. Some kind of monkey.'

There were blank faces all round. Raven recalled the way Kimble had worked at the Adelphi, sending out guesses knowing that people would remember only the ones he got right. Here, shorn of a theatre's trappings and a wider audience, his failure was more conspicuous. But why would he guess at such a thing?

'Not a monkey,' he corrected himself. 'A marmoset.'

Mrs Simpson visibly flinched, while Dr Simpson's expression became tense. 'Marmoset' had been his and Jessie's nickname for their first-born daughter. And this was not known beyond these walls.

'No, not an animal,' said Kimble. 'Only a name. The fondest of names for the fondest of loves.' He looked about himself and gave the subtlest nod: sincere, almost regretful. He issued but one word: 'Maggie.'

At this, Mrs Simpson made a choking noise, as though suppressing an involuntary splutter.

Maggie had died just before her fourth birthday. It began with measles. In her fever she had been unable to swallow, unable to drink, crying out in torment as her parents looked on, helpless.

Mrs Crowe looked at her with concern and confusion, glancing to Sarah also. She understood that there was something she was missing, but she also understood that its import was enormous.

'She says this was not her house. But it is her home still. She remembers another house, not far from here.'

'Albany Street,' Mrs Simpson said, barely a whisper. Raven saw Simpson squeeze her hand for support, though his face was growing stony.

'She was so loved. She knows that. She knows it hurts you that you could not quench her thirst. But the thirst is gone now, and she was there to welcome Mary Catherine when scarlatina took her.'

At this, Mrs Simpson got up, breaking into heaving sobs as she hurried for the door.

Simpson rose too, and Sarah and Mrs Crowe also got to their feet. He looked more than merely concerned for his wife. The professor was vulnerable to upset and could become very low when assailed by memories of the loss of his daughters. There was more to this, though, and it was the same thing that was unsettling Raven. This was intimate knowledge that an outsider should not, could not know. Raven had heard the tales, but only after he had become a trusted member of the household.

Kimble spoke urgently before Simpson reached the door.

'Please, Dr Simpson, I beg of you to stay, though not on my behalf. They wish to speak through me. Maggie and Mary Catherine.'

Simpson stopped, getting a nod from Sarah to assure him she and Mrs Crowe would look to his wife.

Raven felt an overwhelming sense of presence, an energy in the room, though it now had three fewer people in it. There seemed to be a sound in the silence, a rushing in his ears.

Simpson fixed Kimble with a look that was not merely wary but bordering on fear.

'They need you to know that it comforts them to see their brothers and sisters,' Kimble said quietly. 'Though they worry for Jamie, and for Sunbeam. Little Jessie, after her mother. And they wonder also about another boy, another brother. Though he does not live here.'

Simpson looked directly at Kimble and spoke in a tone Raven had never heard in all the years he had known him. It was low, trembling and controlled, but served merely to stress the extent of the fury it was holding back.

'Get him gone from this place.'

If he had been asked before the séance commenced, Raven would have enthusiastically marched Kimble to the front door and tossed him forcefully out of it. Right now, he merely led the man, drifting numbly through the house.

Jarvis was nowhere to be seen, almost certainly having gone to Mrs Simpson's aid when she emerged from the dining room.

'I don't mean to upset anyone,' Kimble said. 'I only say what I'm told, what I hear. Sometimes it feels like a gift, sometimes a curse.'

Kimble grabbed his coat from the rack as Raven opened the door. He felt unnerved by what he had witnessed. Kimble had spoken of things only mentioned in the most private circles of this house. But more troubling still had been the reference to something not discussed even there.

Raven could never forget having inadvertently witnessed a visit by Simpson to a house in the New Town, where he had spied him lovingly bouncing a small child on his knee. Raven had later learned that the professor and his wife had long been involved in quietly finding grateful new parents for the inconvenient offspring of wealthy households: born out of wedlock or from some potentially scandalous liaison. Nonetheless, there had been something about what he'd seen that was more clandestine than merely discreet. Ever after, there had lingered suspicions, unanswered questions that it would serve Raven better to put from his mind.

Raven stepped through the door and onto the broad front steps, in need of fresh air. The house had felt suddenly confining.

He was aware of Kimble's quiet scrutiny.

'Did you just see a white crow?' Kimble asked. 'Or should I say, a white raven?'

'The professor wants you gone,' Raven said, struggling to keep a tremble from his voice. He realised it was from fear.

'Not as much as you, though. The world just became a more complicated place, did it not? And it is vexing you deeply.'

'I have just seen two people I care for revisit their greatest pain. That is what vexes me.'

The little man took a step closer, near enough for Raven to catch a lingering whiff of drink on his breath.

'You would not bother lying to me if you could see what I can.'

'And what can you see, Mr Kimble?'

He gave a small but grave shake of his head. 'I have seldom seen a man with so many ghosts about him. You are surrounded by the dead. It is because you summon them in your thoughts.'

'I am a doctor. It is hardly proof of your gift that I think back upon the patients I failed.'

'Those are not the only ones you think about, though, are they? There are so many, but there is one in particular who follows you everywhere. No matter where you go, he is always there. You are bound together by anger.'

Raven was outdoors now, but he felt the same sense of crowding, of being run to ground.

'You denied him everything. Even his name.'

Kimble spoke quietly, calmly, but Raven heard it as though he was shouting.

'What did he do to you? What did you do to *him*?'

Raven felt something inside him erupt. He grabbed Kimble by the arms and drove him back against the railings.

'Enough,' he said.

Kimble did not stop, though. 'He calls for you, but not by Will Raven. He says you are really Thomas Cunning— '

'DO NOT SPEAK THAT NAME,' Raven yelled, driving a fist into Kimble's jaw.

Kimble spun against the railings and dropped to the ground, silenced at last, at which point Raven heard another voice shouting at him.

'Raven! What in the Lord's name are you doing?'

He turned and saw Sarah, standing just outside the door, an expression of horror on her face.

Raven looked back at Kimble, sprawled on the floor, his mouth bleeding.

It was as though Raven had woken and found himself there, suddenly returned to his senses and confronted by what he had wrought. He felt panic and disgust. He reached down to offer Kimble a hand, but the man flinched and cowered, anticipating a further blow.

Raven took a step away, whereupon Kimble scrambled to his feet and ran.

'What did you do to that man?' Sarah demanded. 'What possessed you?'

Raven couldn't answer, but not because he didn't know.

What had possessed him was something he did not wish to name, but which Kimble just had.

SIXTEEN

aven could hear the thunderous passage of a train beneath the North Bridge somewhere behind him as he descended Leith Street, bound for the Adelphi. Every day it felt like the sound of the city got louder, and he wondered what some wide-eyed traveller from the country or the Highlands might make of it.

Raven's business that afternoon was not medical, nor even strictly professional, but merely another excuse to delay his return home. On the pretext of assisting with Henry's investigation, he had already been to the Department of Rhetoric at the university in search of Professor Lewis, who Dr Cooper had said was an acquaintance of Laurence Butters. Unfortunately, no one had known his immediate whereabouts. However, on the corner of Adam Square he had seen a playbill for the Adelphi Theatre, and it had reminded him of another avenue of investigation. It was one McLevy might already have pursued, but according to Henry the milder weather had brought with it reports of a group of visiting pickpockets operating in the city, and McLevy was concentrating his attentions on that.

'People who have been robbed tend to be more vocal in their complaints about the police's effectiveness than those who have been murdered,' Henry observed. Raven had speculated that the level of public sentiment might soon change, for there was a new pamphlet on sale. This one named Lydia Butters as the dismembered victim. It carried a portrait of her husband, warning of a 'murderer at large' and calling him 'a master of disguises, a man of a thousand faces'.

Henry opined that despite the pamphlet's histrionic tone, its content would paradoxically not be whipping up much panic.

'People worry about a madman on the loose who might kill anyone for any reason,' he said. 'No matter how grisly the details, the moment they learn that it's simply another case of a brute murdering his wife, they can happily ignore it.'

Raven had bought the pamphlet from a boy on the High Street. He had asked the lad who was writing them, but all he knew was that they were dropped off by a cart from the printers, same as the newspapers.

Raven pulled open one of the wide double doors of the theatre and stepped into the lobby, where playbills advertised tonight's performance of *The Beggar's Opera* alongside a list of forthcoming attractions. He reflected briefly on the irony that he had gone into obstetrics because he did not wish to spend his days in theatre. At least in these ones, the dead were just pretending.

The sight of the interior brought to mind his last visit here, which in turn caused him to recall his more recent encounter with Kimble, something he had been unable to cast from his mind. He felt nothing but shame. Whether mediumship or mesmerism, why did he believe it was even his battle? That was medicine for you, and Edinburgh medicine in particular. It conditioned you to conflict. Calls to arms, division and dispute. Too much rallying to defeat a common foe rather than selflessly working for the benefit of a common purpose.

Fortunately, Sarah had been the only one to see his assault, but it was what Kimble had seen that truly disturbed him. His words had shaken all of Raven's assumptions.

As Kimble had implied, it scared him that the world might not operate exactly according to the rules he understood, and scared him more that he had been right to fear his father was not quite gone. Raven did not think he believed in ghosts, but what was a ghost if not a presence, and that presence had never left him.

There were two other people inside the lobby: a young woman sweeping the floor, and a silver-haired man taking down a poster advertising a production of *The Tempest*, due to commence next week. Before it came down from the wall, Raven spied the reason for its removal: Laurence Butters' name against the part of Prospero.

Raven recognised them both from Kimble's performance. The young woman had taken the tickets, while the man was the one he suspected of being Kimble's accomplice. By evening, illuminated only by gaslight, the lobby looked grandly opulent. In the late afternoon he could see how care-worn and tatty it was, paint peeling and carpets threadbare.

'I'm sorry, sir, we are not yet open,' the man said, belatedly noticing him. 'Doors are at seven.'

Raven indicated the poster the man was in the process of removing. 'Is *The Tempest* cancelled?'

'Not at all. Merely an adjustment to the bill.'

'Recasting Prospero, perhaps?'

Raven held up the pamphlet, which did not merely name and picture Butters, but speculated that he had fled the city.

'One week out,' the man mourned with a sigh. 'Fortunately there is an understudy.'

'I gather you need to find a new dresser too,' Raven said, at which the man starkly understood that Raven was not here to purchase tickets. He stopped what he was doing, letting the poster hang half folded over itself.

'Without meaning to be rude, sir, may I ask your purpose here?'

'I have some questions regarding the late Mrs Butters and her missing husband.'

'That is not a subject I can freely discuss,' he replied.

The young woman who was sweeping nearby snorted in disdain. 'Emphasis on freely,' she muttered.

'Has James McLevy been here to speak to you about these matters?' Raven asked.

The man immediately looked tense at the spectre Raven had raised. His eyes went to the young woman sweeping, then back to Raven.

'No, he has not.'

'Then if you would prefer that to remain the case, I would recommend you speak to me in his stead.'

'And you are?'

'Dr Will Raven.'

'What have you to do with McLevy?'

Raven thought of how best to phrase this in order to accommodate his own denial later.

'I am acting on behalf of the police surgeon.'

'I see.' The man extended a hand. 'Daniel Barrington. Actor-manager.'

'And you are?' Raven asked the young woman.

'This is Rachel,' Barrington answered for her. 'My daughter. She works at the box office and sells confectionery during intervals.'

'I am also an actress,' she told Raven boldly. 'I've had parts in four productions.'

'And if you wish it to be five, you will get yourself into the auditorium and make sure the place is clean and ready before doors open.'

Rachel tutted and made for the entrance to the stalls.

'No, please, let her stay,' Raven said. She had been slyly observing Raven since his arrival, and given her variety of duties he suspected those same curious eyes missed little that went on in this place. He also had the impression Barrington would prefer she wasn't around while they spoke.

'What can you tell me about Laurence Butters?'

'He's a fine actor. Hugely experienced, great presence, versatile and dependable. Well, normally,' Barrington added.

'Did *you* know him well?' Raven asked Rachel.

'Him *and* his wife, yes,' she replied, giving her father a defiant look. Raven inferred that she knew more than she said. He would keep that in mind.

'Mrs Butters was kind. She was kind to everybody, wasn't she, Father?'

There was a barb in this, one that Barrington met with a glare. Raven could not decipher it. Perhaps the girl felt Mrs Butters had deserved better treatment from him.

'And what do you know of Laurence Butters' relationship with his late wife?' he asked Barrington. Raven was thinking of the odd, if vague, picture that their neighbour Mrs Bryant had painted.

Barrington pursed his lips, giving it some thought, or perhaps making a show of giving it some thought. 'What does one really know about any man and his wife that goes on behind closed doors?'

'So, you think there was acrimony?'

Raven glanced at Rachel, who was suddenly looking at the floor.

'No,' replied Barrington. 'I mean, obviously there was a problem if he's killed her and chopped her into bits. But I'm saying, nothing that was obvious to anyone else.'

Raven addressed Rachel. 'Was it your impression that there was strife between them?'

She stared at her broom. 'Who's to say,' she replied.

'You never saw them argue, perhaps?' he prompted.

'No,' said Barrington, though he had not been asked. If this was intended to answer for her, then it backfired.

'Never saw them *together*,' muttered Rachel huffily. 'They were married, but they had their own lives, you could say.'

'How was Butters the last time you saw him?'

She shrugged. 'Full of himself, as usual.'

'And how was your working relationship with him, Mr Barrington?'

'Rachel puts it indelicately, but he has a good conceit of himself. He knows what he's worth, or what he thinks he's worth. A tough negotiator. Always looking to chisel a little more money. Keeps his eye on the books in case he's being diddled. If the takings are good, I know he'll be at my door looking for a bonus.'

'It's my understanding he had debts,' said Raven. 'Yet I also heard he reckoned he had money coming to him. Do you know about either of these things?'

Barrington let out an exasperated sigh. 'Laurence owes money and people owe money to him. Always. He likes fine things. I have often thought that even offstage he is playing a part, and he prefers to play the part of someone far richer than himself. Fine dining, fine wines. He has the tastes and posture of an aristocrat, but not the means. As soon as he has money, it is spent. Friends will lend it to him because as soon as he comes into any, it's gone in displays of largesse. Some would call him generous, others profligate. Either way, he is free with his favours.'

'That's one way of putting it,' muttered Rachel, drawing another glower from her father.

'What are you alluding to?' Raven asked.

'She is making mischief and showing off, as usual,' said Barrington dismissively. 'By speaking about things of which she knows nothing.'

'I know more than I care to about Laurence Butters' *favours*,' she retorted. 'I understand the true nature of the man.'

'How so?' asked Raven.

'These are matters I do not care to revisit,' she replied.

She was blushing. She seemed suddenly vulnerable.

Raven glanced at her father, who looked like this was news to him.

'Did he do something to you?' Barrington asked.

'I will not discuss it,' she insisted. 'Especially knowing what he has done since. I do not wish to make myself a target for his vengeance.'

'Anything you tell us could help track him down,' Raven urged. 'You would be safer if we found him.'

'I will be safer if he has no reason to consider my testimony a threat. And unlike some, I will not trade my knowledge for coin.'

'What's she talking about?' Raven asked.

Barrington said nothing, sending his daughter a silent warning that Raven could tell she would not heed.

'You're not the first to come asking questions. That other fellow was here. The one who calls himself the Hoolet.'

'The man who writes the pamphlets? Do you know who he is?'

'Didn't give his real name. Father was the one being free with his tongue.'

'What did you tell him?'

Barrington was tight-lipped, both shamed and furious. Then he spoke, perhaps understanding that his daughter would say it anyway.

'I told him that Lydia Butters had lovers. Many lovers. It was well known,' he stressed to Rachel. 'Someone else was bound to tell him. I might as well make a few bob from it while I try and keep this place running.'

Rachel sneered in disgust. 'Didn't mention you were one of them though, did you, Father?'

Barrington's eyes flitted back and forth between Rachel and Raven, cornered.

'I didn't wish to draw attention to that, no. Especially as . . .'

'What?' asked Raven.

'Nothing. Rachel's mother died more than ten years ago. She cannot expect me to live like a eunuch.'

'That's not all you told the Hoolet, is it though?' she stated. 'Tell Dr Raven why I'm not the only one worried about Butters coming back.'

Barrington sighed. 'I saw him,' he said flatly.

'When?' asked Raven.

'Last night, late, after the performance. I was clearing up and I saw him at the rear of the stage. Just standing, as though waiting for his cue. I called to him, but he rushed off into the wings. By the time I had got up there, he was gone.'

'You're sure it was him?'

'I have seen him in a hundred parts and as many different garbs, but when he's not in character, he's unmistakable. He was wearing a coat he purchased in London. He favours any garment that will distinguish him, and that one is especially treasured.'

Barrington glanced at his daughter again, then back at Raven. 'I told the Hoolet all the speculation about Butters having fled is wrong. As of last night, he was still in Edinburgh.'

SEVENTEEN

arah was surprised and somewhat concerned to receive a summons from Eugenie asking her to visit but to keep it from Raven. She had no wish to be caught in the middle of their marital discord, but when Raven had left after morning clinic, she found herself making her way to the house on Castle Street.

The day was overcast but a little warmer than it had been of late. Sarah found herself longing for the bright early mornings and long evenings of summer. The endless months of winter darkness had as ever worn her down. But despite the promise of summer being on the way, Sarah felt troubled. The séance had unsettled her.

She was not a believer in mystics and mediums, but it was difficult to explain the knowledge that this stranger had managed to glean about private matters within the family. The lack of an obvious explanation did not mean she had to accept a metaphysical one, she knew that. Nonetheless, she felt shaken and just a little less certain than she had been before.

Was she right to believe in mesmerism? There was no explanation for that either and yet it seemed such a benign and potentially useful means of alleviating suffering. There was no attempt to exploit anyone's grief. The intention was to heal, and in the hands of skilled practitioners, the results could be extraordinary. She had read numerous case reports that were convincing, but Raven remained resolutely dismissive. It was collusion or delusion, he said. Nothing more than that. Sarah's own experiences so far had proved inconclusive. Mrs Crowe had seemed entranced, but given her proclivities that could most certainly be self-delusion; while collusion was definitely the word to describe what had happened between herself and Mr Somerville, as a way of mutually negotiating the awkwardness.

As Sarah approached the door she wondered briefly if Raven would be at home. There was nothing to stop him calling in on his way to the Maternity Hospital. She hadn't considered this and so had no prepared excuse as to why she should be visiting.

In the end no excuse was necessary. When she knocked the door, it was Eugenie who answered. She was, for once, not encumbered with a small child and the house was quiet as she led Sarah into the parlour.

When they both sat down, Sarah could see that Eugenie was pale and looked exhausted. Clearly motherhood was taking a toll on her.

'You look tired,' Sarah said. 'Have you been sleeping?'

Eugenie gave her a look suggesting that this was an incredibly stupid question. She sat down and adjusted her skirts around her swollen belly. 'I've been having headaches,' she replied without preamble. 'I have always been prone to them, and the pills and potions prescribed by Will have failed to effect a cure so I have stopped troubling him about it. I was wondering if you might care to try.'

'Me?'

'Yes. I hear you have been taking instruction in mesmerism.'

Sarah wondered where Eugenie would have heard this. Mrs Crowe, no doubt. Safe to say it would not have been from Raven. Sarah presumed that Eugenie knew about his stance on the subject, and pondered whether that explained the secrecy around this visit. An uncharitable part of her wondered if Eugenie intended to use this to her advantage, to drive a wedge between Sarah and Raven if she cared to do so.

'I have only just begun but I'm happy to try,' Sarah said. 'Do you have a headache now?'

'I do.' Eugenie indicated a bowl of water and a flannel sitting on the side table beside the sofa.

'Are we likely to be disturbed?' Sarah asked.

'You mean James? Mercifully he's at my father's house this afternoon and I'm not expecting any callers.'

Sarah took off her coat and asked Eugenie to lie back on the sofa with her head on a cushion. Eugenie draped the damp flannel over her eyes.

'Do you think that Will is alright?' Sarah asked, aiming for a casual tone but unconvinced that she had succeeded.

'What do you mean?' Eugenie replied, sounding wary.

'It's just that he seems out of sorts.'

'You'll have to be more specific.'

'He punched someone.'

Eugenie removed the flannel and sat up again.

'Who?'

'An old man who was causing trouble at Queen Street.'

'A patient?'

'No.'

'Well, thank goodness for that. It would have marked the end of his short career and where would that have left us?'

Eugenie thought for a moment, then asked, 'Is it something to do with this investigation he has embarked upon? The business he's helping Henry with? Although sometimes I think it's all just a ruse so that he doesn't have to come home.'

'Why would he not want to come home?'

Sarah immediately regretted asking this. It seemed too personal, as if she was probing an inflamed wound.

'I don't know. Do you?'

'Why would I? He is hardly likely to discuss such things with me.'

'He does spend a great deal of time in your company.'

'Well, we work together, so that is to be expected.'

Eugenie sighed and flopped back against her cushion. 'I think that he finds family life challenging,' she said. 'It makes me wonder about his own upbringing. I know little about it, and he refuses to discuss it with me.'

'I don't think that his childhood was a particularly happy one.'

'That much I had surmised. But he has his own family now, and whatever happened in his past should not be allowed to spoil the present, don't you think? Perhaps if we had a little more room,' she said, sweeping her hand around the modest dimensions of the small parlour. 'If we had better accommodations, he might feel less confined when at home. He really should have branched out on his own by now. We can't continue to subsist on his assistant's salary alone. Perhaps you could talk to him.'

'Me?'

'I refer to my earlier remarks regarding the time you two spend together. Perhaps you can convince him. Succeed where I have failed.'

Sarah wondered if this was the real reason she was here.

'You want me to encourage him to leave Queen Street?'

'Yes. That is exactly what I want. Preferably before he gets himself dismissed. You're quite sure that man he assaulted wasn't a patient?'

'Quite sure.'

'Who was he then?'

Sarah wondered how to explain what had happened and why.

'His name is Richard Kimble. He was claiming to be a spiritualist medium who could see and hear the Simpsons' dead children.'

'Really? And did they have anything interesting to say?'

'You shouldn't make light of it. He knew a lot about the children and how they died. Mrs Simpson was very upset.'

'Hence the punching.'

'Yes, hence the punching.'

There was silence for a moment.

'I didn't think he was like that any more,' Sarah said.

'Like what?'

'Prone to fits of rage.'

'I would say he simmers rather than rages – at least round here. You've no need to be concerned on my account.'

'I was more concerned about him.'

Eugenie sighed. 'I think that my husband simply needs to decide what he wants and make peace with the decisions he has made. And to stop taking on extra work that attracts no remuneration.'

'You mean the investigation?'

'Yes. Any sign of it concluding?'

'Well, they don't appear to be any closer to tracking down the elusive Mr Butters. He is the prime suspect now. They think that he killed his wife, buried her, and then absconded. Well, buried bits of her anyway.'

'Grisly business,' Eugenie said and shuddered. She stood up and poked at the fire.

'Let me,' said Sarah.

Sarah knelt down at the hearth, added some more coal, and coaxed the flames back into life.

Eugenie stood with her arms wrapped around herself, shivering.

'You're cold,' Sarah observed. 'Can I get you a shawl or a blanket?'

'There's a blanket on the bed. If you could bring that . . .'

Sarah made her way into the hallway only to realise that she did not know where the bedroom was. The first room she looked in was obviously James's bedroom. There was a small bed, with a few wooden toys ranged around the rug on the floor. It looked a little sad and forlorn, probably because the child who usually occupied it was not there. It made Sarah think again of the séance and the damage it had done, stirring up memories that were not easy to bear. Sarah could see no benefit in it. On the contrary, it was creepy and intrusive: a stranger insinuating himself into private pain.

The next room she looked into was Raven and Eugenie's bedroom. Sarah stood by the door for a moment, a strange gnawing sensation in her stomach. She looked at the bed. The cast-iron bedstead; the pillows, blankets, and bolsters. This was where they slept together, lying beside each other every night. Sarah had to admit that she missed that: the closeness, the security of sleeping beside someone else. She suddenly imagined that someone to be Raven, could imagine sleeping with his arms wrapped protectively around her. She began to imagine other things too and felt the heat rise to her face.

Enough, she thought. Enough.

There was a woollen blanket neatly folded at the foot of the bed. As she reached for it, she noticed that on the far side of the room, on the floor, a makeshift bed of sheets and blankets had been made, its rumpled state testament to recent occupation.

When Sarah returned to the parlour Eugenie was reclining on the sofa again.

'I was just thinking,' Eugenie said. 'Perhaps you could ask this medium fellow to contact the late Mrs Butters and find out what happened. Bring the investigation to a swift conclusion.'

'I take it you're joking,' Sarah asked.

'Of course I'm joking. You don't believe in this sort of thing, do you?'

'No. But after the séance . . . I don't know. The whole affair was so disconcerting. And anyway, if Raven was to see Kimble again, I don't know what he would do.'

'I think that we probably do.'

Sarah spread the blanket over the recumbent Eugenie and sat down herself on an armchair beside the sofa.

'Shall we begin?' Sarah asked.

'Begin what? Oh yes. The mesmerism. Please do.'

So not the primary reason she had been summoned here, Sarah thought.

'I think we'll try local mesmerism initially,' Sarah said.

'Whatever you think best,' Eugenie replied.

Sarah reapplied the cold flannel across Eugenie's closed eyes and forehead, stood at the end of the sofa and raised her hands.

She tried to calm her own mind. Her thoughts had to be concentrated on the matter at hand; the mind's attention focused on the patient to increase the remedial power of the treatment. She had to cast all other thoughts from her head. Intrusive thoughts about Raven and why he might be sleeping on the floor rather than in the marital bed.

She began moving her hands from Eugenie's neck to the crown of her head and beyond it, keeping them at a distance of a few inches from the front and sides of the head. She moved around her patient, continuing the hand movements for five minutes or more.

As she did so, she tried to think benevolent thoughts about Eugenie, but it was Raven's face that kept reappearing in her mind. Try as she might to dismiss him, he kept returning.

She dropped her hands, took a deep breath, and tried again.

She thought about the structures inside Eugenie's skull. That was better. Focus on the anatomy of the brain: the cerebral hemispheres, its lobes and convolutions, its membranes and blood vessels. The circle of Willis, the complex arrangement of arteries at the base of the brain. She tried to visualise the pages of her notebooks where she had made detailed drawings of the structures she was now trying to recall. This mental exercise proved to be surprisingly efficacious, and she thought that perhaps it would be worthy of reprisal when she next had the opportunity to mesmerise a patient.

Sarah stepped back for a moment to catch her breath. It was only then that she realised a more prolonged treatment would be unnecessary. Gentle snores were emanating from beneath the cold flannel. Eugenie was asleep.

EIGHTEEN

here was a small boy walking next to his father beneath the colonnade as Raven stepped out through the theatre doors, the child pointing animatedly at a poster for a play about pirates. Once more he recalled the joy of being taken to the theatre by his mother, of feeling that same excitement. It was something Raven would like to bestow upon James, something he would love to share with him, but it seemed so far away, if not impossible. It was Eugenie who ought to take James to joyous things. She deserved that.

The best Raven could do was protect him from harm, and that started with protecting him from the harm Raven himself carried within.

What did he do to you? What did you do to him?

Andrew Cunningham had been Raven's father's name. He had christened his son Thomas, after his own father, who Raven never met. Raven had discarded it like a snake its dead skin. Instead, he had adopted his mother's maiden name and replaced Thomas with Wilberforce, the name she had given him. It was under this new designation that he had reinvented himself after being sent to Heriot's school for fatherless boys. The reason he qualified for its charity had been something else he feared Kimble could see.

In all the years since, only Sarah had discovered his abandoned name, and her lips were the only ones from which he had heard it spoken. He knew she would never have betrayed such a secret, especially not to the likes of Kimble. So how did he know? How did he see?

The thought of Sarah brought him back to mesmerism and her burgeoning enthusiasm; one she shared with no less a figure than Dr Cooper. Nothing felt clear any more. The world was refusing to behave the way he used to understand it. He had seen mesmerism as something it was his duty to stand against and to defeat. But look what his stand against Kimble had wrought.

He was about to cross Broughton Street when he heard someone call his name. Raven turned and saw a man standing with his back against the theatre wall. He had been there all the while Raven stood oblivious: watching, waiting. That alone felt intrusive, but not nearly so intrusive as when he realised who he was looking at.

Flint.

Raven had not recognised him, perhaps because the version of the man he carried in his head was three years out of date, still wearing the last clothes Raven had seen him in. He thought about what Gregor had said, about Flint going up in the world. He was dressed like a gentleman. Or rather, like someone such as Flint imagined a gentleman to dress. Spending the money but not quite getting it right. Spending too much money, perhaps.

Flint stepped from the wall and strode towards him. 'Do you have a passion for the theatre?' he asked. 'Or does it depend who is on the bill?'

Raven remembered that Gregor had said Flint wanted to be kept informed of the investigation, though it seemed unlikely he would have sought Raven out personally merely for that.

'How did you know I was here?' Raven asked.

'I always know,' Flint answered, giving him a thin smile. The remark was much like his new clothes: something intended to give an impression of power and status, but which served merely to draw attention to the bluff.

'If you wished to speak to me, shouldn't you have sent someone to abduct me by now?'

Flint smiled, amused by the memory or perhaps enjoying reflecting on all that had changed in the time since.

'I'd like to think we are both above such things these days.'

'You wish to know about Butters,' Raven said. He did not intend to be coy. He wanted the purpose of this encounter to be discharged as quickly as possible. 'He was seen here last night, backstage. Looking for what, I cannot speculate, but it appears he is still in Edinburgh.'

'That's what I'm hearing too,' Flint stated.

'Then you are not missing anything at McLevy's end. There: that's as much as I know. If you want to find out more, perhaps you should pick up the Hoolet's next pamphlet.'

Raven made to walk away, but Flint's hand reached out and grabbed his arm. Raven batted it away and raised his fists. Flint responded with open palms.

'I know we've had our differences, Dr Raven, but can't we talk over a drink like civilised men? There is something I would like to discuss.'

Flint had never called him 'Doctor' before. He normally dealt purely in threats and intimidation. Clearly the man needed something that he could not simply take, and that made Raven curious.

'You're buying.'

Flint led him across the street to the Adelphi Hotel and Tavern, where he purchased a tankard of beer for Raven and a glass of claret for himself. The tavern was busy, but Flint availed them of a preferred table by means of a mere look towards the men already seated there. Flint might have been absent from Raven's mind these three years, but men of a certain station still knew who he was.

'I gather you are a family man now,' Flint said, taking a sip. 'A son, and another on the way.'

Raven struck Flint with a burning glare. 'Whatever this is, you keep my family out of it, or I will end you.'

Flint returned Raven's stare, unflinching. Raven's mind went back to their last encounter: his knife at the man's throat, Flint's pistol at Raven's belly.

'That's what I like about you, Raven. You've never been afraid of me. Even when you should have been. But I would never harm your family. You are not the only one who has changed. And I have not forgotten your part in the birth of my son.'

'How is the lad?'

Flint took a mouthful of wine, swallowed.

'He died, a year past. Measles.'

'I am sorry.'

Flint's eyes briefly flashed at Raven's condolence, rising to it as though it were a threat. This was a man who could not tolerate being thought in any way weak.

'I have a daughter,' Flint added, conciliatory now. 'She is almost two.'

'And your wife? She remains well?'

He flashed Raven another steely look. 'Thriving,' he muttered, in a way that declared this part of their conversation over.

It was not only Flint's clothes that were different. He appeared richer, more respectable even, but he also looked more burdened since they had last seen one another. Raven felt well qualified to recognise the look of a man feeling pressure from multiple directions.

'Why are you so interested in Laurence Butters?' Raven brushed his fingers against the fine cloth of Flint's jacket. 'You look like a man who must have greater things on his mind than one small debt.'

'I have quite a few irons in the fire these days, yes. But what you fail to understand is that no debt is too small, because if you don't chase the wee ones, it gets around, and folk start thinking they can dodge the big ones.'

'Nonetheless, I was given the impression you had more to occupy yourself than mere usury. Or does lending to actors count as a step up from lending to paupers?'

Raven was hoping to rile him with this, but Flint was nonplussed.

'Butters owes me for services, not a loan. An enterprise I facilitated, and a profitable one by my understanding.'

'What manner of enterprise?'

'That's my business.'

'Very well. But if you wish to redeem your debt, it might help those of us looking for Butters if you were less circumspect about your dealings with him.'

Flint sighed, taking another sip of wine.

Raven wondered why he was being so evasive. He remembered that Flint once had the misguided notion to steal a racehorse using chloroform. In the early days after its discovery there were many misapprehensions about chloroform's powers. Raven had been tempted to encourage this folly merely to lead the man into disaster, but his conscience had dissuaded him on the grounds that it would almost certainly not be Flint himself who got kicked in the head.

'I arranged the use of a venue for him,' Flint said. 'He wished to stage a number of performances – speeches, soliloquies, that kind of thing. I was promised a share of the takings.'

Raven barely stopped himself from spluttering in his beer. 'A theatrical venture? You?'

Now Flint did look irritated. 'I'm not trying to be some impresario. I own the building. If you want to rise in this town, you cannae be a mere tenant, beholden to someone above you.'

'I'll drink to that,' Raven acknowledged. 'But if not a theatrical venture, what kind of business are you running from this building?'

Raven's mind was filling with lurid images, the only kind of business he could picture Flint in charge of.

Flint looked almost pitying. 'You don't understand, Dr Raven. Ownership *is* the business. Property. That's why I wanted to talk to you. I have an opportunity to diversify my holdings, but I do not yet have the funds and I am trying to gather as many assets as I can.'

Raven gaped. Was the infamous money-lender, to whom he was once in hock, now before him soliciting a loan of his own?

'I'm not looking to make an investment,' Raven told him. 'And certainly not with you.'

'I'm not offering one. I've seen where you live. Butters owes me fifty pounds — that's more than you make in a year. But I have not asked you here to discuss Laurence Butters. I wanted to talk to you about someone else: our mutual friend who brought Butters to your attention.'

'Gregor? What of him?'

'A remarkable man,' Flint said. 'Quite unique.'

'Yes, I'm sure he has been invaluable to you down the years.' Raven's fingers ran to his cheek. 'He held me down while your man did this, in pursuit of *my* debt, remember?'

Flint's expression was inscrutable, a mask to hide whatever he felt about the deeds he commissioned.

'Yes. Alec. A man for whom you later did the ultimate kindness, in finally delivering him from his misery. I have not forgotten.'

'Such a kindness that you threatened to use it against me, as I recall.'

Flint's face remained sphinx-like. 'You are an enigma to me, Dr Raven. You help people when there is no advantage in it for you. And yet equally you refuse help when it is offered. Perhaps it is time for that to change.'

For a panicked moment Raven wondered how the man before him could possibly know about Cameron Todd's offer. Then he remembered that Flint had in the past offered Raven opportunities. He had turned them down because he did not wish to be further entangled with the man, and he certainly did not wish to owe him favours.

'I cannot see that Gregor will be of service to you for much longer. Is that your concern? Though I'm sure people will still be afraid of him as long as he walks upright.'

'Gregor has often been compared to Charles Byrne,' said Flint. 'You know who that is?'

'The Irish Giant,' Raven acknowledged.

'I am told the anatomist John Hunter bought his corpse for five hundred pounds, and that was more than fifty years ago.'

'What are you saying?' Raven asked, though it was clear they both understood.

'I have seen Gregor recently, as have you. We both know he has little time left. If you were to help me find a buyer, I would be prepared to offer an equitable split of the proceeds.'

It was what Gregor had always been afraid of. And he must have known that Flint in particular would attempt something like this.

'Gregor has been explicit in his wishes,' Raven said. 'He is haunted by what happened to Byrne. Byrne knew Hunter wanted him, and took steps to keep his body from the anatomists, but he was betrayed by the greed of his friends. I have vowed to ensure Gregor's body does not meet the same fate.'

'Is it truly greed, though, Doctor? Is it not instead the avoidance of a needless waste? Surely it is enough for Gregor to go to his death believing that the fate of his body has been assured by you. Whatever happens after that, he will have no knowledge of it.'

'I would have knowledge of it. Half of Edinburgh must know his wishes. He talks of them often enough. And he is not yours to sell.'

'That's where you're wrong. I have looked after him since he was a boy. Given him employment. Were it not for me, he would have ended up a freak on show.'

Raven could not mask his distaste.

'He made you money for years, but now that he's no longer useful, you wish to sell him like meat.'

'No meat is worth this much per pound,' Flint stated darkly.

He swirled the red liquid around his glass for a moment, contemplating it, then he looked up at Raven again.

'Just so you understand, you are not the only person I have come to with this. I have a man in London, but the share he is asking is greedy and I don't trust him. However, he reckons Gregor is worth at least a thousand pounds. If you are able to find a buyer through your contacts in the world of medicine, I am willing to split the money right down the middle.'

Flint knocked back the last of his wine and put down the glass.

'What could you do with five hundred pounds, Dr Raven?'

NINETEEN

rs Crowe linked her arm around Sarah's to prevent them being separated in the crowd milling about outside the building on Potter Row. They had come to attend the next meeting of the Edinburgh Mesmeric Association, but now had reason to believe they had turned up on the wrong night, or that something very popular was scheduled in the meeting room downstairs. The last time the association had convened, there were maybe twenty people, two dozen at most. This evening there had to be ten times that, trying to squash themselves into the larger room on the ground floor.

'Dr Malham has been out posting bills, promising a demonstration at tonight's meeting,' Mrs Crowe said. 'I would not have imagined such a scheme would prove so effective.'

'Perhaps we shouldn't be so surprised,' Sarah said. 'Interest in mesmerism is growing to such an extent that it has provoked a backlash in the medical press. Dr Raven keeps leaving copies of journals around 52 Queen Street, opened at the appropriate pages, clearly intended for me to find.'

Sarah had seen one in the *Lancet* that morning, and could not help hearing Raven's voice as she read its pompous denunciation:

Careful investigation and consideration of all the experiments drawn to our attention have consistently convinced us that the phenomena are not real, and that mesmerism is a delusion. This humbug should no longer affront the common sense of the medical profession, or dare to show its face in the scientific societies. We thought it long buried and thus it is our duty to stifle these wrong-headed attempts to revive it.

She wondered why Raven could not see the similarities between this establishment resistance to mesmerism and its initial resistance to chloroform. It was largely coming from the same sources: dusty old men, afraid of something new, and especially wary of a power that did not already belong to them.

'I can see two seats free over there,' said Mrs Crowe, indicating a row on the right-hand side of the aisle. Sarah had just approached it when she was all but barged out of the way by two men intent on taking the same seats. They bustled past with an air of entitled self-importance, acting as though neither she nor Mrs Crowe was even there.

Looking at the busy hall, Sarah felt a familiar anxiety, a sense that an avenue she had hoped to travel along was being crowded and closed off by men once again.

Amelia Bettencourt's influence had allowed Sarah's education to go as far as a woman was permitted, but mesmerism offered the chance not merely to learn about a burgeoning field of medicine, but to be in the vanguard. This was not to say that Sarah would be uncritically credulous of it simply because it offered opportunity. If mesmerism proved to be a genuine therapy, then Sarah wanted to plant her own flag before the men fenced it off. But if it was to turn out to be humbug, Sarah wanted to be the one who proved it so, from the inside.

She looked about for any more seats they might have missed, then became aware of an arm waving close to the stage. It was Mr Somerville. He was easily spotted, wearing a matching checked frock-coat, waistcoat and trousers. It was quite striking, tailored neatly to Mr Somerville's wiry figure, though there was a modernity to it that Sarah associated with the look of a younger man. More of Mr Gethyn's handiwork, she suspected.

Sarah turned around to see who Somerville was beckoning, and failing to see anyone behind her, was forced to conclude that it was indeed her. There were two empty seats beside him in the front row, where she and Mrs Crowe joined him.

'That is most obliging of you,' she told him.

'Actually, it was Dr Malham who asked me to keep a look-out and ensure you were accommodated.'

'Thank you anyway,' she said.

Somerville sat down and began – or perhaps resumed – a conversation with two serious-looking gentlemen to his left. She could hear him explain how much busier this was than the last meeting.

'Bankers,' said Mrs Crowe, sotto voce, and Sarah instantly understood why Somerville seemed so keen to impress upon them that mesmerism was in the ascendancy.

It was only now they were seated that Sarah noticed Mrs Crowe was clutching one of those ghastly Hoolet pamphlets. She failed to mask her distaste.

'I know, it's naughty, isn't it?' Mrs Crowe acknowledged, sounding less than apologetic. 'I have a shameless appetite for gossip and scandal. I find few things quite as exhilarating as other people's bad behaviour. My preference is for anything that casts a pall over Edinburgh's upper orders and their hypocritical pretentions. But when that is not available, something gory and gruesome will do.'

Mrs Crowe opened the pamphlet and Sarah glanced briefly at the text. It ran either side of line drawings depicting the artist's impression of the murder, Laurence Butters coming at his helpless wife with a meat cleaver.

'It's implying he murdered her because she was unfaithful,' Mrs Crowe said.

Sarah read a little and then stopped, unable to bring herself to read on.

'The way it's described, it's as though she invited this upon herself,' she said. 'Men are endlessly adept at excusing their own behaviour and endlessly inventive in blaming women for the atrocities they inflict upon them.'

'Yes,' said Mrs Crowe, 'but that is only the half of it. Men are not the only intended readership. It is also for the comfort of women to tell themselves this fate would never befall *them* because *they* do not engage in such sinful behaviour.'

'This claims that Mrs Butters had lovers, plural,' Sarah observed. 'If other people knew this, surely Butters did. Are we to believe he was the poor cuckold who finally met his limit?'

'Unless there was something about her latest lover that particularly infuriated him,' Mrs Crowe suggested.

Sarah sat in silence for a few minutes while Mrs Crowe continued to read.

'Did you ever see him perform?' Sarah asked.

'Oh, yes. Many times. I was introduced to him once. And he was perfectly charming. But I don't imagine many murderers flagrantly advertise their nature, and if anyone could put on a mask to disguise the intentions of his heart, then it would be an accomplished actor.'

Mrs Crowe's eyes widened as something occurred to her.

'I think I saw him recently, at one of Malham's demonstrations,' she said. 'It's possible that he could be here right now, watching tonight's exhibition. Walking among those who are looking for him, hearing what is being said.'

Sarah could not resist turning round and gazing at the crowd, though as she had never seen Butters before, it was a fairly pointless undertaking.

'He would surely not be so brazen,' she said. 'Someone would recognise his face, even in disguise.'

Mrs Crowe did not seem so reassured. 'If you had seen him in a play, you would not believe it was the same man standing in the bar later. There are wicked men who take great pleasure in the practice and genius of their own deceit. Just imagine the thrill of an actor who has made the whole city his stage.'

'Well, I don't believe he's any manner of genius,' Sarah said. 'He's an evil man. I saw with my own eyes what he did to his wife.'

'You saw her body?'

'I saw her foot. It was found at Surgeons' Hall. Butters had unsuccessfully tried to dissolve it.'

Mr Somerville turned around, looking astonished at what he was overhearing, his conversation with the bankers having suddenly ceased. Sarah realised she had spoken a little louder than she intended, but before she had the opportunity to explain, there was a call to order and Malham took the stage.

This evening he wore a black frock-coat and charcoal-grey trousers, a blue neckerchief the only note of colour. He was carrying a cane, which was not something she had seen him with before. He had promised something new tonight, and she hoped he meant more than a mere physical accessory.

After a few words of welcome, Malham paused, then said: 'I must first tell you that I will not be mesmerising any of you this evening.'

He let his words hang there, mutterings of disgruntlement passing through the room like a wave, then quietening again in expectation of what might be on offer instead.

'I do not wish to offer mesmerism up as any kind of spectacle or entertainment, so if that is what attracted your curiosity this evening, you should take your leave.'

There was a shuffle of feet and some low mutterings as a handful of people made their way along their rows and to the exit. Malham watched them with quiet patience, then spoke again.

'Those of us uninterested in mere spectacle are here because we wish to observe and understand the altered state of consciousness that mesmerism induces. The state I call the Garden of Sleep. You will wonder, as I have wondered, what is going on inside the head. What does it feel like from the perspective of those mesmerised?

'To that end, I have subjected *myself* to mesmerism.'

Malham walked closer to the edge of the stage, gripping the cane in his right hand.

'I have wondered for some time, could one self-mesmerise? Initially I thought it impossible, but following many months of diligent practice, I find that I can now induce a self-imposed mesmeric trance. And what I have discovered has been truly remarkable. When self-mesmerised, I enter not a soporific state of dulled senses, but the opposite: a state of heightened awareness. Certain things become more vivid, colours are brighter, sounds clearer.

'It was overwhelming at first, but I have learned to filter out certain unwanted sensations and to focus on others. Naturally as a doctor, that focus has been medical, and the effect has been that when I look at a person, subtle signs become immediately apparent. It is almost as though I can sense their pain: a heightened state of not merely awareness, but shared feeling.'

Malham gave a self-conscious smile.

'As always, there is the fear that what I refer to as self-mesmerism may merely be a form of self-delusion. To that end I would like to put it to the test, and make us all part of the experiment.'

Malham held up his cane, the head of which Sarah could now see was a crystal orb.

'Returning to the self-mesmerised state takes less time on each occasion, but it does require your patience. And your silence,' he added.

Malham held the cane in front of him and stared into the crystal. A stillness came upon him, and a hush fell upon the hall, with the exception of a few stifled coughs which soon settled down. The quiet seemed to grow, becoming less like an absence of sound and more like something created, like a shared responsibility. Sarah became aware of trying to reduce the sound of her own breathing. Was this what he meant them all to do? To focus on their own breathing to the exclusion of all else? She wondered if Malham could, by this method, mesmerise the whole audience and if this was what he intended.

Malham descended the steps from the stage and walked into the centre aisle, every head turning in the rows he passed. There was little need for heightened awareness, Sarah thought, for she could see many people eagerly straining to catch his eye.

He stopped, then he pointed to a man sitting five rows in and spoke.

The theatrical surroundings had made her anticipate an alteration to his voice, the trappings of some hammy performance she associated with showmanship. She realised that part of her was afraid he was going to descend into antics that might bring the whole field into disrepute. Instead, he was quieter than before. Paradoxically, his quiet delivered greater attentiveness. He seemed calm and thus calming.

'It is you, sir. I see, I *feel* fatigue. Weariness.'

The man nodded sincerely.

'Stand up, sir, that everyone might see you.'

Sarah watched the man get to his feet. He looked self-conscious to be standing up in front of an assembly, and yet almost powerless to stop himself.

'Sleep comes but it does not stay,' Malham intoned.

'That's right,' the man agreed.

'You find your rest disturbed.'

'Nightly.'

'And through the day, you feel aches and weariness.'

'*Yes.*'

Sarah heard not merely eagerness in the man's voice, but a near-joyous relief.

'The tonics prescribed for you have been of little use. Would you consider mesmerism as an alternative?'

'If it will help me sleep, for sure I will.'

Malham walked further into the room. People were no longer merely trying to catch his eye, but actively raising their hands. He did not appear to be looking at them, though. He was holding up the cane again, his eyes fixed on the globe. He closed them briefly, then opened them and turned, picking out an older lady to his left.

'You suffer with pain in the neck and shoulders, do you not?'

'Yes indeed, sir.'

She got to her feet without being asked.

'You also suffer headaches which can be severe on occasion.'

'I am a martyr to megrims, sir. They have forced me to my bed.'

'Not once, either. These headaches have caused you to take to your bed several times over the past year, have they not?'

The woman wore a look of surprise, allied to the same mixture of delight and relief exhibited by her predecessor.

'The doctors you have consulted were unable to give a satisfactory explanation for your complaint.'

'They said it was my age.'

'You have taken calomel and Gregory's Powders.'

'I've been prescribed calomel, yes,' she said. She looked astonished that he should know this, and several gasps from the floor indicated that this astonishment was widely shared, presumably by those who did not appreciate that certain doctors in this city prescribed calomel for everything.

'But it only makes you feel worse.'

'Far worse.'

'I would recommend you desist, then. And see whether mesmerism can effect a better cure.' Malham smiled. 'If it doesn't make you worse, it is already an improvement on your current course of treatment.'

There was laughter at this, then Malham picked out another lady, sitting on the edge of the aisle.

'You have joint pain, arthritis.'

His tone was tender, less a declaration of her symptoms for the audience than a voice of understanding. Sarah thought of how Dr Simpson would talk to patients sometimes, letting them know first and foremost that he cared they were suffering.

The woman stood up with a laboured motion, at which point it became clear she required the aid of a walking stick.

'The pain does not rest, does not settle, am I right?'

'It is a shifting pain,' she agreed.

'It moves around the body but sometimes localises to a specific area. Sometimes it travels to your lower back.'

The woman put a hand to where he had just described.

'You have tried many treatments, some of which have provided temporary relief, but your pain has always returned. Do you know what I am about to say?'

The woman laughed, but there was such gratitude in her expression.

'That I would benefit from mesmerism?'

'You would indeed. Come see me, madam, and I will make you well.'

This continued for some time, Malham picking out members of the audience, seemingly at random, and accurately describing their complaints without recourse to the usual diagnostic methods of asking pertinent questions and making an examination. The mood in the room became heightened, people trying desperately to attract Malham's attention as he passed up and down the aisle. They seemed keen to have him tell them what they already knew themselves, and Sarah was beginning to wonder what the point of all this was, when Malham turned and reascended the stairs.

He raised the orb before his face once more, focused upon it, then blinked and seemed to take a moment to re-engage with his surroundings. There was a palpable sense of disappointment as the audience understood that he had ended the trance, and that no one further would be chosen.

Malham looked a little drained, his posture less straight-backed, his expression less bright.

'I am sorry that I cannot continue.'

This provoked a few disgruntled murmurs from the crowd.

'The heightened awareness is both exhilarating and exhausting,' he continued, 'and that which burns bright cannot burn for long. Mesmerism is a powerful phenomenon, and how we might channel it is something we are only beginning to understand. However, what we are increasingly discovering is that mesmerism can prove an efficacious therapy for many ailments where traditional tonics and treatments cannot assist.'

He paused for a moment.

'If I can see what ails you,' he said, 'then I am convinced that I can cure you. I see it as my duty to help the afflicted. Come to me and I will make you well again.'

With that, he left the stage.

There was a moment of quiet, as though the audience was collectively reluctant to accept that the demonstration was over. Then they broke into applause, many of them rising to their feet and cheering.

A man Sarah recognised as Mr Gethyn the tailor then ascended the stage.

He called for quiet.

'If you wish to make an appointment to see Dr Malham here at our new Mesmeric Institute, please leave your name and address at the back of the hall. Thank you.'

Our new Mesmeric Institute? Sarah wondered what role Malham's tailor had managed to acquire for himself.

As she made her way towards the door, she couldn't help being buoyed by the enthusiasm in the room, though her elation was leavened by the thought that no one so far had actually been cured of anything.

TWENTY

he demonstration was barely at an end before Mrs Crowe spotted an acquaintance she wished to speak to, and she bustled off with eager purpose. Sarah would have had to part ways with her anyway. She intended to speak to Malham to arrange another teaching session, but he was now surrounded by members of the audience, and she could see she would have a long wait. She decided she would find him some other time.

There was quite a press at the back too, the main exit choked by people queuing to register their interest. She joined the procession and found herself in step with Mr Somerville.

'That was quite something, wasn't it?' he said. 'He diagnosed all of those ailments in the blink of an eye.'

Sarah thought that he was missing a distinction between Malham describing symptoms and actually making a diagnosis, but it felt churlish to dampen his enthusiasm.

'I'm at a loss as to how that was done,' she admitted. 'I feel I am making progress in learning mesmerism myself, but I fear I have a long road ahead of me before I could ever do something like that.'

'You have to learn to crawl before you can walk, I suppose. But you've the perfect teacher. He's a man of rare talent.'

'It would seem so. It will be instructive to see how mesmerism helps in each of these cases. A record should be kept, don't you think? If there are papers to be published to convince the rest of the profession?'

'You should take that up with the man himself. There may even be a role for a keen mind such as yours. Is that something that you would be interested in?'

'Yes, I think so. It would give me the opportunity to study his work more closely. I could learn a great deal.'

Sarah could suddenly imagine herself presenting papers in front of the Mesmeric Association, and who knew, perhaps one day at the Medico-Chirurgical Society.

'I don't doubt it,' Somerville said. 'You are a woman of surprising capacities.'

'What do you mean?'

'I overheard talk of a foot,' he reminded her. 'Have you a connection to the police?'

'I know the assistant to the police surgeon, that's all. He is a friend of a friend.'

'But you are intimate with the details of this case?'

'At this stage I know no more than whoever is publishing those pamphlets. Mrs Crowe said she saw Butters at one of Malham's previous demonstrations. Are you familiar with him yourself?'

'Not personally. But I did recently see him give a solo perform-ance of speeches from plays.'

'And how was that?'

'Well-attended,' Somerville said, his tone suggesting this trou-bled him for some reason. 'Whatever else was going on with him, he knew how to pull a crowd.'

As they reached the vestibule, they found themselves close behind the two bankers Somerville had invited. They were intent upon their conversation, their braying voices carrying above the hubbub.

'Dr Malham seems an interesting individual,' one of them was saying. 'I mean, you know, American and what-not. Showy, but clearly he's drawing curiosity.'

Somerville smiled at Sarah and raised his eyebrows approvingly.

'My concern is always whether curiosity translates into long-term fees. Medicine is full of fads and overnight sensations. But the level of interest is already impressive, and clearly growing.'

'And what of our Mr Somerville?' asked the first one as they reached the exit onto Potter Row.

Sarah felt something tighten inside her; she was suddenly uncomfortable to be eavesdropping.

'I couldn't get past the suit he was wearing, frankly. That's the thing about new money. The more they spend to look like something they're not, the more obvious they make their provenance.'

'How on earth did he secure Amelia Bettencourt as a guarantor?'

'She has a weakness for waifs and strays, so-called "deserving causes". Her father would have had none of it. I think it is purely to torment him in his grave that she would even entertain going into partnership with someone who is so evidently from below stairs.'

Sarah saw a flush of red around Somerville's neck. His hands bunched into fists. The two bankers were walking, oblivious, towards West College Street. He began to stride towards them.

Sarah instinctively put out a hand and tugged at the cloth of the disparaged frock-coat.

Somerville turned around sharply, glaring at her with unnerving aggression. She let go of his coat but he remained where he was, their eyes locked. They both understood that she had witnessed his humiliation, which engendered a shared feeling of vulnerability. It felt like a dangerous moment.

'Thank you,' he said. His face remained ruddy with anger but his voice was calm, if a little unsteady. 'The worst thing I could have done is behave like the kind of man they believe me to be.'

'I cannot imagine it would have assisted your application for funding either.'

'They don't like it when low men have the temerity to rise above their station,' he said.

'Try being a low woman, Mr Somerville,' Sarah replied.

Somerville's eyes flashed with aggression again, then he let out a laugh, venting tension. 'Touché,' he said.

They stepped to the side, forced closer to the wall and away from the exit by the departing throng.

'How goes the search for funding?' she asked. 'Did they say anything? To your face, I mean.'

'Tonight's success has all but convinced them of the viability of this venture. But no business plan or named guarantor counts as much as a man's name and breeding. Even with Amelia Bettencourt's stature as cautioner, they still seek a surety on my part. They require evidence that I can raise a substantial percentage on my own.'

'And can you?'

'I won't pretend it's not stretching me, but yes. And it will be worth the pain. Harland Malham has great ambitions for the institute. We are at the forefront of a new therapeutic marvel. Edinburgh is world-renowned for its Medical School and he thinks it can be world-renowned for its Mesmeric Institute too. With him at the helm, I think that's achievable.'

'A mesmeric institute on such a scale would be of considerable benefit to a great many people,' Sarah said, thinking of the gratitude and relief on the faces of those present tonight. She showed him the still reddened part of her palm. 'And given my recent experience, a more salubrious location would be welcome too. Where do you hope to move to?'

'Milton House,' Somerville replied, pride and relish in his smile. 'It is up for sale now that the Maternity Hospital has moved elsewhere. You are familiar with the building, I gather. Would it be suitable, do you think?'

'I imagine that it would.'

'I'm due to visit tomorrow. Why don't you come with me? I would value your opinion.'

'*My* opinion? Why?'

Somerville looked deep into her eyes. His own were a rich hazel colour, dark and penetrating. She thought he would be a difficult man to lie to, and a frightening one to disappoint.

'Because you will tell me the truth,' he said. 'You're not afraid to stand up for yourself.'

She was conscious of his closeness. She could smell the newness of his clothes.

'I do stand up for myself,' she said. 'But that doesn't mean I'm not afraid.'

'And yet you persist. I have heard tell that you were once a housemaid. You have come a long way.'

'I am still little more than that. I am permitted to assist at Dr Simpson's clinics, and I help with the children.'

'But you have educated yourself. You are welcome above stairs, invited into certain company.'

'Yes, and I have had to fight for every inch of that,' she told him, feeling indignant, though she could not say why. She felt a need to impress upon him that her struggle had been every bit as hard as his.

'I would not dare suggest otherwise,' he told her, his voice sincere. 'That's why I find you inspiring. Remarkable.'

'Inspiring? How?'

Somerville took hold of her coat where she had taken hold of his, an echo and an acknowledgement of what she had done for him.

'You give me hope,' he said.

TWENTY-ONE

aven bounced about in the back of Dr Simpson's carriage as the vehicle negotiated the rutted lanes around Bathgate. One of the village doctors, Dr Stark, had requested Dr Simpson's opinion about an unusual case, and the professor had jumped at the chance to visit his place of birth. He had retained an almost reverential affection for the town, something that Raven could not understand. Not for the first time, Raven appreciated that Simpson's childhood had been very different to his own.

'I used to deliver bread rolls to all the houses around here,' Simpson said. 'My father owned a bakery, you know.'

Raven did know. Very well and in depth.

'I used to practise my sums in flour spread on the counter in the shop.'

Simpson smiled in reminiscence. Raven wished he had similarly pleasant stories he could recount. Being beaten bloody by his vintner father for dropping a crate of burgundy did not merit the same easy sharing.

They had left the main road some time ago, Dr Simpson insisting he knew a short cut that would save them time. Raven would have preferred the longer route if it saved his coccyx from the pounding it was currently experiencing.

He was grateful that Simpson had shown no indication of knowing about the incident with Kimble. The professor had made no reference to the entire afternoon, in fact, which struck Raven as troubling. Simpson normally liked to dissect events for what might be learned, so it was the mark of a singularly uncomfortable experience that he should wish to put it entirely from his mind, and Raven suspected that Mrs Simpson's reaction had been even more painful.

The carriage drew to a halt outside a small farmhouse and with some relief Raven stepped down into a well-ordered yard. He could hear the lowing of cattle coming from somewhere, and a couple of chickens were pecking about in the dirt.

Simpson stood beside him and took a deep breath in.

'Fresh country air,' he said. 'So good for the constitution.'

Raven was disinclined to agree. All he could smell was manure.

The front door of the farmhouse opened and a man in a tweed jacket approached them, his hand outstretched.

'Professor Simpson. I am so grateful to you, sir. The patient is this way.'

'Lead on, Dr Stark,' Simpson said, and they followed him into the house, Raven picking his way carefully across the cowpat-strewn courtyard.

The house was as well-kept as the yard outside and the smell of fresh bread greeted them as they entered. They were taken up some narrow stairs to a small bedroom which was icy cold as a result of the windows being thrown open to let the air in. The smell up here was far less wholesome than downstairs, despite strenuous attempts at ventilation.

An enormous man was propped up on pillows in the bed, the sheets in disarray around him. The skin of his face and upper chest was a most unhealthy colour, one that Raven was struggling to name. Heliotrope perhaps.

'As I said in my letter,' Dr Stark began, 'the patient is a farmer who, after a long day spent chasing cattle that had escaped their field, returned home in a state of exhaustion, and was subsequently struck down by this curious ailment. I have never seen anything quite like it.'

The man in the bed, as if on cue, groaned loudly, writhed around, coughed and then settled back on his pillows again.

'He's been like this for two days,' Dr Stark continued. 'Restless, complaining of pain in his chest and abdomen.'

'Tell us what you found when you first saw him,' Dr Simpson said, taking his stethoscope from his bag.

'Breathing short and difficult, about fifty inspirations in the minute. A hacking cough with bloody sputa. Pulse hard and fast, about a hundred and seventy in the minute, although that has declined a little since then. Secretion of urine was nearly completely arrested: within the first twenty-four hours he had passed about a wineglassful of a deep red fluid, nearly half of which was blood.'

Dr Simpson sat on the bed beside the patient and felt for the pulse at the wrist. He leaned in, placed the stethoscope on the chest and listened.

'Has the urine increased in quantity?' Dr Simpson asked.

'Somewhat. Still tinged with blood but much less than before.'

Dr Simpson made a thorough examination of the patient and then invited Raven to listen to the chest before all three men repaired downstairs to discuss the case. Throughout, the patient remained silent, oblivious in his delirium.

'Well?' Dr Stark said.

They were standing in the small parlour. The fire had been lit and someone – the farmer's wife, presumably – had left a tray with a teapot and cups, a jug of milk and some buttered bread. Raven was tempted to help himself to some refreshment – it had been quite some time since breakfast – but he resisted.

'What do you think, Dr Raven?' Simpson asked.

Raven tore his eyes away from the tea tray and tried to marshal his thoughts.

'There is considerable hepatization in the lower part of the chest,' he stated. 'But I'm afraid no diagnosis comes to mind that would explain this strange concatenation of symptoms and signs.'

Dr Simpson sat down heavily in an armchair by the fire and sighed. 'Yes. It's a perplexing one, alright.'

Raven was relieved that he had not missed anything obvious. He was six years under Simpson's tutelage, but that sometimes meant he could fail to spot the commonplace while searching for the obscure

'Well, Dr Stark,' the professor said, 'I approve of your treatment thus far and find that I have no further suggestions to make.'

Raven found he was disappointed. He had assumed the professor would be able to pinpoint whatever obscure ailment the farmer had acquired.

'The only thing that comes to mind is a disease of cattle.'

Cattle? Raven tried to recall the various afflictions believed to be transmitted by farmyard animals. Cowpox was the only one he could think of, and this definitely wasn't that.

'When cattle are overdriven,' the professor explained, 'they fall victim to a rapid inflammation of the lungs, liver, kidney, bowels: in fact all organs of the body. It is usually fatal to them. The only way to secure the value of the animal is to slaughter it immediately.'

'Not an option in this case,' Raven said.

Dr Stark drew him a severe look and Raven decided to keep his thoughts to himself from now on.

Dr Simpson stood up again, a prelude to leaving.

'There have been some signs of improvement,' he conceded, 'but with such a severe affliction – I would be surprised if he should recover.'

Raven felt the disappointment of a wasted journey. He took one last longing look at the tea tray and followed Dr Simpson out.

TWENTY-TWO

Raven climbed back into the carriage, Dr Simpson following him after a few moments, having first spoken to Angus, the coachman.

Raven looked out over the fields and hills as they made their way back towards the town. He wondered what it would be like to be a country doctor in a place like this, and shuddered at the thought of it. His ambitions had always stretched beyond provincial medicine. He wished to have an international reputation like Simpson and attend the wealthy in their illnesses as well as the poor. His main interest lay in the evolving speciality of gynaecology: there was plenty of money to be made treating the diseases of women so far largely ignored by surgeons.

The thought brought him back to Flint's offer, which he had not been able to put from his mind. With that kind of money, he would be able to set up his own practice independently of Eugenie's father, and would not have to worry about his income while he built up a roster of patients.

He had given Gregor his word, but Flint's argument had stayed in his head. It mattered what Gregor believed while he was still alive, but after that, what was the difference? His body would only be consigned to the earth to rot and Gregor himself would be long past caring.

Raven had often heard discussion of what was called the resurrectionist's price: the value to medical knowledge accrued from anatomising certain specimens, balanced against the knowledge that they had not consented. From Raven's perspective, it was sentimental and superstitious to care so much – once you were dead, you were dead – and yet there was no question that people felt strongly about what happened to their mortal remains. Burke and Hare resorted to murder because society had become so vigilant over the departed. It became easier simply to kill people and offer them to the anatomist than to rob them from their graves.

In the case of Charles Byrne, the scandal over his theft was so great that Hunter dared not properly dissect his prize. He had paid the resurrectionist's price and yet learned nothing. What if there were vital things to discover about what made Gregor the size he was, and how that growth had sealed his early doom? It was said that no man is truly dead whose name is still spoken. Would it not honour Gregor if his name ever after became attached to a greater understanding of his condition? Or was this merely the siren song of avarice, tempting Raven with moral justifications to debase himself?

'How goes the investigation?' Simpson asked. 'I am hearing all kinds of gossip, and it seems half the city is now claiming to have seen your man Butters.'

With the Hoolet's pamphlets reporting that the killer was still in Edinburgh, McLevy was being inundated with alleged sightings, which was doing little for his disposition.

'The common fear is that his work is not done,' Raven said. 'With Mrs Butters alleged to have been free with her favours, they are painting a picture of him stalking the city in different guises, waiting to avenge himself on all those who cuckolded him.'

'And what of the connection to Surgeons' Hall? Has anything come to light regarding that?'

'Not so far. Though it has emerged that Butters had an interest in mesmerism.'

'Doesn't everyone these days,' said Simpson drily.

'More's the pity,' Raven agreed. 'According to Dr Cooper, Butters attended a demonstration and became quite excited by what he had witnessed. Interestingly, Dr Cooper felt that his intentions were far from pure. Perhaps he thought he could mesmerise his victims.'

Simpson laughed. 'It is my understanding that mesmerism requires a great deal of time and co-operation from the subject: considerably more than for chloroform, which is one of the reasons it is not suitable as a substitute for anaesthesia. If this was a crime of passion, I can hardly imagine Mr Butters in his murderous rage asking his wife to sit still for forty minutes while he prepared his vengeance.'

They were passing a field; through the carriage window Raven watched as a young lad ushered a cow towards a gate. The image brought him back to the farmer and his mysterious illness.

'Have you thought more about this morning's patient?' Raven asked.

'I have thought of little else,' Simpson replied.

'And have you come to any conclusions?'

Raven was waiting for the professor to describe an obscure condition that he had never heard of, no doubt read about in some arcane book or journal. When, as an apprentice, Raven was sent to collect certain texts for the professor from the university library, the librarian often expressed the opinion that the professor was the only one who was aware of the requested volume's existence.

Simpson scratched his head. 'I have no idea,' he said.

Raven must have looked deflated.

'We have to do the best we can with the knowledge that we have,' Simpson stated, 'and that knowledge will ever be incomplete. The medical practitioner can never cease to be the medical student. And you must learn to live with that.'

He looked at Raven with sympathy. 'I said recently that I had nothing more to teach you, Will, but I forgot one last thing; perhaps the most important lesson of all.'

'And what would that be?'

'That sometimes we just don't know.'

TWENTY-THREE

arah's nose was assailed by the smell of wet wool as Henry's jacket began to steam in front of the fire in Raven's consulting room. He had come directly from Greyfriars Kirkyard, where he had spent the morning with James McLevy.

'He's furious,' Henry said, sipping tea and waggling his feet in front of the fire in an effort to dry his damp socks.

'Why?' Raven asked, holding out his cup to Sarah as she poured tea from the pot.

'Because we've been digging up the plots of those recently interred and found nothing. Which means that there are still pieces of Mrs Butters unaccounted for.'

'It's not unreasonable to think that Butters might have used the same stratagem to get rid of the rest of his wife's body,' Raven suggested.

'True, but we have disturbed more graves with no result, and the relatives of the recently deceased are understandably upset.'

'Surely it's understood by everyone why McLevy's doing it. It's not as if he's opening coffins.'

'I hope to God that's not what Butters did,' Henry said, looking suddenly alarmed.

'Unlikely,' Raven replied. 'Opening coffins and adding to their contents would be too much effort for a man working alone.'

'He was a resurrection man once though, wasn't he?'

'In his youth perhaps. Even then it was not a job undertaken alone.'

'How did they do it?' Sarah asked, genuinely curious.

'They would find a fresh plot where the soil was still loose, dig a hole down to the head end of the coffin, use hooks to lever the top part open and haul the corpse out,' Raven said.

'How do you know so much about it?' she asked.

'From the usual source. The repository of all knowledge who sits at the head of the dining-room table.'

'Do you think Dr Simpson was ever involved in such things?' Henry's voice was low, despite the fact that the door was closed and their conversation unlikely to be overheard.

'Well, he was a medical student at the height of it,' Raven said. 'Taught by Knox himself.'

'Hush, Will Raven,' Sarah chided. 'How can you suggest such a thing?'

'Because it might well be true,' he replied, flashing her a mischievous grin.

She punched him lightly on the shoulder. 'Can we get back to the matter in hand.'

Sarah noticed that Henry was looking at the two of them, concern clouding his features.

'What?' Sarah asked.

Henry shook his head. 'Nothing,' he said and sipped his tea.

She knew what troubled him though. It was her easy intimacy with Raven, a married man.

They sat in silence for a while, the only sound being the rain lashing against the window and the crackling and shifting of coals in the fire.

Eventually Henry spoke again. 'If grave-robbing was still a thing, Butters wouldn't have been able to do what he did. Hiding body parts in a freshly dug plot would not have been an option.'

'How so?' Sarah asked.

'Back then the kirkyard had guards posted to patrol the place, and wealthy persons erected metal cages over their graves, so the likes of Butters wouldn't be able to get access to them.'

'Yes, I've seen those,' she said. 'And the tombs and mausoleums in the kirkyard? Did they serve the same purpose?'

'Some of them, yes. Although the ancient ones predate these concerns. They were more about erecting a monument to persons of importance.'

'Have you ever been in one?' she asked. 'A crypt, I mean.'

'Can't say that I have.'

She looked at Raven.

'Our family finances would never have stretched to such an extravagance,' he said. 'Money was always in short enough supply for the living.'

She turned back to Henry. 'What happens to the body if it's kept above the ground?'

'They all decompose no matter where you put them,' he replied.

'And is there space for more than one coffin?'

'In some of the bigger ones. Whole families can be accommodated.'

Sarah thought for a moment, the beginnings of an idea forming in her head.

'So, there's plenty of room inside. No guards to stop you and no digging required.'

'What are you thinking?' Raven asked.

'I think,' she said, 'that perhaps Mr McLevy has been looking in the wrong place.'

TWENTY-FOUR

arah stood outside the black mausoleum, an ancient construction with soot-stained walls. The rain had stopped but the air was still damp. The trees in the kirkyard were heavy with moisture, depositing large droplets on those who were foolish enough to stand beneath them. It was not quite dark yet, but it would be soon. It had taken the best part of the afternoon to track down Mr McLevy and persuade him that this was a notion worth pursuing, though she was already beginning to wish he had dismissed the idea.

This was reputed to be the most haunted part of the graveyard, close to the Covenanters' Prison. The ghost of Bloody Mackenzie was said to patrol the area around the crypt, his soul yet to make the transition to a peaceful afterlife, presumably hounded from his eternal rest by all the Covenanters he had imprisoned, tortured, and killed.

The mausoleum was a circular structure with a domed roof and a hefty iron door which had suffered the depredations of more than a century exposed to the Scottish weather. There was an inscription above the portal which read: *Sir George Mackenzie Lord Advocate during the reigns of Charles II and James VII*, his service to the monarchy evidently what the man inside wished to be remembered for. It had been built against the wall of the kirkyard and was now overlooked by the west wing of the Edinburgh Poorhouse.

Perhaps not the setting that had been envisioned for it when first constructed.

Over the years it had fallen into disrepair, a variety of vegetation having found its way into the lime mortar between the stonework, and a large clump of ivy hung languidly from the roof. The door looked solid enough from a distance but on closer inspection revealed a slight gap around the frame, suggesting it had been opened at some point and then failed to close properly.

There was no knowing if such activity had been recent, but it was the best indication they had found that Sarah's suspicion might be right. Along with Raven, Henry, McLevy and his men, she had taken a short tour of all the crypts and tombs in the place before arriving here, at undeniably the most foreboding sight in the graveyard.

'It had to be this one,' McLevy sighed. Even the redoubtable Irishman seemed uneasy. If there were consecrated places that could nonetheless feel evil, this was one of them.

McLevy had two men with him, both carrying lanterns which had been lit against the growing gloom. The youngest of the two looked as though he had seen a ghost already, probably only too aware of the stories about Mackenzie's poltergeist, a malevolent spirit who was said to physically wound those who ventured too near to his final resting place.

'Well, best get on with it,' McLevy grumbled.

The larger of the two constables set down his lantern and put his shoulder to the door.

'Is this a crime?' Sarah asked.

'Desecration of a tomb?' Raven suggested.

'I think "violation of sepulchre" is the correct legal term,' Henry replied.

McLevy scowled at them. 'A moot point given that I am the law around here. But that said, the procurator fiscal will have my balls on a platter if I start breaking open every vault and crypt in the place. Not to mention the Hoolet having a high time at my expense.'

Sarah wondered whether McLevy's unguarded language meant she had been accepted into the group with no special accommodations or whether he had simply forgotten that she was there.

The burly constable gave the unyielding door another shove. There was the sound of metal grinding against stone as it opened. He stepped back waiting for further instructions, not keen to be the first one in.

Raven picked up the policeman's lantern and squeezed through the narrow opening. Sarah followed, determined neither to be excluded nor to appear afraid, but felt a profound trepidation as soon as she did so. The air was cold and musty. There was another smell too, but she couldn't identify it. Never having been in one before, she was unsure what an ancient tomb was supposed to smell like.

There was a rustling sound, and then the flap of wings, causing her to start. Birds or bats, presumably, unless Old Mackenzie had grown a pair himself.

She had only just recovered when she felt something brush her back and jumped again.

'Sorry,' said Henry. 'Can't see a thing in here.'

McLevy followed Henry with the other lantern. His two associates remained outside.

It was difficult to see much in the dim light. Raven held up his lantern, which illuminated scalloped alcoves in the stonework near the roof. There was some evidence of water ingress causing a mossy discolouration down one part of the wall. A small fetid puddle had formed at the bottom of it.

Raven shone his light around in a circle, taking in the entire circumference of the floor.

'There's nothing here,' Sarah said.

'Apart from us,' Raven replied.

She felt disappointed that her logical deduction had failed to deliver, and she waited for McLevy to rebuke her for wasting his time. But McLevy said nothing. He stood pointing at the ground to one side where a metal grate covered an opening in the floor.

He handed his lantern to Henry and bent down to raise the grille. Part of her wanted it to remain stuck fast and immovable, but it opened with a grinding noise that set Sarah's teeth on edge.

They all leaned over the opening. Stairs led down into blackness.

'I'll go,' said Raven. 'You stay here.'

Sarah wasn't sure who he meant: all of them or just her.

Ignoring what he had just said, she followed down after him before anyone could stop her, taking care on the narrow stone steps. At the bottom, she held tightly onto Raven's jacket as he raised his lantern again, the light of the candle flickering off the stone walls. They were in a vaulted room, a cellar. There were several wooden caskets set on stone plinths. Sarah felt her mouth dry.

'Which one is his, do you think?' she asked. She found that she was whispering and wasn't sure why. It was as though she feared disturbing someone, and not from mere sleep.

'Mackenzie's?' Raven asked. 'Hard to tell.'

Sarah took a firmer hold of Raven's sleeve. 'It's horrible down here.'

'It's not meant for visitors.'

'I don't like it. Let's go.'

'Are you frightened?' he asked.

'Who wouldn't be?'

'It's not the dead we should be afraid of,' he reminded her.

His voice had the same tone and register as if speaking to her in his consulting room. If he was feeling any fear at all he was hiding it well.

He sniffed. 'Do you smell something?'

'You mean something fresher than a hundred-and-fifty-year-old corpse?'

'Indeed.'

There was a more definite aroma down here, one that had only been hinted at in the room above.

Raven walked a little further into the crypt, Sarah shuffling along behind him.

'What's that?' he asked.

Sarah could see something wedged between two caskets. Something wrapped in hessian. Possibly the source of the smell.

She tried to breathe through her mouth but then decided against it, imagining bits of ancient dust and other matter becoming trapped in her throat. She could feel her pulse racing, could almost hear it in her ears.

'Mr McLevy,' Raven shouted. 'I think we've found something.'

Raven put his arm out and tugged at the hessian, Sarah standing behind him and peering over his shoulder. Something had discoloured the weave and initially it seemed stuck to whatever was underneath. Raven pulled again and the material separated, revealing what lay below.

A human torso.

'Talk about balls on a platter,' Raven said, his voice barely above a whisper now.

'Is it Mrs Butters?' McLevy shouted down.

Raven and Sarah looked at each other.

'I can say with some confidence that it's not,' Raven replied.

TWENTY-FIVE

aven approached the university buildings from North College Street, making the short walk from Minto House as soon as the last case of the day had been dealt with. He was only yards from the library when he became aware of a shadow on the pavement as a figure strode purposely into his path. He tensed, years in the Old Town conditioning him to be ready for a fight, but when he looked closer he saw that it was worse than that.

'Dr Raven, if I might have a word.'

It was Christie, looking all the more elongated in the top hat he was wearing, his skin waxy and cadaverous against both the millinery and the black of his coat.

He fished a crumpled pamphlet from his pocket, presenting it with a level of contempt as to suggest Raven himself had published it. It was far from the most recent; old news as far as Raven was concerned, but its contents clearly still high on Christie's agenda.

'"Gruesome remains found at Surgeons' Hall",' he quoted. '"Murder among the sawbones, or a return of the resurrectionists?" Was I not explicit in my instructions regarding discretion in this matter?'

'That had nothing to do with me, or with Dr Littlejohn, I can assure you. I don't know who is publishing these, but we were not his source.'

'I know you're not his source. But you were supposed to get to the bottom of this before anything leaked out.'

'We are making progress,' Raven assured him. 'And the trail is leading ever further away from Surgeons' Hall. The police are seeking an actor by the name of Laurence Butters, who appears to have murdered his wife.'

'I am not interested in who he is or who he has killed. I am only interested in what connects him to the College, and how quickly that connection might be severed.'

Raven decided it would be judicious at this point to omit mention of Butters' past as a grave-robber.

'At this stage we have no reason to believe the connection to Butters is any more than coincidental. The most likely explanation is that Butters somehow acquired access to the building and, seeking out an unoccupied place where he would not be disturbed, happened upon Dr Cooper's office. It is nobody's fault.'

Christie remained looming over him as he pondered this. It felt like Raven was in his thrall as much as his shadow. Christie's was a presence both intimidating and compelling: one that Raven wished to be gone from and yet felt commanded to endure.

'Unfortunately, Dr Raven, in medical politics, perception is everything. The burden of office is that fault does not matter, only responsibility. If this stain is not quickly washed away, people will note that it occurred at the start of my tenure. And if my tenure becomes ever after associated with this, then I will ever after associate you and Dr Littlejohn with failure and disgrace.'

Christie thrust the pamphlet into Raven's hand.

'I do not wish to see any further mention of the College on arse-paper like this. So no matter where the path of this investigation might lead, you do whatever it takes to keep it from my door.'

With that, Christie strode away, though Raven felt as though he had left his long shadow behind.

Raven entered the library, following the same route that he had fruitlessly taken a few days ago. Once again, he sought the

Professor of Rhetoric and once again he discovered the man was not in his office. This time, however, someone was at least able to direct him to where he might be found.

'He is in the courtyard with some students,' said a bearded gentleman he had spoken to on his last visit, a face he vaguely recalled from his own student days. On the surface, this was not the most helpful direction, as the courtyard tended to be thronging with bodies at any given time, but perhaps anticipating this, the bearded man assured him that 'you can't possibly miss them'.

Striding through these halls, Raven felt a heady mix of nostalgia and relief, as he did whenever he trod this ground. Nostalgia for the feeling of excitement and discovery he had known here, the sense of infinite possibilities ahead of him; and relief from the fear of failure that had constantly attended it all. He had attained his degree and continued his training under the best of tutelage, for this was the place he had first encountered Dr Simpson. But in truth, the fear of not realising his potential had never quite left, which was why he was so anxiously pursuing the favour of Dr Christie by doing McLevy's job for him. It was also why he was still giving thought to Flint's offer. He had first encountered him during his time here too.

The discovery at Black Mackenzie's crypt had unfortunately posed more questions than it answered. Part of a male torso had been found, indicating that Butters had killed a second person, but on this occasion there had been no head to identify the victim. McLevy had latched on to the simplicity of the cuckold hypothesis, and to be fair it was all they had to go on while they knew nothing else about the torso in the crypt. But Raven's instincts told him there had to be more to it than Butters finding his wife in bed with someone and murdering them both.

One of the things most intriguing him was why Butters had not fled the city. It was possible his plan had been to dispose of the bodies and then declare that his wife had gone missing or left him. Yet, even though Butters must know his crimes had been discovered, it appeared he was still in Edinburgh, albeit that assumption did come with a large caveat. The Hoolet's pamphlets had ensured a continuing deluge of reported sightings, much to McLevy's displeasure. Butters having been an actor meant that some of the witnesses didn't concern themselves with whether the person they had seen even bore much resemblance to the man. In many cases they had seen someone who looked a bit like Butters when he was playing a particular part.

That could not be said for Daniel Barrington, though. He had worked with Butters for years. And what was more, Butters had run once he knew he had been recognised.

Why had Butters gone back to the theatre? What was he looking for there? And if Barrington, by his own admission (or his daughter's admission, anyway), had cuckolded Butters, should it not have been he who ran away?

Raven recalled the actor-manager's daughter insinuating herself into the conversation, relishing her indiscretion on certain matters while withholding her knowledge about others. For all her saucy cheek and bravado, she was clearly afraid of Butters. Rachel Barrington knew more than she was saying, but it was clear that she was not going to talk to Raven. However, that didn't mean she would not talk to anybody.

There were four young men in flowing white robes standing in the centre of the courtyard as Raven emerged from the building. They appeared to be in an approximation of classical garb, and Raven would have to acknowledge that they could indeed not be missed. In his student years, he had harboured a certain disdain for those studying the arts, wondering what use any of it could be. None of them were going to make a living from it, though perhaps his resentment largely derived from them being the types who did not have to worry about such things.

Professor Lewis was distinct for his less historical dress, though his attire was nonetheless eye-catching, there being something almost dandified about the cut of his suit. It was an extremely modern checked pattern, offset by a green neckerchief. Raven thought of the suit Flint had been wearing, and was struck by the contrasting impressions. Lewis was in his forties, a good ten years older than Flint. Both were wearing garments intended for younger men, but one of them was carrying it off far better. The difference was that while Lewis wore the suit, in Flint's case the suit had been wearing him.

One of the robed young men was declaiming theatrically, the others holding poses around him, like a tableau. It appeared to be a rehearsal.

Raven was waiting for a break in the proceedings before interrupting, but the professor appeared to notice him and signalled to the group to halt.

'Let us adjourn for a moment,' he told them.

'Professor Lewis?' Raven asked.

'Yes, how may I help you?'

'What is this? A Greek tragedy?'

'A Roman comedy. *The Braggart Soldier*. Sebastian here is in the lead as Pyrgopolynices. Are you hoping for a part?'

The professor's tone indicated that they both knew this was far from likely.

'I am Dr Will Raven, assistant to Professor Simpson.'

Raven reasoned that he might as well let that name open a few more doors while he still could.

'He of the chloroform,' Lewis acknowledged.

'Though I am not here on his behalf. I was hoping you might be able to tell me something about a man I seek, by the name of Laurence Butters.'

Lewis stiffened, becoming subtly on guard.

It had occurred to Raven that he could mention Dr Cooper as the reason he had sought Lewis, but he decided he should keep that in his pocket for now, to see how the professor responded.

'The stage actor?'

'Yes. I am assisting James McLevy. The police detective.'

'I have seen Butters in many a role. A fine thespian, to be sure, though I doubt that is what he will be remembered for now.'

'I am trying to find out who he might have had dealings with personally.'

'I only knew him through his work,' Lewis replied, turning away so that he was no longer facing the troupe.

'That's not what your friend Dr Cooper told me. He gave the impression you and Butters were well acquainted. I believe you introduced them to each other at a recent demonstration of mesmerism.'

Lewis's eyes narrowed. He was trying to mask his annoyance at the way Raven had played his hand. His expression then softened, though it looked a deliberate effort.

'Given what has recently come to light, I am sure you understand why one might be disinclined to advertise one's associations with such a man.'

'Entirely, Professor Lewis,' Raven said deferentially. 'I understand the need for discretion, but that must be balanced against the need to apprehend an individual who has proven as dangerous as he has elusive. That is why I am seeking your assistance in understanding more about who he was – offstage. What reason he might have had for his actions.'

Raven stepped further from the robed students, inviting Lewis to join him away from earshot, though they seemed to be paying no attention anyway, engaged in laughter and horseplay.

'I am told his wife was unfaithful,' Raven said. 'Serially so.'

Lewis seemed wearily amused by this.

'I take it that is not news to you?' said Raven.

'It is not news to anyone who has been reading certain scandal sheets.'

'But you knew that before the Hoolet, didn't you?'

Lewis did not deny it.

'How did you know Butters?'

'That is not something I wish to discuss.'

'It seems an innocuous question to me,' Raven argued.

'To you, perhaps, but perspective is everything in certain matters.'

'You socialised with him, though.'

Lewis remained tight-lipped.

'Confidentially, Professor, I fear someone else in Butters' circle has come to the greatest harm. It has not been announced to the public, but there is a second victim. Male. As yet unidentified. I am looking for some clue as to who that might be.'

'Laurence Butters moved in many circles,' said Lewis. 'As did his wife.'

'Did you know her?'

Lewis glanced towards his students, gesturing that he would not be long. Raven did not interpret it as an encouraging sign.

'I know she worked in the theatre too,' he said, 'but I cannot say I knew her. They were not often to be found together.'

'Their neighbour Mrs Bryant suggested the same thing. It was not the portrait of a perfect marriage. I am not asking you to speculate on her infidelities, but can you think of anyone with whom Laurence Butters had a mutual antipathy?'

Lewis wore the same look of weary amusement as a few moments before.

'Are you familiar with *Don Leon*, by Lord Byron, Dr Raven?'

Raven was not. 'The life of a doctor does not leave much time for poetry,' he offered weakly.

'It is a poor life that leaves no time for poetry,' the professor replied. Then he quoted:

'That this little spot, which constitutes our isle,
Is not the world! Its censure or its smile
Can never reason's fabric overthrow,
And make a crime what is not really so.'

'What does that mean?' Raven asked.

'When you understand that, you will understand a great deal more.'

'You are the literary professor. Wouldn't you be the ideal person to explain it to me?'

Lewis glanced at the young men in their flowing robes, then back at Raven.

'I will say this much, then I will bid you good day. Laurence and Lydia Butters were not what they appeared. For some people, onstage or off, their whole life is a performance.'

TWENTY-SIX

he lady on the consulting-room couch had come all the way from Fife for treatment, something she had stressed to Sarah on several occasions prior to the procedure.

'Could she not have had this done closer to home?' Sarah asked, removing the chloroform-soaked flannel from the patient's face.

'I'm sure she could have,' Raven replied. 'Some local surgeon could have had a go, hacked away at it. But such is Dr Simpson's reputation, patients are prepared to travel even for something as simple as a labial abscess.'

Ironically, despite travelling to see Dr Simpson, the patient had been forced to settle for Raven, the professor having departed with his whole family the day before. The mood in the house had not been quite right since Kimble's visit, painful emotions having been stirred up, not to mention difficult questions regarding the intimacy of Kimble's knowledge. Dr Simpson had decided that a change of scene and fresher air were required, and had them all pack for a trip to Argyll.

Raven held up the swab onto which the contents of the abscess had been evacuated.

'Wasn't much in it and it wasn't that inflamed. More cyst than abscess. Probably didn't need anaesthetised for such a small incision.'

Sarah scoffed. 'Easy for you to say.'

Raven looked at her, a hint of devilment in his face. 'Perhaps we should have tried mesmerism,' he said. 'I hear you're becoming quite the adept.'

Sarah ignored the fact he was being deliberately provocative, though she felt a pang of concern regarding his source. Eugenie wouldn't have told him about her visit, surely.

'I would need to develop a greater degree of expertise before attempting to mesmerise for a surgical procedure,' she replied, pretending to take his remarks at face value.

'I'm not sure I would call this surgery. Even you could have done it.' He turned away from her and began to wash his hands.

'Even I? Any more disparaging remarks you want to send my way? Or are you done for the day?'

'You know what I mean about your involvement with mesmerism.'

'I can't say that I do.'

'Look, Sarah, I hold you and your abilities in high regard, you know that. I just think that with mesmerism you're veering into dangerous territory.'

'Because it's something I can do that you can't?'

Raven picked up a towel and began drying his hands.

'This is what I'm talking about. Malham is trying to convince you that you have some special ability when it's all just nonsense. You're being duped and I don't like to see you being made a fool of.'

'I'm not being unquestioningly credulous about this,' Sarah retorted. She was aware that her voice was rising, and she attempted to calm herself. 'I will admit that I don't know how it works but what matters is investigating whether it *does*, and I can see no downside to experimenting. I intend to make a formal study of all the patients treated at the institute. What is the problem with me pursuing this? I'm not doing any harm and there is the possibility of doing considerable good.' She paused, took a breath. 'I suspect it challenges what you believe and perhaps that is the real problem.

I saw how you reacted when Kimble's demonstration upset your assumptions. Perhaps I should be grateful you haven't thumped me.'

Raven bridled at this, the way he always did when she had found her mark. He turned away and began writing his notes.

'Well, it's your time to waste,' he said, as though that was the end of it.

'It's good scientific practice to examine the evidence, is it not?' Sarah asked. 'I'm due to give a demonstration in front of members of the institute, prove to them that a woman can do this as well as a man. You should come. See for yourself.'

'I don't have the time,' he said without turning round. 'We are no closer to identifying the torso from the crypt. I need to find out more about Mrs Butters and the last man she was involved with. Assuming the rumours are true. That's the problem: we have lots of hearsay and few facts.'

'Was Professor Lewis not forthcoming?'

'He was utterly evasive, talking in riddles and poetry. He quoted Byron at me and told me Mr and Mrs Butters were not what they appeared.'

'Byron? Not at length, I hope.'

'Something about a crime that is not really so. He wouldn't be saying that if he had seen the body parts.'

'Is there anyone else who might know something about the Butters' marriage?'

'There was a young woman at the theatre. Worked with both of them. She said she knew more than she cared to about Laurence Butters' true nature but refused to elaborate. She seemed scared of his reprisals, which is understandable, but I also got the impression she was enjoying having a secret. Either way, she wasn't for telling me.'

'Did you annoy her in some way? You seem to have that effect on women.'

Raven ignored her and continued writing.

'How is Eugenie?' Sarah asked.

Raven turned to look at her. 'Why?'

'It's just that the last time I spoke to her she was complaining about headaches. Are they still troubling her?'

He looked at her with some suspicion. 'She hasn't complained of them recently so, no. Why do you ask?'

'Scientific interest.'

Raven frowned, shook his head, and turned back to his notes, saying, 'I don't know what you two are up to and it's probably better I remain ignorant of it.'

Sarah wondered if she should raise the prospect of Raven leaving Queen Street as Eugenie had asked her to do, but now did not seem like the right time.

Sarah lifted the patient's wrist and felt for the pulse. She brushed her finger along the eyelashes, looking for reflex action of the eyelid. There was none. It would be a few minutes yet.

'Perhaps I can help you,' Sarah said.

'Help me with what? Eugenie? I'm not sure anyone is capable of that.'

'No, with the girl at the theatre. Maybe I can get her to speak to me.'

'What are you going to do? Mesmerise her?'

Sarah chose to ignore this remark.

'But I would want something in return,' she said.

Raven swivelled in his chair, turning to face her.

'And what might that be?'

'Come to my demonstration. At the institute. If you remain unconvinced, I won't trouble you with anything mesmerism-related thereafter.'

Raven sighed. 'You think you can get the girl to talk?' he asked.

'I'm sure of it.'

He stuck his hand out for her to shake.

'Deal,' he said.

he front door of the Adelphi was locked, which should not have surprised Sarah but it did nonetheless. Like a church, perhaps, she had expected the doors always to be open. Through the glass, Sarah could see a young woman moving around in the foyer. She knocked on the window and waved. The woman frowned but approached the door and peered through the panel. She unlocked the door and opened it, but only enough to stick her head through.

'If you're looking for Mr Barrington, he's not here,' she said. She sounded impatient, as though women seeking Mr Barrington were numerous and troublesome.

'I'm not looking for Mr Barrington. I came looking for you, Rachel,' Sarah said.

'Do I know you?' The girl seemed suddenly suspicious, and Sarah was worried that she was about to close the door again.

'We have not met but I have some important questions to put to you.'

'Has that man Sanderson sent you?' she replied, her lip curling into a pronounced sneer.

'Sanderson?'

'The Hoolet. Keeps sending folk in various guises trying to get information out of me for his pamphlets.'

So, William Sanderson was responsible for the inflammatory

pamphlets, thought Sarah. That would fit. They were full of exaggeration and gory detail, much like the stories the man had previously been associated with. He had been the editor of the *Edinburgh Courant* in the recent past and had threatened to print stories full of innuendo and salacious rumour about enemies of the paper's then proprietor, Sir Ainsley Douglas. After Sir Ainsley's untimely death, Sanderson found himself surplus to requirements and had evidently found some other means of peddling his wares.

'I can assure you that I have nothing to do with Mr Sanderson.'

'So, who are you then and what do you want?'

'I'm assisting Mr McLevy with his enquiries.'

'Assisting McLevy? A woman? You must think my head buttons up at the back.'

'On the contrary. I think you may have valuable information. There have been developments in the enquiry. More lives may be at risk, and what you know might help prevent further atrocities.'

The young woman bit her lip and then opened the door a little wider.

'Well, you're welcome to ask but I'm not sure what I can tell you.'

She led Sarah through the foyer and into the theatre itself. The plush carpet seemed worn in places, but overall the atmosphere was one of opulence and grandeur, even if that grandeur was a little faded.

Sarah tried to imagine standing on the stage, members of the audience listening intently to what she had to say, rapt attention focused on her. She could see the appeal.

Despite disagreeing with him, Raven's comments about mesmerism still prodded at her. Was her own desire to be of significance affecting her judgement? Was she craving being taken seriously to such an extent that she was losing perspective? She thought not. Until it could be clearly demonstrated that mesmerism was a fraud, she would pursue it.

She thought about the demonstration and now began to ponder

whether her deal with Raven was a mistake. If the patient selected was unsuitable in some way, if things didn't go as planned, he would never let her forget it. He was not always gracious in triumph.

A door at the side of the stage led them through to the dressing rooms and beyond those the manager's office.

Rachel unlocked it using a key from a chain round her neck. The office was much less salubrious than the rest of the theatre: a careworn desk, teetering piles of paper, playbills and a large safe.

Rachel sat down and invited Sarah to do the same. She produced a small flask from a pocket in her skirt, took a swig from it and then replaced it.

'So, what do you want to know?' she said. She sat with her arms folded tight against her chest, as though signalling her reluctance to divulge anything.

Sarah cleared her throat. 'You knew Mrs Butters well?'

'Well enough.'

'Were you aware of her extra-marital affairs?'

'She was less than discreet.'

'Do you know who she was involved with most recently?'

'She didn't tell me his name. Natty dresser, she said. She liked her clothes and her costumes, and she admired many a well-dressed man.'

'Doesn't really narrow it down,' Sarah said.

'What? In this town? I should think that it does. All the men dress as though they've just come from a wake.'

This was largely true, Sarah thought, but less so since Mr Gethyn had opened for business.

'And was Mr Butters aware of his wife's many . . . indiscretions?'

'Yes. And she of his. They didn't have a conventional marriage, if you know what I mean.'

Sarah didn't. 'It was an arrangement?' she suggested. 'That they both were free to have other . . . partners?'

'Something like that.'

'But then why would Mr Butters kill her?'

'Secrets. Lies. Money. Revenge. Take your pick. Working in a playhouse you become familiar with all the reasons people resort to murder.'

'And what about you?'

'Me?'

'Were you ever part of this . . . arrangement?'

'What? With Laurence Butters?'

She started to laugh. Not the response Sarah had been anticipating. Anger perhaps, but not laughter. She was, after all, impugning the girl's virtue.

Rachel evidently sensed no threat to her reputation. She continued to laugh. Sarah could think of nothing humorous about it.

'It's just that my colleague Dr Raven felt that there was something about you and Mr Butters that you were reluctant to speak of,' Sarah said, trying to explain her line of questioning.

'You think that he attempted to outrage my modesty or took liberties?'

She snorted and wiped her eyes. She sat for a minute, then became suddenly quite serious. 'I did witness something, as it happens. Disturbed me quite a bit at the time. I mean you hear about this sort of stuff, don't you? Especially working in the theatre. But hearing about it and seeing the evidence for yourself? Different things, aren't they?'

'I'm not sure what you mean.'

'I saw him with a man. They were pleasuring each other.'

'I see,' Sarah said. She suddenly thought of Raven's garbled quote from Byron. A crime that is not really so.

'I must have seen Laurence Butters wear twenty different costumes,' said Rachel. 'Transforming himself night after night. But his greatest disguise was Lydia. His relationship with her was a sham, a cover. Theirs was not a love match: it was a marriage of convenience.'

'm glad to see you haven't brought another box,' said Raven, as Henry joined him and Sarah in the kitchen, having been escorted down the stairs by Jarvis. It was an indication of the recent regularity of his visits that the butler was no longer announcing Henry or fetching Raven to the hall to greet him. 'I can just about tolerate a decomposing foot in my consulting room, but an entire torso in the kitchen would have Mrs Lyndsay banning us from the place in perpetuity.'

'I bear only curiosity,' Henry replied. 'And among my questions is how Butters transported that torso from his home to Greyfriars. What manner of actorly trickery he might have engaged to avoid suspicion.'

Raven slid a plate of fruit loaf towards him while Sarah poured Henry a mug of tea. He accepted both with the familiar gratitude of someone never sure when his duties would allow for his next bite. It was a trait Raven had come to recognise in the medical profession. They ate like hungry dogs, falling with unseemly haste upon anything offered.

'How would you have gone about it?' Sarah asked. 'Had you decided to bring our recent discovery all the way here from the police office on the High Street?'

Henry thought about it, though perhaps this was merely a pretext for chewing another mouthful of fruit loaf.

'A handcart and a crate,' he said.

'And would you have had any concern about walking through the city with such a thing?'

Raven recognised the tone. She already knew the answer and was merely walking him through it.

'Perhaps if the weather was hot and the smell attracted attention,' said Henry. 'Though I would easily be able to explain my business to any policeman.'

'Yes, but the weather is not warm,' she observed. 'And I cannot imagine the sight of someone wheeling a crate would ever attract much attention. Butters might be renowned for adopting many personae and disguises, but he would also know that sometimes it is possible to hide in plain sight.'

Henry nodded his acknowledgement.

'Your note said you had news,' he said, turning to Raven.

Raven glanced at Sarah, whose visit to the theatre had proven more fruitful than his. The thought unfortunately reminded him of the quid pro quo, which he was not looking forward to. He was unsure how he would cope with watching her demean herself through a display of mesmerism, but nor could he renege on a deal with her.

'I spoke to Professor Lewis, who was strangely evasive, and not merely because of Butters' crimes.'

'Yes,' said Henry. 'You reported that he was given more to allusion than elucidation.' His tone suggested that Raven better have greater reason to summon him here than to tell him something he already knew.

'Sarah has discovered the cypher to the riddles in which he was speaking.'

Henry put down the second slice of fruit loaf that had been on the way to his mouth.

'Mr and Mrs Butters' marriage was for show,' said Sarah. 'Butters' amorous inclinations were not towards women.'

Henry's response mirrored Raven's when he heard the same information: a moment of surprise and then the realisation that this was somehow inevitable; it made sense of everything Lewis had said yet he had not been able to see it.

Upon returning from the theatre, Sarah had found the lines from Byron that Professor Lewis had quoted, working from Raven's garbled recollection: '*And make a crime what is not really so.*'

As she had read them aloud, Raven had recalled Professor Lewis's distinct appearance and guarded manner.

'I can well understand his reticence,' said Henry. 'For perhaps Butters' secret is a secret held also by Lewis. It was courageous enough of him to even leave you this trail of breadcrumbs.'

'The pious regard it as a crime against nature,' said Sarah. 'Though it would seem strange indeed for God to decree that a man following the dictates of that nature with which he was formed should be punished with death.'

'Officially, that is the penalty for sodomy,' said Henry. 'Though in truth it is only likely to reach court in the event of a scandal. Nonetheless, it always carries the potent threat of ruin. And therefore Butters protected himself with a sham of a marriage.'

'My question is what Lydia Butters got out of this arrangement,' said Raven.

'A companionate marriage,' Sarah suggested. 'And licence to indulge herself, it would appear. Mrs Bryant said she saw many male visitors, who could have been there for relations with either one of them.'

'But that is just it,' Raven said. 'If Butters' real desire was for men, he would not be angry with his wife for taking lovers. The motive everyone has been assuming falls to dust. Butters entered into a years-long marriage purely to create a façade. He is a man used to presenting a face to the world when a different truth lies beneath. Onstage or off, such pretence requires enormous self-control. He is both calculating and disciplined. It is therefore difficult to equate such qualities with a man who would murder two people in a crime of passion. We should be looking for a calculating motive for a calculating crime.'

'Blackmail,' suggested Sarah. 'As Henry said a moment ago,

the great threat to such men is discovery: scandal and ruin. Rachel Barrington witnessed him in flagrante delicto at the theatre, backstage. He may have been calculating, but in the heat of lust, anyone can lose their judgement.'

Raven looked to see if Sarah's eyes flitted towards him as she said this, but she remained fixed upon Henry.

'Butters would have had knowledge of other men in this city,' she went on. 'What if one of them threatened to expose his proclivities, and Butters killed him for it?'

'Then why would he also kill his wife?' Henry asked.

Raven had an answer. 'If the blackmailer was his wife's lover. Perhaps money was partly what she got out of the marriage: a home and lifestyle she could not have afforded on her earnings as a seamstress. Butters was coming into money, possibly a great deal of money, and she would have known that. It could be that she and her lover saw the chance to take him for all he had.'

'That would certainly call for a calculating solution,' Sarah acknowledged.

'All of this might be so much clearer if we knew who the second victim was,' said Raven. 'Have you anything to go by? Distinguishing marks? A scar?'

'No,' Henry answered. 'With just the torso, I can only estimate his height to be between five foot five and five foot ten.'

At that moment, Mrs Lyndsay swept into the kitchen, causing a hush to fall upon the room, a silence that felt guiltily conspicuous. Mercifully she stayed only to fetch a stack of dinner plates, then was swiftly gone again.

'I would have thought she was used to morbid topics,' said Henry.

'Medical topics, yes,' said Sarah. 'But the dead are another matter. She is very superstitious, and she interprets any general disrespect towards the dead as a show of disrespect towards her late husband. Spend enough time in this kitchen and you might develop the impression he was the only man ever to die; a tragic fate to befall someone who was apparently a saint when he walked the earth.'

Raven heard the bitterness in Sarah's tone, which derived from the years she was directly under Mrs Lyndsay's rule. Mrs Lyndsay was very strict with the maids, even though the Simpsons shied away from the starchy formality that might be practised in other households. Her tendency was to speak only when spoken to, perhaps a legacy of previous employment. As a result, she often moved through the house unheard, unnoticed, a passive, silent witness to its dramas. Raven imagined she must be a great repository of knowledge, but not one that would be easily unpicked, for she was loyally discreet. That said, he could imagine someone gaining her confidence a lot sooner than they might Jarvis's.

Sarah and the cook could not be less alike. Mrs Lyndsay was someone who believed in the correct order of things, and that included her notions regarding the place of women. Sarah's status in the house had long since changed, but there were times when Mrs Lyndsay affected to have forgotten this. He could therefore understand Sarah's spikiness, but his own impression was of a woman who profoundly missed her late husband and spoke warmly of him to anyone who would listen. In Raven's experience, indulging her to do so was a small price to sit in the warmth of her kitchen and be favoured with bread and cakes or anything else that might be going spare.

With the sound of her footsteps long enough departed, Raven thought it safe to return to the matter at hand.

'Lydia Butters' head was found in the same graveyard. Surely the other head must be somewhere around there too.'

'McLevy has ruled out further such ventures,' Henry told him. 'He does not have the manpower to be opening every mausoleum and mort safe in Greyfriars.'

'I wonder where else he might have attempted to dispose of body parts,' Raven said. 'He was doing it on a piecemeal basis, attempting to find a dissolving agent at Surgeons' Hall before presumably spying a freshly covered grave in Greyfriars, which must have awakened memories of his nefarious youthful pursuits.'

'I suppose we have our medical forebears to blame for the

introduction of mort safes,' said Henry. 'Protecting the dead from the body-snatchers and the anatomists.'

Raven sighed, his thoughts turning to the temptation that had loomed over him since his meeting with Flint.

'Perhaps this is a medical perspective,' he mused, 'but are we doctors the only ones who are not so precious about the fate of human remains?'

Sarah shrugged. 'Like any woman, I know well what it is to be defined by your body,' she said. 'But your corporeal form is not the whole of you, and therefore once you are gone, it is no longer yours. I would have no objection to being anatomised.'

'I have a cousin in the army,' said Henry. 'Returned from India, where he witnessed many different religions and cultures. There are Hindus who dispose of the departed by pushing them into a sacred river, and Zoroastrians who leave bodies on a mountainside to be eaten by vultures.'

'So there is no grave,' Sarah observed, intrigued.

'I can understand that,' Raven said. 'I find the idea of head-stones and other such monuments rather sad.'

'They're supposed to be sad,' Sarah replied.

'What I mean is, why would one wish to come to their grave to remember a person? It is a place where we never knew them, only the sadness of their loss. Surely the true monument to someone is the ways in which they live on: the marks of their contribution, hearing their name years later, spoken with affection and respect.'

'For most people a headstone will be their only monument,' Sarah said. 'If they even have that much.'

'Many mariners request to have their bodies cast overboard,' said Henry. 'No grave but the sea. And I have read that the Norsemen were sometimes cremated on burning boats. Pyres are common in many cultures, in fact.'

'Butters took a foot to Surgeons' Hall to test the efficacy of dissolution,' said Sarah. 'Would he not also have experimented with flame?'

'Possibly,' said Henry. 'But the body is difficult to completely destroy by burning. I have seen the aftermath of fires in this city: powerful blazes that brought down a building and yet the bones of those who perished remained intact. He would not have enjoyed any greater success trying to cremate his victims in his own hearth.'

As Henry spoke, Raven thought of where else Butters had been.

'Dr Cooper was away fishing in Fife on the morning the foot was found in his office,' he said. 'And yet I recall the room being warm.'

Henry understood.

'His furnace had been lit.'

TWENTY-NINE

s Raven trailed Henry once more into the bowels of Surgeons' Hall, he became conscious that he was trying to cushion his own footfalls and wincing slightly at the blithe sound of his companion's as they reverberated about the walls. He knew that it was improbable that they should come and go entirely unseen, but felt that the less conspicuous they could be, the more comfortable he would feel.

The corridor was lined with busts and paintings of the College's great seventeenth- and eighteenth-century alumni. Raven noted that all of them were long dead, and considered that there were a few surgeons he could stand to see so honoured if that were the requirement. There had been little love lost between the surgeons and the emerging discipline of gynaecology, with the likes of Professor Syme manning the barricades to defend against what they saw as an infringement on their territory. Archibald Christie had made it clear that he was not in post to pour oil on those troubled waters, which was why Raven had no desire to antagonise him further by having to explain their business here today.

He saw a bow-legged old fellow ambling towards them with a bucket gripped in both hands, back bent with the effort of its awkward weight. Raven didn't recognise him and with the man's head down was optimistic that this would remain mutual.

'Hello, Patrick,' Henry hailed him cheerily. 'How are you doing?'

The man looked up and put down his bucket with a dull thump. It looked to be full of balled-up papers, but the sound of it indicated something more solid beneath. Upon a closer look, Raven could see a layer of grey between gaps in the paper.

'Dr Littlejohn,' he replied, so loudly that it felt to Raven like it must be audible on Clerk Street. Was the man deaf? 'I'm still keeping myself off the slab, so can't complain.'

'Delighted to hear it,' Henry replied.

'And what of you? Still helping out Dr Struthers?'

'I'm at the police office most days, yes.'

'Well, I suppose it's one way of staying the right side of McLevy,' he said with a wink, then picked up his bucket again and went on his way.

'What was that about?' Raven asked, irritated.

'Just politely passing the time of day,' Henry replied, confused. 'Patrick's been here for ever. What's the problem?'

'The problem is that we need to be discreet. I'd have come in the dead of night if I thought we could get in and out without Corpus knowing.'

Henry's colour paled. He had indeed momentarily forgotten the clandestine nature of their errand, and as he resumed his progress down the corridor, Raven noted that his footsteps were quieter.

Henry knocked Dr Cooper's door and then entered. Dr Cooper had company, an individual who took their arrival as his cue to depart. He was a neatly dressed, squirrelly-looking man, skittish in his manner. He did not acknowledge the visitors but did stare at each of them as he departed, the intensity of his gaze an odd combination of startlement and scrutiny.

'Who was that?' Raven asked as they stepped inside.

'Name's Gethyn,' Cooper said.

'A surgeon?'

'No. Not medical. He's my tailor.'

Raven recalled Cooper saying he had met Butters at Gethyn's house.

Dr Cooper had answered politely but did not look pleased to

see them. For a moment Raven had a glimpse of what it must feel like to be McLevy; the difference being that McLevy clearly relished the fear and discomfort his presence provoked. Raven far preferred the effect Dr Simpson generated, his manner making people feel better even before he had dispensed any words, never mind medicine.

Raven thought about the last time they spoke, how it was Cooper who had mentioned Professor Lewis. He briefly wondered whether Cooper had the same reason to play down any association with Butters, then recalled that Cooper had four children; one of his two sons already a doctor and the other set fair to follow.

'How may I help you today, gentlemen?' Cooper asked.

'We need to have a look in your furnace,' said Henry.

'My furnace? Help yourselves. Happily, I hadn't bothered to light it today as I won't be here long enough to make it worth my while. I have a class to teach and will be going home soon after.'

Raven and Henry approached the thing. It was an iron tower with a pagoda-like top above a horizontally split two-part door, and beneath that a drawer for the ashes.

Henry was just crouching down to pull out the drawer when the office door flew open and a tall, spindly figure stood beneath the lintel.

'Whatever you're doing, you can cease it at once,' Christie boomed. 'You are here without my permission and I consider your presence nothing short of trespass.'

Henry got to his feet, his posture apologetic. 'Dr Christie, sir, we merely wished to conduct a quick search of—'

'I will not countenance any further speculative excursions beneath my roof,' Christie commanded. He strode deeper into the room, bearing down on Raven.

'When last we spoke, Dr Raven, you were at pains to stress how none of your discoveries pointed to any connection between this Laurence Butters and the College.'

'That remains the case,' Raven assured him, 'other than Dr Cooper admitting he was briefly introduced to Mr Butters, and had seen him perform on the stage. However, we have reason to believe that Dr Cooper's furnace may have been used in the disposal of body parts relating to— '

'I ordered you to keep this from my door,' Christie all but spat at Raven. 'But instead you come here seeking to further establish the connection between this revolting business and our venerated institution. I realise I should not have expected better of a mere obstetrician, but as for you, Dr Littlejohn, I am disgusted by your betrayal, and it will not go unanswered. Now be gone, the pair of you.'

Henry looked shrunken in the face of Christie's onslaught, contemplating the consequences not merely of this, but of failing McLevy too. Raven knew it would not be much better for him either. It would be impossible to set up a new practice in this city if no less than the head of the College of Surgeons had decided to blacken his name. In medicine, reputation was everything.

But with that thought, Raven realised that he still had a card to play. He would not have wished to sacrifice it for this, but he understood that it was now or never.

'Dr Christie, I would speak to you alone,' Raven said quietly.

'There is nothing I wish to hear from you,' he replied.

'You will want to hear this.'

Henry looked at him with a mixture of confusion and hope as Raven gestured to Christie to join him in the corridor.

Christie was not a man who had got where he was without considering every opportunity, and he strode out of the office with an expression warning Raven that this had better be worth his while.

'I assume you are aware of John Hunter's great prize,' Raven said. 'The Irish Giant.'

'Of course. Largely a trophy from which very little was learned, as I understand it. What does this have to do with— '

'I know of another,' Raven said.

'Another giant?' Christie asked, his features animated.

'There is a man,' Raven said quietly, 'comparable in stature. He has outlived Byrne, but his end is drawing near.'

Christie looked intrigued. 'An opportunity to learn what Hunter missed, perhaps. But the dissection would need to take place soon after death, before significant deterioration of the tissues. How long would transportation likely take?'

'He is here in Edinburgh.'

'And would this individual agree to donating his body?'

Raven looked away briefly, unable to meet the man's eye as he replied. 'Certain arrangements have already been made,' he said. He could not bring himself to lie outright. 'But payment is expected.'

Part of him hated himself as he spoke, but there was so much at stake. Here was a chance for Gregor's name to go down in history and for important discoveries to be made about his condition, as well as for Raven to assuage Christie's rage by facilitating something likely to be prestigious for the man. And, of course, there was the matter of the fee, which would not only pay for his own practice, but would keep Flint in his debt thereafter.

All of this would come at the cost of breaking his promise, but did that really matter if, as Flint suggested, Gregor went to his death believing it would be honoured?

'I must caution,' Raven said; 'this man knows his worth, and as his friend I would not see him sold cheap. Hunter paid five hundred pounds, and that was seventy years ago. My man has those he wishes to provide for once he is gone. He considers himself worth at least a thousand.'

Christie sucked his teeth, gazing down the corridor at the busts and paintings; perhaps seeing his own there more clearly now.

'A thousand pounds seems excessive, even for a specimen such as this.'

'There are other interested parties,' Raven said. 'But for now, only I have his ear.'

'Then for now you shall also have mine,' Christie said, his expression indicating that their discussion was at an end and Raven ought to be already gone. Raven did not move, however.

'There is another condition. We need to search that furnace.'

Christie tutted and dismissed him with a cursory wave, his thoughts already on greater things. Raven took that as assent.

Henry crouched once more in front of the furnace and carefully opened the two-part door.

'What did you say to him?' he asked, a mixture of relief and incredulity still writ large in his expression.

'That is confidential,' Raven answered. 'But suffice it to say you owe me.'

'I don't doubt it.'

Henry peered inside the furnace then prodded the cavity with a poker. The only thing to emerge from the machine's black maw was a dull clanging.

'It's empty,' Henry reported redundantly.

'Try the drawer beneath,' Raven urged, worrying that having been forced into this deal with the devil, he would have little to show for it in the end.

Henry slid the drawer out with surprising speed and ease. It was clear why.

'Also empty,' Henry declared with a sigh of resignation.

Then they looked at each other.

'Patrick,' they both said.

They rushed from the room and down the corridor, finding the old porter emerging from another office, the bucket still gripped in his hands.

'Is that ashes?' Henry asked.

'Aye.'

'From Dr Cooper's furnace?'

'Among others.'

'And where do you dispose of them?'

'I don't. The dustman does.'

Raven's heart sank. They should have remembered this was the case.

'Course, he's not been for a couple of weeks,' Patrick said. 'Have you lost something?'

Patrick escorted them to the rear of the building, where he showed them the dustbin where the collected ash was stored awaiting collection.

'We'll clean it up after,' Raven assured him.

'After what?'

Raven tipped it on its side, causing a mass of ash to pour out onto the flagstones, beneath a plume of dust. They stood waiting for the air to clear, bits of ash already clinging to their hair and their clothes.

Henry knelt down and ran his hands through what had been spilled, finding nothing but cinders. Raven shook the can, disgorging more ash amid another cloud. There was a short interlude of coughing until the dust settled again. Henry resumed his search and this time his fingers found something solid. He picked it up, blew on it and held it out for Raven to see.

It was grey and thin, looking much like a wooden ember until Henry brushed some more of the ash away.

'That looks like mandible to me,' said Henry.

'What?' asked Patrick, who had been watching proceedings from a safe distance.

'It's a portion of the lower jaw,' said Raven.

'Suggesting that some of the body parts were indeed subject to fire.' Henry held up the fragment, balefully examining the only fruit of their effort thus far.

'McLevy ought to be grateful that we found this much,' Raven suggested.

'Ought to be, yes,' Henry agreed. 'But he won't. Not least because this doesn't move us any further forward in identifying the second body. I can't imagine some obliging neighbour recognising him from this, can you?'

'At least it's something,' Raven said, 'and there might be more.'

'I imagine so,' Henry agreed, looking far from pleased.

'Isn't that a good thing?' Raven asked.

'Not if you're the one who now needs to take the whole lot back to the police office to sift through it properly.'

THIRTY

The young woman's face was puffy, her hands and feet also markedly swollen.

'When was she admitted?' Raven asked.

Matron stood beside him at the edge of the bed, having directed him to the patients she wished him to prioritise at the beginning of his Minto House ward round.

'This morning.'

'Have the true pains commenced?' he asked.

'Only within the last hour or so.'

'Protein in the urine?'

'Lots of protein, not much urine.'

'Bloodletting, antiphlogistics and diuretics,' Raven ordered. 'The Simpson recipe against the supervention of convulsions.'

Matron handed him the ward book for him to write his instructions in.

The next patient was one he had delivered himself the previous afternoon. There had been considerable haemorrhage immediately after the placenta was extracted, requiring a large dose of ergot and manual compression of the uterus. Raven flexed the fingers of his right hand at the memory of it. It had been quite the struggle to get things under control.

'And how are we today?' he asked the woman while looking at the chart clipped to the bottom of the bed.

'Tired. Thirsty.'

'Are you keeping to your bed as instructed? It is important to refrain from all movement.'

The patient scoffed. 'I hardly have the energy to sit myself up.'

'She was a bit restless last night,' Matron said, 'but a dose of laudanum settled that.'

'Any further bleeding?' Raven asked.

'Only what would normally be expected.'

Raven allowed himself a smile at Matron's matter-of-fact response. It was like an unspoken conspiracy to conceal from the patient just how close she had come to death.

His ward round was followed by a breech delivery. Progress was slow and the after-coming head required a bit of manipulation, but once delivered, both mother and baby were doing well.

After that, he made his way to Matron's office, glancing at the clock as he sat down to write in the ward register. It was almost six. He had arrived at the Maternity Hospital several hours before, hoping for a brief ward round followed by a swift retreat. He should have known better, but as long as he got his notes down without delay or distraction, he would be on time for Sarah's demonstration at the Mesmeric Association.

Not that he had any true desire to be there, but it was reciprocity for her mission to the theatre. Were it not for that, he would have found a reason, any reason, not to go. If Sarah wanted to spend her time waving her hands in front of people's faces, that was up to her, but Raven wanted no part of it. And now he was going to be dragged into bearing witness to this flummery. And suppose she did manage to put some poor dupe into a trance, what was Raven supposed to say to that? Did she really imagine that he would change his mind on the strength of that alone?

He could not disappoint her, though, and not just because he had given his word. For all that he thought it was humbug, he also knew that it meant a lot to her, and more so that she would be under pressure, required to conduct this demonstration in front of a number of people. A friendly face would be all the more appreciated, and much as he disapproved of mesmerism, he wanted to show her solidarity.

Raven had barely picked up his pen when Matron wrenched open the door without knocking.

'She's fitting,' Matron said.

Raven didn't need to ask who she was referring to. The swollen woman.

By the time he reached the ward, the convulsions had ceased but the woman did not rouse.

Raven drew off some blood in the hope of relieving and reviving the patient, but the convulsions returned, were prolonged and left the patient in deep coma.

Raven listened in for the foetal heartbeat and found it to be present. The patient's extremities were cold, the pulse rapid and weak.

'How far advanced is the labour?' he asked.

'She still had some way to go.'

Raven conducted an examination. Unfortunately, the matron was correct. The cervix had only opened to the diameter of about a shilling.

'What are you going to do?' Matron asked.

'What else can I do? I'm going to try and extract the child before it succumbs too.'

THIRTY-ONE

Dr Malham sat behind his desk and dismissed Sarah's concerns with a wave of his hand.

'I have already selected a suitable candidate,' Malham said with that smile he tended to deploy when expressing an opinion others were likely to disagree with.

They were in the little office upstairs from the main association meeting room where the mesmeric demonstration was due to take place.

Sarah turned to Mrs Crowe, who was standing beside her looking as confused as Sarah felt.

'But Mrs Crowe has kindly volunteered to be my subject,' Sarah said. 'We have discussed this already and I thought that you had agreed.'

'Yes,' Malham said. 'But she is a woman.'

'I am aware of that,' Sarah replied.

Malham sat back and steepled his fingers in front of his mouth as though contemplating further.

'I have given this matter careful consideration,' he said, 'and I believe that your demonstration will be all the more impressive to the association should you succeed in mesmerising a member of the opposite sex.'

Should she succeed? It appeared that even Malham had his doubts about the outcome of her efforts. Then she remembered her sham of an attempt with Somerville. Malham was letting her know he had not been fooled.

Sarah opened her mouth to protest but Malham raised a hand to forestall her.

'Trust me, Miss Fisher. All will be well.'

He took out his watch. 'It's nearly time. Mrs Crowe, might I suggest you take a seat below? We are about to begin.'

Mrs Crowe looked at Sarah, giving her arm a comforting squeeze. 'I'm sure you'll do wonderfully well, my dear,' she said, before disappearing through the door.

Sarah felt the knot in her stomach tighten. With Mrs Crowe as her subject, she had been confident of success, but now the spectre of failure loomed large on the horizon.

'So, who is the subject?' she asked. 'Is it someone I know?'

'All will be revealed,' Malham said, rising from his chair. He seemed to be enjoying her discomfort, as though this were all some kind of game to him.

He checked his watch again.

'Shall we?' he said and held the door open for her.

He ushered her downstairs to the meeting room, where a number of chairs had been laid out in a semicircle. Mrs Crowe was the only woman there. The rest were the medical men of the association, a hostile energy emanating from them like a fire with a blocked flue. All had severe expressions, as though they had already concluded that this was a waste of their time.

Raven was not among them.

aven looked at his watch as he finally emerged from Minto House, calculating how long it would take him to get to Potter Row. Sarah's demonstration would already have started, but it was his understanding that it took a long time to induce a trance. That, in fact, was one of the obstacles to mesmerism being any use amidst the demands of modern medical practice, so if he made it there in time to witness the trance itself, and any effects that were supposedly manifest, then that might be enough. As long as he showed his face.

Darkness was falling as he hurried down the broad stairs into the driveway. The house had once belonged to the Elliots of Minto, or so he had been told. He didn't know who they were or had been, far less why they had abandoned their town residence and permitted it to be used as a surgical hospital, a dispensary and now a maternity hospital. The grand driveway had no doubt played host to carriages conveying the gentry to supper parties and dinners. The house's current inhabitants usually turned up on foot, whether in labour or not.

As he hastened his stride, the motion caused him to feel the weight of the watch in his pocket. Sometimes there was another weight to it beyond the physical. It was the only thing that remained of his father: the man's sole bequest, albeit an involuntary one, for he had made no will or indeed any plans regarding his death. It

had come a good deal sooner than Andrew Cunningham anticipated; and such a waste, as he hadn't drunk quite every bottle in
the house before he met his end.

Raven did sometimes wonder why he held on to the timepiece
given his hatred of the man, even having gone to some lengths to
protect or retrieve it. He kept it as a symbol, really: of where he
had come from and where he wanted to go. Of the man he was
determined to become, and of the man he was determined *not* to be.

As he approached Argyle Square, he became aware of a drunk
meandering along the pavement thirty or forty yards ahead. The
burden of the watch made him think of Kimble and how he had
said Raven was surrounded by ghosts.

You denied him everything. Even his name.

It still troubled him how Kimble had known the things he did,
as though he had either seen inside Raven's mind, or truly seen
the presence of his father.

*No matter where you go, he is always there. You are bound together
by anger.*

Raven did not want to believe either of those things were
possible, and yet there was no doubt that the man's words had
rung true.

Raven checked his stride as he neared the drunk, the man's
unsteady motion emphasised by the swaying of his long coat. Then
Raven almost tripped over his own feet as he realised that the
meandering figure was none other than Kimble himself. He was
momentarily startled. First Flint, now Kimble. He seemed to have
developed a means of conjuring people from the ether just by
thinking about them. Kimble would no doubt have offered a supernatural explanation for this, but Raven favoured a rational one.
Perhaps some deeper part of his mind had recognised Kimble at a
distance, and it had been that which prompted his previous
thoughts.

It was the coat, he realised. Raven remembered it from his visit
to Queen Street. That must have been what he had recognised.

The man was long in his cups, in a sufficiently advanced state of refreshment as to be oblivious of Raven's presence as they passed on the pavement. He was rolling home from some tavern.

It occurred to Raven that this might be an opportunity to demand answers as to how Kimble knew certain things, but he could not afford to stop. He could not disappoint Sarah, and besides, even drunk the man might not spill his secrets.

He cast a glance back, watching Kimble disappear into Scott's Entry, a narrow alley leading towards the Cowgate. He was soon out of sight, and Raven knew it was wisest to put him out of mind, stop worrying about what Kimble said and how he had divined it.

Dr Simpson's words came back to him then: *Sometimes we just don't know.*

He knew he needed to let it go. Just as he ought to let go this animosity towards mesmerism. As Sarah said, what was the harm? His argument had been that time was wasted pursuing something that was nonsense, but how much research was about eliminating possibilities until we had whittled down to what must be true? Perhaps the same would hold of mesmerism: if there *were* causes and effects, and they could be separated from the bizarre and outlandish claims of the likes of John Elliotson and indeed Mesmer himself, then what remained might be of value. And if anyone could discern that, it would be Sarah.

Raven noticed two figures approaching from the other direction, less of a collision hazard due to the brisk purpose in their gait. He wondered if they were late for something too.

Then they turned down Scott's Entry.

It was not his problem, he told himself. For all he knew, Kimble lived in one of the buildings in the close and was already climbing his stairs out of sight. And the time to show his face at Sarah's demonstration was ticking rapidly away.

But Raven had instinctively recognised what he was looking at, just as they had instinctively recognised what they saw: a man in a fine coat, insensible with drink, staggering into the growing darkness of an alley.

Raven wore a scar on his face that was a permanent reminder of what could happen in such places. What wouldn't he have given to have someone come to his aid that brutal night.

'Dammit,' he said.

He turned on the ball of his foot and struck out, back towards the alley.

THIRTY-THREE

alham stood in front of his colleagues and called the meeting to order. Sarah recognised the showman's instinct in waiting for the ensuing silence to be not only complete, but on the cusp of uncomfortable before filling it. That way, not only did he have their absolute attention, but also their gratitude.

'Gentlemen of the Edinburgh Mesmeric Association,' he began, his American accent setting him apart as much as his dress, 'I thank you for attending this evening, where we shall put certain matters to an objective test. We are here tonight to interrogate the thesis that not only can mesmerism be taught to those outside the medical profession, but that the skills required can also be taught to women.'

There was a cough from someone in the audience, a deliberately audible throat-clearing. Sarah wondered whether it was intended as a subtle declaration of scorn.

'There have been doubts cast regarding the feasibility and the wisdom of teaching these skills to laypersons, and doubts have also been raised about whether such abilities can be taught to the fairer sex. Can a woman, with her weaker constitution, with her relative lack of neurovital power, be effectively instructed in the art of mesmerism?'

Sarah stood beside him and tried not to entertain any notions of failure or disappointment. She could sense the collective scrutiny of the audience and felt the colour rise in her cheeks. That weasely creature Gethyn was in the front row, staring at her with his beady eyes. He was Dr Malham's tailor but of late seemed to have nominated himself the man's high priest. As such he was developing an envious animosity towards Sarah for the interest Malham showed in her, Gethyn clearly regarding her as some sort of rival.

She became aware of the door opening at the back of the room and looked up, hope rising, but it was not Raven who entered. Mr Somerville was holding the door open for a middle-aged man who was walking with crutches. His left leg seemed shorter than the right, his knee slightly bent and the foot everted at an awkward angle.

His progress to the front of the room was slow, his crutches loud on the wooden floor. The man was evidently in some pain and his face contorted in a grimace as he sat with some difficulty in the chair provided for him.

He laid his crutches down then extended his injured leg in front of himself, rubbing at the muscle on the front of his thigh.

Mr Somerville took a seat at the back of the room beside Mrs Crowe. Sarah was glad of another confederate amongst this small gathering of hostile men, but it was Raven she really wanted to see.

'Good afternoon, Mr Jameson,' Malham said, addressing the man with the crutches. 'Thank you for agreeing to join us and to permit us to make our little experiment.'

Something inside Sarah felt hollow as she made the deduction. Malham then turned to his audience.

'This gentleman fell from a horse five months ago and sustained an injury to his left hip and thigh. He was two weeks confined to bed and was then able to move around with crutches. However, his symptoms did not resolve further, and he has been left with a degree of lameness and considerable pain.'

Sarah watched Mr Jameson's progress to the front of the room with a growing sense of alarm. This did not seem like a simple case of inducing mesmeric sleep. Would she be expected to cure him? And here, now, in one session? Would anything less than that be deemed a failure?

She wondered why Malham had selected this patient without any prior discussion, without giving her any warning – and without, she realised, stipulating to the audience what success in this experiment would look like. Would a reported reduction in pain and discomfort suffice, or would the patient have to dance a jig before they were satisfied?

Why would Malham take such a risk? she wondered.

Then she realised that he was taking no risks precisely *because* he had not defined terms in advance. He would not want her to fail, she reassured herself, because should she succeed he could claim his tutelage to be at the heart of it. That would seal his ambition to open the association's doors to many new pupils he might train, including women.

Malham took a step backwards, an indication that Sarah should begin. She thought he would retreat to the sidelines, but instead he remained at the centre, which made her feel all the more scrutinised. That was when it dawned on her that Malham might indeed have reason to see her fail in front of the assembled association. It would emphasise the extent of his own unique gifts, demonstrating that his talent could not easily be replicated by others. His place at the head of the association would be assured.

Sarah looked at the expectant faces surrounding her, predominantly grim and even more predominantly male. She took in Mr Jameson's crutches and their implications, upon which the room seemed to close in around her.

She had the smothering sensation that she had walked into a trap.

THIRTY-FOUR

pproaching Scott's Entry, Raven saw that Kimble had most definitely not reached the sanctuary of his own home. As he entered the alley, he watched the larger of the men strike Kimble on the back of the head with a short cudgel, acting before Raven had the chance to call out a warning. Kimble fell forward with a drunk's reflex, somehow managing to cushion his fall and roll onto his back. His arms came up to protect himself as his assailant swooped down, intent on raining further blows to beat away his resistance and render him unconscious.

'Haw!' Raven shouted. 'Get away from my father!'

He was not quite sure where this last had come from. He had a notion that if he pretended such a connection, the two assailants would assume a greater determination and purpose on his part than from a mere passer-by. He hoped that would be enough to make them run.

Kimble looked up groggily, as if trying to make sense of the new arrival.

The man with the cudgel rose to his feet and began striding towards Raven. He muttered something to his accomplice as he passed, and the other one put his foot on Kimble's chest to prevent him escaping amidst the distraction.

Raven was aware of the weight of his knife inside his coat. It would be a gamble. If he drew it, the man might run off, but if not, who knew how it might go? The thought took him back to another alley, five years ago in Berlin. A life and death moment: his life, someone else's death.

I have seldom seen a man with so many ghosts about him. You are surrounded by the dead.

Raven had long ago vowed not to add to their number.

The approaching ne'er-do-well was taller than Raven, and even in the fading light he could see that the man's skin was pockmarked and scarred, his nose flat and misshapen. Raven recognised the visage of a man who had been in a great many fights. He would be used to pain and injury, thoroughly acquainted with the sensation of being punched in the face. But Raven had been in a great many too, and was willing to bet his face was prettier because he had won more of them.

He raised his fists in a defensive boxing stance, drawing his opponent's eye as the man prepared to swipe with his cudgel. Raven's purpose, however, was not defence but distraction. With the man's eyes on Raven's fists, he dropped and drove a straight leg into his knee. The contact produced a crack that reverberated off the alley's walls. Then, as Raven planted his foot again, he sent his outstretched fingers – the full force of his arm and shoulder behind them – into the man's windpipe.

The man dropped to the ground, the cudgel clattering alongside him.

This second blow had the intended effect of eliminating both opponents, because having seen his larger companion taken down rapidly and painfully, the smaller one stepped off Kimble, turned and fled.

Raven put out a hand to Kimble, who reached up to him from the cobblestones beneath. His eyes still looked glassily unfocused. More than that: tearful.

'Michael,' he said.

'We need to get you home. Where do you live?'

'Michael,' Kimble repeated, sobbing. 'It's so good to see you.'

'I said, where do you live?'

Kimble took a moment to think about it, as if dredging the answer up from the darkest depths of his memory.

'Merchant Street,' he said.

Raven recognised the address. A left turn at the end of the alley and then another hundred yards. It was no distance, but the man was bleeding from a head wound. Raven had to make sure he got home safely and knew he ought to tend to the wound too.

He would have to break his promise to Sarah. It wrenched at him, but it was the right thing to do.

THIRTY-FIVE

arah tried to focus on Mr Jameson but simply could not. She realised she was beginning to panic, forgetting to breathe.

'I need a moment,' she said. 'Some air.'

She began walking towards the door, which prompted grumbles around the room: the sounds of assumptions being vindicated. Glancing at their faces, she felt relief that Raven was not among them. It struck her that the reason he had not come might be that he did not wish to witness her humiliation.

Mr Somerville rose to his feet and opened the door for her. Sarah thought about passing right through it and running away.

Somerville leaned towards her and spoke under his breath. 'This whole city is full of bastards who want to see you fail,' he said, a coarseness to his voice lending it conviction. 'But the only thing they'd like more is if you didn't even try.'

She met his eye and felt something powerful in the sincerity of his expression, as though energised by it. As she turned and walked back towards Mr Jameson, she understood what it was. It was someone else's belief in her.

She took a couple of deep breaths and asked the patient to do the same. She asked him to relax his shoulders and make himself as comfortable as possible. Malham looked at her and raised an eyebrow. This was a slight deviation from the usual script but as he had made some changes himself without any prior consultation, she felt no qualms about making a few adjustments of her own. In truth she was buying time to calm herself and to settle her own mind.

Fortunately, the patient had not heard Malham's statements about her inherent female inadequacies. She smiled at him, and the smile was returned. She explained what she was going to do and was faintly aware of Malham's expression at what she had omitted. All this business of making passes with her hands felt redundant, something for the benefit of observers rather than the subject. She had been reading James Braid's accounts of the process he was calling 'hypnosis', which made no reference to it. Her instincts told her that it was all about the eyes and the concentrated still-ness. Waving one's hand around was surely a distraction to both.

She held the man's gaze, matching her breathing to his. After several minutes nothing had changed, and Sarah could feel a rising anxiety in her chest. She tried to ignore it, to focus again on the task at hand, and not to think about the medical gentlemen seated around her, watching for any mistake, ready to criticise, to scoff at her efforts, to dismiss her and her entire sex.

She focused on Mr Jameson's face, forced herself to notice small details: a slight scar on the top lip, a patch of stubble that his razor had missed, the flesh just beginning to sag around his jawline.

He blinked a couple of times and then, to her great relief, his eyes began to close.

She looked at his twisted leg and before she could consider the wisdom of it, she lifted the limb and gently straightened it out, moving the foot into a more natural position. She felt no resistance, no tension in the muscles. She held the leg like that for several minutes, aware of a few murmurs from the small audience.

She gently placed the leg down again and then asked Mr Jameson to open his eyes. This he did slowly, then looked around as though expecting to find himself transported somewhere else.

'Is that it?' he asked, disappointment all too evident in his tone.

'Yes,' she said. 'Sometimes several sessions are required before any change can be detected.'

She looked to Malham. He said nothing, his expression inscrutable. She wondered again what he wanted to happen. Success or failure? She couldn't be sure. And if it was failure, she had handed him the perfect explanation, for she had deviated from his instruction.

Sarah bent down and picked up Mr Jameson's crutches. She handed them to him and helped him get to his feet. She thought that his leg looked a little straighter, his foot less splayed.

He took one tentative step and then another. He looked at her with a curious expression, as though something was amiss.

'It seems less painful,' he said, in a tone of pleasant surprise. He handed her back his crutches and took a few steps without them. There were gasps from the floor.

He turned to face the audience.

'A definite improvement,' he told them.

He turned to Sarah and gave her a small bow.

Sarah felt a huge sense of relief. Someone in the audience began to applaud. There was a slight delay before others joined in.

'Bravo!' someone shouted. She was fairly sure it was Somerville. The applause grew louder.

Sarah looked at Malham. He was smiling for the room, but he did not look happy.

THIRTY-SIX

aven sweated as he helped Kimble up the steep and narrow stairwell. It would have been a hard enough climb on his own, but was far more of a challenge while supporting a swaying individual who seemed in permanent danger of tumbling all the way back down. And of course, his rooms had to be on the fifth floor of the tenement.

'It's always the top,' he mumbled to himself, something Dr Simpson would say on home visits, usually with an indomitable cheeriness that Raven did not share.

The building was a better one than many around these parts. It was not quite so well appointed as Butters' residence, but a far cry from the kind of slum he was all too familiar with. Nonetheless, the dwelling was small, just a room and kitchen with a small bed set in an alcove.

Raven helped the man to a seat at his small, square kitchen table and turned on the gaslight so that he could see to dress the wound.

The cut had bled messily, as scalp wounds tended to, but it was nothing serious. Raven estimated that Kimble's disorientation derived far more from alcohol than from the blow to the back of his head. Going by the look and smell of him, he had been drinking all day; perhaps for several days.

Raven put some water into a bowl and used some rags to clean away the blood. As he dabbed carefully at Kimble's hair, he noticed that there was a slight swelling around his jaw. The sight of it caused something in Raven to burn with shame.

A quick search in a cupboard revealed that, fortunately, the man kept a small medicine box, including a bandage. As Raven dressed the laceration, he looked at the walls, which, as in Butters' home, were adorned with theatre playbills. They all advertised an act named 'The Mysterious Lembik', showing a figure in a cloak, arms outstretched, power emanating from his fingers. Beneath each was the name of a theatre in a different city: Glasgow, Newcastle, Manchester, Carlisle, Liverpool. Three of them included an image of a woman floating in the air, held there only by whatever spell the magician was casting. 'Newton defied!', the copy claimed, boasting of an astonishing levitation, among other wonders that would dazzle the audience.

Lembik sounded an exotic name, Eastern European perhaps. Raven remembered that Kimble had trouble recalling his address. He wondered whether the man was renting these rooms from the magician, or being allowed to stay here while Lembik performed elsewhere. Perhaps that was what theatre folk did as they moved from city to city, though if that were so, it seemed odd that Lembik's home should be so modest. The posters all cited prestigious theatres, indicative of his name being a draw.

Then it struck him: Lembik – Kimble. It was a mere anagram.

He had once been a magician, an esteemed illusionist. Now he was a drunk pretending to speak to the dead.

'Michael,' Kimble said, 'where have you been? I haven't seen you in so long.'

Raven was about to tell him he was not Michael, but Kimble was fading from consciousness, falling asleep in front of him.

Raven helped him to the alcove bed, where he laid him down, fully clothed, though he did manage to slip the man's shoes off to avoid muddying the sheets.

There was a small sideboard close to the alcove, upon which sat three framed pictures. One was a line drawing, showing a young man of around Raven's age, or maybe a couple of years younger. From the resemblance, he assumed it to be a younger Kimble until he looked closer at the one next to it, depicting a young boy, maybe around ten. It was unquestionably the same individual, painted in colour by an affectionate eye.

This, he guessed, was Michael.

The third picture was of a woman.

Raven looked again at the posters. That was when he recognised that they showed the same woman being levitated. Kimble's wife, he assumed, the boy's mother.

Raven tried to tug the sheet from beneath Kimble, intending to cover him against what cold the night would bring. He was too heavy, so Raven fetched Kimble's coat and laid that upon him instead.

As he did so, Kimble rolled over and his eyes opened.

'Michael,' he said again.

'I'm not Michael,' Raven replied softly.

'I know,' Kimble said, his voice faltering, regretful.

THIRTY-SEVEN

here was a thrill still running through Sarah, even half an hour after the demonstration had ended. It was as though the fear she felt had been transmuted into something else, a powerful emotion repurposed to drive her through what she had to do, and there remained an excess of it.

Sarah wanted to talk to Mr Jameson some more but soon found she could not get near the man. The medical men had gathered around him, asking questions and prodding at the injured but now improved leg. Mr Jameson didn't seem to mind, happy to demonstrate his ability to walk short distances without the aid of his crutches.

'My legs felt heavy before,' he had told her. 'I felt like I was carrying them instead of them carrying me. Now it doesn't feel that way.'

Sarah had many questions she wished to ask but had not got the chance before he was surrounded. She was unclear as to what exactly had effected the improvement.

The attention was all on Malham now, though. The members of the association were congratulating him, as though she had been merely his instrument.

'I surprised Miss Fisher with an unexpected subject in Mr Jameson,' he said. 'But only because I was confident in my assessment of what I had taught her. I wished to test her, but it was a test I was sure she would pass.'

'To have procured such capabilities in a woman,' said a voice ringing with wonder. 'This will surely bring patients and pupils flooding through the doors.'

The speaker was the oleaginous Mr Gethyn. Sarah was instinctively wary of the Welsh tailor, whose conduct towards Malham was beginning to remind her of a stray dog in search of a new master.

'We should inform the newspapers,' Gethyn suggested. 'Worthy of a few lines in the *Scotsman* and the *Courant*, surely.'

Malham looked uncomfortable at the notion.

'I am not convinced we should place Miss Fisher under that kind of public scrutiny,' he said. 'Besides, we do not wish people taking undue note of her sex and thus regarding her practice as some kind of novelty.'

'I take your point,' Gethyn agreed. 'I am reminded of Samuel Johnson's remark about the sight of a woman preaching being like a dog walking on its hind legs. It is not done well, but you are surprised to find it done at all.'

Gethyn turned to Sarah, as though belatedly remembering she was there.

'I mean that as a compliment,' he said, 'in that in your case, it *was* done well.'

Sarah decided she had had enough. She still felt exhilarated, as though she had a surfeit of energy that she did not know what to do with. She wanted to jump up and down, quite possibly on Mr Gethyn's head. Instead, she decided she would settle for some fresh air.

She stepped out of the room and into the entrance hall, where she found Mr Somerville standing alone, someone else who had decided he was surplus to requirements.

He doffed his hat grandly, which made her smile.

'It seems an inadequate gesture,' he said. 'For she who made the lame to walk.'

'I cannot rightly say what I did or quite how I did it,' she replied.

'But Mr Jameson is improved. That is what matters.'

'It would matter more if I understood how. I suspect the answer lies in the relationship between the mental and the corporeal.'

'Then it is much the same as when you felt weak and unsure of yourself shortly before your great feat.'

'Perhaps. I owe you my thanks for that, Mr Somerville. I drew strength from your words.'

'The strength was entirely yours, Miss Fisher. I merely reminded you it was there.'

'But what you said . . . It was precisely what I needed to hear in that moment. How did you know?'

'I recognised a kindred spirit. You draw strength from the desire to prove that people are wrong to underestimate you.'

Mr Somerville looked towards the open door. Darkness had fallen, though the sky was clear.

'Let me accompany you,' he said. 'Make sure you and your bag have no further misadventures. Where are you bound for?'

Sarah was grateful for the offer. She had not been looking forward to the journey.

'Queen Street.'

'I will summon a cab.'

'Oh, that is not necessary.'

Sarah said this but could not truly say why.

'You would rather walk?'

'The air is mild tonight,' she offered by way of explanation. In truth, she was feeling something that she did not want to end, which it surely would as soon as she was home. The sense of everything that had happened tonight was still running through her. But also, she would have to admit, she was enjoying the presence of Mr Somerville, and did not want that to be over too soon either.

It was a pleasure to be walking through this part of the city after dark without fear or its attendant haste, able to take in the sense of it at leisure. It was like a walk along Princes Street in the daytime. Like any woman, Sarah had to be permanently conscious of how dangerous the Old Town could be, especially at this time of night. Mr Somerville did not seem to have any such cares, and not merely because he was a man. Other men were as wary as she on these streets. She wondered about the past he had alluded to, which was when it occurred to her that perhaps he was not fearful because he had once been the thing everyone else was afraid of.

Being in his company, she felt the sense of something both powerful and dangerous that ran deep beneath the surface. A complicated man. She knew that it had transformed her to hear his words, his demonstration of belief in her.

She thought of another dangerous and complicated man. He had not come. And now she thought she knew why.

This whole city is full of bastards who want to see you fail.

That had not been Raven's wish; it was actually something worse. He had stayed away because he could not face seeing her succeed.

THIRTY-EIGHT

aven was putting on his coat when Sarah accosted him in the hallway.

'You didn't come last night,' she said.

Her face wore a steely look he knew only too well. The truth was that he had gone to the association offices after he had finished with Kimble, but by that time it was too late. There were only a few men milling about outside, and there had been no sign of Sarah.

Raven had approached one of the men, asking if the demonstration was over. The man he had spoken to was notably dandified in his dress and spoke in an American accent. Raven deduced this to be Dr Malham, wondering if all his countrymen were so flamboyant in their appearance, or merely the ones hungry for public notice. He was told that he had indeed missed the demonstration but if he was interested in the mesmeric cure, an appointment could be made. Raven had politely declined.

'I heard it was a great success,' he told Sarah, hoping that a conciliatory tone might help.

'Was that why you didn't attend?' she replied. 'Perhaps you didn't want to witness something that would force you to reappraise your stance on mesmerism.'

'Of course not. If you must know I made strenuous efforts to be there but was delayed.'

'By a case at the Maternity Hospital?'

'That and something else. The fates were conspiring against me.'

She stared at him as though waiting for a more coherent explanation. Fortunately he had one: the act of a good Samaritan.

'It was Kimble,' he told her. 'I encountered him drunk and witnessed him being assaulted in the street. I intervened and made sure he got home safely.'

Sarah stood with her arms folded, her growing anger evident. This was not the response he was expecting.

'Kimble? The man *you* assaulted on the front step of this very house? His well-being took precedence over your commitment to me? Or was it your need for absolution?' She looked to be on the verge of tears. 'Either way, we had a deal,' she said. 'You said you would come.'

'I couldn't just leave him. He had taken a blow to the head.'

'Right. Of course not. Although I wonder, if it hadn't been him, would you have found something else to delay you?'

'That's unfair.'

'Fair is making good on your promises.'

She turned away from him then, giving him no opportunity to further defend himself.

He wanted to pursue her and demand whether she would have preferred he leave a vulnerable man to the predations of violent criminals, but knew that it would do no good. When Sarah was feeling self-righteous, there was no reasoning with her. He had failed to meet his end of a bargain: that part was inarguable, and she would use it to trump all other considerations, because Sarah was never in the wrong.

No good deed ever goes unpunished, he told himself. He grabbed his hat and headed for the door.

The walk to the High Street helped clear his head but he was still feeling aggrieved by the time he entered the surgeon's room at the police office. Henry was already there, the torso from the crypt on the table before him.

Henry looked up as Raven entered. He was wearing a long leather apron and was wielding the tools of his trade: a scalpel and a pair of dissecting forceps.

'This is the strangest post-mortem examination that I've ever undertaken,' Henry said.

Raven walked round the table examining the evidence from all sides.

'What do you reckon the poor chap did to deserve this?' he asked. 'Was it a crime of passion? One of necessity to preserve a secret? Or was it a premeditated murder with a mercenary motive?'

Henry looked up from what he was doing.

'At this juncture, your guess is as good as mine.'

'Also, does it count as desecration of a grave if you're adding rather than taking away?'

Henry rolled his eyes.

'Have you found anything that might help identify him?' Raven asked.

'No. I don't know who this is or why he died. But I think I might know how.'

'Not decapitation then?'

Henry ignored this and gestured for Raven to come closer. He was pointing at something on the torso. It was an opening, slightly ragged, about an inch and a half in length, under the left nipple, between the sixth and seventh ribs.

'It extends into the chest, so I presume that is how this poor soul met his end. Although I'm just getting started. Might know more once I open him up a bit.'

Raven took a look and then drew back.

'Whoever he was, he's really starting to stink.'

'Undeniably,' Henry agreed.

'I don't know how you stand it, Henry,' Raven said, removing his handkerchief from his pocket and using it to cover his nose and mouth. 'I'd take a difficult delivery over this any day of the week.'

'Like most things, you get used to it. Although I'm told the smell hangs around a bit on one's clothes. Problem is, if you're the one wearing them, you cease to notice.'

Raven retreated to the corner of the room and, judging himself to be at a safe distance, put his handkerchief back in his pocket.

'Do you think that is one of the reasons why you remain unmarried?'

In all the time Raven had known him, Henry had shown an uncanny ability to avoid romantic entanglements. He displayed an almost monk-like devotion to his work and his studies.

Henry looked as though he was giving this some thought.

'The smell of decaying corpses is not known for its aphrodisiac properties,' he said. 'And I think I would struggle to find a woman who might share my interest in dead bodies.'

'Not to mention sewers,' Raven added. 'Don't forget your fascination with drains.'

'Quite the catch, aren't I?'

Henry bent over the torso again, sticking his forceps into the chest wound to determine how deep it was.

'In truth, any woman would be lucky to have you,' Raven insisted. 'And many women have scientific interests. Look at Sarah.'

Henry gave Raven a knowing look. 'I think Miss Fisher's romantic inclinations lie elsewhere.'

'What do you mean?'

'I hear she's seeing someone. Don't know the name, but he's involved with the mesmerists, apparently. A smartly dressed individual, according to someone who saw them together.'

'Malham?'

'As I said, I don't know the name.'

'Well, this just gets worse and worse.'

Henry straightened up and put his instruments down. 'Why? What is it to you?'

'I'd just rather she didn't associate with cranks and quacks.'

'It's not really up to you who she associates with, though, is it?'

Raven was somewhat taken aback by Henry's insistence on this point. 'No,' he said, trying to defend his position, 'but I don't wish to see her humiliated or hurt.'

Henry gave him that knowing look again. 'I think that Sarah is quite capable of taking care of herself.'

'Have you anything more to show me or can I leave now?' Raven asked.

'As I said, there might be more to report once I've completed my examination, but in the meantime, there is this.'

Henry made his way to the other side of the room. Raven followed, giving the torso as wide a berth as possible.

'This is what I managed to recover from the ashes,' Henry said, indicating several fragments of bone laid out on a tray. 'A few bits of the cranium, a portion of the lower jaw that we saw before, fragments of several cervical vertebrae, a shirt button, and this.'

Henry held up a block of mineral teeth. He looked rather pleased with himself. Raven didn't see how this discovery would help.

'I suppose it tells us he was not in the first flush of youth, so that would rule out any younger lovers Mrs Butters might have taken.'

'Look closer,' Henry urged, holding up the false teeth so that Raven could see the underside.

'It that a set of initials?'

'Indeed it is.'

Raven strained to decipher them.

'AD?'

'Yes. There is a great skill in manufacturing a comfortable set of dentures. The dentist responsible for these has branded his merchandise.'

'I don't see how this helps.'

'In order to make a set of dentures, a model must first be obtained. The models are usually kept in case of accident.'

Raven saw what his friend was getting at. 'The dentist will

have a record of who these teeth belong to,' he said. 'How many dentists are there in the city?'

Henry handed him a list. 'There are twenty-five, though the good news is that I doubt all of them undertake this kind of work. The bad news is, no fewer than four of them have the initials AD.'

THIRTY-NINE

o Sarah, the empty rooms of Milton House felt even more spectral and haunted than the black mausoleum in Greyfriars Kirkyard. This was because she knew the stories of many of those who had perished here. Having been the site of the Maternity Hospital for six years, it had been witness to many untimely deaths: new-born infants and their mothers wrenched from life long before they should have been. The arbitrary nature of death and disease seemed all the more poignant here, and her impotence in the face of it all the more profound.

The circumstances of the women who had come here to be delivered were often sobering: no suitable place for a baby to be born, no family support, no one to assist; or those society shunned for becoming pregnant without a wedding ring to sanction it.

The women were frequently undernourished and poorly clothed, suffering from a variety of ailments that complicated their confinement. Sarah often wondered about the seemingly insatiable appetite men displayed for prosecuting war when famine and pestilence were doing such a good job on their own.

'You know your way around,' Mr Somerville observed as he followed her through the downstairs rooms.

'I spent quite a bit of time here. Dr Simpson encouraged my interest.'

What she didn't say was that it was Raven who had, at a practical level, provided her with support and instruction. It was he who had taken the time to explain and to teach when she had visited.

'And do you still attend the new hospital? Where is it now?'

'It moved to larger premises near the College last year. But no, I don't go there very often now. I don't seem to have the time to spare these days. I'm kept busy at Queen Street.'

She wondered if that was actually true, and had to concede that there was likely more to it. Raven still invited her when there was an interesting case to see, but since his marriage to Eugenie such opportunities seemed to have steeply declined.

'Why the move?' Mr Somerville asked.

'Minto House is bigger. Three storeys, fifteen rooms.'

'Well, lucky for us this place remains vacant. It would make a suitable home for the new institute, don't you think?'

Mr Somerville gave her a warm smile, inviting her opinion with the impression that what she had to say actually mattered.

They were standing in one of the larger downstairs rooms, which had previously been used as a ward. There was a landscape painting still hanging on the wall, testament to its having been an elegant drawing room at some time in the past.

'Yes, I think that it would,' Sarah said. 'More than adequate for the treatment of patients and the instruction of students. Its legacy in housing previous medical institutions further commends it. What do you think yourself?'

'I can but agree,' Mr Somerville replied. 'The only thing lacking is a room large enough to accommodate Dr Malham's demonstrations, but perhaps that is a happy problem to have. He has scheduled a public appearance at the Assembly Rooms, as even the large hall in my Potter Row premises is inadequate to the level of interest he is attracting.'

Mr Somerville proffered a handbill advertising the event, billing it as 'an exhibition of the astonishing phenomenon that is revolutionising medical practice'. She noted that there was an admission fee and tapped the bill where the price was printed.

'Is this entirely wise?' she asked. 'Dr Simpson says you can tell the difference between someone who is demonstrating science and someone who is selling spectacle quite simply by which one is charging money for it.'

'There are costs to hosting such events,' Somerville replied. 'Even those demonstrating science have overheads to consider. But it will all be worth it should the exhibition attract the right patrons. If the institute is to function on the subscribers model used by the Infirmary and the Maternity Hospital, these are the very people Dr Malham needs to convince.'

Sarah knew he was right. Charitable institutions relied upon the deep pockets of their wealthy patrons.

She wandered through to one of the rooms at the rear of the building, now devoid of all the medical paraphernalia that it used to contain.

'This was the delivery room,' she said. She remembered watching Raven at work, a calm demeanour maintained even in the most challenging of circumstances.

'Your late husband was a doctor, wasn't he? Is that what sparked your interest in the healing arts?'

The mention of Archie felt like an uncomfortable jolt, as though by thinking of Raven when the question was posed, she had been caught out in an act of infidelity.

'My husband was a doctor,' she said, 'but my interest in medicine predated my marriage.'

'You must miss him a great deal.'

'I do,' she said, feeling tears begin to form. It was not merely the memory of Archie that moved her, but the solicitude of Mr Somerville.

She blinked them away.

'It's hard being on your own again, isn't it?' Somerville said, shaking his head. 'Only those of us who have been through it can truly understand the pain involved.'

'How long since your wife died?'

'Three years. More or less.'

'Does it ever get easier, do you think?'

Somerville sighed. 'I find the pain never dulls, but the gaps become longer between its visits.'

'Do you think that you will ever marry again?'

The question was out of her mouth before she had time to think about it.

'I had thought not. But now I'm not so sure.'

He was looking at her with an intensity that Sarah found both intriguing and alarming.

'I'm not convinced that marriage is compatible for a woman with ambition,' she said, lowering her eyes and hoping to truncate the discussion of this topic.

Somerville paused for a moment before responding. 'I appreciate the great difficulties you face in attempting to take on the medical establishment,' he said.

'Do you?' She looked at him again. Her tone was disparaging. She wasn't sorry about it. She doubted any man could truly appreciate the struggles a woman faced when attempting anything beyond marriage and motherhood.

'I only mean that I was born without many of the advantages other men enjoy,' he explained.

'Not quite the same though, is it? There are still many benefits attached to being a man, however lowborn.'

'That's true,' Somerville conceded. 'But perhaps mesmerism is a chance for both of us to turn the tables.'

'How so?'

'You, for once, are being treated on a par with men by being offered tuition and the opportunity to practise your new skills and I . . . I have the upper hand for a change.'

'In what way?'

'I am going into partnership with Dr Malham, to be joint owners of the new institute. You have seen the interest he is generating, and word of your own gifts is bound to spread too.'

'What do you mean by a partnership?' Sarah asked. 'I thought you were buying this place yourself.'

'We are both bringing different things to the arrangement. He has something I do not have, in that without him, Milton House is just a building. But for now, I have something he does not: the means to secure the purchase. That gives me the whip-hand. Malham is from a wealthy family back in America, and he is concluding a property sale in New York in order to invest in Milton House. But until he is able to buy out my share, I will be taking a percentage of all of the institute's earnings.'

'What is the percentage?' asked Sarah.

'Sixty,' he replied with a grin. 'Do you know how it feels to have a man like that worried *I'm* in a position to take advantage of *him*?'

Sarah smiled back, though she could confidently assert that no, she did not know how that felt.

'So Malham is to be named in the deed?' she asked, wondering about those snobbish bankers, and whether Amelia Bettencourt knew about this.

'Yes. Though it does not change my arrangement with the bank. Essentially, I am lending him the share under a private agreement and taking a percentage of earnings in lieu until he pays me back.'

'So it is an informal loan, then. Doesn't that carry risks?'

'I have some experience with such arrangements,' he replied, his voice oddly distant all of a sudden. 'It would be safe to say I am more comfortable in that aspect than in dealing with banks, though I am hoping that changes in time.'

'Shall we continue with our tour?' Sarah suggested, and led the way to the stairs.

As they climbed, Somerville continued to expand upon his plans for social and financial advancement.

'To be an owner of property: that is how you thrive in this city. You need to be the person whose say-so is required for other people to pursue their business. You need a stake.'

'So you wish to become a landlord?'

Somerville laughed. 'You make it sound altogether less grand and certainly less honourable than I was imagining.'

They walked around the upstairs rooms, largely in silence. There was not much left to be said about the suitability of Milton House for their purposes. It was undoubtedly a desirable premises for the institute. But there was something about Somerville's arrangement and his other commercial aspirations that bothered her, though she was struggling to identify exactly what.

They descended the stairs and stepped back out onto the oval driveway at the front of the house, another reminder of its having once been the private residence of a wealthy man. Sarah wondered if there had been quite so many buildings surrounding it when the place was first built for Lord Milton. Presumably it had enjoyed a better outlook back then, hemmed in as it was now by Old Town dilapidation.

Sarah pulled on her gloves as they headed towards the Canongate.

'In this city,' she said, 'people are revered merely for having wealth. No one ever questions how it was acquired.'

Somerville stopped walking. 'Do you doubt my intentions? This—' He waved his hand to take in the house behind them '—is not merely a money-making scheme.'

'I know that.'

'I won't pretend that I'm proud of everything I've done, Miss Fisher. But I would ask any man or woman who judges me what decisions they would have made when faced with the difficulties I have encountered in my life.'

'But that's exactly my point,' Sarah said. 'What is grand and honourable about joining the ranks of those prosperous landlords who extract money from the needy, who have to pay the insultingly high rent demanded of them in order to live in these slums?'

Somerville seemed taken aback at her sudden passion, but she ploughed on regardless.

'Dr Littlejohn believes everything is connected,' she told him, 'from open sewers to open veins. Crime, violence, disease: it can all be traced back to poverty, the conditions people are forced to live in. Not everyone has the wherewithal to fight their way above it.'

'You think I don't care?' he asked. There was no anger in his voice despite Sarah's accusations, just a deep sadness. 'I lost my wife and my son, both to illnesses that run rampant in these streets. I am not ignorant of the realities of life in this city.'

Sarah felt suddenly less sure of herself, her own anger dissipating.

'My daughter is all I have left,' Somerville said, 'and I have vowed to protect her. The only way to do that, as far as I can see, is to protect myself – and to do that I need to acquire both money and status.'

Sarah looked at his face, could see the grief etched in the lines around his eyes. She felt sorry for his loss, but she still could not let his cynical world-view go unchallenged.

'Perhaps you ought to be building a better city for her to live in, rather than trying to protect her from those who live here now.'

Somerville paused for a long time, giving deep thought to what she had just said. When finally he spoke again, his voice was soft, almost tender.

'You are a dangerous woman, Miss Fisher.'

'Why?'

'Because growing up in this city, my survival strategy has always been to appear more fearsome than those who would threaten me. It has served me well. You are suggesting an altogether different path, one that is treacherous for being unfamiliar.'

He looked into her eyes. She was suddenly aware of his proximity, his face close to her own. For a moment she thought he was going to kiss her, but there was a shout from the street nearby, a scuffle of feet, and he stepped away. If not for that, she was sure he would have. And she was not sure she would have objected.

FORTY

llan Davidson stood close to the windows where the light was best, Raven remaining to one side of him to avoid casting a shadow. He was looking through a magnifying glass at the surviving section of the dental plate, wearing a strained expression as he turned the object back and forth.

Mr Davidson was the fourth and final of the city dentists whose initials were AD, and the one Raven had been the most optimistic about after two fruitless days of enquiries. Alistair Dunn and Allan Daniels turned out not to construct such plates themselves, and while Anthony Dawson did, he was not in the habit of marking his work with his initials for later identification. He had been scornful of the notion, in fact. 'It strikes me as a wee bit preening and self-important,' he had said. 'We are not creating artwork or jewellery here. It speaks of a strange kind of pride, to secrete your signature inside the person of a patient. But to each his own.'

Allan Davidson had a practical justification for the practice, however.

'I see a lot of patients for repairs of other dentists' poor work. If someone turns up with a plate and claims I was the one who made it, I can very quickly verify whether this is true.'

Davidson let out a long slow breath through his teeth and handed the fragment back to Raven.

'These are my initials, clearly, but I'm afraid this is not my handiwork. I'm sorry.'

Raven felt something in him crumple.

'You say this was taken from a victim of Laurence Butters?' the dentist asked.

'We believe so. He attempted to destroy it in a furnace.'

Davidson nodded, giving it some thought. 'From what I understand about the case, it is likely to belong to Mrs Butters' lover, is that right?'

'Yes. What of it?'

'That being so, it is likely the victim also worked in the theatre. People in that world do tend to move around. So, unfortunately, you may have to broaden your search to every dentist in Scotland, and possibly beyond.'

'That's likely to be a lot of ADs,' Raven mourned. 'Why couldn't the initials have been XV?'

The dentist gave him a look of solidarity. 'I'm sorry I couldn't be of more assistance, Dr Raven. And do pass on my regards to Dr Simpson.'

Raven stepped back out onto George IV Bridge feeling weary. Contacting every dentist in the country was a task beyond his resources, and not one that he imagined McLevy would be inclined to pursue. His frustrations were exacerbated by the thought that his broken bargain with Sarah had been for nought. He was no further forward despite her contribution, one that had come at the unanticipated cost of her no longer speaking to him.

They were civil in front of patients, but any attempt at conversation beyond the strictly professional was rebuffed. Such silences felt all the more stark with the Simpson family still from home. They had yet to return from their sojourn in the country.

Not that Raven had failed to extend an olive branch. He had apologised again for missing Sarah's demonstration, while trying to make her understand his obligation to help a man in danger.

Sarah had shaken her head and given him that look, the one that suggested she was despairing of his lack of comprehension.

He passed a doorway, faintly wondering why it seemed familiar and trying to think of which delivery he might have assisted somewhere in the building. Then he realised it was Kimble's home.

Sarah had been sore and scornful about his intentions towards the man, rightly guessing he had been seeking redemption of some kind. Raven had done his penance, but still could not get Kimble out of his mind: the portraits on his sideboard, the playbills posted on his walls. Initially he assumed he had encountered a man living alone. Then he had come to grasp that what he had seen was a man living with loss. A lonely man seeking solace in a bottle.

As though carried automatically, Raven found himself ascending the stairs to Kimble's rooms. Reaching the top, he knocked on the door and turned the handle, finding it open.

As he stepped inside, he saw Kimble get to his feet. There was a bottle of whisky on the table, the seal freshly broken and a generous dram poured into a glass. There was a plate off to the side. Kimble had just finished a meal, or perhaps it had been finished some time ago and he had not yet cleared it.

The man looked at him quizzically. Not alarmed, but surprised.

'Mr Kimble? I was passing. I don't know if you recall— '

'Will Raven,' Kimble interrupted. 'The doctor haunted by many ghosts. And given to fits of rage.'

Raven wondered if this meant Kimble had no recollection of their encounter two nights ago.

'I'm sorry,' Raven said. 'It was unconscionable of me to assault you. I was angry and lost control of myself.'

'On that occasion, you were not angry so much as afraid,' Kimble said. 'People are fearful of that which they do not understand, and sometimes that fear manifests itself in violence. However, you saved me from far worse the other night. Let us say the ledger is even.'

'So, you do remember. I thought you might have been insensible with the drink.'

Kimble glanced at the dram in front of him. 'When people say they have no recollection of their conduct when drunk, they are simply lying to themselves rather than taking ownership of their shame. I have never been so drunk that I cannot remember what was done or said both by me and to me. And believe me, I have been very drunk, very often.'

He lifted the bottle.

'Will you join me in one?'

'Yes,' Raven said, taking a seat. 'If only so that it is one fewer you can drink tonight.'

'Are you here to save me then, doctor?'

'You're a man seeking oblivion. I have seen it before, enough to know that only you can save yourself from that.'

Kimble gave him a dry smile of acknowledgement and produced a second glass from a cupboard. 'Indeed,' he said, pouring. 'That's not why you've come, is it? What you really seek is to discover how I knew those things about the Simpson family, and about yourself. It troubles you deeply that you don't understand.'

Raven took a sip. It was decent stuff, not the gut-rot he had feared.

'I am a man of science and medicine. It is my mission to understand, to seek answers and explanations.'

'But what happens when the explanation is troubling to your deeper understanding, a challenge to all that you have come to rely upon?'

'Dr Simpson says sometimes we just don't know. I am beginning to see the wisdom in that.'

'And yet,' said Kimble.

'I have a friend who has immersed herself in the practice of mesmerism. She cured a man who was unable to walk without aid. I know what she did, but not why it worked. No one, in fact, knows by what process the effect was procured. That troubles me.'

'But surely the effect is what matters?'

'That's what she would say too.'

'So why does it trouble you?'

'Because I distrust it. Like I distrust your claim to be in contact with the dead, telling people you are talking to their lost loved ones.'

Kimble took a sip. 'Again, is it not the effect that matters? Is not the comfort they derive more important than how that comfort is procured?'

'It troubles me if the effect is something independent of that which is claimed as the cause.'

'Would it ease your discomfort were I to tell you how I know the things I shared?' Kimble asked.

'Were you actually to tell me, that would astonish me more than anything else.'

Kimble smiled approvingly. 'You are learning. So allow me to teach you something more. I owe you that much.'

Kimble produced some cards, seemingly from nowhere. He laid them upon the table, a jumbled spread of wands, swords, cups and pentacles.

'Choose one.'

'At random, or are you to discern meaning from my choice?'

'That is up to you.'

Raven tapped the Knight of Cups.

Kimble cleared the others so that only Raven's card remained on the table.

'Was there a reason you chose it?'

'You tell me.'

'The knight. Simultaneously of some importance and yet a junior figure. A roguish one too, hence he is sometimes called the knave. But he is also seen as a prince: son to the king and queen. He whose best time is yet to come, but not yet fully his own man. He has his ambitions, but nothing is certain. Everything in this world is precarious. It can be gone like that.'

Kimble snapped his fingers and the card disappeared. One moment it was in his hand and the next it was gone.

'Bravo,' Raven muttered drily. 'Was that the lesson? Or are you going to tell me where it has gone?'

'No. The lesson concerns this coin.'

'What coin?' Raven asked, seeing none.

Kimble snapped his fingers again and opened his palm. A silver shilling had materialised there. He placed it down on the table between them, stark against the wood.

'Together, we are going to make this vanish.'

Raven eyed it carefully. Kimble passed his hands over it, back and forth, left and right. It made Raven think of the descriptions of mesmerism that he had heard. He wondered if this was a subtle, off-hand way of mesmerising a subject, by making them focus on hand movements when they thought they were focusing on something else.

'Actually, to do this we need some salt.'

Kimble lifted the salt cellar and placed it on top of the coin. He then produced a napkin – again, unsettlingly, from nowhere – which he draped over the salt cellar.

'Now, concentrate your mind on the coin,' he said. 'Three, two, one.'

Kimble snapped his fingers and lifted both salt cellar and napkin away in a dramatic sweep.

The coin was still there.

Raven wondered if the bottle of whisky was not the first Kimble had opened today.

'I asked you to concentrate,' Kimble said.

'So it's my fault the trick didn't work?'

'Let's try again.'

Kimble put the salt cellar and napkin over the coin once more.

'This time you count,' Kimble said.

'Very well,' agreed Raven. 'Three, two— '

Before Raven could finish, Kimble slapped his palm down hard upon the salt cellar, enough to surely damage his hand. Instead, Raven saw that the napkin was spread flat against the table, the salt cellar gone.

Kimble lifted the napkin away. The coin was gone too.

He folded the napkin carefully and handed it to Raven.

'Where did the salt cellar go?' Raven asked, amazed.

Kimble raised his eyebrows. 'How fickle you are, Dr Raven. Previously you were wondering what had happened to your card.'

Kimble's eyes went to the napkin. Raven unfolded it and revealed the Knight of Cups.

Raven could not help but let out a laugh, some simple, childish part of himself delighted by the trick. He thought of James and how he would love to amaze him like this when he was old enough to appreciate it.

'Will you tell me how it was done?' he asked eagerly.

'That is not the lesson. The lesson is that a logical, scientific man such as yourself is easily manipulable by a practised deceiver. It is the magician's job to make you not only concentrate on the wrong thing at the crucial time, but to look in the wrong place for the explanation. You must change the way you think about the mystery you are trying to solve. Make no assumptions, and never look at it from the same angle twice.'

FORTY-ONE

tanding room only,' Somerville announced with satis-faction as he led Sarah towards what he described as Malham's dressing room. It was not a term she was used to hearing in the context of one preparing for a medical or scientific procedure, but nor was the venue. They were at the Assembly Rooms, where the broad expanse of the lobby was teeming with people, the ballroom already accommodating consid-erably more than could have fitted inside the room where he last demonstrated his gifts.

Sarah and Mr Somerville found Malham in front of a full-length mirror, examining himself from every angle. Gethyn was standing behind him holding the crystal-topped cane, his face a picture of beatific adoration.

Malham turned to the new arrivals, his arms spread wide.

'What do you think?' he asked.

He was dressed all in white. White suit. White shirt. White cravat with crystal tie-pin.

Sarah didn't know how to respond. Fortunately, Somerville stepped into the breach.

'Striking,' he announced. He sounded taken aback, though not necessarily in a good way. 'It's . . . very dramatic.'

'That is precisely what we were aiming for,' Gethyn replied, clearly delighted with Somerville's assessment.

Malham turned his attention to Sarah now, waiting for her input.

'It's . . . remarkable,' she said, hoping that the ambiguity of her comment and lack of enthusiasm in her tone would convey her reservations. She worried that Malham's attire was a bad omen, a signal that he was drifting from the realms of scientific demonstration towards theatrical entertainment. There was also something troubling about his colour choice. White struck her as worryingly messianic.

She could hear Raven's voice in her head recounting the important tenets of scientific experimentation: rational thought, judgement, verification, doubt. Those who were convinced that they had all the answers were invariably wrong, he said. Malham's conviction was thus becoming unnerving.

'When taking the stage, it is so important to make an impression,' Gethyn stated.

'I thought you were a tailor,' Sarah said. 'What do you know of the stage?'

Gethyn briefly narrowed his eyes at her, but when he spoke, he made every effort to conceal his irritation.

'Theatre has always been a passion of mine,' he replied.

'I know little of such things,' Somerville said, 'but I do know the importance of how a man presents himself.' He turned to Malham. 'Are you sure this is the right way to go?'

Sarah could have grabbed him and kissed him for articulating what she was feeling herself. The reputation of mesmerism was in this man's hands, and if he turned it into a farce, it might never recover.

Malham brushed away his concerns. 'Have no fear, Mr Somerville. I know what I am about. A little stagecraft is called for when addressing such a large crowd.'

This reassured Sarah a little and Somerville tipped his hat by way of acknowledgement.

'Then we shall leave you to your final preparations. Good luck.'

'I can assure you, Mr Somerville, that luck does not come into it.'

Just as they were about to leave there was a knock at the door. A small man with glasses made a tentative entrance.

'Sorry to disturb, Dr Malham, but a member of the audience has become unwell. Can you come?'

Malham was looking at himself in the mirror again, adjusting his cravat.

'My dear sir, most of the audience will be unwell,' he replied. 'That is why they come to see me.'

'I think that it's quite serious,' the man persisted. 'Someone has collapsed.'

For a fraction of a second Malham looked alarmed, but this was quickly replaced by irritation.

'I really can't afford to be disturbed at this juncture. I have to begin the delicate process of self-mesmerism. Miss Fisher has a command of medical knowledge to rival many a doctor. Sarah, can you deal with this please?'

The man did not seem happy that Sarah had been designated Malham's substitute, but given the lack of an alternative he bade her follow him.

The ballroom was even more crowded now, and the atmosphere was oppressive, too many bodies crammed in together. A group had gathered at the side of the room, a woman lying on the floor in the midst of it.

'She said she felt lightheaded and then collapsed,' someone said as Sarah approached. It sounded like a simple faint, a common enough occurrence when so many women insisted on the tight lacing of their stays, but it still had a tendency to cause a collective panic when it happened. What was needed was someone to take control, be the voice of reassurance. Sarah was eminently suited to the task, but as a woman this was not initially appreciated. Several men were attempting to sit the unconscious woman up.

Sarah had to intervene. Loudly.

'Let her be. It is better to let her come to without moving her,' she said. No one seemed to be paying much attention. Sarah was about to elbow her way in when a voice commanded: 'Stand aside. Let this lady through.'

It was Somerville, a man whose voice and presence brooked no refusal.

Sarah pushed past the onlookers. The recumbent woman was young and pale, her face damp with perspiration. Sarah felt for a pulse. Slow but steady. She elevated the woman's legs, taking care not to expose anything beneath her skirts, and guarded her against further interference. Somerville was creating a bit of space around them, pushing the surrounding crowd back. Sarah felt a brief moment of angst. Flattered as she was by Malham's faith in her, if she had misconstrued the problem here, the fault would be hers alone. He should really have come and assessed the situation himself before leaving Sarah to deal with it.

The woman started to move, opened her eyes.

Relieved, Sarah helped her to sit up. Someone offered a glass of water. Someone else proffered a hip flask, suggesting a bit of brandy would do the trick. Sarah accepted the water and guided the woman to a chair. She asked that some windows be opened to improve the stuffiness of the room.

When her patient had suitably recovered, she found her own seat beside Somerville.

'Well done,' he said. He smiled and it warmed her.

Sarah settled into her seat, grateful to be in Somerville's company. He had been unstinting in his support of her and she in turn felt oddly protective of him. She had seen him disparaged by the bankers, underestimated by those who considered themselves above him in class and status. She admired his determination but was concerned about the wisdom and viability of his arrangement with Malham, confused that he should be so relaxed about effectively lending the man a fifty per cent stake in the Mesmeric Institute against no physical collateral. She wondered what Somerville was not telling her about himself, and wondered too if she had any right to ask.

Contemplating the dangerous side of one man's nature brought another man to mind. She hadn't mentioned to Raven that she was coming to this event this evening as there was still too much ill-feeling between them. There was little doubt that he knew about it none-theless, as the demonstration had been well advertised, via newspaper advertisements and bills posted around town. These, she realised, would have been among the overheads Mr Somerville alluded to.

It did not sit well with her when she and Will were on bad terms, and she suspected that he was struggling with something. Ordinarily she would want to help, but she was finding it hard to get over her hurt.

She understood that Raven needed to help Kimble when he witnessed him being attacked, that in good conscience he could not have walked away. And yet, while she was a believer in the expression 'Where there's a will, there's a way,' she knew the opposite of this tended to hold too. When people didn't want to do something, they were quick to welcome fresh obstacles.

She thought that if it had been some random stranger, she might have found Raven's act of charity easier to bear. But that it had been Kimble, a man for whom Raven had developed an unhealthy fascination, made it that bit harder to take. Raven was seeking to make amends, which was understandable. What hurt was the sense that Raven felt a greater urgency to do right by Kimble than to do right by her.

Sarah became aware of the dimming of the gaslight in the chandelier above her and the audience became quiet as Malham took the stage. He looked almost ethereal in his white suit, presum-ably the intended effect. The stage was stark, empty except for a row of chairs. This was a relief, as Sarah had been wondering what showy accoutrements Malham might have assembled, in keeping with his choice of dress.

He waited for complete silence, then tapped his cane three times, loudly, on the floor of the stage. He reprised his introduc-tion from the previous demonstration, held the crystal close to his face, stared intently at it for several minutes, then lowered it slowly.

'I have now entered the garden of sleep, a state of consciousness that permits me to see what others cannot. It gives me a unique ability to divine the nature of illness and to effect a cure. Is there anyone here present who wishes my help?'

Sarah watched a host of hands raised around the auditorium.

Malham grabbed the lower end of his cane and pointed the crystal tip at a member of the audience, who responded with an eager expression.

'Oh, thank you, sir,' the man said. 'I am sore troubled with— '

'Do not tell me,' Malham commanded, firm but gentle in his tone. 'Pray join me on the stage if you wish to be healed.'

Sarah watched as the man made his way to the stage. He was young and thin, his jacket hanging off his narrow frame. He stood in front of Malham, who reached out and placed a hand on the man's head. Malham closed his eyes. Everyone waited.

Suddenly Malham stepped back, as though his hand had received a shock from a galvanism machine.

He pointed his cane at the man and said: 'I see you. I see you.'

The man on the stage coughed. More than a nervous cough. A deep bronchitic rumble. He took a handkerchief from his pocket and wiped his mouth. The audience remained silent, waiting for what came next.

'You are a Scotsman by birth,' Malham intoned.

The man nodded his head.

'Until recently you resided in London, is that right?'

'Yes,' he confirmed, which prompted a few impressed mutterings from the floor.

'You have enjoyed good health and have passed through scarlet fever and measles without any negative impression being made upon it.'

The man nodded again, beginning to look a little disconcerted that Malham should know such things. He wasn't the only one.

'Your constitution remained unbroken until an attack of fever four years ago. Since then, you suffer from cold, poor appetite and a chronic cough.'

'That is correct, sir.'

Malham turned to the crowd, which was rumbling with sounds of astonishment.

'The diagnosis is tuberculosis.'

'How did you know, sir?' the man asked.

Malham turned back to him. 'I told you. In the garden of sleep I have the ability to see what others cannot. And by taking you into that garden with me, I can offer you a therapy beyond what others have been able to provide.'

Dr Malham led the man to one of the chairs and bade him sit. He placed a second chair directly in front of his subject, sat upon it and proceeded to mesmerise him. Malham was getting faster at it. The man's eyes began to close and his head drooped in a matter of minutes, perhaps no more than five. There was a degree of restlessness from the audience, but no more than a susurrus of whispering, mostly people expressing wonder and confusion at how Malham could have ascertained what he did.

To Sarah's surprise, when Malham stood up, satisfied his subject was entranced, he walked away and climbed down from the stage, leaving the man motionless on his chair.

Malham then called forth a gentleman who proceeded towards the stage with a pronounced limp, labouring his way up the stairs. Malham placed the crystal to his head as he looked the fellow up and down.

'Your limp is the result of a fall. Something to do with a railway line,' Malham suggested.

The man's face lit up in astonishment. 'I was a labourer on the line between Edinburgh and Newhaven,' he confirmed.

'Where you suffered a fracture of the right femur. It healed, but there remains a lingering ache in the thigh that has never quite resolved.'

'That is correct. It troubles me all these years later.'

'Join me then, in the garden of sleep.'

Malham induced another trance, the first fellow still peacefully at rest to the right of the stage.

Once again Malham returned to the auditorium, where this time he called upon a frail-looking young woman.

'I feel weak all the time,' she told him.

'And yet the truth is you are strong. For you survived a bout of smallpox as a child, did you not?'

Her eyes widened in amazement. 'I did.'

'And you also survived rheumatic fever several years ago. You are troubled by a cough with bloody sputum, you suffer breathlessness, difficulty climbing stairs.'

'Holy Mary, mother of God,' she said, crossing herself. 'You can tell all that just by looking?'

'In the garden of sleep, I see everything.'

At this point Mr Somerville turned to Sarah. 'How is he doing this? he whispered.

'I have no idea.'

'I diagnose that you have morbus cordis, a disease of the heart,' Malham told the young woman.

She tearfully agreed that this was the case. 'That is exactly what the doctor told me,' she said, with the clear implication that the doctor had not been able to help her.

'To survive all that you have done takes great strength, a strength that I can help you find again within yourself. Join me now, as these others have done.'

Sarah was struggling to understand what she was witnessing. Malham's previous demonstrations had been impressive, but they had consisted of him making vague diagnostic pronouncements with talk of pain, headaches, and fatigue. This tonight was something quite different. He was talking in specifics, exhibiting a detailed knowledge of medical ailments past and present.

As the case histories were revealed, it was quite clear that these were details Malham could not possibly discern from observation alone. Sarah had a sense of something unsettling at work. Malham said it was self-mesmerism and talked about the garden of sleep, but this did not feel anything like the mesmerism she had been learning herself.

Sarah remembered a previous time she had felt like this. It was when Kimble performed his séance. She understood now what had troubled Raven about it. It was both powerful and frightening, and in the realms of his medical and scientific understanding, there was no explanation for it.

Once the young woman was asleep, Malham returned to the first gentleman, the young man with tuberculosis. He placed both hands on the man's chest, then bade him: 'Awaken, sir.'

The young man's eyes opened. He looked blearily at the audience, as though taking a moment to remember where he was.

'How do you feel now?' Malham asked.

The man sat up straight in his chair, placing his hands to his chest where Malham's had been a few seconds before.

'I feel better,' he said. 'I do. I feel much better.'

The audience responded with enthusiastic applause.

Malham then demesmerised the railway man, who upon being asked how he felt, climbed to his feet and began to walk across the stage, his movement smoother, his limp altogether less pronounced.

'The pain is considerably less,' he declared.

Finally, he awoke the young woman.

'I am breathing freely,' she announced, a broad smile upon her face.

Within seconds, almost the entire audience was on their feet in rapturous applause.

Sarah spotted Gethyn at the side of the stage looking worshipful: a true disciple.

She was feeling less than reverential. In fact, she was feeling afraid. Each of Malham's subjects had undeniably attested that they felt better, but that was not what she was overhearing in conversations all around her, nor what would be described in homes and taverns tonight and breathlessly spread across Edinburgh tomorrow.

They weren't saying Malham had made these people feel better. They were saying he had cured them.

FORTY-TWO

'So you were the Mysterious Lembik,' Raven said. 'Illustrious in your day.'

'Indeed I was.'

'You performed at some prestigious theatres.'

'Those were barely the half of it. They are the venues I still have memorabilia for. I played in many more places.'

'"Newton defied",' Raven said.

'Yes. That was the illusion that made me.' Kimble took a drink, then looked at the amber liquid. 'And this is what unmade me.'

'Levitation,' said Raven.

'I made a woman float above the stage. Quite the crowd-pleaser. Many levitation illusions had been constructed before, but I devised one that for a time defied explanation. As I said, it is the magician's job to make the audience seek that explanation in the wrong place. They thought perhaps there were very fine wires suspending her. But I was able to demonstrate that there were not by running a brass hoop the length of her horizontal body as it floated above the boards.'

'I think I've seen something similar,' Raven said.

'Oh, I don't doubt that you have. My illusion was stolen. Suddenly magicians were performing it up and down the country, many of them better than I had.'

'And that was why you took to drink?'

'No. Drink was how it got stolen.'

Kimble had looked brighter and more animated as he performed the trick with the salt cellar and as he spoke about the levitation illusion. Now it was as though he had aged in a matter of moments. A silence grew, and Raven felt like a door was closing. He put a foot in to stop it.

'Who is Michael?' he asked.

Kimble raised his eyes, fixing them on Raven's. Much passed between them in that brief moment. Raven saw a man considering flight, even if not physically, and then glancing across to the sideboard, perhaps understanding how much Raven had already deduced.

'Michael was my son. My boy.'

Kimble took another sip of whisky, then gulped the lot before pouring another generous measure.

'The pain is so great, sometimes I'm overcome with the burden of his memory, and other times his memory is the only thing that keeps me going.'

'I am sorry,' Raven said, uselessly.

'I had hoped he would follow me one day.'

'He resisted?'

'Oh, no, he was an apt and eager pupil. I don't think I was ever happier than passing on what I had learned and watching him master it. Seeing the excitement in his face as he came to understand the principles. He would have been among the best there ever was. Better than Robert-Houdin or John Henry Anderson, the Great Wizard of the North. But cholera took him. That was when I began to drink.'

Kimble glanced at one of the posters showing the woman being levitated, the one who also appeared on the sideboard.

'For a while, performing was all that sustained me, all that sustained both of us. Me and Gloria, his mother. It was a distraction. But afterwards I needed to dull the pain. Then I began to need it earlier and earlier in the day. I became sloppy, and not merely in my performance. Much of what is vital happens offstage. I became careless.'

Kimble's eyes glazed, his mind somewhere else.

'Was there some kind of mishap?' Raven asked tentatively.

'A disastrous one, yes. But not in the manner you are thinking. We magicians must be fastidious in our preparations, but also in our security: in keeping our secrets, transporting our equipment between shows. But drunks are fastidious only about ensuring they have drink.

'I remember the moment when I turned up to a new theatre, in Nottingham, and discovered that one of my trunks had already been opened, the padlock disabled. I saw the hasps hanging loose and knew I was undone. The secret of my levitation effect was gone.'

He gave a bitter smile.

'It was simply a piece of metal, Dr Raven. One that was bent in an unusual way, allowing manipulations of that hoop that it might apparently pass back and forth unhindered by any support that could be holding Gloria. Just a simple piece of metal, and yet the thing it was truly holding up was my whole world. Everything fell apart by degrees after that. Gloria left. She said it was my drinking and my failing performances, but I know that the largest part of it was that I looked so much like Michael. Every time she looked at my face, she saw his, and it hurt her too much to bear.'

Kimble glanced towards the portraits: Michael as a boy, and as a young man, presumably not long before he was lost.

'I was unable to get work, but frankly I didn't much care. Nothing mattered. I missed Michael so much that I started to believe I could sense him. It was so tantalising, as if the barrier between us was paper-thin and there might be a means by which he could pass through it and return to me.

'Around then, I saw a medium perform in a theatre in Carlisle, and he claimed he could sense Michael too. He passed on words that Michael was speaking to me then and there, and it felt so warming, so nourishing for a while. Just for a few blessed moments. That's the problem when you sell illusions, though: I very quickly understood what he was doing. But I also understood how powerful it was, how it had made me feel. I knew that other people would wish to feel that way too.'

'So you ceased being Lembik and became merely Kimble? Selling people's memories back to them as the work of the spirits.'

Kimble gulped back another dram.

'It's a living,' he said.

'If all it does is keep you in whisky,' Raven told him, 'that's not a living. That is a long, slow death.'

Kimble refilled his glass.

'All living is a long, slow death, Dr Raven.'

FORTY-THREE

arah approached the dressing-room door, unsure whether she really wanted to go in. Somerville entered ahead of her, keen to give Malham his hearty congratulations, but Sarah was too confused to feel in any way celebratory.

They were obviously a little late. Others had gained entry before them and from the tone of the voice currently speaking, not everyone in the audience had been impressed.

'Surely you can see, sir, that what we have all borne witness to tonight is not what the Edinburgh Mesmeric Association is seeking to promulgate.'

Sarah stepped a little further inside and saw that the speaker was one of the doctors from the association meeting she had attended. What had Mrs Crowe said his name was? Sarah couldn't recall.

'What we should be seeking to promote,' the man continued, 'is the benefits of mesmerism administered by medical practitioners. The air of mystery and the unworldly is a dangerous distraction and liable to dissuade people from seeking help or seeking to become involved.'

For the first time that evening Sarah genuinely felt the urge to applaud.

Malham seemed to accept this criticism with surprising equanimity. His brow remained unfurrowed, his facial expression placid and calm. Sarah wondered if he was still in some kind of self-imposed trance, his conscious mind still happily ensconced in the garden of sleep.

That said, in truth there was little need for Malham to stir himself and attempt a defence, as Gethyn seemed keen to jump into the fray on his behalf, the growling mongrel guarding its master.

'Dr Malham is raising the profile of mesmerism far higher than you and the rest of the association could ever dream of,' Gethyn insisted. 'The Edinburgh Mesmeric Association needs Dr Malham far more than he needs it. I predict that there will be a queue at the door tomorrow longer than ever before. So, have a care, sir, or Dr Malham may take his talents elsewhere.'

Malham roused himself at this point, keen to smooth any feathers that Gethyn might have ruffled.

'Thank you, Mr Gethyn, but I have no intention of leaving Edinburgh quite yet.' He patted Gethyn on the back and squeezed his shoulder. 'Perhaps you would do me the service of seeking out the house manager to collect our share of the takings.'

Gethyn nodded. 'Of course, Dr Malham.'

He breezed past Sarah and marched down the corridor with a renewed sense of purpose.

Malham smiled at the disgruntled doctor. 'Do please forgive my intemperate friend. Mr Gethyn has a tendency to speak from the heart when he should be more guarded.' A look of concern then shrouded Malham's features. 'Loyalty is to be valued,' he went on, 'but I sometimes worry about what lengths that man might go to on my behalf.'

Malham's apology was interrupted by a knock at the door and the return of the bespectacled man who had previously brought the news of the unwell audience member. He gave Sarah a curt nod, the only acknowledgement she was likely to get, and addressed Malham.

'There is a gentleman who wishes to see you, sir.'

Malham sighed. 'The rigours of the demonstration have left me quite drained. Please tell the gentleman to come to the association offices tomorrow. I will see him then.'

The messenger seemed disinclined to do that. He cleared his throat.

'It's James McLevy,' he said.

Malham shrugged, failing to appreciate the significance of the name, but he was alone in this. The mere mention of it sent a palpable ripple through the room.

'James McLevy, the police detective,' the bespectacled man clarified, clearly not relishing the prospect of telling the police officer that he would be denied entry.

'A police detective?' Malham repeated. 'What on earth does he want with me? I suppose you'd better show him in.'

'You must excuse me,' Somerville whispered to Sarah. 'I have matters to attend to.'

He left the room without further explanation. Sarah was not surprised. Had Raven been with her, he would likely have done the same. She wondered about Somerville's relationship with the detective, given the troubled past he had alluded to, and briefly thought about leaving herself. Interactions with Mr McLevy were often fraught affairs, but her curiosity got the better of her, as it so often did.

McLevy entered the room a few minutes later, by which time Malham had sat himself down on a chair and was massaging his temples.

'Good evening, Dr Malham,' McLevy said, exhibiting a decorum that Sarah had not previously witnessed. 'An impressive display if you don't mind me saying. Even more impressive was the make-up of the audience you've got out there. The great and the good of Edinburgh, and all were enraptured. Landowners, politicians, newspapermen. I think I even saw the provost. Though I also caught sight of one or two less savoury individuals. You're not in hock to a man named Flint, by any chance, are you?'

Malham frowned and shook his head. 'Never heard of him,' he said.

McLevy noticed Sarah standing at the side of the room.

'Miss Fisher, you do appear in the most unlikely places,' he said.

Malham turned to look at her, as though only just noticing that she was there.

'You are known to the police?' he asked, clearly dismayed that this should be the case.

'Miss Fisher has proven resourceful to certain of my enquiries,' McLevy replied, 'for better or worse.'

'How intriguing,' Malham said. 'Miss Fisher, there is more to you than you choose to disclose.' He stared at her for a moment then turned back to the detective. 'And to what do I owe the honour of your visit, sir?'

'I was hoping to obtain your opinion regarding the suitability of mesmerism for the treatment of a long-standing and recurrent complaint,' McLevy said, indicating the area around his lower back. 'An injury sustained during a chase. A burglar, one of the few that got the better of me. I've long been known as McLevy the thief-taker.'

'Indeed,' Malham said.

McLevy looked disappointed, clearly expecting more of a response.

'As I said,' he continued, 'an injury sustained in the line of duty. Many years ago, now. But it still pains me. Worse in bad weather. Can predict a coming storm.'

'Well,' Malham said, leaning forward in his chair, 'we can't have the city's leading detective incapacitated in this way. You must come to the association, and I will see what I can do.'

'I would be most grateful. I have tried half the doctors in this city and got no better.'

'Mesmerism often succeeds where established methods have foundered,' Malham contended. 'That is why the medical establishment is fearful of it.'

'I am nothing if not open-minded, as Miss Fisher can attest.'

Sarah was grateful she wasn't eating when McLevy said this, or she might have choked. She merely smiled and inclined her head.

'In fact,' McLevy continued, 'having seen you divine information seemingly from the ether tonight, I was wishing you could do the same with regards to the whereabouts of Laurence Butters.'

Malham gave a frown, a mixture of concern and not a little puzzlement.

'Laurence Butters? The actor? What about him?'

'You're not aware of the recent murders?' McLevy asked, astonished.

'Well, of course I have heard of them. But you must forgive me, Mr McLevy, I have been so preoccupied of late that I have not followed the story closely.'

'Two bodies have been found, or parts of them. Butters remains loose in the city.'

'And this Laurence Butters is the murderer you seek?'

'Indeed. Butters' wife, Lydia, was the first victim to be discovered. We have subsequently found a second, male, as yet unidentified. Do you know Butters? Have you made his acquaintance?'

'He attended one of my early demonstrations and we were briefly introduced. He expressed a profound interest in my work. Perhaps too profound.'

'How so?'

'He asked me to teach him mesmerism, but I refused. Make no mistake, Mr McLevy, I am keen to share what I have learned, and our new institute will require as many capable practitioners as I can confidently train, but there's the word: confidence. Mesmerism is not a discipline to be shared lightly. One must be sure of the hands into which one places something so powerful.'

Malham's concerned expression deepened.

'Something troubled me about Butters, about his nature, and possibly his intentions. I got the strong sense that it would be unwise to thus empower him, and so I rebuffed his approach. He did not take it well.'

'Did he become aggressive? He remonstrated with you?'

'No. That would have troubled me less. Rather, there was something quiet and understated about his response. It is said silent waters run deep. I think silent menace runs deep too. Now you are telling me this man has murdered his wife and one other person?'

'That we know of.'

'Then I might need more than Mr Gethyn to protect me,' Malham said. His tone was light, but his concern was obvious.

'Mr Gethyn? He is your bodyguard?'

Malham shook his head. 'No. I was speaking frivolously. Mr Gethyn is an enthusiast for mesmerism, and as such, he is sometimes a little over-effusive in taking my side, that's all. My levity is perhaps inappropriate. We should not make light of the danger. I had no notion this Mr Butters was capable of such deeds, or I might have sought protection.' Malham paused for a moment. 'Perhaps there is a way I might protect myself, though.'

'What do you mean?' McLevy asked.

'When first you mentioned my helping you look for Butters, I took it as the light-hearted comment you presumably intended. But now that you tell me Butters is the man you seek for these murders, I feel it is imperative that I attempt to assist, not least for the purposes of self-preservation.'

McLevy looked a little unsure at this sudden turn of events. 'Well, I don't suppose it can do much harm,' he said.

Malham reached for his cane.

'You mean here? Now?' McLevy asked, looking conspicuously uncomfortable.

'The sooner the better, wouldn't you say?'

'Very well. I will permit you to try. But what happens here must not leave this room,' he added.

Sarah took a seat, wondering what on earth Malham was going to do now. She was reminded of Raven's listing of Elliotson's faults, how his experimentation into mesmerism subsequently veered into mind-reading and clairvoyance.

Malham settled himself back in his chair. McLevy remained standing by the door, perhaps in readiness to make his escape should they all be discovered attempting to ascertain the whereabouts of a murderer in this way.

Malham held up the crystal-topped cane and stared at it as he had done before. Within a few minutes he began shaking his head, as though he was experiencing some difficulty putting himself into the trance state. Then he began wincing, as if experiencing physical pain. What took mere moments onstage was taking far longer. McLevy looked at Sarah, seeking reassurance that all was well. She had none to give him.

They continued to watch Malham squirm, Sarah wondering at what point it might be wise to intervene. Then there seemed to be a breakthrough, a lessening of his distress, and his eyes closed.

'I have now entered the garden of sleep,' he said, his voice just above a whisper. 'But it does not feel as welcoming as it has previously been. It is the same place and yet not familiar. I warn you, Mr McLevy, I will not be able to stay here for long. Not in the presence of what I have found here. I feel such violence, such rage. I feel the human body rent apart, broken down. I see part of a jawbone.'

McLevy looked at Sarah as if to ask: Did you tell him this?

She shook her head. She knew about the pieces of bone recovered from the ashes at Surgeons' Hall because Raven had told her, but she could not see how Malham could have found out about it.

'At the heart of this rage burns envy,' he continued.

'It doesn't take a trance to work that out,' McLevy muttered, clearly far from impressed by this performance. 'He killed his wife and likely her lover.'

'This is not a mere jealousy of the heart,' Malham intoned. 'Of lust and passion and common infidelity. This is something else. A love for one that becomes a hate for all else.'

McLevy looked as though he wanted to be elsewhere, regretting being part of this. He began to shuffle his feet and seemed to be on the point of leaving. Sarah doubted that he would be attending the association offices any time soon for treatment of his back pain.

Then Malham came out of his trance, opened his eyes, and stared directly at the policeman.

'I am sorry, Mr McLevy,' he said, shuddering a little. 'I could not stay, could not tolerate the presence I felt there. It was like standing too close to a fire. And what disturbed me most was that this rage is not spent. These two victims will not be the last.'

FORTY-FOUR

aven had barely touched his whisky, but he felt almost
drunk from everything else he had imbibed during his
brief visit. His head was swimming with it, so much
so that he was almost halfway home before it occurred
to him that somewhere during their encounter, Kimble had effectively admitted his mediumship was fake.

Whether Kimble was telling him mesmerism was fake, that was
another matter. *You must change the way you think about the mystery
you are trying to solve*, he had cautioned. Raven thought of what
Sarah had read about James Braid in Manchester, contrasting that
with Mesmer and his bathtub full of iron filings, to say nothing
of the circus Elliotson had made of University College Hospital.

What had most affected Raven was Kimble's sadness: his
crushing pain and his pitiable sense of loss. He was a man who
preferred not to make anything obvious, and Raven appreciated
Kimble's method in encouraging him to seek new ways of deduction
rather than simply be told the answers. But there was one thing
over which he had given Raven explicit clarity, and it felt like the
easing of a burden or the receipt of a blessed gift. Perhaps he could
even call it the exorcism of a ghost, for there was one fewer of
those following Raven when he left Kimble's building.

The man had treasured every minute with his lost son, while
Raven was squandering what was in his grasp through pointless

fear. He could see now how absurd it was for him to worry about what he might pass on to James, the legacy of his own upbringing. Kimble had spent maybe twenty years with Michael and would give anything for another minute with him now. Raven had spent much of his son's young life avoiding him, afraid of the effect he might have, afraid of truly being the boy's father.

No more.

He began to sweat from the pace he was setting, and it was all he could do not to break into a run in his impatience to be home.

As he came through the front door, Raven was greeted by the familiar sound of James fussing discontentedly somewhere in the house. He recognised the half-crying that was either the beginnings of a greater tantrum or the tail-end of one that was taking time to exhaust itself.

Eugenie emerged from the parlour to greet him. This was as often a harbinger of trouble as of a warm welcome. He pulled her into his arms, his hand automatically going to her belly.

'Is all well?' he asked.

'With this one, yes,' she said, though there was an unspoken corollary, perhaps concerning the fussing he could hear from elsewhere. 'She's turning somersaults,' she added. Eugenie had simply decided that the child she was carrying would be a girl. 'I think she intends to be an acrobat. Perhaps she will join the circus.'

'Wouldn't that please your father,' Raven said.

Eugenie responded with that mischievous grin, that secret smile she kept for when they discussed something only the two of them shared.

She was far happier with him of late since he had announced his firm resolution to finally leave Queen Street; more so that he had a plan for doing it without her father's financial assistance. For in truth, content as she would have been to receive his money, Eugenie also had a desire to consolidate her independence from a father who had always been too controlling for her liking.

'Where is the boy?' Raven asked.

'Just follow the sound.'

Raven went to James's room. He was sitting on the carpet, still fussing, tears and mucus drying on his face. He filled his lungs at the sight of his father, ready for a renewed bout of vigorous bawling now that there was another pair of ears to hear it.

Raven swept him up into his arms and held him. James seemed momentarily startled by this unaccustomed show of affection. Raven hugged him again, and the child made an odd noise which he realised was a chuckle.

He felt a tug as James tightened his arms around Raven's neck.

Raven understood not only what was happening now, but what had been happening before. The boy had instinctively reacted to Raven's unease, whereas this time what he had sensed was something calming.

The Mysterious Lembik truly was a magician.

Eugenie appeared in the doorway, failing to hide her surprise at what she was witnessing. He could hardly blame her for that. She looked pleased, though there was something else in her face, a note of caution.

'Is everything alright?' he asked.

'You might not be cherishing him quite so much when I tell you what he's done.'

'What?'

'I try to keep him out of your study. But sometimes I turn my back for ten seconds . . .'

She held up a sheet of paper, ragged down one side where a section had been ripped away. 'Your class certificate from the university. I'm afraid he got hold of it. He is no respecter of documents,' she added, trying to make light of it, yet indicating she anticipated Raven would not.

Raven shook his head and offered her a smile, savouring the feeling of James's warmth against his chest. 'I kept meaning to put it in a frame,' he said. 'My own fault. Besides, it's kept more for sentimental reasons rather than necessity.'

He looked at the damaged sheet and began to read from it.

*I hereby certify that Mr Wilberforce Raven
very regularly attended my course of lectures
on Midwifery and the diseases of women
and children at the University of Edin
during the winter session of 18
Signed: Professor James Yo*

'I would tell you he is sorry, but this was an hour ago and James will have forgotten. I doubt that he even has a notion that it was wrong.'

Raven looked at the certificate again, which was when he saw that far from having reason to be annoyed, he should be thanking the boy.

'He has done me a service. He is a better detective than James McLevy.'

'What do you mean?'

'I've just come from seeing the dentist Allan Davidson, working my way through Henry's list of ADs. I forgot that we were dealing with a mere fragment of a dental plate. What if there was a missing letter? What if I should not be seeking an Alistair Dunn or an Anthony Dawson, but an Alistair Douglas Morrison or an Anthony Donald Thomson?'

'Or an Adam David Sheldrake,' said Eugenie.

Raven gaped, because she had rendered it so obvious.

The man was a good friend of Eugenie's father. Cameron Todd boasted one of the most prestigious medical practices in the city, and Adam Sheldrake by far the most lucrative dental practice.

Preening and self-important, Anthony Dawson had said. That described Sheldrake perfectly, and there was no question that he was the type to mark his handiwork with a personal signature. Unfortunately, as well as preening and self-important, he was also the most avaricious, self-seeking and determinedly unhelpful man in the city.

FORTY-FIVE

he following afternoon, as he made the short walk to Dublin Street, Raven recalled the time Sheldrake first came to his notice, shortly after he had started as Simpson's apprentice. Raven had suspected the dentist to be involved in something unspeakable and had been on his way to confront him when he was abducted by Flint's men and ended up delivering the money-lender's son instead.

Flint. There was a man who had not lain awake worrying about the corrupting influence he might have on his offspring, far less what his wife had to say about anything. But then Raven remembered that he was on the verge of entering a business arrangement with the man, and not one that permitted him to strut upon the moral high ground. Besides, who was to say that Flint was not a good father. Raven knew nothing about that side of the man, and among the lessons he had learned from Kimble today was not to make assumptions based on what merely met the eye.

Raven entered the brightly painted and well-kept close and ascended the stairs to the first floor, where Sheldrake had his surgery. He heard the man's voice even as he approached the door, though it was not the haughty tone he associated with the man. Rather it was something altogether more appellant.

'I can assure you, Mrs Aubrey, that the procedure is entirely safe, and I must warn you that the pain will only get worse, to say nothing of the danger of infection.'

'I'm not afraid of infection, Mr Sheldrake. I'm afraid of not waking up. And if there is greater pain, then at least I will be alive to feel it.'

Raven entered in time to see a timid-looking woman making for the door, Sheldrake pursuing her with a pleading expression. Raven had facilitated her exit by holding the door open – not, he realised, the most judicious prelude to announcing himself.

'Mr Sheldrake, my name is Dr Will Raven. I am assistant to— '

'Dr Simpson, I know. We've met.'

Raven had been unsure whether Sheldrake would recognise him, as guests at Simpson's soirées did not always remember the evening's lesser players. Evidently Raven had not left an impression for the right reasons, for Sheldrake's tone was far from welcoming. He vaguely recalled a disagreement, Sheldrake objecting not so much to the substance of Raven's argument as to Raven having the temerity to take a contrary position at all.

'What do you want?' Sheldrake asked.

Raven understood this was not the opportune time to honestly answer that question and opted to defer for a moment.

'What troubles your departing patient?' he asked.

Sheldrake rolled his eyes to the heavens. 'Physically, very little. The rotten tooth that pains her could be easily extracted – it's already loose – but she has always been an anxious type. In the past she has willingly submitted to anaesthesia but it appears she has been reading hysterical nonsense about chloroform being dangerous, and nothing I say can persuade her otherwise. You know how it is once women get a notion in their heads. But what makes it worse is that she has also been hearing about some American mesmerist, a Dr Malham. You know of him?'

'Indeed. I have a friend who is under his tutelage.'

'You give it some credence, then?' Sheldrake asked.

'Good God, no,' Raven replied, eager to ingratiate himself, though he felt uncomfortably disloyal disparaging Sarah's enthusiasm.

'If Mrs Aubrey is to be believed, on stage at the Assembly Rooms, Malham cured everything from morbus cordis to tuberculosis, then made a lame man walk as an encore.'

Raven scoffed for Sheldrake's benefit, though his thoughts turned to what he had heard about Sarah's impressive feat at her mesmerism demonstration. He had privately speculated whether the patient might have been a fake, planted there by Dr Malham to dupe not only the observers, but Sarah too. However, it transpired that the man Jameson had been seen by other doctors in the city and his complaint had been genuine. He was now reportedly walking with greater ease.

'Surely she does not believe Malham can cure her toothache?' Raven asked.

'She does at least understand that the tooth is rotten. But she wants me to engage this Dr Malham to mesmerise her for the procedure because that would be safer than chloroform. It is intolerable. Even if I did not consider mesmerism to be poppycock, I would not be able to entertain such a notion, as it now seems half the city is in search of Malham's services.'

Sheldrake gazed out of the window and sighed, perhaps watching his patient and her fee disappearing up Dublin Street.

'Anyway, what can I do for you?' he asked.

'It is a matter regarding a dental plate of your construction.'

'You require one to be made?'

'No. It concerns one you made already.'

Raven produced the fragment, offering it to Sheldrake. He took it and held it briefly up to the light of the window.

'Yes, this is my work, most definitely,' he said. 'Who did you say it belonged to?'

'I didn't. That is what I am trying to ascertain. This is all I have to go on. It belonged to a man, that's as much as I can be sure of.'

'And what became of him?'

'You are aware of the recent murders in the city? The remains found at Greyfriars and in Surgeons' Hall?'

Sheldrake stared at the object again, as though it had been transformed into something altogether less benign.

'Good God.'

'Henry Littlejohn suggested you might be able to identify the patient from your moulds.'

'I should think so, yes.'

Sheldrake kept turning the plate in his hands, his expression changing from mild disgust to something more calculating.

'Do you have access to the moulds?' Raven asked. 'I mean, are they stored here in the surgery?'

Sheldrake handed back the plate and stood with his arms folded. It was not the stance of a man who was about to give Raven what he wanted. Not without getting something in return.

'You say you have a friend with a connection to this Dr Malham?'

Oh dear God, Raven thought, even as he nodded his affirmation.

'Then I can identify the owner of this plate just as soon as I am in possession of Mrs Aubrey's extracted tooth.'

A light drizzle began to fall as Raven climbed the steep slope of Dublin Street, the heavy clouds matching his own sense of gloom. It was as though Sheldrake had passed on his feelings of exasperation. Once again, the keys to progress in this matter were in Sarah's hands, but how could he persuade her to assist him? It was not merely a matter of apologising; he had enough practice with that for it not to be an impediment. More confoundingly, he needed to work out the riddle of what it was Sarah felt he needed to apologise for.

Even if he got past that, there was still the question of what Sheldrake expected. Raven doubted that even a co-operative Sarah could persuade Malham to assist in a dental extraction, given the waiting list to see him was growing all the time, as was no doubt the size of the fee he was commanding. Would Sheldrake expect

Raven to pay for that? The wisdom of such an expenditure gave him pause, which brought him to the biggest question, which was whether it would even work.

Then Raven realised why it would: Mrs Aubrey already believed that it did. That was the secret. Sheldrake had suggested that the extraction would not be particularly painful, so it was not that mesmerism needed to render her insensible to pain and trauma. It was simply a means of ensuring her co-operation. If mesmerism was what made Mrs Aubrey sit still and open her mouth for a procedure that would take a matter of seconds, it would have done its job.

Suddenly he saw what Sarah had tried to tell him, when he had been too pig-headed to listen: it didn't matter what mesmerism was, only what effect it had. He could see now that his attitude had not only been stubborn, but unscientific. Sarah had believed Raven would find any excuse not to witness her demonstration because he was refusing to engage with a proper examination of the practice.

Finally, he understood what it was he needed to apologise for.

FORTY-SIX

r Sheldrake was looking Sarah up and down in that nakedly evaluating manner to which certain men felt they were entitled, as though she were an item on the butcher's counter, or perhaps a farm animal at auction. She suspected the final judgement would not be approving.

'You said you would get me Malham,' he said, addressing Raven as though she wasn't even there.

Mrs Aubrey was looking at her too, making no effort to hide her disappointment. Sarah wondered what promises Sheldrake had made the woman, or whether she had readily accepted the expedited and inconveniently early-morning appointment because of unrelenting pain in her mouth.

'The agreement was that I would provide a mesmerist,' Raven replied. 'This is Miss Fisher. She has been trained personally by none other than Dr Malham himself.'

Raven's tone was reverential, suggesting he was in awe of the man whose name he invoked, something Sarah knew was far from the truth. She was prepared to forgive him this deception, for her own scepticism of Malham was fast rising to meet his.

It was not the only thing she had been prepared to forgive, hence her co-operation here this morning. Though she said nothing to Raven, Sarah privately felt she had been a little unfair in not accepting his reason for missing her demonstration. In truth this was partly because Raven wasn't the only one angry with Kimble. She blamed the man for the upset he had caused in the Simpson household and may have been tempted to punch him herself had the opportunity arisen in the days after the séance took place. Mostly, however, she had forgiven Raven because she knew she needed him on her side.

Given the exaggerated reports she was hearing about what she witnessed at the Assembly Rooms, she was beginning to harbour doubts regarding Malham's intentions and the consequences for the reputation of mesmerism. Admittedly it was not Malham who was making outlandish claims for the power of what he practised, but she knew his showmanship had been designed to encourage others to make them on his behalf. If Malham was indeed a charlatan, then she could not think of anyone who would put more effort into proving it than Raven. The only problem she had foreseen was how insufferable he was likely to be about it, but happily he had been the one who came cap-in-hand to her.

Mrs Aubrey looked markedly unimpressed, though it was Sheldrake to whom she directed her disappointment. He, after all, was the one who would be charging her a substantial fee.

'I wish to be mesmerised by Dr Malham alone,' she told him.

Sheldrake was straining to mask his frustration, but Sarah knew Raven would be sharing it if the dentist did not get what he wanted.

'I completely understand, Mrs Aubrey,' Sarah told her brightly. 'Why settle for the student when you can have the master? I will make a referral for you directly. I believe the first available appointment is three weeks hence.'

It was as though these words precipitated a twinge in the rotten tooth. Mrs Aubrey put a hand to her jaw and looked at Sarah enquiringly.

'Trained personally by Dr Malham, you say?'

It took Sarah considerably longer to induce a trance than for Mr Sheldrake to pull her tooth. Sarah flinched as she watched him grip it and tug, waiting for the cries and fury.

Mrs Aubrey's eyes did immediately open as the tooth came free, but her expression was of immediate relief. Mesmerism had done its job.

As soon as she had departed, Raven presented Sheldrake with the broken plate, which he accepted with a degree of satisfaction, a man who knew he had gotten the better part of a deal.

'Do you construct many such plates?' Sarah asked him, wondering how long he would be rooting through moulds and how confident they could be in his identification.

'Not many, no,' Sheldrake replied. 'This kind of work is far from cheap, and there are only two types of people prepared to go to that level of expense: those to whom the money matters little, and those to whom their appearance matters a great deal.'

Sheldrake was rooting through a wall press, taking out moulds and placing them on a broad table next to the chair recently vacated by Mrs Aubrey.

'It has been suggested that, as the victim was Lydia Butters' lover, he might be another actor,' Raven said. 'Would that narrow it down?'

'It would indeed,' Sheldrake replied, though his expression turned sour, like he had bitten into something unpleasant. 'I did make a plate for an actor some years ago. Not an individual one would wish to be associated with these days. Let me try that one first.'

Sheldrake selected one of the moulds in front of him, carefully lowering the fragment onto it.

The dentist frowned as it slotted into place.

'Indeed, as I suspected.'

'It is a match?'

'Yes. Though perhaps not the answer you were looking for.'

'How so? Who does the mould belong to?'

Sheldrake turned it over so that a name was visible on the underside.

'Laurence Butters.'

FORTY-SEVEN

o we have been looking at this entirely the wrong way,' Sarah said, striving to match Raven's stride as they ascended towards Queen Street. His pace indicated an appetite, for neither of them had eaten yet today. 'We have been thinking that Butters was the perpetrator when in fact he was the victim all along.'

Raven nodded in agreement. 'Someone murdered Butters and most likely killed his wife too, perhaps because of what she had witnessed.'

It was a shocking reversal and yet now that she knew it, it seemed staggering that they had not seen it before.

'We must send McLevy a message,' Raven said. 'Though he will not be pleased. We have wasted days looking for the wrong man and the wrong motive. We've been asking ourselves who Butters wished to harm, when in fact the question should have been who wished harm upon Butters.'

'Or his wife,' Sarah suggested. 'Let's make no assumptions there either. How did we all miss this?'

'Most of the time, the simplest explanation is the most likely. Sadly, a great many men murder their wives, and Lydia was found first. It was a reasonable deduction to make. And Butters' clothes were removed from his home, to make us think he had taken them when he ran from his crime.'

'But he was seen,' Sarah said. 'Multiple witnesses reported sighting him around Edinburgh.'

'That's true,' Raven acknowledged. 'As McLevy keeps pointing out, the man of a thousand faces and supposed master of disguise kept being spotted. But if there is one thing that I have learned in recent days, it is that the eye can be tricked, and that people can see what's been suggested to them. Once the story got around and everyone was on the look-out for Butters, then Butters is who they saw.'

They returned to 52 Queen Street in time for breakfast ahead of the morning clinic. The house felt unsettlingly quiet with the family absent, especially at mealtimes. Sarah could not remember the last time Dr Simpson had taken such a trip without a sick patient waiting at the end of it.

She entered the dining room to find Raven already seated at the table. A newspaper was spread out in front of him, but he seemed more intent upon draping a napkin over the salt cellar. He was placing his hand down tentatively on it but then pushed it away when he became aware of Sarah's presence. He held up the teapot.

'Would you like some?'

Sarah nodded then took a seat.

'Don't you ever have breakfast at home?' she asked.

He looked at her, a slight frown replacing his smile. 'I much prefer my first meal of the day to be taken in relative peace,' he replied. 'And I know that Mrs Lyndsay dislikes it when there is no one here to appreciate her cooking.'

Sarah took a sip of her tea. 'How is Eugenie?'

'Huge. Tired. Keen to be delivered of her burden.'

'It must be soon now.'

Raven leaned forward to grab a piece of toast. 'Imminent.'

Lizzie bundled into the room bearing a tray with dishes of scrambled eggs and sausages. She placed it onto the table and then looked at the pair of them, shaking her head.

'There's too much for just the two of you,' she said.

'Let me be the judge of that,' Raven replied. 'I've hardly eaten anything these past few days and find that I'm ravenous this morning.'

Lizzie tutted and left the room. Sarah speared a sausage and spooned some egg onto her plate.

'Can you pass the salt or is its positioning part of some experiment?' she asked.

Raven handed her the salt cellar.

'Thank you. What exactly were you doing with it?'

Raven swallowed and wiped his mouth with his napkin.

'I visited Kimble again,' he said softly, spoken like an admission.

'Again?'

'I was passing and thought that I ought to check up on him.'

Sarah took another sip of her tea. 'I realise your intentions towards him are noble,' she said. 'But you will understand if I remain a little conflicted, given the pain he caused in this very room.'

Raven looked at her, his face grave. 'Kimble is in more pain than anyone in this household,' he said. He picked up the salt cellar and turned it over in his hand. 'He showed me a trick. He said he would make a coin disappear. He draped a napkin over a salt cellar, placed them both over the coin, then drove his palm down hard onto them. When he lifted the napkin, both the salt cellar and the coin had disappeared. This happened not on a stage but two feet in front of me.'

'Did he tell you how it was done?'

'He told me there's more value in me learning to work out these things for myself. I suspect that applies to how he knew certain secrets about me and about this household, because he did own that it was trickery.'

'He admitted as much?'

'He confided in me,' Raven said, putting the salt cellar down beside the matching mustard pot. 'He lost his son to cholera and started to drink. As a result, he lost his wife and his career. He was a magician, but he turned his hand to mediumship. It is a dishonourable inverse of conjuring: convincing the vulnerable that his tricks are real, and his illusions mean something deeper.'

'He is not the only one doing that,' Sarah said.

'Do you mean Malham?' he asked, surprised at her apostasy.

'I do. And if you even think about saying I told you so, I will skewer you with this fork.'

Raven held up his hands in a gesture of compliance and Sarah proceeded to describe all that she had witnessed at the Assembly Rooms.

'He did the same thing Kimble did in this room,' she added, 'divining information that he could not possibly deduce from observation alone. No real therapy was demonstrated, but the audience, in their amazement at his diagnoses, ascribed the power of cure to mere trances. I realise you must think me a fool. You were sceptical from the start and now you are vindicated.'

'I disagree,' Raven replied. He placed his hand on hers and squeezed it. 'We are approaching this from different directions but we have the same intention: to find what is genuine, what might be valuable about mesmerism and separate it from charlatanry.'

Sarah withdrew her hand and busied herself pouring them both more tea.

'It was my enthusiasm for the possibilities of mesmerism that made me vulnerable to falling under Malham's spell,' she said. 'But that spell is well and truly broken.'

'I realise this must be painful for you,' Raven told her. 'I am given to understand that you and Malham were becoming close.'

Sarah hastened to clarify. 'I have been instructed by him, and I may have been impressed by him, but no more than that.'

'I see. It's just that Henry told me you were seen in the company of a smartly dressed man, and I assumed— '

'Oh, that wasn't Malham.'

Too late, Sarah realised her response had told him more than she intended.

'Who, then?'

Sarah felt herself blush. 'It must have been Mr Somerville. I suppose I have been in his company rather a lot recently. He is a . . .' She wasn't sure how to put it. A businessman? A property owner? 'He is in the process of purchasing Milton House. He has an arrangement with Malham. They are going into partnership to create a mesmeric institute.'

'Somerville?' Raven said. 'I don't believe I've had the pleasure. Are you . . . well acquainted?'

'I think we are becoming friends. He is a widower, so we have that in common. And we both know what it is to be struggling against those determined not to open their doors to the wrong sort. I think you'd like him. There is much about him that reminds me of you.'

Sarah sat back in her chair, watching Raven's face, assessing his reaction.

'I'm not sure that constitutes a commendation,' he said.

'I simply mean he is endeavouring to rise above his humble beginnings.'

Sarah picked up her cup and stared into the amber liquid. 'I'm concerned about Malham,' she said, happy to get away from the previous subject. 'He has made himself the centre of mesmerism in this city and I realise that I know very little about him. Why is he here? Why is he not demonstrating these remarkable talents in New York? Or Boston? I need to understand how he knew those things and diagnosed those patients. If I can deduce that much, then I can distinguish it from mesmerism, and perhaps mitigate some of the damage he has done.'

'As you suggest, it's probably the same trick as Kimble did here. Kimble dresses it up as talking to the spirits. Malham talks about the garden of sleep: mesmerism is merely the cloak Malham puts around the same thing.'

'But how did he do it?' Sarah asked.

'I wish I knew. Dr Simpson saw through the tricks Kimble did onstage, but what he effected here in this house was something different.'

'What did he do at the Adelphi?'

'Oh, just some nonsense with cards and envelopes. There was also a strange business whereby he was locked in a cabinet and yet some musical instruments appeared to play themselves. That was obvious, in that the whole thing took place in the dark, so some unseen confederate was working with him. But how Kimble knew the things he did about this family, that's a harder thing to explain.'

As Raven said this, Mrs Lyndsay came in. She looked askance at the food that had not been eaten and began to clear the table.

'There's a simple enough explanation, if you ask me,' Mrs Lyndsay said, indicating that she had overheard, as she so often did. 'But it's one that most people are reluctant to accept.'

'And what would that be?' Raven asked.

Mrs Lyndsay shrugged, as though the answer should be obvious. 'The dead speak to Kimble, and he listens. He sensed the children that used to be here, same as he sensed my Arthur, God rest him. He knew Arthur was close by me and kindly acted as a conduit, letting him communicate with me from the other side.'

'When was this?' Sarah asked.

'It was the day he first came here. You remember? He made a scene in the hallway, shouting at Dr Simpson, and the professor being the kindly man that he is, recognised a soul in distress and asked Jarvis to bring him to the kitchen for a bit of breakfast.'

'I think it was his partaking of a liquid breakfast that caused the trouble in the first place,' Raven said.

Mrs Lyndsay ignored Raven's interjection.

'We got talking and he said he felt something right away. It was amazing, the things he knew about my Arthur.'

'Was that all you talked about?' Sarah asked.

'Oh, we talked about all sorts. Such a kind man, most solicitous. The time quite ran away from us.'

Raven and Sarah shared a look.

They said nothing until Mrs Lyndsay left.

'She knows everything that goes on in this house,' Sarah said. 'She is a repository of knowledge about all that has happened in this family.'

Raven nodded sagely. 'Once Dr Simpson had agreed to the séance, Kimble set about finding out the information he would need,' he said. 'The illnesses, the nicknames. Malham's information could have been procured in the same way. Because although at the time what they each said seemed remarkable, in the cold light of day it was remarkable only that they knew it.'

FORTY-EIGHT

Dr Christie greeted Raven with an unexpectedly eager look; one might even say he appeared welcoming as he marched towards him down the corridor, the man's shoes clack-clacking upon the tiles. Raven knew it would not last. Christie clearly assumed he was here to talk about a different matter, and he couldn't tell him what he wanted to hear regarding that either.

It did not take long for Christie to interpret Raven's grim expression.

'Is this concerning the murders?'

'I'm afraid so, sir.'

Having informed McLevy of what Sheldrake was able to tell him, Raven had decided to get another unpleasant errand done while he was in this part of the town. Little as he relished the task, he knew it would be worse should Christie learn of the news from someone else first.

'The second victim has been identified as Laurence Butters.'

Christie's thin, gaunt face turned even more grey than usual as the cogs turned in his head. He knew that while Butters was believed the murderer, the connection to Surgeons' Hall remained remote; now all possibilities were back on the table.

'And have you any other news? How is the health of the large specimen we discussed?'

'I will let you know as soon as is appropriate,' Raven replied.

Though Raven had tried to disguise it, Christie detected the note of conflict in his tone.

'I would not have thought you squeamish about such things, Dr Raven. Perhaps it is fortunate then that there exists the lesser discipline of man-midwife for those lacking the fortitude to be surgeons.'

Raven bridled at the insult. 'If I exhibited discomfort, it is in listening to the eagerness with which you anticipate the death of a fellow human being.'

Christie sneered. 'My anticipation is entirely centred on what we might learn from anatomising a remarkable corpse. And I object to the implication that I have anything less than respect for this man. Indeed, I will endeavour to ensure that the knowledge gleaned will prove a lasting monument to him.'

Raven knew who was more likely to be memorialised should Gregor's wishes be ignored. That was the only monument Christie was interested in.

Having delivered his news to Christie, Raven proceeded to the university, seeking a second audience with Professor Lewis. As Kimble had pointed out, if you were trying to unlock a deception, you had to revisit the same information from a different perspective. This time he was directed to a small theatre on South College Street behind the main college buildings.

There were several students in costume on the stage, with Lewis seated alone in the auditorium as he trained an eye upon proceedings.

Raven glanced around the theatre. It was small compared to the Adelphi or the Theatre Royal and lacked the ornamentation of the other two.

Raven sat down beside Lewis, who looked immediately wary.

'Does this place belong to the university?' Raven asked.

Lewis paused as though trying to decide whether it was wise to answer any more of Raven's questions, then said, 'We are renting it from a Mr Somerville.'

Raven's surprise gave him away.

'You know him?' Lewis asked.

'Only through a friend. We have not met.'

Raven was still trying to process the news that Sarah was becoming close to another man. He wasn't sure he believed it was purely friendship. Although initially relieved that it wasn't Malham, that relief had now been replaced by concern about who this Somerville was.

He was torn, though. Raven had a duty to protect her, as he had promised her late husband Archie. But that did not mean every man Sarah associated with ought to be disapproved of. She deserved more supportive behaviour from him than that.

'What is this Somerville like?' Raven asked. 'What age is he?'

'Older than you, younger than me. Smartly dressed. Not exactly flamboyant but handsome enough. Exquisite tailoring. Looked like Gethyn's work, so he has some taste.'

'And what of his manner?'

'He drives a hard bargain. I offered him a split of the takings, but he insisted on payment in advance: a flat-rate minimum and a share on top. We'll be lucky to break even, but we don't do it for the money.'

Somerville was evidently a lot cannier than Flint had been in venturing into this business. In the latter's inexperience, he had been foolish enough to agree to a split with Butters, a share that had never materialised and now never would.

'Are you planning a show, Dr Raven? Is that what you came to ask me about?' There was a weary note in Lewis's voice, emphasising how unlikely this was. 'Or is it perhaps something else that has brought you here today?'

'I understand the Byron quote now,' Raven said. 'What it implied about Laurence Butters and his marriage. And I understand why you chose to convey the information with such subtlety and discretion.'

A moment of acknowledgement passed between them.

'You will therefore understand,' replied Lewis, 'why I must not betray certain confidences. But if you still seek to identify Butters' second victim, give me a name and I might be able to tell you whether he moved in particular company.'

'I have a name,' Raven said. 'Laurence Butters.'

Lewis's reaction was much the same as Raven's own, and indeed Sarah's, Henry's and McLevy's: a shocked surprise followed by a dawning inevitability.

'Someone has deceived us all,' Lewis said.

'I need to know who would have wanted Laurence Butters dead. Who he might have associated with. When was the last time you spoke to him?'

'I last saw Laurence a few days before . . . his death.' Lewis paused, sadness in his face as it dawned on him that his acquaintance was no longer merely a fugitive but gone for good. 'We had a drink in the Red Lion Hotel on Shakespeare Square, behind the Theatre Royal.'

'Was there anything odd about him? Anything troubling him?'

Lewis shifted in his seat. 'He told me he'd seen a dead man.'

Raven's eyes widened, wondering why Lewis had omitted this before.

'I didn't think much of it at the time,' he went on. 'Laurence was given to hyperbole and liked to be mysterious and elliptical. He knew how to keep an audience in his grip. Even if it was an audience of one.'

'What did he mean by it? That he had seen a ghost?'

'He would not elaborate, but had he seen a ghost I would expect him to seem more alarmed. He struck me as a man enjoying a secret.'

Raven paused for a moment, trying to work out what Butters might have been alluding to, then said, 'If I were to ask you to speculate, in the light of everything that we now know, what would you guess he meant?'

Lewis made a dismissive gesture. 'I will not encourage any investigation that leads to men of certain appetites being placed under scrutiny and accusation.'

'It's too late for that,' Raven replied. 'McLevy knows about Butters' appetites now. If you don't want him charging around asking awkward questions, the best thing you can do is help me end the investigation sooner rather than later.'

Lewis sighed, knowing Raven was right.

'Laurence seemed pleased, as though seeing this dead man heralded an upturn in his fortunes. And by a dead man, I suspect what he meant was someone who had reinvented himself. Someone with certain proclivities, who had put that part of his life behind him. Butters would have had the power of information over him, and if I were to speculate, as you put it, it would be that Butters was expecting to be well paid to keep his secret.'

'But whoever it was found a cheaper and surer way of silencing him,' Raven said. 'Any notion who might that be?'

'If it was someone from his past, my guess would be another actor, or former actor. A gentleman who now works in a different field and might have much to lose from such a disclosure.'

'The men you allude to are drawn from circles wider than the theatre, surely,' Raven said.

'Yes, but you are looking for someone who understands the power of artifice. We were all deceived because this man posed as Butters after his death.'

Raven now knew why the master of disguise kept being seen. The killer wanted him to be. Butters' clothes had been taken not just to make it look like he had packed a bag for his escape. Barrington had mentioned the distinctive garment Butters had worn.

Suddenly Raven understood Kimble's salt-cellar trick because this illusion worked by the same principle. For the napkin, one had only to substitute Butters' jacket. The illusion was not in making something disappear: it was in making the observer believe it was still there when it had already gone.

FORTY-NINE

arah finally found a quiet moment to sit down. She slipped off her shoes and rubbed her tired feet. She had been at the association offices all afternoon, assessing and mesmerising some of the patients who had queued for hours waiting to be seen. It was satisfying work, as most of those she had treated appeared to experience some immediate benefit regardless of the nature of their complaint. The problem was the time required for each treatment. It was a lengthy process.

There was a gentle rap at the door and Malham came in. Sarah slipped her feet back into her shoes and tried to appear relaxed. Having decided that she did not trust his motives, she found it difficult to be in his presence for fear that her feelings were somehow conspicuous.

Fortunately, Malham seemed oblivious.

'What a day,' he said, clearly delighted. 'I've had to turn people away, told them to come back tomorrow. The move to the new premises can't come soon enough.'

'We're going to need more mesmerists,' Sarah replied.

'We will have to accelerate your training, Miss Fisher. You will soon be required to instruct others in the art of mesmerism as well as treating patients. I am going to need your full attention, your complete commitment to the institute.'

'What do you mean?'

'I mean that you must work for the institute to the exclusion of all else.'

'Leave Queen Street?'

Malham looked directly at her. 'What we are doing here is nothing short of revolutionary. We are shaking the very tenets of medicine to their core. We will have the pill-mongers quaking in their boots.'

To Sarah's ears this sounded like an ill-advised declaration of war.

'Surely mesmerism complements rather than replaces other forms of medical practice,' she suggested.

Malham laughed. 'My dear Miss Fisher. We have barely scratched the surface. There is still so much that mesmerism can achieve.'

Sarah wasn't sure what he meant by that, but it had her worried.

'You would abandon conventional practice entirely?'

'I wish to concentrate on the most effective method of producing a cure. I care little for conventional wisdom or what my fellow medical practitioners may think of me.'

'Did you struggle to have your treatments accepted in America? Is that why you came here?'

Malham looked troubled at this. He quickly regained his composure but Sarah had seen enough to suspect there must be a story behind that reaction.

'Edinburgh medicine is renowned the world over,' he said. 'If I can succeed here, I can succeed anywhere.'

'True enough,' Sarah said, though she noted that he had not answered her question.

Malham took his watch out of his pocket. 'The evening is almost upon us, and I have much to do. Divest yourself of all else, Miss Fisher. Mesmerism is clearly the future for both of us.'

I'll be the judge of that, thought Sarah as he swept from the room.

★

Sarah stood at the window and watched Malham stride down Potter Row. She lifted her jacket from the peg and made her way towards the stairs, keen to get back to Queen Street. Did Malham really expect her to cast Dr Simpson aside and devote herself entirely to mesmerism? He was a fool if he thought that was the case.

She passed Malham's office, the door still wide open. She spotted a ledger on his desk, the one that Mr Somerville took to every demonstration containing details of the patients who had expressed an interest in being treated, as well as those who had been mesmerised.

Sarah stood at the top of the stairs and listened. All was quiet.

She turned and made her way back to Malham's office, where she stood over the open ledger and listened again for any noise in the building. There was none, so she let her finger run down the list of the most recent entries. She could see nothing untoward, just the names of those treated that day. She flipped back several pages and something caught her eye: not the names of the patients but the diagnoses noted down beside them.

Bronchial complaint. Heart disease. Broken leg. She recognised the symptoms of the patients who had been picked out by Malham at the Assembly Rooms, but they had been listed in the ledger before the demonstration took place. Evidently they had been present on previous occasions and had given their details at the end. Their names, addresses and the nature of their complaints were all written down.

Sarah became aware of a presence and looked up. Gethyn was standing in the doorway.

'What are you doing?' he asked, his tone accusatory.

'I'm just checking that the details of my last patient were correctly entered into the ledger,' she said, smiling at him.

Gethyn did not look appeased. She knew that he did not like her. Resented her in fact. He had been taught the basics of mesmeric technique by Malham, but even with the institute becoming so busy, he had not been entrusted with treating any patients yet. He seemed envious of Sarah's success and of Malham's obvious interest in her.

She closed the ledger and stepped out from behind the desk.

'Good day, Mr Gethyn,' she said as she passed him, still hovering menacingly in the doorway. He grunted something incomprehensible in reply.

Sarah made her way down the stairs, worried that he might follow her. She was looking behind as she approached the front door, which was why she almost collided with Mr Somerville on his way in.

'What's the hurry? Is there a fire?' he asked. He smiled at her, obviously in a much better mood than Gethyn.

'I'm running a little late, that's all.'

She looked over her shoulder again but there was no one there.

'Then allow me to escort you. I'm in no particular hurry myself.'

Though the prospect of some time spent in Somerville's company was a pleasant one, Sarah knew she needed to be alone for what she had in mind.

'That is kind of you, but I have some errands to run.'

Somerville accepted her excuse without protest. 'I hear the place has been busy today,' he said. 'The result of Harland's performance at the Assembly Rooms, no doubt. It all augurs well for our move to the new institute, don't you think?'

'Indeed.'

'The timing could not be better. I have just now concluded the purchase of Milton House.'

'Dr Malham certainly knows how to generate interest.'

'It is most fortunate that our paths crossed when they did,' Somerville replied.

'And yet it is surprising that someone so remarkable should forsake New York or Boston for Edinburgh.'

Somerville seemed happy to disregard this. 'Edinburgh's medical reputation goes before it,' he contended.

'Yes, but Edinburgh's population is relatively small. Surely there is more money to be made, larger crowds to attract in bigger cities.'

He looked at her closely for a moment. 'What is your concern?'

'Did the Assembly Rooms display strike you as odd in any way?'

'Odd? I would have said mysterious and inexplicable. Hence it is the talk of the town.'

'But medicine is seldom made a spectacle,' Sarah informed him.

'Dr Malham has a talent for showmanship,' Somerville said. 'I will admit that much. And I know the stuffed shirts over here might find that rather vulgar, but Americans are simply more direct about selling themselves. To me, that's no bad thing.'

'Yes, but where does the medicine end and showmanship begin? The boundaries are becoming blurred, and you are making a great investment on the basis of what one man can bring to this practice, to this phenomenon of mesmerism. If this man is not quite what he seems, what would that mean for you?'

Somerville smiled at her, as though there was some secret she was missing.

'I appreciate your concern for me, Miss Fisher. But you have no reason to worry on my behalf. As I told you before, it is the property that matters. If the circus should move on, and the interest in mesmerism proves a passing fad, a building can always be turned to another purpose. I got where I am today by making sure everyone who owes me understands that I expect a return on my investments. Those who didn't pay me back – and they were precious few – did so because they died before they could make good on their debts.'

s Raven left the little theatre, he spotted a distinctive figure ahead of him on Nicolson Street. It was a shape he had once been permanently on the lookout for, a looming presence that in the past would have seen him dart into the nearest doorway. Now, recognising Gregor triggered a different response. People stopped to look at him as he went past, perhaps no longer entirely because of his size, but because he looked in danger of imminent collapse. He was struggling, steadying himself with a hand on the wall every few paces. This remarkable individual who had once struck terror into those who beheld his great frame was now a pitiable creature.

Raven could not say that Gregor was a good man, but he was not sure he could say that of himself either. Though no one could call Gregor a gentle giant, he had on occasion shown tenderness and concern. And he had once shaken Raven from his own moral cowardice, pressing him to visit the most difficult kindness by ending the life of a suffering man.

Undoubtedly Gregor had done good things. He had saved Raven from harm, and he had saved Sarah's life. Most of all, he had taught Raven that even those who first appeared to be monsters were complex creatures. That the layers beneath the skin of every man could never be judged by appearance alone.

Gregor had paused again at the entrance to the York Hotel,

allowing Raven to catch up with him. He was carrying a bottle, a bag and a loaf wrapped in paper.

'That looks an expensive bottle of whisky, Gregor,' Raven said.

The giant looked down at him and smiled. 'Aye. I have become so much wealthier of late.'

'How so?'

'Well, if the definition of a rich man is someone who could not spend all his money in a lifetime, then I have become rich. When you are buying what may be your last bottle of whisky, you can afford to be extravagant.'

Raven was about to dispute this, but Gregor stopped him.

'Do not lie to me and tell me I have years yet, Doctor.'

Raven nodded. There was little point in denying what was obvious to both of them. There had been several occasions over the previous few years when Raven had thought that Gregor's time had come, but the man always seemed to defy expectations. That was until now. It was quite clear that there would be no further reprieves.

'Fair enough,' Raven said. 'At least let me carry your bag for you. I'll escort you home.'

'I am not bound for home,' Gregor said. 'It is a pleasant afternoon. I am going to sit beneath a tree and enjoy the air while I still can.'

He lumbered off in the direction of Nicolson Square, Raven at his side. As they entered the gardens, everyone else seemed in a hurry to leave, so there was no difficulty finding somewhere to sit. Gregor lowered himself gently onto a bench and let out a long sigh. Their slow progress along Nicolson Street had left him breathless.

Gregor waited a few minutes until his breathing had slowed, then uncorked the bottle with his ruinous teeth. He spat out the stopper, heedless of where it fell. Raven took this as an indication that he had no intention of recorking it.

Gregor took a swig of the whisky then offered it to Raven.

'That is kind of you, Gregor, but I must decline. I have much to do. Need to keep a clear head.'

Gregor took another swig and then wiped his mouth on his sleeve.

'I see McLevy's getting desperate,' he said, putting the bottle down and producing a pamphlet from his pocket.

Raven took a look at it, already fearing the worst.

'It says that McLevy's been consulting with psychics,' Gregor said, amused. 'Someone called Malham. Hoping his gift of second sight might shed light on the Laurence Butters murders.'

Sarah had mentioned this, although she implied that McLevy had exhibited a certain reluctance and was adamant no one should find out.

'God help us,' Raven said. 'There will be hell to pay when McLevy sees that. I wonder how Sanderson found out about it.'

'I'm guessing from what the Hoolet says that the detective has yet to find Laurence Butters.'

'Oh, we've found him,' Raven said. 'And as this information is likely to be in a pamphlet soon enough, I may as well tell you: Butters is dead. He was dead when you first went to his door. Someone – the person who killed him, presumably – made it appear that he was still alive.'

'Flint won't be getting his money then,' Gregor reasoned. 'I would like to have found him. I don't like leaving a job unfinished.'

'I imagine Flint will be more disappointed than you.'

'I don't know about that. The last time we spoke he didn't seem too troubled. I got the impression he has bigger matters to contend with, and funds coming in from other sources.'

'You saw him recently?'

'He came to visit. Brought me a bottle and some cured ham.'

Gregor noted Raven's surprise.

'Flint remembers who his friends are,' he explained. 'I know you would find it hard to believe anything good about him, but he has always done right by me. You would do well to remember that. He is a dangerous enemy but he's loyal too, honourable in ways many people would not understand.'

Raven found all this rather difficult to hear, but he could

not judge Flint for his intentions without judging himself for his own.

Gregor took another glug of whisky and then fell into a fit of coughing. He really was not long for this world.

Looking at him suffer and slowly deteriorate, Raven felt something more than pity: he felt guilt and shame. It was far easier to rationalise Gregor's wishes when he was out of sight, an idea rather than a flesh-and-blood man.

Raven could not lie to himself. If he went through with the plan he had concocted with Christie, he was no better than the body-snatchers: selling someone's remains against their express wishes.

He thought again of what was called the resurrectionist's price and realised that it was not one he was willing to pay merely to finance his practice. Nor could he found his future upon something so dishonourable. It would be like building a house on cursed ground, or upon a plague pit. No matter how well he built it and how long it stood, he would always be shamed by the knowledge of what lay beneath his feet.

He knew this change of heart would make an enemy of Flint, but he had been an enemy of Flint before. Of more concern was that it would also make an enemy of Christie. That was something he had to accept, however, because Raven's justification for selling Gregor was a lie that he could no longer tell himself. It didn't matter that once he was dead Gregor would never know what happened to his remains. What mattered was that Raven would *always* know.

'Flint was in very good fettle, when last I saw him,' Gregor continued. 'Unusually so. I think he's seeing a lady.'

'Presumably without his wife finding out. Or has she been forced to accept that as part of the arrangement?'

Gregor looked confused. 'His wife? She died years ago.'

'But I met with him only last week, and when I asked about his wife, he said she was thriving.'

Gregor shook his vast head. 'Flint doesn't like to look weak.

He didn't want to invite your pity. He's very mindful of how he is perceived, especially these days.'

'What do you mean?'

Gregor considered his answer.

'Maybe it's just because he knows I won't live to tell, or that I know nobody worth telling, but Flint has confided in me. He isn't merely going up in the world. He has made himself anew, cutting ties with his past. To those finer people in whose company he now moves, he is not presenting himself as Callum Flint.'

'Then what is he calling himself?' Raven asked, but even before Gregor answered, an awful realisation began to dawn, all of the disparate clues he failed to notice assembling themselves before his eyes.

'He has taken his late mother's name,' Gregor said. 'Somerville.'

Raven felt as though a void had opened beneath his feet.

'Are you alright, Dr Raven? You've gone a bit peely-wally.'

Raven reached for the whisky bottle.

'I think I need a drink,' he said.

FIFTY-ONE

arah made her way to the New Town, reciting the names and addresses from the ledger so that she wouldn't forget them. She had not had the chance to write anything down before Gethyn's inquisitive interruption. That man really did make her feel uneasy in precisely the way Somerville made her feel calm.

As she crossed St Andrew Square, she felt the hairs rise on the back of her neck. She had the unmistakable sense that she was being watched. She stopped and looked around but couldn't see anything; just strangers going about their business. She counselled herself that this fear was simply because she was doing something surreptitious, indirectly spying on Malham.

Trying to think about things rationally, she knew that Malham was nowhere near here, and even if he was, he could not possibly know her purpose. However, if her suspicions were correct and he was to spot her going into one of the addresses on her list, he would immediately understand what she was about.

Then she really might have reason to worry.

Sarah approached a townhouse on Northumberland Street and pulled the bell, hoping that Betsy still worked here. Betsy was someone she knew from her own days as a housemaid, when they would run into each other in shops and on errands. She had chosen this address for that reason. It would be easier to get what she wanted from someone familiar.

'Sarah! To what do we owe the honour?'

Betsy had changed little in the time since Sarah had last seen her. She was fresh-faced and rounded, which might give the impression she dined well and spent much of the time in the fresh air, but neither of these was likely to be the case. Although she had never met him, Sarah knew that Mr Cruikshank was a banker and liked to keep his money close. He was notoriously parsimonious when it came to feeding his staff.

'Did you wish to speak with the master?' Betsy asked.

Sarah smiled and shook her head. 'It's actually you I need to speak to, Betsy. Well, you and whoever else among the staff might be able to help.'

'Oh,' Betsy said, clearly surprised by this. 'What might you need help with?'

'There was a caller at Queen Street the other day, but the gentleman failed to leave his card. I have been given to understand that the same gentleman called in here.'

'Many people visit this house,' Betsy stated.

'Yes, but this would be an American gentleman. Finely dressed, very charming.'

The housemaid's eyes lit up. She clearly recognised the description.

'Yes, there was a gentleman,' she admitted, 'but I'm not supposed to . . .'

She became furtive, looking around as though she too might be being watched. She opened the door a little wider and indicated that Sarah should step inside.

She led Sarah to the kitchen, where there were more staff preparing the evening meal.

'Miss Fisher here is asking about the American gentleman,' Betsy announced to them.

They all paused what they were doing and looked at Sarah.

'It's alright,' Betsy said. 'Sarah is a good friend. She works for Dr Simpson.'

The professor's name had the usual emollient effect.

'There was an American came here,' the cook said.

That small piece of information earned her a severe look from the butler.

'We're not supposed to talk about it,' he said.

'Why? What happened?' Sarah asked.

'See, he came to the house when the master was not at home,' Betsy explained. 'But instead of simply leaving, Dr Malham offered to treat anyone who might benefit from the mesmerism. Agnes there suffers something terrible with the gout and he put her in a trance.'

'It made such a difference,' the cook said.

The butler sighed and shook his head, his attempts to ensure discretion apparently wasted.

'Dr Malham asked us to keep it a secret,' he said. 'That he had been in and treated some of us. He said the master might take issue with his ministering to the staff without his express permission.'

'Did Dr Malham ask about Mr Cruikshank's health?' Sarah asked.

'He did indeed,' Betsy admitted.

'And what did you tell him?'

'There wasn't much to tell,' Agnes interjected. 'The master is as fit as a flea.'

'It's true,' Betsy added. 'He'll outlast us all.'

Sarah was confused. The tuberculous man who had appeared on stage did not fit this description at all.

'It's just a pity,' said the butler, 'that the same cannot be said for his son.'

Sarah left the Cruikshank house more convinced than ever that Malham was not the man he claimed to be. There could be no question: Malham's amazing diagnostic abilities had a rational explanation. He used the same method as Kimble, which was that he had simply gone and asked. As Raven so succinctly put it, the information that had been revealed was not in itself remarkable, only that he should know it.

But what would she do with this knowledge? Who could she tell? Obviously it would be damaging to Malham, but he would not be the only casualty. Mesmerism itself could be dealt a mortal blow.

As she walked along the street, she again had the feeling that she was being watched. She chided herself for her fear. There was no reason to think that her activities would have given anyone cause for concern.

To reassure herself, she looked back. That was when she saw Gethyn. He dodged out of sight, but not fast enough.

He had been watching her, had seen her take an interest in the ledger and had followed her. He had seen her come out of the Cruikshank house.

She feared it might have been worse than being seen by Malham himself.

The words Malham said at the meeting came echoing back.

I sometimes worry about what lengths that man might go to on my behalf.

FIFTY-TWO

aven found himself at the front of the police office on the High Street with no recollection of having conveyed himself there. He wondered if this was what mesmerism felt like, his mind dissociated from his bodily functions. He had left Gregor to finish his whisky alone but felt numb and detached, as though he had drunk half the bottle himself. Maybe he had, but there wasn't enough whisky in Scotland to block out the enormity of what he had just learned.

He stood at the door and tried to marshal his thoughts. It was imperative that he share Lewis's revelations and discuss the implications for the case. There was still a murderer to be found. Everything else would have to wait.

He was directed to the police surgeon's room at the back of the building, where he found Henry and McLevy standing over a corpse.

Henry looked up as Raven entered, taking in his shocked expression and misinterpreting the cause. 'No need for alarm,' he said. 'This one's complete so I don't think it relates to the Butters murder.'

McLevy was grimacing. 'The smell off him would gag a tramp,' he said. 'I think he's been stewing in his own juices for quite some time.'

'Perhaps we could repair to your office, Mr McLevy,' Raven suggested. 'I have some news.'

As soon as they entered McLevy's office, his face became thunderous.

'I don't care what news you've got,' he said to Raven. 'You can get that shite out of here.'

Raven wondered at his sudden rage and then remembered that he was clutching Gregor's copy of the Hoolet pamphlet.

'I knew it was a bad idea,' McLevy continued, 'letting that man get involved. And there's no keeping a secret in this town.'

'You mean Malham?' Henry asked. 'Did he reveal anything of use?'

McLevy scoffed. 'His supposed psychic powers revealed absolutely nothing. And I'm fed up with people asking me about it.'

Henry held up his hands, indicating that he would probe no further, but McLevy had not finished. He pointed at the paper in Raven's hand.

'That arse-wad of a pamphlet suggests that Malham divined all kinds of obscure information, but he gave me nothing I did not already know.'

'I think that's his speciality,' Raven said. 'It's what he does on stage.'

'What do you mean by that exactly?' McLevy asked. 'How does he do it?'

'He gathers information. In some respects, he's as much a detective as you are, except that his trick is to pretend he knows nothing when he first walks into the room.'

'The sleekit bastard,' McLevy said, venom in his tone. 'So, the man's a fraud?'

'It would seem so,' Raven agreed. 'Although mesmerism or hypnosis, whatever you want to call it, does seem worthy of further investigation. But the rest of it . . .'

Henry looked at McLevy. 'Did you try the treatment yourself?'

'Mesmerism? No. I've been too busy with all this. And I certainly won't be trying it now.'

Raven realised why Sarah had been so concerned about Malham's behaviour. He thought about her success with Mr Jameson and the many uncharted pathways between mind and body. It was wrong that the potential benefits of this treatment were being obscured by Malham's behaviour. There was so much yet to be learned about the human body and the process of healing. Malham and quacks like him were muddying the waters, getting in the way.

'You claimed to have news,' McLevy grunted, impatient now.

'Do tell,' said Henry eagerly. 'You looked like you'd seen a ghost when you first came in.'

'Not a ghost, but Butters said he had seen a dead man.'

'What nonsense is this now?' McLevy spluttered.

'That's what he told Professor Lewis shortly before meeting his end. Lewis believes Butters was referring to someone who had reinvented himself to disguise who he really is. He reckoned Butters was intent on blackmailing this person: extorting money in exchange for silence about certain proclivities.'

'That would explain a sudden windfall,' Henry suggested.

'And he may have done it before,' Raven added. 'Butters had a history of coming into money and then spending like a king.'

'If that's the case then it's a surprise Butters didn't meet his end sooner,' McLevy said. 'It's a dangerous business, blackmail.' He rubbed his chin. 'Who could it be? Someone at Surgeons' Hall?'

'Possibly,' said Henry. 'But bear in mind we're dealing with someone who lacks medical training.'

'Sounds like a surgeon to me,' Raven said.

McLevy threw him a look.

'Let's try to think about this logically,' Henry continued. 'Going by what Professor Lewis said, we are looking for someone who has presented themselves anew. Someone to whom such a revelation would be damaging, and presumably someone no one would suspect.'

'Well, that doesn't exactly narrow things down,' McLevy grumbled.

'Lewis suggested it might be someone who'd once been an actor,' Raven said, 'due to the illusion whereby he made it appear Butters was still alive and roaming the streets of Edinburgh.

Someone who had taken Butters' distinctive jacket and worn it to create such an effect.'

'It worked too,' Henry said. 'We've wasted several days looking for someone who was already dead.'

McLevy fixed Henry with a glare indicating how much he appreciated being reminded of this, and growled his next remark.

'So, we are looking for someone who had presumably appeared on stage with Butters at some point and been his lover off it.'

The detective grabbed his hat and headed for the door. 'Looks like I'm off to the theatre,' he said. 'See yourselves out.'

They waited until the reverberations of his heavy footsteps had receded.

'Talking to McLevy is like handling explosives,' Raven said.

'You can never be sure what's going to set him off,' Henry agreed. 'But I detect there is more on your mind than Butters and McLevy. What's wrong?'

Raven briefly considered dissembling or denying, but Henry knew him too well.

It was hard to accept even as he heard the words spill from his own mouth, but Raven could now see the sense of it, all that he had missed. Flint and his new clothes. A man craving respectability. And what was so wrong with that?

He had always assumed that what Flint sought was notoriety, to keep his money-lending clients in tremulous fear, but really what he sought was acceptance, a seat at the high table.

There was a part of Raven that could not begrudge him that, given the divides and injustices of this city. Pursuing Sarah, however, that was beyond the pale. The thought of her in the arms of this violent, tempestuous man made him shudder.

But she had lain in Raven's arms, and he was a violent, tempestuous man too.

Sarah's words echoed in his mind.

He reminds me of you.

'Good God,' said Henry. 'I can see why you're troubled. Callum Flint?'

'You should see her when she talks about him, Henry. There's such affection there. She seems happy.'

'Don't you want her to be happy?' Henry asked.

'Yes, of course I do. But it is also my duty to protect her, and that includes ensuring she is not deceived.'

Henry gave Raven a penetrating look. 'When people learn an inconvenient or upsetting truth, they are seldom grateful to the person who conveyed it, especially if they can question that person's motivations. You might succeed in driving Sarah away from Somerville, but no one will be the happier for it. Not Sarah, certainly not Flint, not even yourself. And though in time she might come to understand why, she might not forgive you for it.'

Raven saw the truth of this. It was not up to him who Sarah associated with. A voice reminded him that there had been a time when he feared his own close association with her might threaten *his* respectability. That as a doctor, he could not marry a housemaid.

So, in his cowardice, he had forfeited the right to judge Flint or Sarah in this matter. But he still had a duty to protect her. And that he would definitely do.

FIFTY-THREE

aven stifled a yawn as he made his way along Nicolson Street. He was on his way to Surgeons' Hall and was not looking forward to his reception there.

He had slept fitfully the night before, though for once the interruption to his rest was caused not by James but by Eugenie. She'd been unable to sleep, kept awake by the baby kicking inside. Her time was near at hand. Labour could begin any day, or it might be weeks yet. Raven wasn't sure which he would prefer.

Eugenie's restlessness had set Raven's mind to running. He was still unsure what he should do about Flint, but there was one issue which had become clear and upon waking he had found his will resolute.

He paused at the door of Surgeons' Hall and took a deep breath. He was unsure whether his decision would be considered wise or foolhardy, but his conviction that it was the right thing to do could not be shaken. He should really have seen it before now.

Patrick the porter opened the door for him as Raven approached the entrance hall.

'You've no' found more bits, have you?' he asked.

'Fortunately not,' Raven replied.

'Are you here to see Professor Christie?'

Raven confirmed this with a nod. He hadn't made an appointment, meaning Christie didn't know he was coming, but given recent events the porter didn't ask. He led the way down the corridor, past the meeting room and library, to Christie's office.

Christie was reading a letter at his desk when Raven entered. He looked up and frowned but said nothing until Patrick left them alone.

'To what do I owe this unexpected pleasure?' he asked, his impatient tone indicating he considered it to be anything but. 'Are you any closer to identifying the murderer? I hear that McLevy has called in a psychic to assist in his investigations, which suggests a degree of desperation.'

'We have made some progress,' Raven said. 'We think that the perpetrator may have been an actor in the past.'

'An actor? Well, I suppose there is some solace to be found in that.'

'Solace?'

'Yes. The link to Surgeons' Hall becomes ever more tenuous. I have never heard of anyone taking a path to surgery from the stage. I cannot imagine anyone ascending from tuppenny theatre to operating theatre,' Christie added, clearly delighted with his wordplay.

Raven found the man's smugness deeply irritating. It was plain he cared only about his own reputation and that of Surgeons' Hall. His interest in the murder appeared to begin and end there.

Christie leaned forward in his seat. 'What of the other matter?' he asked.

'That is why I'm here,' Raven said. He had been concerned about the repercussions of crossing this individual, but looking at him sitting there, marinating in his own conceit and complacency, Raven became even more convinced that this was the right thing to do. 'I'm afraid that I am the bearer of bad news.'

Christie looked taken aback. 'He died? Already?' There was a brief, calculating pause. 'Is he long buried?'

Christie revealed much about himself in saying this, voicing the idea of exhuming a body before he could think better of it.

'No. He's still alive. Just.'

Christie's relief was quickly replaced by irritation. 'Then what is the problem?'

'He does not wish to be anatomised.'

'What has that to do with anything? Is this about money? Is he demanding a higher price?'

'Quite the opposite. He says that he no longer needs the money. In fact, when last we spoke, he seemed confident that he had sufficient wealth to meet all of his needs. Such as they are.'

Christie said nothing for a while, regarding Raven with a combination of scrutiny and suspicion. Then he said, 'The Irish Giant went to his death content in the knowledge that his wishes would be carried out. There is no reason we cannot all three of us get what we want from this.'

He had modified his tone, but this still felt like a demand rather than a suggestion.

'There is a very good reason,' Raven replied. 'My friend has requested he be buried at sea, and unlike what happened to Charles Byrne, I intend to see that his wishes are honoured.'

Christie sneered at him. 'It is a lot of money to give up, Dr Raven.'

'My self-respect has a higher price.'

Christie tutted. 'Your intentions are noble but misguided, and frankly selfish. You have a responsibility to more than just your friend. I think you should focus on the knowledge we would all gain.'

'I am more concerned about the knowledge I would have to live with.'

Christie sat back in his chair and regarded Raven with an appraising eye. 'You are young yet, Dr Raven, so I can forgive an element of naivety.'

Raven stood his ground under the man's intense stare. 'What you call naivety I would call conscience.'

The sneer returned, letting Raven know what Christie thought of his conscience.

'When I speak of naivety I do not mean with regards to your

self-righteousness. I mean with regards to your misapprehension that this will not happen anyway. You are merely denying yourself your share. If that is a price you are happy to pay for your principles, then the more fool you, but understand that I will obtain this specimen regardless.'

Raven could feel his anger building. 'This *specimen* has a name. One you evidently do not know, so good luck finding him without it.'

Christie laughed. 'His name is Gregor. I may be new to the city but a man so remarkable and conspicuous took little time to identify. How much longer do you think it will take me to discover where he lives? But if you can find the good sense to simply tell me his address, then I'm sure I can find the grace to overlook this ill-advised interlude.'

Raven could feel his hands forming fists at his side.

'If you come looking for him, you will find me standing in your way.'

Christie did not appear troubled by this.

'I would warn you, Dr Raven, that *in my way* is an extremely dangerous place to stand.'

FIFTY-FOUR

aven checked his stride to keep close to Sarah as they made their way along George Street, concerned she might get separated from him as they approached the Assembly Rooms. Part of him wilted a little at the sight of so many people clamouring to witness Malham's latest deceit.

'How is Eugenie?' Sarah asked.

Raven sighed. 'The same. Ready to burst.'

'Do you think Dr Simpson will be back in time?'

The professor had remained in the country, and Raven had not yet heard word of when the family would return.

'I think that Dr Simpson has other things on his mind. Obviously I would like him to be here but I'm not anticipating any difficulties. Her last was not a difficult birth. I'm more concerned with her response to the news that the funds I was to start my practice with will not be materialising.'

'What funds?' Sarah asked.

Raven realised he had said more than he intended. He had forgotten that Sarah was not party to any of the deliberations regarding Gregor, his imminent demise or what should be done with his body. He thought for a moment about telling her of his deal with Flint, that it had been her Mr Somerville's idea to sell Gregor's remains, but he realised that this arrangement reflected equally badly on him. Henry's words also came back to him: he would make none of them happier by revealing Somerville's true identity.

'It doesn't matter,' he said. 'Eugenie's father has offered to help. I'd rather not be in his debt, but perhaps I'm being unrealistic. How else is someone like me going to realise that kind of money?'

The crowd thickened outside the main entrance and Raven did his best to guide Sarah through.

'I have confirmation of how Malham diagnosed those people,' she said. 'I spoke to household staff who told me he had visited, charming everyone while subtly soliciting information regarding those upstairs. It is exactly as we suspected.'

'You're doing better than me. Progress remains slow on the Butters front.'

'Still no suspects?'

'We think that he was blackmailing someone. Probably an actor.'

Raven was regarding the mass of people funnelling through the foyer when another possibility presented itself. What if the man they sought was not an actor, but nonetheless someone with an appreciation of the theatrical? He recalled Barrington telling him Butters had worked all over the country. Had Malham been in London at some point before coming to Edinburgh? Could he be the 'dead man' Butters had spoken of?

Then Raven caught himself. He realised he was in danger of letting his own dislikes and prejudices get in the way of clear thinking, something that had threatened to be his downfall in the past. Henry was adamant that the murderer was not a doctor, and even the snootiest London physician would accept that a medical degree from Harvard constituted appropriate qualification.

Besides, Sarah had told him all about Somerville's partnership with Malham. The American was from a wealthy background, so simply paying Butters off would have been considerably less troublesome than killing him.

On that score, Raven continued to wonder what proof Butters might have had that would not precipitate mutual ruin were he to reveal it. He was surprised Butters' previous blackmail victims did not simply call his bluff. Perhaps some of them had.

Raven's ruminations ceased abruptly when he saw Flint moving towards them through the crowd. Sarah saw him too, grabbing the man's arm and presenting them to each other before Flint had the chance to back away.

'Will, this is Mr Somerville. Mr Somerville, this is my good friend Dr Will Raven.'

Flint looked briefly horrified then quickly hid it behind a mask of politeness.

Raven extended a hand, luxuriating in Flint's discomfort. He had never before held the whip-hand over this man, but a few words now would ruin him in Sarah's eyes, and Flint knew it.

'Delighted to make your acquaintance,' Raven said, grinning. 'Sarah has spoken of you, but I suspect she has barely scratched the surface. I am sure there is a great deal more to know.'

Before anything else could be said, Gethyn, the tailor, appeared at Sarah's side.

'Miss Fisher, Dr Malham requests your presence at once,' he said. His manner was officious and unsmiling.

Raven recalled the man's furtive nature as he had emerged from Cooper's office. He remembered too what had subsequently been discussed and wondered whether Gethyn had loitered nearby as he and Henry carried out their search.

Sarah had told Raven how Gethyn worshipped Malham. Raven now had an answer for who might have informed the American about the jawbone. Chances were, Gethyn was also the one who told Sanderson about Malham's supposed psychic intervention with McLevy, for it surely served Malham's public renown to have such feats reported.

'I'm sorry, I'll have to go,' Sarah said to Raven and Flint. 'Perhaps you two might take this opportunity to get better acquainted.'

She smiled at them before turning to follow Gethyn through the crowd.

Raven turned to Flint. 'Shall we take our seats, Mr Somerville?' he asked brightly.

Flint glared at him with a look that was intended as a shot across his bows, but was itself an acknowledgement of Flint's vulnerability to Raven. And as they walked into the hall and found somewhere to sit, Raven glimpsed another possibility. Was Gregor sent to Butters' home to provide a cover story for Flint? Had the money-lender sent his own man ostensibly to collect payment, thus indicating he believed Butters to be alive when in truth he had already killed him?

Flint: a man who had recently reinvented himself as Somerville, a 'dead man' who had made himself anew, and whose new-found respectability would suffer from the revelation of a secret past. Perhaps that secret past was nothing to do with carnal appetites, but simply that Butters was threatening to tell polite society the same truths Flint knew Raven could tell Sarah.

Then Raven realised he was doing it again: trying to fit the facts around people he did not like or approve of. First Malham, now Flint. In medicine or in any other enquiry, you didn't go looking for what you *wanted* to be true, not least because that way you might miss the truth when it was right in front of you.

Before he could muse any further, the houselights dimmed, and Gethyn appeared from behind the curtain.

FIFTY-FIVE

arah found herself backstage at the Assembly Rooms again, in the dressing room that formed Dr Malham's inner sanctum. There was an obvious difference this time, however: members of the association were conspicuous by their absence, and Malham was entirely alone when Mr Gethyn ushered her in. Sarah wondered if his acolytes were no longer welcome or perhaps simply no longer necessary. Malham's version of mesmerism had taken on a life of its own.

Malham turned to her, his expression severe.

'Miss Fisher,' he said, 'something has come to my attention, and I think it is important we have mutual candour. I do not wish anything to distract me ahead of tonight's demonstration.'

Gethyn remained hovering by the door. His usual air of loyalty and latent menace seemed to have been replaced by a malignant sense of anticipation. Sarah recognised it from her schooldays. She was reminded of a girl in her class, the eagerness in her face as she awaited the teacher meting out punishment to someone she had told on.

'I am informed you noted certain names and addresses from the ledger, and that you subsequently visited a household on Northumberland Street.'

'And how did you come by this information?' Sarah asked, glancing towards the tailor. 'Did it reveal itself to you in the garden of sleep?'

Malham ignored the barb. 'Mr Gethyn was only looking out for both our best interests. He is aware of the damage that can be done by unfortunate misunderstandings.'

'My understanding is that you sourced medical information from the household staff.'

Gethyn spoke up in an angry rebuke. 'You're ruinously jealous,' he seethed. 'You had your glorious moment with Mr Jameson, but you could not stand to see Dr Malham distinguish himself as being so much more advanced in his talent. The conditions he diagnosed two nights ago could not be known to household staff. How ridiculous. What do they know of medical matters?'

'You'd be surprised how much household staff know about the people they serve. There's little you can hide from those who do your laundry.'

'Well, you would know all about that I suppose,' Gethyn replied.

If this comment was meant to shame her it had the opposite effect.

'Yes, I would,' Sarah replied, straightening to stand just a little taller.

Malham interjected, his tone conciliatory.

'What you discovered is partly true,' he said. 'I did visit certain houses, but you have misapprehended. It's not about me gleaning information, but about establishing contact, getting a sense of people. The garden of sleep can be like walking through the thickest morning fog. I think everyone in Edinburgh must understand how that can be. You do not know whether a shape looming before you is a person or a pillar. I need something that helps me find those souls in the gloom.'

He paused, letting that sink in.

'They are putting up the House Full notices outside. There are even more people inside tonight than last time. We are building something here, Miss Fisher. Something I would like you to be part of.'

Sarah met his gaze. 'I fear that we are deviating far from mesmerism, and I worry that this—' She struggled to find a suitable word ' —escalation is threatening what we are trying to build. Mesmerism is about a connection between mind and body. It needs to have credibility in people's minds before it can mend their bodies, and that credibility is at risk if they come to believe it is merely stagecraft and showmanship. What happens on the stage will not be replicated should they seek treatment at the institute.'

'You are absolutely right, of course,' Malham said. 'People need to have faith in it, because the greater the power they believe mesmerism to have, the greater its effect as a therapy.'

Sarah was struggling to feel reassured.

Malham turned to Gethyn. 'Mr Gethyn, go and make the announcement. It is almost time.'

Gethyn looked delighted, as though he was party to certain information that no one else knew. Which was probably true and equally concerning.

Malham faced Sarah again. 'Sarah, if I am successful, what you will witness tonight might disturb you, but do not let fear cause you to run from the truth of it. It is the future of medicine. We have had two thousand years of useless potions, of leeches and bloodletting. Is it not time for something better?'

Sarah walked from the room alongside Gethyn, the tailor looking puffed up by this role that he had been given.

'I think you fancy yourself John the Baptist, announcing the Saviour,' Sarah said quietly. 'Mind out you don't lose your head.'

Gethyn snorted, his only response to her warning.

They parted ways as he headed for the stage and she the auditorium.

There was a vacant seat between Raven and Somerville in the front row. It was not the only thing between them. Neither of them looked particularly at ease in the other's company. She wondered what they had talked about. She hoped Raven had not been too forceful in his views on mesmerism, or Somerville too effusive in his enthusiasm for Dr Malham.

As she approached, she saw other familiar faces in the rows

nearest the stage, including several doctors she recognised. Word of this event had brought in a number of medical men, their arms folded, ready to be unimpressed. Further back she saw Mrs Crowe and James McLevy.

As Sarah approached her seat, Gethyn was already on the stage calling for silence. He had to shout to make himself heard. No one paid him much attention. It was not him that they had come to see.

The low hubbub of conversation was suddenly snuffed when Malham stepped out from behind the curtain. Sarah noted that such drapery had not been deemed necessary before, only a few chairs. There were chairs tonight too, also in front of the curtain. Perhaps Malham had ruled the rest of the stage redundant or even a distraction. An optimistic part of her wondered if he had already taken on board her concerns about stagecraft and showmanship, and that what he had in mind tonight would be less dramatic.

Malham reprised his previous feats, diagnosing and then mesmerising two people plucked from the audience. Once again there was astonishment at his ability to discern information at a glance. He told them all things that he could not, should not know. As before, the patients were revived at the same time and reported themselves to be feeling better.

The applause was thunderous, but Malham was not finished. He ventured into the auditorium a third time and summoned to the stage a heavy-set gentleman who was seated in the front row. This time, however, there was a look of growing concern upon Malham's face. Sarah wondered whether he had accidentally picked the wrong man. This was not the source of Malham's distress, however.

'You suffer from pain, yes?'

'Yes, yes, I do. Terrible pains in my stomach.' The gentleman placed his hands over his abdomen, indicating the source of his trouble.

'The pain is so severe at times that you struggle to eat.'

'Well, yes, that's true.'

'Your sleep is disturbed.'

'Sometimes.'

'The fatigue you experience is unremitting.'

The man nodded.

'No one has been able to supply a diagnosis,' Malham said, shaking his head.

'My doctor cannot tell me what is wrong,' the man agreed.

Malham paused for a moment. He looked troubled.

'There is a growth,' he said. 'A tumour in your abdomen.'

The man put a hand to his mouth. There were gasps from the audience.

A woman who had been seated beside the heavy-set man began to cry.

Sarah asked Raven to pass along his handkerchief, which the woman gratefully accepted.

'I'm his wife,' she explained.

'Am I going to die, sir?' the man asked.

Malham did not answer. He stood with his cane gripped in front of his face for a long time, his eyes focused upon the crystal. Then eventually he turned to the man.

'What is your name, sir?'

'Godfrey. Charles Godfrey.'

'Mr Godfrey, I will not lie to you. Unlike some of my fellow countrymen, I am not in the business of selling a single cure for everything. Mesmerism alone will not be enough.'

The man blanched, looking quite vulnerable and exposed as he sat on the stage. Malham was not done, though.

'But I believe there is something I can do. In the garden of sleep, it becomes clear how close we all are to one another. How I can almost see inside a patient's body, penetrate the flesh with my mind and read the stories that are told beneath. Their medical histories are written within them, clear as day. Thus, when I sensed your ailment, I also perceived how I might remedy it.'

The curtain drew back, to gasps from the audience. A draped table sat on the stage, a silver tray on top of it. To Sarah it looked like an operating table. Or an altar. She hoped ritual sacrifice was not going to be Malham's next trick.

It was then she noticed the mirror hung above the table, angled to allow the audience a direct view of the table and what was about to happen there.

'For some time I have wondered, if my mind can go beneath the skin, might I meet a patient in that garden of sleep, and access healing in a way no doctor has been able to before? Will you let me try, sir?'

Mr Godfrey nodded, rather helplessly, Sarah thought. Under such circumstances, in front of all these people, it was probably more difficult to say no and to retreat.

Gethyn stepped forward and helped the patient up onto the table. Once Mr Godfrey was settled, Malham began to mesmerise him, taking longer than he had with the previous two. Once satisfied that he was sufficiently under the influence, Malham gave Gethyn a signal and the Welshman helped the patient lie down.

Malham then picked up his cane and stared for a long time into its crystal top, the room becoming deathly quiet but for a few suppressed coughs.

Malham closed his eyes for a few seconds, and then opened them again, his expression serene and yet concentrated.

He put the cane down and stood behind the table. He placed one hand on Mr Godfrey's face, closing his eyes. Sarah was uncomfortably reminded of seeing the same thing done to the recently dead.

'Deeper,' he said. 'We must both go deeper.'

Malham placed his hands on the man's abdomen.

'It is again as though I can see beneath the skin. More than see beneath the skin; as though I can feel beneath it.'

Malham's breathing became heavier.

'The tumour is pressing upon the stomach and the liver. This is the source of his illness, and it is mortal unless the tumour can be removed.'

There was a low murmuring from the audience, a collective recognition of the likely implications of such a diagnosis.

Sarah looked at Mrs Godfrey, who was now whimpering quietly into Raven's handkerchief.

'Surgery is impossible,' Malham continued. 'No surgeon will enter the abdomen, for even if they succeed in removing the tumour, the patient will surely die.'

At this point Dr Malham pulled up Mr Godfrey's shirt to expose the bare flesh underneath, revealed in all its portly detail and clearly visible to the audience by virtue of the suspended mirror.

What was he doing now? Sarah looked at Raven, who shrugged his shoulders.

Malham placed his hands directly upon Mr Godfrey's abdomen.

'It feels so close, as though I might reach in and touch it. I can see it in my mind's eye. The shape of the tumour. The colour of it. I feel as though my fingers could penetrate through the skin, through the integuments and reach the tumour itself.'

Malham was breathing more and more heavily.

There was not a sound from the audience now. Even Mrs Godfrey was silent.

'I can see beyond, I can feel beyond, as though if I were just to reach in— ' Malham gave a gasp. Somewhere in the audience a woman screamed.

In the mirror, Sarah could see that the fingers of Dr Malham's right hand had penetrated the abdomen as far as his knuckles, blood instantly pooling around the wound.

Malham himself looked alarmed by what was going on.

'My God,' he said.

Several people got to their feet.

'Do not approach,' Malham warned, sounding fearful.

He placed his left hand above the right, strain on his face as he began to pull at something. A grisly length of bloody matter began to emerge. Malham continued pulling until he held the whole thing, whatever it was, in his left hand. He then removed his right hand and grasped the skin, holding the wound closed.

From his breathing he sounded on the point of exhaustion, staring in disbelief at the object in his left hand. He dropped it onto the silver tray as though afraid of it.

He placed both hands on the patient's abdomen once again, closing his eyes in intense concentration. Then slowly, gently, he pulled his hands away. Malham picked up a cloth and wiped the blood from Mr Godfrey's skin. There was no wound.

Malham gazed in confusion at his own bloody hands, as though they were alien to him.

Then he looked at the patient.

'Mr Godfrey. Come forth from the garden.'

The patient slowly opened his eyes and Gethyn rushed to help him sit up. Malham showed the patient what was on the tray. The man looked slightly stupefied and not a little afraid.

His wife rushed towards the stage, climbing the steps at the front. She hugged her husband and then threw her arms around Malham.

'You have saved him, sir. You have saved him.'

Malham staggered back, on the verge of collapse. He took hold of his cane and used it to support himself. He was shaking, endeavouring in vain to steady his breathing and consequently struggling to speak.

'My apologies, ladies and gentlemen, I cannot continue,' he said, whereupon the curtain fell.

There was stunned silence in the hall, people trying to make sense of what they had seen. This lasted several seconds before there was a gradual rise of applause and then rapturous cheering.

Sarah could hear some of the association members in the row behind. 'What was that?' one asked his colleagues, but none of the doctors present could offer any rational explanation for what had just occurred.

Mr Somerville was staring at the closed curtain, transfixed. He turned to Sarah, eyes sparkling with astonished delight.

'I have no notion as to what I have just witnessed but listen to the audience. The man is a wonder.'

Sarah was unsettled by what she had witnessed too, but this was because she knew something others did not: that Malham's intention was to deceive. She had no notion how he had managed this surgical feat, but there were two things she knew for sure: that Malham was extraordinarily dangerous and that he had to be stopped.

FIFTY-SIX

he house was on the east side of George Square, a handsome three-storey terrace comfortably south of the Old Town's stink and squalor. Gregor had been right, Raven reflected with some bitterness. Flint had indeed gone up in the world.

The front door was opened by a housekeeper. Raven gave his name and was admitted, though he had not been invited. He found that the title of Doctor opened many doors.

Raven stepped into the front hall and regarded the pleasant interior with some envy, comparing it to his own cramped accommodations. He thought of his years of diligent study and the long hours of demanding work. The rewards he had accrued were far smaller than those evidently acquired as a result of criminality.

The housekeeper walked towards the rear of the building and knocked on a door on the right.

'A gentleman to see you, Mr Somerville. His name is Dr Raven.'

Flint appeared moments later, the fury in his face quickly masked before his housekeeper could see it.

He affected a polite smile. 'And what is it regarding?' he asked.

'A mutual acquaintance,' Raven answered, enjoying the man's discomfort.

Raven then heard a clatter of quick footsteps and saw a tiny figure emerge from the same doorway. A little girl was behind Flint, peeking out at Raven from the safety of her father's legs.

Raven felt everything become immediately more complicated.

'Margaret, can you take Isabelle through to the parlour while I have a chat with our visitor?' Flint asked.

The housekeeper led the little girl away by the hand. Isabelle continued to stare at Raven until he was out of sight.

'This way, Dr Raven,' Flint said, his voice cheerful.

Raven followed Flint into a bright and tastefully furnished parlour. His mind conjured images of the less than salubrious Fountainhall tenement where he had delivered Flint's first child.

Flint changed as soon as he closed the door.

'You have found where I live and seen what I have here,' he said, a look of steel in his eyes. 'Well done. Now imagine what I would do to protect it.'

'You don't need to labour the point,' Raven replied. 'I know all too well who you are and what you are capable of.'

Flint wore an odd expression, fading anger giving way to a mixture of scorn and regret.

'You have no idea what I am capable of. I am more than the man you once knew.'

'Yes, I gather you are a man of property. Purchasing the old Maternity Hospital and going into partnership with Dr Malham. I understand you have effectively advanced him half ownership of Milton House. Surely a riskier undertaking than you're used to.'

'Not from where I was sitting last night. People will pay handsomely for the attentions of a miracle-worker, and I will be taking sixty per cent of that until Malham's debt is paid.'

'The man is a charlatan.'

'What should I care so long as he brings in money?'

'Because why would you trust a fraud? Have you been mesmerised yourself, that you believe someone intent upon deceiving the whole city would not seek to deceive you too? It is my understanding that his name is on the deed.'

Flint went to a bureau and opened a drawer. From it he produced a familiar object: the same Forsyth pistol he had once pointed at Raven's head. He brandished it with both purpose and pride, a treasured possession but also a totem of power and resolve.

'And should he fail to satisfy me,' Flint said, 'I will prevail upon him to withdraw any claim on it. Malham is like many in your profession, Doctor: the scion of a wealthy family, with little experience of life's harsher realities. Right now he is in partnership with Somerville, but should he in any way displease me, he will discover who he is truly in business with.'

Raven stared at the pistol, then looked Flint in the eye.

'It must be difficult presenting one face to the world, all the while fearing you might accidentally reveal the other.'

'Both of them are the truth, Doctor.'

Raven decided now was the time to broach his true purpose here.

'I wonder which one Miss Fisher would prefer.'

Flint's face changed. He glanced at the pistol as though it had transformed into something unfamiliar and seemed in a hurry to divest himself of it.

His anxious expression was the same as at the Assembly Rooms, when Sarah had presented them to each other. It struck Raven that he had only seen Flint look so vulnerable when his wife was in labour: when he had been truly afraid of losing something that he valued. Hard as it was to admit it, Raven could see that Flint genuinely cared about Sarah. Or cared about what she thought of him, at least.

'What is your business with Miss Fisher?' Flint asked, placing the gun back in the bureau and locking the drawer.

'I have known her for six years. She is very dear to me, so I take a keen interest in her well-being.'

Flint turned and faced Raven again. 'Then you should have no worries on that account,' he said. 'Her well-being is my chief priority. I could provide for her as well as anyone in this city.'

Raven scoffed. 'I doubt you know anything about her wants and needs. She requires so much more than the financial support of a man. She wishes to educate herself. To be a doctor.'

'I know well how she wishes to rise above her station in life. It is an ambition that we share. I respect her for it. I would support her, not hold her back.'

'You will never be worthy of her.'

'I don't doubt it. But there is honour in endeavouring to be, is there not?'

'What do you know of honour?' Raven asked. But even as he spoke, he remembered Flint putting himself at risk when it would have been easier to leave a dying man behind. And Gregor saying of him that Flint was honourable in ways others would not understand.

Dr Simpson's words on this occasion offered no comfort. *Sometimes you just don't know.*

'Look, it's not for me to tell her who you really are,' Raven said. 'But I will not see her deceived.'

Flint's manner was unusually imploring. In this, more than his clothes or the other trappings he had gathered to himself, he looked like a different person.

'Then let me tell her myself. On my own terms.'

Raven let him wait for a moment, though he already knew his answer. It was why he had come here, after all.

'I will grant you that much, but it will come at a price.'

'What price?'

'Five hundred pounds.'

'Five hun—? You're extorting me? *Me?*'

Raven remained silent, waiting for him to work it out. He watched the dawning moment as Flint realised what Raven meant.

'You're talking about Gregor.' Flint laughed and shook his head. 'You want my share. You're made of sterner stuff than I thought.'

'I don't want your share. There will be no share. Gregor is not to be sold, but his remains disposed of respectfully in accordance with his wishes. That is the price of my silence. But I warn you it is a silence that will expire in a few days. You have to tell her soon.'

Flint looked as though he was totting up numbers in his head, assessing his options. Wondering whether to comply.

'I could silence you permanently, Dr Raven. Perhaps you should remember that.'

'Ah, now that's the Callum Flint I'd like to introduce Sarah to. A vicious piece of work who deals in threats, intimidation, and violence.'

Flint sighed. He looked worried he had betrayed himself, or simply let himself down.

'I don't like being cornered. You know that. And nor do you, Dr Raven. We are more alike than you would care to admit. You have held a knife to my throat, and I had no doubt you would have cut me rather than concede ground.'

'Touché,' Raven said. He didn't like to be reminded of the less reputable aspects of his character either.

'I have striven to be a better man,' Flint implored. 'To leave the criminal I once was behind.'

'You said yourself, both are the truth, and Sarah deserves to know that. Tell her who you are. If she still wants to be associated with you after that, then it is no longer my concern.'

FIFTY-SEVEN

arah was beginning to feel both conspicuous and conspicuously alone as she stood outside the house on Hill Square. It was a bright enough afternoon and this was far from being an insalubrious part of the city, but the memory of being followed by Denzil Gethyn remained uncomfortably fresh in her mind. She assumed Raven had been delayed at the Maternity Hospital, but as his status as a doctor was going to be crucial to gaining admittance, this was one visit she could not carry out by herself.

She saw him hurrying around the corner, a look of apology in both his expression and the urgency of his gait.

'What kept you?' she asked. 'A difficult case?'

'That would be one way of describing him.'

'Describing who?'

Raven gave her an odd look, conflicted, as though reluctant to discuss it.

'You never did meet my old acquaintance Mr Flint, did you?'

Sarah had not, but she had heard enough to know he was a thoroughly nasty piece of work.

'You're not having dealings with him again, are you?'

'That remains to be seen. He tells me he's a changed man.'

'And do you believe him?'

'That will not be for me to judge. Shall we?'

Raven ushered her forward and together they climbed the steps to the townhouse's front door. They were at the home of Charles Godfrey, the beneficiary of what the Hoolet's latest pamphlet described as 'Dr Malham's Miraculous Mesmeric Surgery'.

Sarah was of the opinion that it was not enough merely to assume Malham had perpetrated some manner of deception. In her commitment to scientifically evaluating mesmerism, she needed to ascertain the truth of Mr Godfrey's medical condition before and after his visit to the Assembly Rooms.

The door was answered by a housekeeper, a squat, round-faced woman, her expression unwelcoming.

'My name is Dr Will Raven. I work with Dr Simpson, and this is Miss Sarah Fisher. We would speak with Mr Godfrey, if the master of the house is home.'

'He won't see you,' she said. 'I've already had to turn away Dr Graham, as well as several other doctors who have beaten a path to this door ever since his cure. Mr Godfrey wants nothing to do with any of you, and given how little use your profession has been, he has made it clear that he would welcome a prolonged absence of your ilk while he recovers.'

'He remains well then?' Raven asked, but the woman was already closing the door.

'I suppose we should have anticipated as much,' he mourned. 'Every doctor in the city is talking about this.'

'What is the significance of Dr Graham?' Sarah asked. 'Is he eminent in a particular field?'

'No,' Raven replied, brightening. 'He must be Godfrey's own physician.'

Within the hour they were seated in Dr Graham's consulting room. He was a younger man than his grey hair might indicate; slight of build, with a calming presence, though he seemed rather exercised by recent developments.

'Mr Godfrey would not let me examine him,' he confirmed, shaking his head. 'Wouldn't even let me in the house. Me – his physician for more than a decade. To make matters worse I have already had two patients today say they suspect they are suffering from the same manner of complaint, worried they might die if they are unable to rapidly procure an appointment with Dr Malham.'

'Were you present at the Assembly Rooms?' Sarah asked him.

'No, but I have heard about little else since,' he answered, lifting a medical journal to reveal a copy of the Hoolet's new pamphlet beneath it. 'Some colleagues and I asked to examine what was removed from Mr Godfrey's abdomen, but Dr Malham refused.'

'On what grounds?' Raven asked.

'He said that as he alone had removed the tumour, he alone had the right to dissect and examine it. He promised to share his findings, but nothing has been forthcoming.'

'How was Mr Godfrey when you last saw him?'

'Much as he always is when he has cause to call me. Suffering from recurrent stomach pains, resultant I would say of his over-rich diet and fondness for burgundy. He has a tendency to become anxious regarding his business dealings, which precipitates certain symptoms and an urgent summons to myself. I give him the same advice every time: fresh air, a light diet and try to delegate some of his work. He never acts on my advice, but he usually gets better whenever his latest business worries pass.'

'So you didn't suspect he had anything seriously wrong with him?' Raven asked.

'No, and certainly not a tumour. But the problem is, there is no way of proving that either way. It would be a brave doctor who declared anything for certain about the state of that man's insides.'

Dr Graham pointed to the pamphlet's description of 'a miracle that will transform all of medicine'.

'It says here that Malham forced his fingers inside Mr Godfrey's abdomen and drew out a length of diseased tissue. And then he healed the wound without stitching it.'

'So it would seem,' Sarah said.

'It's impossible,' Dr Graham insisted. 'And yet every account I have heard has described the same thing. Can they all be mistaken?'

'We were there,' Raven told him. 'The account in this pamphlet describes what we saw. But what we saw and what took place may be two different things.'

'I don't think many people will be questioning what they saw. The excitement of it all may already have coloured their recollection of events. What is needed is a detached, rational and sober perspective.'

Raven thought for a moment.

'I think I can get us two out of three,' he said.

FIFTY-EIGHT

I t was three days since Malham's feat of miraculous surgery.

Raven was picking his way carefully down the steps of Fleshmarket Close, glancing instinctively over his shoulder as was his practice in the narrow alleys of the Old Town, particularly this one. It was far from the darkest or most disreputable conduit, but he had once been attacked here, so the sight of these surroundings always spurred a heightened vigilance.

He clutched Sanderson's latest pamphlet, which excitedly reported that Mr Godfrey was now fully recovered and in great spirits. Of course he was, Raven thought. Mr Godfrey had been feeling understandably awful having been told he had a fatal tumour, and he was now feeling much better after coming to believe it had been removed. But whether there was anything to his symptoms, indeed whether there had ever even been a tumour, was immaterial. Considerably more significant was that a patient's treatment and recovery continued to be the subject of a scandal sheet's front page, something more commonly the preserve of sensation, outrage and horror.

Raven was on his way to seek out its author, identified thanks to Sarah's endeavours. He entered the cramped little tavern halfway down the steps to Market Street, a howff where journalists were known to gather, and where William Sanderson reportedly still drank, maintaining old ties and dependable sources.

Raven was prepared for this to be merely the first port of call in his search, hoping someone in here would know where Sanderson might be found, but he saw that he was in luck. The once editor of the *Courant* was sitting alone, nursing a whisky, the latest editions of his own former title and of the *Scotsman* open before him. The newspapers and his drink sat on a large table, big enough for at least six to sit around. The man was still used to holding court.

Though he was long fallen from his esteemed position, he did not look like a man in reduced circumstances. He remained immaculately dressed; inappropriately so, Raven always thought, for someone whose job consisted of so much sifting through dirt.

Raven placed the latest pamphlet down in front of him by way of announcing his arrival.

Sanderson looked up to see who had occasioned this interruption, his face a combination of annoyance and restless curiosity. It was the latter Raven was relying upon. Sanderson was first and foremost a newsman, not someone who would ever let his emotions get in the way if there was the scent of a story in his nose.

'What can I do for you, Dr Raven?'

'I've been reading about medical miracles, and I'm worried I'm going to be out of a job.'

Sanderson wore an expression that was half smile and half sneer.

'What do you want?'

'There is something I'd like to know.'

'Then you've come to the wrong place. I sometimes pay for information, but I don't sell it, other than in print.'

'Is Harland Malham paying you?' Raven asked. 'He ought to be. You're proving yourself quite invaluable in spreading word of his supernatural abilities: from psychically assisting McLevy's enquiries to removing tumours with his bare hands.'

Sanderson gave him that same look, simultaneously amused and contemptuous.

'He hasn't paid me a penny, but I am making money from him hand over fist. His deeds are selling pamphlets by the thousand.

I'm making more from this game than I was being paid next door at the *Courant*.' Sanderson took a sip of his whisky. 'Malham sells,' he told Raven. 'Even more than murder. People will always want to read about remarkable deeds and a man's rise to prominence.'

'For sure,' said Raven. 'But once they've had that, there's only one story they'll want to read more.'

'And what might that be?'

'His downfall.'

FIFTY-NINE

aven noticed Sarah glancing at the clock. It was almost time, but the man of the hour was yet to emerge, and he feared the audience might soon begin to grow restless.

They were gathered in the anatomy lecture theatre at the university, awaiting a medical demonstration by a new practitioner, a man of remarkable gifts. The event had enjoyed considerably less fanfare than Malham's triumph at the Assembly Rooms. It was not advertised at all, in fact. No bills, no leaflets, no notices in the newspaper. Select spectators were there by invitation only.

The venue had been chosen so that everyone could enjoy a direct view of the table. There were those who had wondered about the mirror above Malham's stage, mirrors being well-known tools of illusionists. But as Raven had learned, the illusionist's secret is always to make the audience look in the wrong place for the solution.

Others had wondered about the drapes around Malham's table. There were no such coverings here. The table was an aged wooden thing, stained in places from prolonged use. There was no silver tray either, just a bucket.

Cooper and some other surgeons were present, alongside medical men, not all of whom had been at the Assembly Rooms. Most were deeply sceptical about what they had seen or heard but no one could provide any credible explanation.

McLevy was also in attendance, sitting among the doctors with a glowering impatience. It was often said indulgently of ill-humoured individuals that they didn't suffer fools gladly, but if there was something McLevy suffered less, it was anyone making a fool of him. What he had seen at the Assembly Rooms three nights ago had not pleased him, particularly in light of the pamphlet that had told all Edinburgh he had engaged Malham as some kind of psychic consultant.

Raven wandered across to ask if he had any news. McLevy rolled his eyes.

'I've spoken to a theatre critic of my acquaintance,' he said. 'The man could name every actor who has appeared on the Edinburgh stage in twenty years, and he's a gossipy so-and-so at that. The problem is, Butters got around. He mostly performed in Edinburgh, but he went wherever there was work to be had. London, Bristol, Liverpool, you name it. He was in Cardiff before he came here.'

Raven glanced up and saw that Sanderson was seated on one of the benches. They exchanged brief nods of acknowledgement.

Also present was Flint. Or Somerville, as Raven was having to counsel himself to think of him, at least until Sarah knew the truth. As far as he was aware, the man had not told her anything yet.

Raven noticed a door at the back of the room open and allowed himself a smile as two familiar faces quietly snuck into the lecture theatre. They were uninvited but had nonetheless learned of the event, just as Raven had intended they should. Dr Harland P. Malham and his slavish acolyte Mr Denzil Gethyn took their seats at the back of the auditorium, trying to remain inconspicuous.

Sarah looked at the clock again. She tapped Raven on the shoulder.

'Where is he?'

'I'll just go and check.'

Raven exited through a side door and proceeded along the corridor to the room set aside for the man they were all waiting for.

It was empty. Kimble had gone.

Raven was about to utter an oath when he glimpsed movement through the window. He ran from the room, through the entrance hall and out into the courtyard, where he saw Kimble making his way towards the street.

Raven caught up to him.

'Where are you going?'

'I can't do this,' Kimble said, sounding plaintive.

'Of course you can. You've been doing this all your life. You showed us last night and you said yourself it's simple stuff.'

'There are more than just you and Miss Fisher out there today,' Kimble replied. 'It's so long since I did this sort of thing in front of an audience.'

'You were performing at the Adelphi a fortnight ago, in front of many more than are gathered here.'

'That was different. Any idiot can do mediumship. This is the real thing. I haven't done it in years. I don't feel well. I'm shaking like a leaf.'

Kimble held up his hands, which were visibly trembling.

Raven realised what was wrong.

'When did you last have a drink?' he asked.

'Not since last night. I thought it was time I started trying to cut down. I reckoned if this goes well, maybe I can think about getting back to, you know . . . But that's just raising the stakes, making it worse.'

'I think that's a noble intention, Mr Kimble.'

'Please. It's Dickie.'

'Abstinence should be encouraged, and it's something I can help you with. But maybe this is not the moment to start. Wait here.'

Raven placed two hands briefly on Kimble's arms then ran back inside, where he headed for the library. He doubted medical students had changed much since he was among them, and he fervently hoped one particular tradition had been maintained.

Raven found what he was looking for behind a volume entitled *A Treatise on the Liver*. He pocketed the bottle, vowing to replace it with a larger one as soon as he had the chance. It was less than half full and likely contained some cheap gut-rot, but it would serve for his purposes.

Ten minutes later, Kimble was ready to perform in a new kind of theatre. He didn't look much like a surgeon, dressed as he was in a baggy, ill-fitting jacket, but he was about to perform an operation nonetheless.

'Gentlemen,' he said, calling the room to order. At Raven's request he did not acknowledge that there were two women in the room. One was the patient, which was less of an issue, but he did not wish to draw any added attention to the presence of Sarah, sitting somewhere she was not supposed to be. Women as a rule did not grace the lecture rooms of the university.

'Thank you for granting me your time and for the opportunity to appear before you this afternoon. All my life I have found that objects do not behave in my hands the way they behave in those of others. What I wish to show you today is something I've been wary of sharing with anyone, but having learned of the remarkable Dr Malham's feats at the Assembly Rooms I realised I am not alone.'

Kimble had learned of these feats from Raven, who had described what Malham had done in as much detail as he could remember. Kimble had simply smiled and said: 'Now, tell me again. And this time describe exactly what you saw. Not what you *think* happened.'

Kimble walked around the table, taking in the whole audience, looking into their eyes. He spoke quietly, as he had done at the Adelphi, forcing their attention.

'One of the miracles of the human body is its ability to repair itself. We've all suffered injuries that got better in time. Though many of us have scars, how many cuts to our skin leave no trace? This is what I have studied, and I have learned that the fabric of matter is not as we assume.'

Kimble looked to Mrs Crowe. She had been most obliging when Sarah told her what they intended.

'I am told we have a patient,' Kimble said.

Mrs Crowe stepped forward onto the floor of the theatre. She was wearing a coat, which she dispensed of to reveal a loose cotton shift beneath. Kimble led her by the hand and helped her up onto the table, where she lay flat on her back.

'Have you been well?' he asked her.

'Generally. Though I have of late suffered from a discomfort here,' she replied, touching a point in the middle of her abdomen.

Kimble's face was calm, serene. He placed folded sheets above and below the area she had indicated.

'May I place my hands upon you, madam?' he asked.

'Certainly.'

The cotton shift was pulled up, the folded sheets ensuring that only a small strip of abdominal skin was revealed to the audience. With such a select group of predominantly medical men present there was no response to this. Raven wondered if Malham had chosen a male patient for his demonstration to avoid any hint of scandal. Baring even a patch of female flesh at the Assembly Rooms may well have provoked one, overshadowing his true purpose.

Raven cast a quick look at Sanderson. If the man had been hoping for something more salacious, he would be disappointed, but he would have a story worth telling nonetheless.

Raven watched as Kimble placed his hands on Mrs Crowe's exposed flesh. He had had his doubts about her. She seemed flighty, an irrepressible gossip, but her agreement to be part of this had seen her rise considerably in his estimation.

Kimble's eyes were closed, as though scanning Mrs Crowe's insides with his mind.

'I sense something beneath the surface,' he announced. 'Something that would surely prove fatal were it permitted to remain.'

Mrs Crowe looked alarmed and tried to sit up.

'Do not be afraid,' Kimble told her. 'I need you to lie still and remain calm. Close your eyes and imagine yourself to be somewhere beautiful, somewhere peaceful. I promise you will feel no pain.'

Kimble took a deep breath, holding up both of his hands where they could be seen.

Raven noted that everyone in the operating theatre leaned forward as one, their eyes fixed upon Mrs Crowe's middle.

Raven could afford to look at the audience because he had no need to observe the procedure itself. Kimble had demonstrated it for him the day before, taking him through it stage by stage. Sarah had been the patient then, but Kimble had expressed a preference for someone less lean. 'The plumper the better,' he had said.

Kimble now placed his right hand upon the flesh of Mrs Crowe's abdomen and then, exactly as Malham's had done, his fingers disappeared into it, until it seemed that all four fingers had entered to the depth of his knuckles.

'They are simply folded back,' Kimble had explained to Raven. 'The soft flesh around creates the appearance of them having gone through. What really sells it, though, is the blood.'

The blood arrived right on cue, appearing from the wound around Kimble's fingers. In truth it was coming from inside a flesh-coloured sleeve he was wearing over his thumb.

'What are you doing, man?' one of the surgeons in the audience cried out. 'It is folly to enter the abdomen.'

Kimble ignored him. He brought his left hand down over his right and proceeded to pull a bloody, fleshy object from the 'wound' he had made.

'My God,' someone said. 'What is that? Is it a tumour? A piece of intestine? Has the idiot butchered her?'

Raven noted that, despite the protestations, no one tried to intervene. It probably helped that the patient remained completely composed. There was none of the thrashing and wailing all of these men would have witnessed in this room in the days when surgery was performed without chloroform.

'Silence, please,' Kimble insisted. 'The most crucial stage is at hand: causing the flesh to repair itself. Interfering with that could be catastrophic.'

There was silence in the room once more. Kimble closed his

eyes. His face became anxious, and everyone leaned forward in their seats again.

'Oh dear. Oh, good heavens.'

There was palpable concern around the room. In Malham's demonstration, nothing had gone wrong.

'It is not done. This is not all.'

Mrs Crowe's eyes opened, which seemed to exacerbate the growing anxiety among the spectators.

'We certainly cannot leave *this* inside the patient,' Kimble announced.

He put his left hand to the wound again, and this time from within he produced, not more fleshy matter, but . . . flowers. Yellow, orange, purple, blue. More and more flowers, which he began tossing into the air, a cascade.

Mrs Crowe's eyes were wide now with amazement and delight. Kimble had failed to tell her about this part.

'What on earth have you been eating, madam?' he asked.

'Someone did tell me there was too much flour in my diet,' she said, joining in the fun.

'And still, what's this?'

Kimble reached in again, and this time produced a paper parasol, which popped open with the press of a button. This he gave to Mrs Crowe while he wiped the blood from her undamaged skin with a cloth.

'Are you feeling quite well,' he asked.

'Never better.'

'I'm not sure precisely what was ailing you,' Kimble said. 'Whether it was the parasol, the paper flowers, or the chicken gizzard. Better out than in, though, that's what I say.'

There was laughter now from the doctors, while the surgeon who had voiced his concern appeared relieved and slightly embarrassed. Even McLevy wore a look of grim satisfaction.

But there were three people in the room who did not look pleased at all.

Two of them were Malham and Gethyn.

The other, looking most thunderous of all, was Flint.

Sanderson had seen enough and was making his way to the door. Raven intercepted him.

'Did I not give you quite a story?' he said.

'You did indeed,' Sanderson admitted. 'And a deal is a deal. What is it you wanted to know?'

'Who told you about McLevy consulting Malham regarding the Butters case?'

Sanderson sighed and glanced across at the mesmerist.

'You didn't really need to ask me that, did you, Dr Raven?'

'I just needed confirmation.'

'No, you didn't. Mostly you wanted me to see this. It's good for me either way. The rise and the fall: they both keep the presses running.'

Sanderson was right about Raven's main purpose. He had sought Sarah's thoughts on the matter first, though. 'If Sanderson publishes this story, it could finish off mesmerism entirely in this city,' he had warned.

Sarah had been sanguine about it. 'We are performing this procedure to remove a nasty little tumour,' she said. 'Mesmerism won't survive with it still attached. Whether it survives after its removal will determine its true worth.'

'How did you do that?' one of the doctors was asking Kimble. Several of them were crowding around the table, another of them having a good poke at Mrs Crowe's still-exposed abdomen before she slapped his hand away.

'Much as a joke ceases to be funny once it's been explained,' Kimble said, 'the wonder of an illusion evaporates once the method is known.'

This drew groans from the onlookers, but Kimble would say no more. He helped Mrs Crowe adjust her clothing and get down from the table.

Raven knew the method, but most importantly, so did Malham.

He saw him approach Flint and beg his understanding. 'He is a magician,' Malham was saying. 'He has just admitted as much.

Simply because someone can recreate the *appearance* of a phenomenon through trickery does not mean the phenomenon does not exist. His trickery is a low and underhand attempt to discredit me.'

Flint was looking the way Raven had often seen him before. He was not someone given to explosions of temper, even before he had begun pretending to be more civilised. Flint was always concerned with control, the violence within him all the more frightening for being barely concealed beneath a calm surface. For all he had talked of not caring whether Malham was a fraud so long as the money came in, he had been forced to confront how these things might be mutually exclusive, and had just witnessed the value of his investment begin to plummet.

Flint restricted his reaction to a mere four words, but they were nonetheless devastating to Malham.

'Our arrangement is void,' he said.

Kimble sauntered across to where Raven stood, an unfamiliar smile on the magician's face. He was clearly elated by the experience of performing.

'I was hoping Dr Simpson would be here,' he said. 'I wish to offer my apologies. I've done a lot of thinking since you came to my aid that night, and I have come to understand the hurt I caused. When you are too wrapped up in your own pain, you can justify anything.'

He paused for a moment and scratched his bristly chin.

'I thought I was drinking to forget my loss, but I realise that I was also drinking to blot out the shame. No amount of whisky can shield me from the truth of it, though. To practise mediumship is to dishonour the very thing that once gave me pride and self-respect. To sell one's illusions as supernatural powers is an affront to the noble art of magic.'

SIXTY

aven was in Queen Street Gardens with Eugenie and little James, enjoying the unusually warm sunshine of the late afternoon. James was in good humour, shrieking and chasing pigeons again. Eugenie was seated on a bench, fanning herself with the Hoolet's latest pamphlet.

Raven watched James collapse in a fit of giggling as the latest flock of birds he was running at took to the air. Raven realised that he looked at his son with different eyes now. He no longer felt afraid about being the child's father.

He considered how much had changed since he was last in these gardens. Before Gregor had shown up that day, Raven had come to believe that Flint was no longer a part of his life. Maybe he ought to accept that Callum Flint *was* no longer a part of his life, but that, unfortunately, Callum Somerville might be. That still very much depended on how Sarah responded when Somerville came clean.

The thought of Gregor brought him back to Christie and their fraught last encounter. Unlike Flint, Christie did not have a crew of ne'er-do-wells, henchmen and mercenaries to prosecute his will. He had merely been attempting to intimidate Raven into giving him what he wanted, but it wasn't going to work. Christie would not get his prize, but unfortunately nor would Raven be getting Christie's money. He had accepted that Eugenie's father would have a say in his future.

Dr Simpson's words echoed again: *Sometimes you just don't know*. Raven was having to make his peace with that on a number of fronts. He was about to strike out on his own after years of mentorship, so maybe this was what it truly felt like to be your own man. A world with fewer certainties, where the delineations that marked black and white, right and wrong, would never be clear again.

The Hoolet's new pamphlet illustrated the point perfectly, its front emblazoned with the question: 'Was Dr Malham's Medical Miracle Genuine?' as it invited readers to make up their own minds. Sanderson was playing both sides, something he was adept at. He knew that people who wanted to believe in mesmerism would do so, and people who wanted to believe in Malham's other powers would not care what Kimble had demonstrated.

Raven spotted James's attention shift and saw Sarah enter the gardens. James ran at her and she lifted him high then swung him round, much to his delight. She paused in front of Eugenie, James sitting contentedly on her hip.

'How are you, Eugenie?' Sarah asked.

His wife shielded her eyes and looked up. 'How do you think?' she said, indicating her swollen belly. 'This heat is intolerable. Tell me, Sarah, you must know some tricks. How do I bring this on?'

'My grandmother used to say that raspberry-leaf tea would get things started, but surely you don't have much longer to wait.'

'Each day seems like an eternity,' Eugenie sighed. She rested her head back and closed her eyes.

James had begun to squirm, so Sarah released him to run at the pigeons again. Raven watched her walk towards him, her smile fading as she handed him a letter.

'I've just received this,' she said. 'From Malham.'

Raven opened it and scanned the contents.

My dear Miss Fisher,
Following the events at the university I have had time to take stock of my conduct in recent weeks, and I have come to the conclusion that you are correct that my showmanship has not

served the cause of mesmerism or of our planned institute. My intention with these public events was solely to raise interest in the practice, but I would concede that mesmerism's credibility is fragile, and that is why I would like to reiterate my offer to give you a greater role. It is my sincere desire that the institute should flourish and therefore I implore you to accept my offer of a position there, where the emphasis will strictly be upon mesmerism and nothing more.

Yours,

Dr Harland P. Malham

Raven folded the letter and handed it back to her. 'He actually sounds chastened,' he observed. 'I wouldn't have thought him capable of humility, but I have been wrong about a few people of late.'

Sarah rolled her eyes. 'Oh, Will, it is as well I am not as easily fooled as you. Malham is merely trying to appeal to Mr Somerville through me. He hopes that if I accept a post at his institute, Somerville will reconsider.'

'And is he minded to? Have you spoken to him of late?'

Raven was searching for any indication that Somerville had told her the truth, but her manner was too calm, and it would surely have been the first thing she mentioned.

'We spoke this morning,' she said. 'He is not withdrawing from the institute entirely, merely pulling out of the arrangement that would make Malham co-owner of Milton House. Instead, he intends to be merely a landlord. He is meeting Malham at the Adelphi Theatre this evening to discuss matters.'

'Why there?'

'The Adelphi has not been doing well of late and Malham indicated there might be an investment opportunity, but in truth I suspect it is merely a pretext for talking Somerville around, trying to persuade him to reconsider the partnership. If so, he is wasting his time. My understanding is that Somerville will not be swayed, and certainly not by me.

'I am relieved, to be honest,' Sarah went on. 'His deal with

Malham had me uneasy. I do not see how Mr Somerville could be quite so sanguine about such an arrangement.'

Raven understood exactly how he could be so sanguine but could not tell her why. If their agreement was currently being dissolved, it ought to be Malham who was relieved. He would never know what danger he might have put himself in: danger from which neither conjuring nor mesmerism could have saved him.

'It sounds like it might be for the best,' Raven said.

'I will hear all the details tomorrow. Mr Somerville has asked me to meet him. He said he has something he'd like to discuss.'

'Sounds important,' Raven said, trying to disguise his own anxiety over the prospect.

Raven wandered across to where James was poking at a slug with a stick. Sarah walked with him. As they reached the boy, she nudged Raven's elbow and pointed at something on the street. A carriage was pulling up outside No. 52.

Raven smiled at the sight of the figure emerging from the brougham.

'Dr Simpson,' Sarah said. There was familiar warmth in her tone. 'He's quite unmistakable in that sealskin coat, though it's surely too warm a day for such a thing.'

Raven watched as the professor helped Mrs Simpson down from the carriage, the sight of him distinct even at a hundred yards. Then he realised: at the Assembly Rooms, even as Raven had counselled himself, the truth had appeared right in front of him and he hadn't seen it.

'Is he back, then?' Eugenie called from the bench. 'Maybe he can tell me how to get this little interloper out.'

Raven didn't respond. His mind was elsewhere.

'It is the coat that is unmistakable,' he told Sarah. 'Not the wearer. Just as Butters' murderer intended.'

Sarah gave him a puzzled look.

He was thinking about the rain-lashed night when Flint's son was born: on that night, Raven had been abducted because he borrowed the professor's coat. Flint's men thought he was Simpson.

'What are you saying?' Sarah asked.

'Lewis suggested the murderer was an actor, someone from the theatre who understood the power of artifice. But who else might understand how much we associate a person with a particular garment?'

It took her no more than a moment.

'A tailor.'

SIXTY-ONE

aven hailed a hansom cab on Queen Street and requested to be taken to the police office. He asked for all haste, but this did not prove forthcoming until he offered to supplement the fare. Despite this, the streets were busy, so progress was still frustratingly slow.

He found Henry and McLevy present as expected. Less so was the presence of Dickie Kimble.

'What are you doing here?' Raven asked him.

'Helping with enquiries,' Kimble replied.

McLevy cleared his throat. 'As I'm looking for someone who worked in the theatre, I thought perhaps I would be wiser seeking the insight of an illusionist practised in the art of deception rather than a deceiver pretending to have insight.'

'I've been making a few things apparent,' Kimble said, producing a coin seemingly from thin air.

Raven ignored this flourish. 'About that,' he said. 'We've been looking for an actor when we should have been looking for a tailor. It's Gethyn.'

McLevy fixed him with a sceptical stare: not dismissing the idea, but not instantly convinced either.

'How do you work that out?'

'Lewis speculated that Butters was talking about someone he

knew from his past, someone who had reappeared. Gethyn set up in Edinburgh only recently. And he's a Welshman.'

'My theatre-critic friend told me Butters performed for a spell in Cardiff,' McLevy acknowledged.

'Gethyn is an acquaintance of Dr Cooper,' Raven added. 'He must have known when Cooper was away fishing in Fife and therefore when his office would be empty.'

'A tailor,' said Henry, seeing another angle. 'Someone not medically trained but handy enough with a blade.'

Raven acknowledged the point, but he wasn't finished.

'Dr Cooper told us that when he came to Malham's demonstration, Butters had seen something that could change his life. We thought he was talking about mesmerism, but it was that Butters had seen Gethyn.'

McLevy had heard enough.

'Let's go,' he said.

McLevy led them out of the office and down towards Gethyn's shop, three of his officers in tow. They stood out on the busy High Street in their three-quarter-length dress-coats and top hats, but it was the sight of McLevy that caused pedestrians to make way.

There was a clerk closing up the shop as they reached Gethyn's premises, a look of alarm on his face as he glanced up and realised they were heading his way.

'Mr Gethyn's not here,' the clerk said, in a tone that indicated he hoped it wasn't himself they were here for.

'Where is he?' McLevy asked.

'I don't know. He hasn't returned from lunch. I was taking the opportunity to close early.'

'Do you know where he lives? It is an urgent matter.'

The clerk looked relieved, as though he had been expecting a rebuke for his planned act of lassitude. He offered up the information without any hesitation, as people tended to when McLevy was the one asking.

Ten minutes later they were climbing the stairs at the address on Lothian Street, close to the university and almost halfway between Surgeons' Hall and Greyfriars Kirkyard.

Gethyn had rooms on the first floor of a handsome building, indicative of a man who was making good money. A man with a lot to lose.

McLevy knocked firmly. When there was no response, he tried the handle and found it unlocked. He called out, 'Gethyn? Are you in there?'

There was no reply. There was no noise at all.

McLevy and his officers entered first, making a sweep of the rooms. The others followed on when it became clear that the place was empty.

'The clerk said he left at lunchtime,' Raven reminded him.

'Well, we know who we're looking for now,' McLevy said. He ordered one man to stay in case Gethyn returned, then led the others down the stairs, assigning them places to enquire after Gethyn's whereabouts: taverns, Malham's institute and the railway station.

Raven, Henry and Kimble, now surplus to requirements, found themselves back out on Lothian Street.

'What made you think of a tailor?' Kimble asked, his eyes lively with curiosity.

'Butters had a distinctive jacket that he often wore. A tailor would understand that anyone wearing it might be mistaken at a distance for the man associated with it.'

'Though he needn't have bothered,' said Henry. 'Once the story started to spread, people all over the city claimed to have seen him. A rumour on its own would have sufficed.'

'The sightings only happened *after* a witness saw him in that jacket,' Raven pointed out.

'Who was the witness?' Kimble asked.

'Your associate Mr Barrington, the actor-manager at the Adelphi. He told me he saw Butters in the backstage area.'

Kimble frowned. 'If merely being recognised as Butters was Gethyn's intention, it strikes me as risky to go to his place of work. Someone might mistake him for Butters at a distance, but in a venue where people knew him well, there was surely a danger that someone would immediately recognise he was an impostor wearing Butters' clothes – and there was but one way he could have acquired them.'

'Barrington said he only saw him briefly, then he fled. Because Gethyn could not afford Barrington seeing him up close,' Raven realised.

'There had to be a reason he would take that risk,' Kimble said.

Then Raven saw it.

'Gethyn was searching for something. Something he knew Butters had: the proof upon which his blackmail was founded. But why would Butters hide such a thing at the theatre and not at his home?'

'Perhaps,' Henry suggested, 'it is rather that Gethyn searched the theatre because he failed to find anything at Butters' home. But he may not have had long to search, as he also had the disposal of two bodies to occupy him.'

'Was anything unusual found at the house?' Kimble asked.

'There was a padlocked trunk which had been broken into,' said Raven. 'It contained nothing but old playbills and newspaper cuttings: notices and reviews of Butters' performances.'

'Money?'

'There was no room. It was rammed full.'

Kimble raised an eyebrow.

'Yet it had been padlocked,' he said.

SIXTY-TWO

arah had been left alone in the gardens with Eugenie and James, Raven having successfully flagged down a passing cab some time ago. She could only assume McLevy's name had been mentioned, there being no other explanation for such a feat at this time of the day.

Eugenie was still seated on the bench, her eyes closed. She looked exhausted, and Sarah did not wish to disturb her, so she focused her attention on James. He had tired of chasing pigeons and was now pulling up daisies with his pudgy hands. Sarah sat down beside him on the grass and started to pluck some of the daisies herself, chaining them together. James began to watch the process of linking the stems together before grabbing them and ripping them apart. This seemed to please him enormously, so Sarah began repeating the process.

'Excuse me?'

Sarah looked up to see a boy enter the gardens.

'Are you Miss Fisher?'

Sarah nodded and held her hand out for the note he carried.

'Who is it from?' she asked.

'I don't know. A smart gentleman at the Adelphi Theatre.'

She opened it and read, keeping one eye on James, who had begun to wander off, trailing after the messenger who had now left the gardens.

Dear Miss Fisher,

I require your assistance at the Adelphi Theatre. If you can, please come without delay for it's a matter of some urgency.

Also, I do not wish to alarm you, but if you should encounter Mr Gethyn, please stay away from him. I believe he is in a most agitated state of mind and I understand he bears you a great deal of ill-will.

Yours,

Callum Somerville

Sarah was confused. What could Mr Somerville require of her? Perhaps he was contemplating purchasing the theatre. She knew he respected her judgement, though that would hardly be a pressing matter. But as for Gethyn, Somerville didn't know the half of it.

Sarah looked back to where Eugenie was seated on the bench, noticing her grimace and watching as her hands grasped at her abdomen. Sarah picked up James, who immediately began squirming in her grasp, but she held on to him and made her way over to his mother.

'Eugenie? Are you alright?'

Eugenie shook her head. 'I think something is wrong.'

'Have your pains started?'

'I think so. But it's more than that.'

She gazed up at Sarah in an oddly unfocused way.

'Sarah, I can't see you.'

SIXTY-THREE

'He may not be an actor, but Mr Gethyn has made all of Edinburgh his stage,' Kimble said as they climbed the stairs inside Butters' close, off Nicolson Square. There was a smell of cooking from one of the other dwellings, a normality to the place that was oblivious of the deeds wrought here. Such deeds had no monument, the world washing around them like waves erasing footprints on sand.

'I would see him perform his final act on the gallows,' Raven replied, though he worried about the start Gethyn had got. The clerk said he had not returned after lunch, so if he had got on a train, he could be as far as Newcastle by now.

They had gone back to the police office to retrieve the key to Butters' flat, but when they got there, Henry found that he did not know where McLevy had put it. This had not seemed to trouble Kimble, however, and he had bade Raven lead him there regardless, while Henry remained in post.

When they reached Butters' door, Kimble produced a small metal implement from his coat pocket. 'There are few doors a magician cannot open. That is why we learn to be scrupulous and resourceful about securing our equipment. Most of the time,' he added, with a baleful twitch of his brow. Raven recalled how Kimble had lost the secret of his levitation illusion. Having seen the man's talents, he thought it a great shame that he had lost his career as well as so much more.

Less than two minutes later, Kimble had the door open and they made their way inside.

Raven felt a shiver and not from the temperature. Being here again made him more uncomfortable than when he had visited with Gregor and been shown body parts beneath the floorboards. Now Raven had a more vivid picture of what had happened in this place. Two people had been murdered within these walls: murdered and then butchered, by a man who would stop at nothing to protect his secret.

Raven now knew who that man was, but his secret remained elusive.

'Show me this trunk,' Kimble said.

'I warn you, it contains only— '

'Mere mementos, I know.'

Raven led him into the kitchen but was dismayed to see the trunk was not there.

'Did the police clear the place?' Kimble asked.

'I don't think so. Henry would have said.'

He recalled Henry talking about their search, mentioning how Mrs Butters' clothes remained but her husband's were gone, all part of Gethyn's deceit. He went to the bedroom and there they found the trunk pushed up against the wall, the padlock still hanging from its broken hasp.

Kimble lifted the trunk and upended it, shaking sheaves of loose papers carelessly about the floor until it was empty. Butters' life, in glimpses and fragments.

The magician let out a sigh.

'I did tell you,' Raven said.

Kimble gave him a small, dismissive shake of his head.

'Dr Raven, when are you going to learn to look at what is in front of you and not what you *think* you are seeing? As I told you before, make no assumptions, and never look from the same angle twice.'

Raven looked at the empty trunk, then at the pile of playbills and newspapers, wondering which of them he was failing to see properly. Kimble had made quite a mess, but perhaps not as big a mess as he ought.

Raven looked at the trunk again, which was when he finally saw what had been missed. It was not as voluminous as it appeared, the floor of it sitting higher than the exterior suggested.

'A false bottom,' he said.

Kimble felt carefully inside, then removed a panel of wood that was sitting neatly upon four supports, one in each corner. He handed the panel to Raven, revealing what was hidden beneath.

Raven was about to bemoan that it was just another newspaper, but he had learned Kimble's lesson.

It was a copy of the *London Illustrated News* from the week ending Saturday April 17, 1852. 'Magician Sought After Rival Dies in Theatre Fire', stated the headline, beneath which ran three wide columns of text, the majority of the page taken up by an artist's etching of the blaze.

Raven moved closer to the window where the light was better.

'My eyesight is not what it was,' said Kimble. 'What does it say?'

Raven scanned the copy, impatient for the details that might make sense of its being sought by Gethyn. '"Nigel Alton, a magician known as Alton the Uncanny, was found immolated after Hammersmith's Regency Theatre burned to the ground on Sunday last,"' he read aloud. '"Police are seeking a fellow magician, the Mighty Imhotep, whose real name is Peter Ingram." These names mean anything to you?'

'The Mighty Imhotep is familiar, though I never knew him. As for the other one, not a thing.'

'The two were rivals, it says. Ingram accused Alton of stealing one of his illusions. "Alton's remains were found in the charred embers of the theatre, identifiable only by scraps of his clothing and a ring he wore. Several witnesses saw Ingram on Monday boarding a train at Euston Station in his distinctive purple top hat and cape."'

It remained unclear what made this blackmail material. Perhaps Gethyn had been Ingram's tailor, and possibly his lover.

Raven turned the page, at which point he almost dropped the paper.

'A dead man,' he said.

Taking up a quarter of the page was a line-drawn illustration of the deceased magician, and though it said his name was Nigel Alton, the visage was unmistakably familiar. It was that of Dr Harland P. Malham.

SIXTY-FOUR

arah looked around in the forlorn hope that Raven might have returned but there was no one else to be seen. They were alone in the gardens.

'Wait here,' Sarah said. 'I'm going to get help.'

James continued to struggle in her arms as she carried him across Queen Street. She started naming the cakes and biscuits that Mrs Lyndsay would have in her kitchen, getting him to repeat the words to her. That was enough to focus his attention for the brief time it took her to reach No. 52.

She handed the child to a very bemused Jarvis, explaining as quickly and succinctly as she could what the problem was, then hurried back to retrieve Eugenie.

Sarah led her slowly and carefully out of the gardens and across the street. They had to stop several times, the pain of her contractions causing her to double over.

Jarvis held open the door as they approached.

'The child is in the nursery,' he said. 'Dr Simpson is waiting for you in the downstairs consulting room.'

This last proved untrue. Dr Simpson appeared behind Jarvis and escorted Eugenie to the consulting room himself. 'Come away, now,' he said. 'Let's see what ails you.'

He helped her up onto the examination couch, his brow creased in concern.

'Sarah here says that there is a degree of blindness,' Dr Simpson said.

'Things were a little blurry this morning,' Eugenie admitted. 'Now I cannot see objects clearly at all.'

'Your face is swollen,' Dr Simpson observed.

'As I cannot see it, I'm not really in a position to judge.'

'Headaches?' he asked.

Eugenie groaned as another contraction gripped her.

'She has been suffering from headaches,' Sarah confirmed.

'Will has failed to mention any of this to me,' Dr Simpson said. 'Was he aware? Did he check the urine for albumin?'

'I don't think he knew about the headaches.'

Dr Simpson looked confused. 'Why was it kept from him?'

Sarah felt a reluctance to admit her part in all this, but she knew that she had to. It would not do to compound her mistakes.

'Eugenie had asked me to treat her headaches with mesmerism. She knew that Will did not approve so she didn't tell him. And neither did I.'

'And you did not appreciate the significance of her symptoms.'

It wasn't a question. It was a statement of fact. Sarah realised that with mesmerism she had been dabbling around the edges, working with insufficient knowledge, while keeping important information from Raven. And now Eugenie was gravely ill.

The initial treatment for Eugenie's complaint – amaurosis complicating acute albuminuria – was bleeding. Sarah held the bowl as the blood trickled from the vein in Eugenie's arm. As Sarah watched the blood pool and thicken, she felt waves of guilt and shame wash over her. She had been so focused on what she wanted, what she thought mesmerism could do for her personally, that she had missed more important things.

She had missed the significance of Eugenie's symptoms – premonitory symptoms of puerperal convulsions – and had been blind to the fact that Malham was a self-obsessed maverick, happy to sacrifice the good that hypnosis might do for the sake of financial gain and the fame that attended his spectacular performances.

The hypnosis of James Braid – sober, scientific, and applied solely for the benefit of the patient – was what she should have been concentrating her attention on. Instead, she had been swept up and duped by Malham, the consequences of which would be far-reaching and potentially catastrophic.

She felt as though she was being punished for her hubris. The considerable gaps in her knowledge had been laid bare and she knew now that she would never be satisfied being some enthusiastic dilettante at the peripheries of medicine. She wanted to be competent, useful. She did not want to be in this position again.

Much to Sarah's relief, Eugenie's vision improved considerably after the bleeding and she insisted that she felt better. Her headache had abated but her pains were increasing in frequency.

'We should send for Will,' Sarah suggested.

Eugenie groaned and shook her head. 'There is time yet.'

Dr Simpson evidently did not concur.

'I would fetch him if I knew where he was,' he said.

'He was going to the police office,' Sarah said.

Dr Simpson called for Jarvis and instructed him to send an urgent message. As soon as Jarvis left the room the summons became even more imperative. Eugenie began to convulse.

SIXTY-FIVE

aven showed Kimble the line drawing, his hands trembling as he held the paper. He felt as though he needed independent confirmation that he was not falling for another illusion.

'That bears an uncanny resemblance to the American mesmerist Dr Malham,' Kimble said. 'Except that it would appear he's not a doctor, and that his name is not Malham.'

'Nor is he even American,' Raven added.

There was a small obituary. It stated that Alton was the son of a Somerset doctor, with a brother who followed in their father's footsteps. Alton, however, disappointed his family by instead pursuing a career as a conjuror. He enjoyed modest success, playing music halls and small theatres. The tone was sympathetic, in light of his demise, but the implication was that he had been overshadowed by more gifted performers. None of which shed any light on how he could have turned up in Edinburgh six months after burning to death.

Kimble let out a dry chuckle. 'My son Michael was always in a hurry to know when he would be ready for the stage. I remember when he was about thirteen, he proudly told me he now knew thirty tricks. "How many do you know, Father?" he asked me. I thought about it and told him seven.'

Raven failed to see the relevance of this. He assumed Michael's reaction must have mirrored his own.

'See, it's not the trick, it's the story you construct around it that creates something magical, so if you study a magician's work, you'll see the same trick over and over again.'

Suddenly Raven understood. Alton and Ingram got into a dispute, perhaps over the theft of an illusion, and in the ensuing altercation, Alton killed the other man. He knew he would face imminent discovery and therefore the rope. But he was an illusionist. He dressed the body in his own clothes, placed his ring on the dead man's finger and set fire to the theatre. Then, donning Ingram's distinctive hat, he made sure he was seen at Euston. He need not even have boarded a train.

'Like the salt cellar,' Raven said. 'The illusion is in making people believe something is still there, in this case Ingram. For why else would someone who had just committed murder walk through a railway station in a purple top hat and cape? He knew that was all anyone would see. And he would repeat the same trick with Butters.'

'As I'd wager he also intends to do with Mr Gethyn, whose sudden disappearance takes on a darker hue.'

'Gethyn?' Raven asked. 'Malham has no dispute with him. Gethyn worships the man.'

'Yes, but now Butters has been revealed as a victim and not a suspect, Malham needs someone new to take the blame for his deeds. I would wager all the whisky on Islay that Gethyn is already dead.'

Raven realised that this was not the only trick Malham meant to repeat. When Butters saw Malham perform, he understood how popular Malham was becoming, how much money he was likely to make, and reckoned he would enjoy a portion of that. Butters had blackmailed people before, but he fatally underestimated Malham. Flint had made the same mistake.

'He might not stop at Gethyn, either,' Raven said. 'Somerville offered Malham a stake in Milton House, with Malham saying he would pay him once he had concluded a property sale in New York. Somerville used to be a money-lender: the type accustomed to making threats, not fearing them. But he has been duped like the rest of us. There is no property in New York, and if Somerville dies, there will be no record of what Malham owed him. As Somerville has not yet amended the partnership agreement, Malham would own fifty per cent of Milton House outright without having paid a single penny. It's possible he intends to murder Somerville and let Gethyn take the blame for everything.'

At that moment, Raven heard a tentative knocking from somewhere behind him, followed by a voice calling from the flat's front door.

'Hello?'

A breathless young lad ventured uncertainly inside, a messenger.

'Dr Raven?' he asked.

'Yes.'

'Thank God. I've been all across the town and back. It's your wife. She has gone into labour.'

'At last. She will be much relieved. Is all well?'

The boy looked confused. 'How would I know? I've been running about trying to find you to give you this message. I've been all the way up to the police office and then here. All I know is that she's at 52 Queen Street and you've to go there.'

Raven looked at his watch and then at Kimble.

'We can stop off at the Adelphi en route. Warn Somerville.'

The young boy was still hovering, hoping for a tip. Raven fished about in his pocket and pulled out some coins.

'Did the other gentleman find you?' the lad asked.

'What other gentleman?'

The boy shrugged. 'Doctor something. He was in there asking after you when I spoke to Dr Littlejohn.'

Even as the boy spoke, Raven heard footsteps from the close and looked through the open door. Coming up the stairs were four individuals, not one of whom he would wish to encounter in an Old Town alley.

Raven rushed to close the door, but the first of them got there before him, the others barrelling through behind.

One of them gestured to the boy, slipping some coins into his hand and cupping his ear to whisper a message. The boy immediately fled, rushing out and down the stairs. From the colour he had turned, Raven knew he would not be going to raise the alarm.

SIXTY-SIX

Sarah had never witnessed such a severe seizure. She had experienced a brief period of euphoric relief when Eugenie said she felt improved, but now her guilt was revisited upon her tenfold. There were deficits in her knowledge, but she knew enough to understand how serious this was — both for the mother and for her unborn child.

'Loosen her clothing. Raise her head. Open the window,' Dr Simpson demanded, reaching for the chloroform bottle.

It took Sarah a moment to decide what to do first, a long purgatory of indecision and hesitation. She felt overwhelmed. This was all her fault.

'Sarah!'

Dr Simpson's voice penetrated the panic in her head. She threw open the window, bunched up the pillow underneath Eugenie's head and loosened her dress as much as she could.

Dr Simpson handed her the chloroform and a piece of muslin. 'We must subdue the excitability of the nervous system,' he said.

Sarah's hands shook as she dripped the chloroform onto the cloth. She placed it over Eugenie's nose and mouth, terrified of giving too much and making an already serious situation worse.

The knot in her gut twisted some more as she looked into Eugenie's contorted features. Her jaw was clamped tight, her face grotesquely twisted, her eyes rolled back in her head.

Dr Simpson listened in to the foetal heart with his stethoscope and then began rummaging in his bag. He pulled out a pair of forceps.

'We have to get this baby out,' he said.

SIXTY-SEVEN

s soon as the messenger boy was gone, one of the men closed the door and the rest fell upon Raven and Kimble. Two of them grappled Raven into submission, a third taking hold of Kimble while their leader retrieved two chairs.

Moments later, Raven found himself bound to his seat, thick rope cutting into his arms and his ankles while Kimble was being similarly restrained alongside him. The thought of what had recently happened to two other people in this place was prominent in his mind.

Raven didn't recognise any of their assailants and had no notion what he or Kimble had done to incur their displeasure. Then the leader, a gnarled-looking man with a thick grey beard, finally broke his silence, speaking in a Glasgow accent.

'Dr Raven, we're looking for an auld pal of yours by the name of Gregor.'

And now Raven understood.

He had been wrong about Christie. His threats were not empty, and he did indeed have a crew of ne'er-do-wells, henchmen and mercenaries to prosecute his will. It must have been the head of the College of Surgeons himself who had asked after his where-abouts, as Henry would never have given Raven's location to this crew.

'I don't know who you're talking about,' Raven spat.

Greybeard gave a nod, and one of the men drove a fist down onto Raven's thigh. Pain shot through him, though he was determined not to cry out. He was not sure he could muster such fortitude a second time.

'Maybe I've not been clear. Big fella. Quite distinct. Ring any bells?'

Raven eyed him defiantly. It earned him another punch to the thigh.

'I'd like his address. Now.'

In that moment Raven deduced that Christie did not intend merely to discover where Gregor lived. It did not take four men to beat information out of someone. These men meant to go to Gregor's home and finish him off so that Christie could take possession of the body before it was even cold.

SIXTY-EIGHT

arah looked at the tightly swaddled bundle held in Mrs Simpson's arms, the baby pale, still and quiet. There was a silence to the room that should have felt like a relief but instead seemed unsettling.

She looked over at Eugenie, who was still unconscious. Sarah couldn't be sure whether this was the result of the convulsions or the chloroform. Nor could she be sure whether Eugenie would ever wake up. Only time would tell.

'There is nothing more to be done,' Mrs Simpson said.

Sarah had to accept that she was right, but it was difficult to peel herself away. She wished she had some compelling task to occupy her, some reason to be elsewhere.

With that thought, she remembered Mr Somerville's urgent message. The Adelphi was only ten minutes' walk away and there was still light.

Sarah grabbed her coat and set off along Queen Street. She strode quickly, giving off an air of purpose and haste as was always her practice when walking alone. She knew that it would not ward off malefactors but held on to the notion that it might at least cause them to choose an easier target.

When she reached the Adelphi, there were no lights on in the foyer, which struck her as odd. Then she remembered what day it was: Monday, when Edinburgh theatres were usually closed. She wondered how she would get in but presumed the building must be open as Somerville had sent his message from here. She tried one of the doors and found it locked, but the one next to it opened with a push.

Sarah stepped into the gloom of the foyer, lit only by the fading daylight of Broughton Street, itself largely in shadow. She could see a glow around the doors leading to the stalls. The house lights were on.

'Mr Somerville?' she called, stepping inside.

The stage was dressed for a play, with painted screens depicting a classical landscape, a castle dominating the foreground.

'Mr Somerville?' she called again.

Then, looking to the stage, she saw something that troubled her. Sticking out from behind one of the flats was what looked like a foot.

Sarah proceeded cautiously down the aisle and climbed the short staircase to the centre of the stage. She could now see that there were two feet jutting out from beneath a heavy brown dust-sheet.

'Mr Somerville?' she called a third time, her voice now tremulous as she approached.

There was no movement beneath the sheet. She looked at the shoes: brown polished leather, criss-crossed with leather laces. She had to stifle a sob as she recalled seeing Mr Somerville wearing a pair just like them.

Sarah crouched down at the far end, and with a growing dread peeled back the cloth. Beneath it lay a body, blood pooled beneath the head. It was not Mr Somerville but Mr Gethyn, his throat cut.

Sarah opened her mouth to scream but felt it immediately covered by a firm hand holding a cloth, as another arm looped around her waist, pulling her tight to the body behind her. She recognised the smell immediately: chloroform.

Sarah drove an elbow into her attacker's ribs and tore away from him, but he was too quick. He threw himself on her from behind, bringing her crashing painfully to the floor and pinning her there with his weight, her forehead pressed to the boards.

'You betrayed me, Sarah,' he said. 'I would have made you a pioneer, the leading woman of a revolutionary movement, but you chose to burn it all down.'

He brought up the handkerchief again and held it there. Sarah struggled, tried to pull her head away from the cloth, tried not to breathe. Malham gripped her by her hair, pulled her head back and thumped it viciously against the floor. The room swam in a haze of pain and disorientation. He replaced the handkerchief and gradually all became dark.

SIXTY-NINE

reybeard was crouched in front of Raven, staring into his eyes as though trying to read whether he was about to acquiesce. If so, he would see only conflict.

Gregor did not have long to live, but if Raven gave up his address, the man might die within the hour. Equally, if Raven held out and remained bound here, Flint might die too. Not to mention the fact that his wife was in the process of birthing their child.

Raven did not want Flint to die, he realised with some surprise. And not just because Sarah was starting to care for him, or at least for the man he was pretending to be. For weren't we all the men we were pretending to be?

Just ask Thomas Cunningham.

Saving Flint, a man he had long detested, and who now had designs on Sarah, would come at the cost of his promise to Gregor. Christie would get his prize, and for considerably less money, Raven was sure; none of which would come his way. Another untidy compromise, but one he had no choice but to make.

Raven was about to disclose Gregor's address when Kimble beat him to it. Or rather, it would be more accurate to say that Kimble disclosed *an* address.

'I know the man you mean,' Kimble said. 'He lives in Hatter's Close, off Carnegie Street.'

Raven shot Kimble a look demanding to know what he thought he was doing.

'This one is too full of anger and pride,' Kimble told Greybeard. 'I fear how much violence he would let you inflict on him as the price of his principles. I, on the other hand, am happy to sell mine cheaper. Now let the pair of us go.'

'Not until we've got our man.' Greybeard thrust this face into Kimble's. 'So if you're lying, speak now, because we'll be back, and next time it won't be fists.'

'I'm not lying,' Kimble lied. Raven had recognised the address he gave. It was half a mile from here, and nowhere near where Gregor lived. He was trying to steal them some time.

'We'll know soon enough,' Greybeard said. He took two more lengths of rope and used them as gags, tying them tight around Raven and Kimble's mouths so they would not be able to call for help.

Raven waited until the sound of the departing footsteps had long faded, then tested how much noise he could still make. His cries were muffled, hopelessly so. He shuffled and shook in the seat, which made a scraping sound on the floor, but knew that even if he kept it up constantly, it would not be enough to prompt a complaint from below. He wasn't even sure there was anyone home. Those cooking smells had come from the other side of the close. He gave up, as all he had achieved was to turn his chair away from Kimble's.

Raven was in a state of abject despair. His thighs ached, his mouth was bleeding at the corners where the rope pulled his jaws apart, and those were the least of his problems. Kimble's gamble had failed, and by the time Christie's men returned, angrily minded to make good on their threat, Malham would have killed Flint.

'Should we get a move on, then?' Kimble asked.

Raven turned his head to see how he could be speaking, and saw that the magician had stood up from the chair, his ropes fallen away around him.

Raven would have gaped had his mouth not been wedged apart already.

'You thought I had a confederate for my cabinet illusion, didn't you?' Kimble said. 'As I've told you before, it's never done the way you think.'

SEVENTY

hen Sarah opened her eyes once again, she found she could not move or speak. It was not the effect of chloroform, however. She was lying on the stage, her hands and feet bound tight, her mouth gagged with a length of rough cloth torn from a dust-sheet. Her head pulsed with pain from where it had been struck against the floor and the skin around her mouth stung, burned by direct pressure of the chloroform-soaked handkerchief.

Her attacker was nowhere to be seen, but he had revealed himself. Too late she had seen the truth of it. *Someone who understood the power of artifice*, Raven had said. A fraud. A charlatan.

A murderer.

She felt dampness beneath her and realised that it was probably Mr Gethyn's blood. At least she had not met the same fate. Yet.

Then she reasoned that this was most likely because Malham had something worse in mind.

You betrayed me, Sarah. That was how Malham viewed her efforts to get to the truth. But vengeance aside, she could not see how her death would benefit him, or why he had killed Gethyn. He had a plan though; she knew that for certain. She would be dead already otherwise.

She could not move, could not call for help. All she could do was pray for intercession, pray for rescue. Pray for Raven.

Sarah felt a renewed surge of fear as she heard a noise from the back of the stalls and saw the doors to the foyer slowly open. Then her heart leapt as she saw that it was not her attacker. Rather, it was her deliverance.

Mr Somerville stepped into the stalls, looking curiously around. He did not appear to see her at first.

'Dr Malham?' he called out.

Sarah tried to scream, making whatever noise she could through the gag.

Somerville looked to the stage, his eyes widening in confusion and disbelief when he saw her.

Her own eyes were blurring with grateful tears as he ran towards her, calling out her name. Then, as he crossed the stage, mere feet from reaching her, Mr Somerville disappeared.

SEVENTY-ONE

inutes later Raven was running towards the North Bridge, having decided that by the time he found an available carriage he could be halfway there on foot. He had sent Kimble to find McLevy, the magician in possession of the newspaper that would explain all, even to a thrawn and stubborn Ulsterman.

Every step was taking him closer to Princes Street, where he knew he would need to make a choice.

Eugenie was in labour, which was not so surprising. They had known it was imminent. But that a messenger had been sent to the police station suggested urgency. Whether that urgency was being conveyed in Raven's capacity as a father or a doctor could mean very different things, and the messenger had shed no light on the matter.

His wife might be in difficulty, so he had the perfect reason to go directly to her, despite Flint's predicament. Under such circumstances no one would blame him for it. But just as Gregor would never have been aware had Raven broken his promise, it didn't matter what anyone else thought, only what he knew of himself.

Besides, Eugenie had gone into labour at Queen Street, and the professor was back. Raven could not delude himself that there was something he might do that the professor could not, any more than he could delude himself about the scale of the danger Flint faced. The only element in question was whether he was already too late.

Flint had dressed himself in fine clothes and moved in higher circles in his attempt to leave behind the man he had once been. He had fooled people who could not know better. But the problem was that he had also fooled himself. In the world he had left behind, nobody would have dared try to clear their debt to Flint by murdering him.

Raven ran beneath the Adelphi's colonnade, where he found the foyer dark but the door open. Malham must have picked the lock, as it would have piqued Flint's suspicion had they needed to break in.

As Raven entered the gloom of the lobby, he could see a glow of light around the doors to the stalls. He wondered why Malham had chosen this place to meet Somerville if he had murder in mind. In Hammersmith he had found himself with little choice. After killing Ingram, perhaps in the heat of the moment, burning the theatre had offered a means by which he could make himself appear the victim, fake his own death and be reincarnated as someone else.

Raven cracked the lobby doors enough to peer through and see Malham standing on the stage, his back to the auditorium. He was holding a can of something: lamp oil, from the smell of it. He was dousing the scenery, the curtains and the props, throwing it around with urgency and little care.

He was dressed in an unfamiliar overcoat, a drab affair covering a typically flamboyant suit beneath. Protection from the oil perhaps, given the carelessness with which he was dispersing it.

There was no sign of Flint. Was it that Raven had got here in time, finding Malham setting a trap? Or was Flint already dead, lying somewhere behind the flats.

From the sound of the oil can, it was almost empty. Raven's initial intention had been to take Malham by stealth, but now he knew he needed to act.

Malham placed the vessel down and reached into a pocket of his overcoat, producing a box of matches.

Raven strode through the doors, causing Malham to pocket the matches and turn around. He looked warily at Raven, doubtless recognising him from Kimble's recreation of his mesmeric surgery. Raven could tell he was calculating, wondering what Raven was doing here, how much else he knew. Raven had to stop him reaching for those matches and choose his moment, or simply keep him talking until McLevy and his men got here.

'Can I help you?' Malham asked.

'I am Dr Raven, a good friend of Miss Fisher,' he said, walking towards the stage. 'She told me you would be here. Is everything alright?'

'Well, yes and no,' he replied in what Raven now knew to be his fake American accent. 'I was supposed to meet with Mr Somerville, but he has not appeared and I have grounds to worry.'

'I am more concerned for our own well-being,' Raven replied. 'There is a strong smell of oil about the place. We might be wisest to remove ourselves.'

Malham stayed where he was. 'I think it's just paint that you smell. This is a theatre, after all. I'm thinking of buying it. Why don't you come up here and I'll give you a tour?'

That was when Raven knew Malham was the one waiting to choose *his* moment.

Raven stopped dead, halfway down the aisle, and Malham saw that he knew.

Malham reached into his pocket, producing not the box of matches but a pistol, and as he raised the weapon, Raven recognised it as one that had been pointed at him twice before. It was Flint's pistol, which he had been so attached to and would not have been easily parted from.

It felt unsettlingly incidental: Flint was a figure who had long menaced Raven's thoughts, who had loomed so large in his mind. Now he was learning of his death under circumstances where it meant so little and made no difference.

He recalled Flint's pride in describing the gun's properties.

This pistol has a Forsyth percussion lock. It uses fulminate of mercury instead of priming powder. So there is no delay between my pulling this trigger and the charge firing.

As Malham took aim, Raven realised it was not merely the bullet that presented a danger.

He dived as Malham fired, throwing himself behind a row of seats as he heard the pistol's report. Then he heard the screams and saw a glow on the edge of his vision.

Raven climbed to his knees and peered over the seat-backs, from where he saw the mesmerist on stage presenting a greater spectacle than he had ever offered before. He was engulfed in flame, but this was no illusion.

In his terror, Malham was trying to run from the fire, but the source of the fire was himself. The flash of the pistol had ignited the oil on his coat. He crashed against the flats stage-left, causing them to burst into flames, then fell against the curtains, igniting them also as he dropped to the floor. The fire spread rapidly about the stage and the walls where the oil had been spilled. Malham was soon so completely engulfed that even his screams ceased.

Then one of the burning flats crashed forward, revealing a bound figure lying motionless on the boards.

Raven felt something cold pulse through him as he saw that it was Sarah.

He ran to the stage, heedless of the growing heat. Raven crouched at her side, pulling away the gag. She was breathing but barely conscious. He tugged at her bonds but they would not be quickly loosed, so he picked her up bodily and carried her, as all the while the blaze grew fiercer at his back.

She began to rouse and splutter as he made it out onto Broughton Street, her eyes swimming and unfocused. He saw that her mouth had angry red marks around it, and not from the gag. Chloroform.

'You're safe now,' he told her, setting her down on the flagstones.

Sarah coughed, struggling to say something.

'Don't speak,' he said. 'I'll find some water.'

Sarah shook her head and managed two rasping words.

'Somerville. Trap.'

He had wondered what she was doing at the theatre, but like Flint, it appeared she had been lured. He did not wish to think what horror she had witnessed in there tonight, but at least she had been spared Flint's fate.

'I know,' he said solemnly, working to untie her hands.

Sarah pulled them away and pointed them insistently at the theatre, drawing on all her strength to speak again.

'Somer . . . ville.'

Raven's heart sped up as he understood the implications. She knew Flint was in there and she had not seen him die. He had to go back inside.

SEVENTY-TWO

aven tied a handkerchief around his nose and mouth as he hastened into the foyer, beyond which he could already sense a near-overpowering heat. He stepped through the doors, looking at the flames spreading higher, growing fiercer, then he ran towards them.

He might tell himself he was doing it for Sarah, or even for Flint's daughter, but he was not. In being forced to consider how Sarah perceived Somerville, and in hearing Gregor speak fondly of Flint, he had glimpsed that there was a liberation to be found in forgiving your enemies. If you did not, you were never free of them. Raven had not allowed himself to forgive Flint, so he knew now that if he did not at least try to save the man, far from there being any liberation, Flint would be with him for the rest of his days.

Raven climbed onto the stage, staying to the right where the fire had not spread entirely, but would soon enough. He ran behind the flats, hoping to find Flint bound and gagged somewhere backstage.

He felt the heat growing in its intensity, smoke catching in his throat. He could not stay in this place.

He glanced across the stage at Malham's burning body. The scheme he devised had instead consumed him. But how exactly had he bested Flint? He would not have been an easy man to over-power, even taken by surprise, and Malham must have anticipated as much.

Then Raven realised what Sarah had been telling him.

Malham had asked Flint to meet him in a theatre. It was an environment he knew well: a place where he could quite literally lure him into a trap.

Raven crouched down and looked for breaks in the floorboards. There they were: a discontinuation of the lines where a trapdoor was inset. He felt for the indentation and found the catch. It dropped away on its hinge, swinging in and down.

Raven peered into the gap. The drop to the floor beneath the stage had to be ten feet, but there was something directly beneath him. A crate. Raven jumped down on top of it and then to the floor.

The crate's lid was secured by a metal rod running through the hasps. He pulled it free, throwing the lid to the ground. Immediately there was frantic movement within, Flint rearing at him before falling back again. He was confused and disorientated, his head bleeding, and not merely from the fall. Malham had bludgeoned him with something.

Nor was he alone. Beside him was Gethyn's body, dressed in a suit Malham had previously worn.

Raven hauled Flint over the edge of the crate, only for the man to collapse to the floor.

'My leg,' he managed to say. 'It's broken.' He sounded groggy, weak.

Raven helped him to his feet, but Flint collapsed again immediately. He could not walk even with support.

The heat was becoming fiercer. Raven heard a bang as something crashed onto the stage above.

Raven pivoted Flint's midriff against his right shoulder, placing his left arm around the man's back. Then with all his strength, he lifted the man he had hated most these past six years and carried him through the bowels of the theatre, up a staircase and out into an alley.

The burden was heavy, but he knew that these were the last steps he would ever have to carry it.

SEVENTY-THREE

The carriage ride along Queen Street took only a few minutes, but the sensation of movement in the cool air helped Sarah clear her head.

She was starting to feel better, but was unsure how much of that was down to relief; firstly at her own survival and then that Raven had managed to rescue Mr Somerville.

There was a tender lump on her forehead and her throat hurt from the smoke, but she had suffered less than others. There was blood plastered to Somerville's head. He was conscious but barely so, looking blearily at the houses on the street as the carriage passed. And as for Mr Gethyn . . .

Raven sat beside her, a reassuring hand upon hers, but its comfort was bittersweet, for she knew that while the worst was over for her, it might yet still await him. She wanted to tell him, but each time she tried to talk he silenced her. She knew he would find out soon enough.

The carriage pulled up outside No. 52, and even from this distance she could see a red glow in the eastern sky where the Adelphi burned. Jarvis must have noticed it, for he was already standing on the step outside the front door looking along Queen Street.

He took in the condition of the arriving passengers and ran to assist. Sarah waved him away, directing him to help Raven, who was covered in soot and coughing like a consumptive. Between them the men half-carried, half-dragged Mr Somerville into the hall.

'What's happened?' Jarvis asked, struggling to take it all in.

'Help me get him into the consulting room,' Raven wheezed.

Sarah swallowed, knowing she had to speak now.

'It will need to be the waiting room,' she told him in a hoarse whisper. 'Eugenie is in the consulting room.'

Raven gave her a concerned look. He could tell from her tone that there was more to be said.

'How bad is it?' he asked, fear in his voice as Jarvis helped him lay Somerville down on the waiting-room floor. 'Sarah, please. Just tell me what has happened.'

There was no way of sugaring this pill. 'Eclampsia,' she said.

'Oh, God.' Raven pulled away from her grip and ran to the consulting room. His face had drained of all its colour.

Dr Simpson was sitting by the bed, keeping watch over Eugenie.

'I think that she may still be under the influence of the chloroform,' he explained. 'But the convulsions have ceased.'

Raven looked over at the crib.

'And the child?'

Sarah brushed past him and picked up the swaddled bundle. She handed it to him.

'You have a daughter,' she said.

Raven looked down at the child, his child, and tears formed in his eyes. The baby stirred. A tiny grimace contorted her face and then she settled again.

Raven looked over at Eugenie.

'Let's hope she still has a mother,' he said.

Dr Simpson had been as reassuring as it was possible to be under the circumstances. Things had gone as well as could be expected. Now all they could do was wait and hope.

Raven could not sit still. Sarah knew him too well to imagine he could simply await events. He had to be busy. Dr Simpson understood as much too.

'I suggest you go and tend to Mr Somerville's wounds,' he said. 'Better for you to be occupied. I'll continue to sit with Eugenie.'

Raven had looked conflicted about this but his trust in Dr Simpson won out in the end. He slouched from the room, Sarah following at his back.

As soon as they were out of Dr Simpson's hearing, Raven stopped and turned to Sarah.

'I can't bear to look at her,' he said. 'I have let her down, neglected her well-being by concentrating on other things. Had I not been so distracted I would have realised what was going on.'

Sarah laid a hand on Raven's arm. 'It's not your fault. You didn't have the full facts. She asked me to mesmerise her for the headaches she was suffering. I withheld information about her symptoms that would have alerted you. If anyone is to blame here, it's me.'

Raven shook his head. 'I cannot accept that. She's my wife and I'm the doctor here, not you.'

Sarah felt the sting of his words even though they were not intended to hurt. Her own lack of knowledge had played its part and she would not be convinced otherwise.

They entered the waiting room to find Somerville still splayed out on the floor. There was a sheen of sweat on his face, his eyes squeezed shut.

'How bad is it?' Sarah asked.

Raven examined the leg. 'He has fractured the lower end of his tibia. Not much displacement but a great degree of pain and loss of power in the leg.'

'Does he need a surgeon?'

Somerville's eyes snapped open at the mention of this. He did not seem to relish the prospect.

'I'm not going to lose my leg, am I?'

Raven shook his head. 'No. Your injury is easily managed. Couple of pasteboard splints and a looped bandage. Although it will take some time to heal.'

'Better than being dead, as I surely would be had you not dragged me from that place.'

A look passed between the two men, some moment of acknowledgement that seemed more complex than Sarah could fathom.

They set to work, though Sarah insisted on administering a
dose of laudanum before they commenced. She helped Raven splint
the leg before seeing to Somerville's scalp wound herself. She knew
that even though she was recovering from the effects of chloroform,
her suturing would be neater than Raven's. The sewing she was
taught at school had proven useful: just not in the way originally
intended.

She was about to apply her needle when Somerville held up his
hand.

'Miss Fisher, there is something I need to tell you.'

Raven remained hovering at the door. 'Perhaps now is not the
time,' he said.

Sarah looked up at him. 'Dr Raven, go and see to your wife. I
can manage here.'

Raven hesitated for a moment but then left them alone. Sarah
wondered if his reluctance to leave was to do with Eugenie or
because he knew what Somerville was about to say.

'I would prefer to see to your wound first,' she told him. 'Can't
this wait?'

Somerville coughed and shook his head.

'This has waited too long already.'

here was no such thing as an easy funeral, but Raven had always known this one would be particularly difficult, the onerous burdens of guilt and regret adding to his sense of loss.

As he looked around, his sadness was augmented by an element of anger. A tragic death and a life worthy of commemoration, yet the church was sparsely populated: maybe a dozen people at most for someone who had died in their twenties.

Across the aisle, he saw Eugenie's father staring back at him accusingly, in that moment no doubt regretting that his daughter had ever set eyes on him.

It was because of Raven that Cameron Todd was sitting here today, of that there could be no denial, but he could console himself that he was far from the only doctor in the church.

Not all of them had come to pay their respects, however.

The deceased had not been a wealthy man, but there was a strong case that he had been one of Edinburgh's more prominent citizens. It would also be fair to claim that he was an individual who had made an impact on a great many lives. Usually not for the better, admittedly, but that was true of half the feted men whose statues adorned the city's streets.

Raven's mind went back, as it often did, to that night in the alley when he first encountered Gregor. The giant had held him while another man cut Raven's face as a warning to make good on a debt owed to Flint. In that moment, and for a long time after, Raven would have happily wished death upon all three of them. Now two of them indeed lay dead, but each of their passings had brought Raven unexpected regret and difficult lessons.

It would have been impossible for him to imagine such a thing that night as he held his face together and bled into the rain. Harder still to imagine that he would one day risk his life to save the man who had sent them.

That man was positioned just yards away, seated on the edge of the aisle in a wheeled chair, his bound leg held out in front of him. Flint was paying for the funeral, something he had promised his long-term employee he would do. Raven had little doubt he had made this promise purely to ensure he had control over Gregor's body for a subsequent sale, but despite the change in circumstances, Flint had remained true to his word.

Somerville, Raven corrected himself, having determined to think of the man by his new name. Somerville had remained true to his word.

'Callum Flint died in that fire,' he had told Raven.

'We shall see,' had been Raven's reply. Whether he wished merely to leave his name behind or also his brutal practices remained in question, and Raven wished him to know that.

Looking at Flint now, his thoughts went to the night he had rescued him from the fire, after which he had watched Eugenie lie there and not known whether she would recover. It chilled him to consider how easily he might have been standing in a different church, looking at a smaller coffin. It should not require the threat of having something taken away to make one truly value it, but it was often the case. Those hours waiting for Eugenie to wake up had been among the longest in his life.

He recalled how young James had appeared at the door, having woken up in an unfamiliar place and found his way downstairs in search of his mother. What would either of them do without her, Raven had wondered, helpless.

James had seen Eugenie lying on the bed and run towards her, a look of confusion on his face when Raven restrained him. 'She's sleeping,' he told him, but James did not understand why he couldn't simply waken her. Raven had been able to offer a unique distraction, though.

'Come and meet your sister,' he said.

Raven had carried James across to look in (admittedly mild) curiosity at the tiny sleeping figure in her cot. Raven, for his part, had gazed upon her with pure adoration. He had learned not to fear being a father to his son, and while the prospect of raising a daughter held no fewer terrors, he was resolved to overcome those too.

And then mercifully, gloriously, Eugenie had roused.

A little later James clung on to his legs and watched as Raven delicately handed Eugenie their daughter, feeling like the richest of men, if not a wealthy one. His fortune was the three other people in that room. Up until then, Raven's ambition had been an entity in itself. Now he understood that the desire to build a career ought to serve a deeper purpose, and his was clear. He needed to start his practice as soon as possible. Much as it pained him to have to leave 52 Queen Street, he knew his priorities lay elsewhere.

In that moment, he had decided he would accept Cameron Todd's money, though it still rankled. Eugenie's father would always see himself as being above him, Raven's practice a mere subsidiary of his own. But he would still rather that than have his autonomy and live with the knowledge of having betrayed Gregor.

Raven looked at the oversized coffin sitting at the front of the church and allowed himself a moment's satisfaction. Thanks to Kimble's misdirection as they sat bound in Butters' kitchen, Christie's hired hands had not got to him.

Once he had been sure that Eugenie was settled, Raven had made his way to Gregor's house, intending to warn him and to see what assistance he might provide. But when he arrived, he found that Gregor had died sometime that day. Perhaps mere hours before, for his body was barely cold.

It had been Gregor's wish to have a Christian funeral service, and Reverend Guthrie had agreed to officiate. Also in accordance with Gregor's wishes, there had been an intimation in the *Scotsman* announcing both his death and the subsequent funeral service; an intimation that Raven suspected might present temptation to those not minded to honour the giant's wishes.

'Can we trust the Reverend Guthrie?' Raven had asked Simpson, having laid out the full truth of the matter.

'He is as incorruptible a fellow as you are ever likely to meet,' the professor had replied. 'But every man has his price.'

Raven looked around the church and sure enough, there was Christie, sitting close to the back. Unlike Dr Todd, Christie was not here because he had been press-ganged to help swell the numbers and he was not a man noted for attending the funerals of the impoverished and the unknown. There was no sign of Greybeard and the others, but Raven knew Christie was as resourceful as he was sleekit, and not to be underestimated.

Raven had seen him the day after the fire at the Adelphi. He had accompanied Henry to Surgeons' Hall to inform both Christie and Dr Cooper that the investigation was at an end and the College no longer implicated. It was information that Henry was capable of conveying on his own, but there was something else Raven wanted Christie to know.

'Do pass on my regards to your acquaintances,' Raven had told him, taking him quietly aside while Henry proceeded to Cooper's office.

'I have no idea which acquaintances you could be speaking of,' Christie replied. He stood close to Raven, meeting his eye and addressing him in a manner that acknowledged he knew exactly which acquaintances Raven was speaking of, and that Raven could prove nothing. 'I hope you enjoy your moment of pride and right-eousness,' Christie went on. 'But the moral high ground can make for treacherous footing. And as for pride, you might wish to be sure the matter is concluded before you indulge yourself.'

With that Christie had given a thin and bitter smile.

'Gregor had been dead a while before I found him,' Raven had added, lying. 'I think he might be past his best.'

'His best?' Christie scoffed. 'Even as a skeleton, providing a trophy to match Hunter's would far exceed anything the man achieved in life.'

Yes, unquestionably, Christie still had plans.

The Reverend Guthrie conducted the service with a grace and sincerity that would have pleased Gregor, then he announced that there would be a eulogy. Raven panicked briefly, wondering whether Gregor had misinterpreted some offer he had made, or whether Raven himself had failed to comprehend a request. Then he saw that an usher was helping Somerville to the front of the church. He was in no state to ascend the pulpit, so he struggled upright and gave a brief address to the sparse congregation.

'People in this town knew Gregor,' he said, 'or knew the sight of Gregor at least.'

His voice was calm but insistent, a man used to being heeded but at the same time eager to persuade.

'He was hard to miss,' Somerville went on. 'People would see Gregor and see someone to be afraid of. But Gregor was often the one who was afraid, for he was always different, an outsider. I knew him from when he was a boy, an orphan, mocked as much as he was feared as he grew up – and kept growing.

'Gregor was often a man who found himself on the wrong side of the law. I will not lie about that in the house of God. People had a right to fear him, for he was at times a man of violence: a criminal, who worked for a money-lender.'

Somerville appeared to directly address Sarah as he said this.

'It is not lost on me as I stand in this place that Jesus' only act commissioned by anger was to throw the money-lenders from the temple. But nor should we forget that in the end, even in a state of mortal agony, His last act was to comfort the criminals alongside him. So do not judge Gregor if you knew nothing of him.

'Gregor was a man who lived much of his adult life aware that his time was limited. He took an interest in Charles Byrne, the Irish Giant, and knew how young he met his end. It is true none of us know the day or the hour, but we can at least comfort ourselves with the possibility of how far off that day and that hour might be.

'People think because Gregor could best most men, he had nothing to be afraid of; that he did not need to be courageous. But in living with that knowledge Gregor was the bravest man I ever knew. So hereafter, whenever his name is spoken, it is courage I will first think of. Not strength, nor stature, but courage.'

Somerville was helped back along the aisle, not looking directly at anyone as he progressed. Raven could see why. The man's eyes were misted. To his surprise, Raven's were becoming so too.

This was an impairment he could not afford, however. He needed to stay alert and keep his eyes fixed on that oversized coffin.

The Reverend Guthrie concluded his service, then the time came for the pall-bearers to shoulder their burden. Raven was to lead them, supplemented by men from the undertaker Somerville had engaged. But when Raven heard footsteps and looked to the doors, those were not the men who filed into the church and took hold of the coffin.

Christie and Guthrie exchanged the briefest of looks. Every man did have his price, even those of the cloth.

Raven recognised them, though he knew Somerville would not. Raven had not told him of the threat. He knew Somerville could have brought men in, but the most important thing was Gregor's dignity. He had wanted a service that conferred respect upon his passing and commemoration. One that descended into a mass brawl on the steps of the church would be a desecration.

Raven said nothing as he helped carry the coffin solemnly through the church and out onto the street. As he passed Christie, he stole a glance at him from the corner of his eye. The man wore a look of quiet satisfaction as he observed Raven, powerless to do anything other than Christie's bidding, obediently conveying his coveted prize to the waiting cart.

As he stood outside the church and watched the cart drive away, Raven was filled with many memories and not a few regrets. One was how long he had thought of the departed as 'Gargantua', seeing him as a monster and not a man afflicted by a medical condition. A second was that he had been tempted so long by Flint's offer. A third was that Gregor had been alone at the end. But in that moment, Raven's greatest regret was that he would not be there to see Christie's face when he opened the coffin and found that it was full of manure.

THE FIRTH OF FORTH

TWO DAYS EARLIER

SEVENTY-FIVE

I t's the salt-cellar trick again,' Raven told Sarah. 'This time the illusion is not in Gregor's body disappearing, but in making Christie believe it is still there.'

The air was cold, catching in Raven's chest, but his throat was improving after the ravages of the Adelphi's smoke, and Sarah was over the worst of her experience too. The lump on her head was flattening, though there was still a hoarseness to her voice.

They were sitting in a fishing boat off Newhaven. Gregor's remains lay close by them on the deck, wrapped in sailcloth and weighed down with stones. He would be buried at sea, or at least out in the Forth, in accordance with his long-held desire.

The professor's purchase of Viewbank, a house close to Newhaven, had been an attempt to escape the rigours of his practice, but had in fact seen him minister to the local fisherfolk. As a result, the fishermen's assistance had not been difficult to procure. Nor was securing the co-operation of the Reverend Guthrie once Simpson had told him of Christie's unconscionable intentions. Guthrie was eager to assist. Eager also to take Christie's money, which would go towards the funding of his Ragged Schools, which aimed to feed, clothe and educate the poor children of the city.

After Gregor's intimation was published, Guthrie quietly let it be known to Christie that he was aware of the value to medical science that was in imminent danger of being lost. The Reverend made it clear that though an undertaker had been hired to convey the coffin to Greyfriars, where Somerville had purchased a plot and a headstone, this task might instead fall to men of Christie's own choosing, should he make a suitable donation.

'Every man has his price,' the professor had said. 'Or so someone like Christie will believe.'

Raven was conscious this would thereafter put the churchman in an awkward position with Christie once his part in the deception became apparent, particularly with money changing hands. However, Guthrie said he would be happy to tell the head of the College of Surgeons that his contribution should be regarded as a penance for plotting to desecrate the body of a man against his express wishes. He would also convey that such a penance would ensure Christie's actions did not come to the notice of the police.

'Does McLevy know about any of this?' Sarah asked, indicating the shrouded corpse.

'McLevy's been too busy with other matters.'

'What did he make of all your revelations?'

'He's been telling the Hoolet and all the newspapers that he suspected Malham all along, and that the psychic detective consultation was merely a strategy for getting close to the man.'

Sarah laughed. 'He should write a book,' she suggested. 'He's adept at spinning a yarn.'

'Talking of yarn-spinning – what of Mr Somerville?'

'What about him?'

'How do things stand between the two of you now?'

Sarah looked across the water. Raven could tell that she was considering her answer carefully.

'I still consider him to be a friend.'

Raven could not have said precisely what answer he wished to hear, but he knew this was not it. It told him nothing either way, and he suspected this was what she intended.

'A friend?'

'Yes. I'm a great believer in redemption.'

Sarah met him with a look that gave Raven the unsettling impression there was nothing about him she didn't know.

'And what of yourself?' she asked. 'Now all this is over, what's next? You know you can't stay at Queen Street for ever, however much you might like to.'

'I'm aware of that.' He sighed. 'I have resolved to accept Dr Todd's money and his oversight after all.'

'But that's not what you want?'

'What I want is to do what's best for my family, and setting up my own practice is therefore an urgent priority. Though it will hardly be my own practice with Eugenie's father looking over my shoulder. I can't imagine he'll let me do anything remotely risky, with his reputation and his money at stake. I'm not likely to make great strides in gynaecology like that, am I?'

'What if there was another way?'

Sarah wore an expression Raven recognised. She had something in mind that would probably get both of them into trouble.

'What do you mean?'

'I've been thinking about something Mr Somerville said. To become someone in this city, you need to have a stake. You need to be a participant in the game, not a piece on the board. I have the money. What if I were to invest in your practice?'

Raven felt tantalised by possibility, excitement vying for primacy with a wariness learned the hard way.

'And what would you want in return?'

Sarah looked out across the water once more, for longer this time.

HISTORICAL NOTE

he mid-nineteenth century witnessed a resurgence in interest in mesmerism, and the Scottish Curative Mesmeric Association met throughout the 1850s in an attempt to promote its benefits and encourage its application. It is thought that the introduction of the anaesthetic agents ether and chloroform, which were both more efficient and more reliable, led to a decline in the surgical use of mesmerism, although its medical use persisted.

A resistance to the use of anaesthetic agents to relieve the pain associated with normal labour lingered into the early 1850s but subsided once it became known that Queen Victoria inhaled chloroform during the birth of her eighth child, Prince Leopold, on 7 April 1853.

The crime depicted in this book is very loosely based on the murder of Dr George Parkman, whose dismembered and burned remains were found in a laboratory at Harvard Medical School in 1849. A dental plate assisted in the identification of the body.

Charles Byrne, the Irish Giant, suffered from acromegalic gigantism, and died in 1783 at the age of twenty-two. He knew that the anatomist John Hunter wanted his corpse and so made arrangements with his friends that his body be buried at sea. His coffin was intercepted on the way to Margate, Hunter reportedly having paid £500 to the undertaker to steal the body from the casket and replace it with stones. Byrne's skeleton remains part of the collection at the Hunterian Museum in London.

There was a great interest in the paranormal in the UK during the 1850s, largely imported from America via touring acts such as the Fox sisters and the Davenport brothers. What we now know as Spiritualism was founded by the Fox sisters, who performed by cracking bones in their feet against wooden floorboards, causing a rapping sound that they attributed to spirits. It is from this that the phrase 'Knock once for yes, twice for no' derives. The Davenport brothers were famous for a cabinet illusion similar to that performed by Kimble, one which relied upon subtly gathering a loop of rope in their hands while they were being tied up.

Dr Simpson attended a theatrical performance by a spiritualist medium in Edinburgh about this time, and did indeed ruin the show by debunking the deception in a manner much as depicted here.

The mesmeric surgery performed by Malham was inspired by the fraudulent practice of 'psychic surgery', long popular in the Philippines and Brazil. This sleight-of-hand deception involved fake blood and animal parts, and was used to convince patients that tumours had been removed. Countless victims subsequently died from cancers that they mistakenly believed to be cured, including, in 1984, the American entertainer Andy Kaufman.

The Adelphi Theatre on Broughton Street did indeed burn down in the spring of 1853, though presumably not in the circumstances depicted in this book. A new theatre was built, opening as the Queen's Theatre in 1855, but it was also destroyed by fire the following year, as was its successor in 1857. The next theatre built on the same site was given the charter to dub itself the new Theatre Royal, opening in 1859. It was destroyed by fire in 1865 but rose again the same year, only to be burned down once more in 1875. Yet another theatre was opened on the site in 1876, burning down in 1884. At some point you might take the hint, but it was rebuilt once more and stayed fire-free until 1946. Part of the new St James Quarter abuts the site now. Just saying.

ACKNOWLEDGEMENTS

ur thanks as ever go to the wonderful team at Canongate and especially our editor Francis Bickmore for letting us write what we want and then making it better.

Our ongoing gratitude goes to Sophie Scard, Caroline Dawnay and Charles Walker at United Agents for their invaluable feedback and support.

Thank you to Rachel Barrington, who very generously bid in a charity auction to have her name included in the book.

And finally, we would like to offer our thanks to the National Library of Scotland for their magnificent digitised archive – especially the maps.

'The immersive world of Ambrose Parry just gets better and better'
Jess Kidd

CANON‖GATE

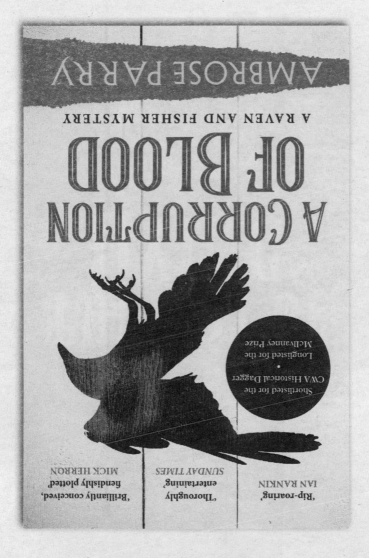

AMBROSE PARRY

A RAVEN AND FISHER MYSTERY

A CORRUPTION OF BLOOD

Shortlisted for the
CWA Historical Dagger
•
Longlisted for the
McIlvanney Prize

'Rip-roaring'
IAN RANKIN

'Thoroughly
entertaining'
SUNDAY TIMES

'Brilliantly conceived,
fiendishly plotted'
MICK HERRON

'Full of twists and turns'
EVENING STANDARD

'Gripping'
SUNDAY EXPRESS

THE ART OF DYING

'Victorian Edinburgh comes
vividly alive – and it's a world of pain'
VAL McDERMID

AMBROSE PARRY

'Wonderful'
The Times

CANON GATE

AMBROSE PARRY

'Victorian Edinburgh comes
vividly alive – and it's a world of pain'
VAL McDERMID

THE WAY OF ALL FLESH

'Astonishing'
MARK BILLINGHAM

'Won't let you go until the final page'
S.J. PARRIS

'A rip-roaring tale'
IAN RANKIN